LUCIFER'S WAR

BY
MELINDA M. SNODGRASS

Lucifer's War was first published by Tor Books in 2008 under the title The Edge of Reason.

Second edition was published by Prince of Cats Literary Productions in 2020

This third edition contains some new and updated scenes.

Thank you for reading!

<u>Credits</u>
Cover Design: by Fakel Barros

Since the first moment that humans left the trees and began to walk upright, a secret war has been fought.

On one side of this ancient battle are the Old Ones, malign entities that feed on the suffering of humankind. Their weapon? Magic and religious fanaticism. The only force able to hold them back is the ancient order of the Lumina. Dedicated to the liberation of the human spirit, they employ reason, understanding and technology to stop the superstitious rampages of the Old Ones.

When Officer Richard Oort of the Albuquerque Police Department rescues a mysterious teenage girl from a trio of inhuman hunters, he's hurled into the crush of this primal battle. Recruited by the Lumina to serve as their newest paladin, Richard joins a handful of unlikely allies, including an adolescent sorceress, an enigmatic billionaire, a sexy coroner, and a wandering god with multiple personalities.

And then there's Richard's boss. Damon Weber is a handsome, intelligent, and honorable man and Richard falls hard for him. Even knowing his feelings will never be reciprocated.

The Old Ones and their righteously intolerant pawns seek to destroy Richard—or subvert him to their cause—ruthlessly expending all the powers of magic and organized religion at their disposal. As the gates between the universes shred apart, it may be up to Richard to save humanity from the endless horror of the next Dark Age.

THE CAROLINGIAN BOOK 1
LUCIFER'S WAR

NEW YORK TIMES BESTSELLING AUTHOR
MELINDA M. SNODGRASS

The Sleep of Reason Produces Monsters.

Francisco Goya

CHAPTER ONE

DARK AS SIN

I N HER MISERY Rhiana Davinovitch decided she wanted to die. She had been running for three hours now. Her hunters were slow, which meant she kept well ahead, but they never tired, unlike her human muscles and tendons. Eventually, they would wear her down and she would die. That time had just about arrived.

Rhiana drew in a shuddering breath across a throat made tight and sore from exhaustion and raked the hair out of her eyes. Despite the chill of the mid-November night, her hair was moist and slick against fingertips aching with cold.

For the first time in an hour, she looked up from the sidewalk where her gaze had been desperately focused as she tried to place each foot carefully in front of the other without tripping or falling or losing the steady rhythm of her half walk, half run.

She was surprised to find herself in the business plaza set between Albuquerque's two main shopping malls. She stood in the median of Uptown Boulevard, which ran between the Uptown Center building on the north and the City Place building and ABQ Uptown on the south.

She had escaped from the trailer in the South Valley in the early evening. They had been keeping her, hoping she'd finish the work, but after her escape they seemed to have decided that silencing her was more important. So, they'd summoned the hunters. She'd tried hitchhiking, but no one would stop. Once she reached the populated areas of Albuquerque she had hammered on doors, but no one had answered. She realized that the creatures who hunted her had trapped her in a field of darkness and fear that no human would enter. No one could help her.

She reckoned she had covered somewhere between fifteen and seventeen miles. She could go no further. Without volition her hand went into the pocket of her coat. The metal of the pennies was sharply cold against her skin. If she could feed, she might be able to fight, but there were no people nearby for her to use. A wave of cold brushed against the exposed skin of her face and hands. She glanced up at the bare branches of the trees. They stretched motionless toward the cloud-filled sky. Rhiana looked to the west and watched as one streetlight after another blinked out. The exterior lights on the Uptown Center building faded and died.

They were coming.

✧ ✧ ✧

Officer Richard Oort stood at the driver's side of an early two thousands Toyota junker. The blue paint had been faded by decades in the New Mexico sun, and there was a long crack across the front windshield, a gift from the state's notoriously rock-strewn highways and byways. It was illuminated by the flashing lights on the police cruiser parked directly behind it.

This particular November night, Richard and his partner, Sterling Bond, a heavyset man in his his forties, had responded to a call from the upscale neighborhood at the foot of the Sandia Mountains about suspicious people casing the area and clearly up to no good. The suspicious people turned to be four Hispanic teenagers, two boys and two girls, in the old car.

Sterling stood on the front porch of one of the McMansions talking with the owners. The couple looked to be in their fifties, dressed in pajamas with robes thrown over, and they reeked with entitlement and bad taste. The house was a testament to that; it had too much of everything from the *chile ristras* hanging by the huge front double doors, to the wooden ladder emulating a pueblo ladder, to the round squat tower that suggested a kiva. It was Santa Fe style on steroids.

And it wasn't alone in its pretension; more McMansions marched along the winding street. The large boulders that littered the shoulders of the towering mountains were their only accommodation to their location. Richard was from Rhode Island, and even after more than two years in Albuquerque he still found the severe west face of the Sandias to be strange and intimidating. Mountains weren't supposed to be this… threatening. Though they were pretty when they caught the light of the setting sun and turned a rich, dark pink which was the reason for their name. *Sandia* meant watermelon in Spanish.

Richard shook off his wandering thoughts and turned his attention back to the license in his hand. The driver was one Raphael Ortega, age nineteen.

"So, Raphael, what are you doing up in this neighborhood this late at night?" Richard asked in Spanish.

The girl in the back seat wrinkled her nose and said in the same language, "You speak Spanish funny."

"Yes, I learned to speak Spanish back east so mine is more Castilian than the dialect here in New Mexico. But clearly, you understood me." He looked back at the driver. "And you haven't answered my question."

"We were just looking at the city lights. It's pretty from up here." The boy's tone tipped between whining and blustering.

The boy wasn't wrong. In the valley below, the city gleamed like scattered jewels. In the west, the peaks of three extinct volcanoes seemed to float against the stars, their rounded peaks dark silhouettes against the moonlit sky.

The homeowners raised their voices, and he heard the woman say, "I keep an eye out."

The husband added, "I'm sure they were casing us. Looking to rob us."

The boy in the backseat muttered in English this time. "We ain't no thieves."

At almost the same time Sterling said, "Don't worry, folks, we'll run 'em out of here." He flipped closed his notebook and walked down to join Richard at the curb. "So, *amigos, comprende* beat it? Otherwise ..." He pulled his cuffs off his belt and dangled them in front of the kids. "*Se hablo* under arrest?"

Inwardly Richard cringed at the terrible accent and mocking tone. He gently edged Sterling aside, and said, "Look, the Elena Gallegos picnic ground is just up the road from here. You'll have a great view from there and no one will object."

He watched the expressions flit across the young faces. Comply? Object? He held his breath, hoping they would pick wisely. He really didn't want these kids to have an arrest record for just being kids. Reuben nodded, rolled up the window. Sterling and Richard watched as they made a U-turn and left the neighborhood, the taillights vanishing around a curve as they headed back to Tramway Road.

"First, it's '*se puede decir*.' That's 'can you say' in Spanish. And they weren't doing anything wrong, much less illegal," Richard said quietly.

"First, don't lecture me, Rhode Island, and whether it's right or wrong they were in the wrong neighborhood. We did everybody a favor." Sterling shook his head at Richard's expression and clapped him on the shoulder. "There's an all-night Denny's down on Menaul and I could use a cup of coffee. Its colder than a witch's tit out here." Sterling headed for the cruiser.

"A favor? How do figure that?" Richard snapped.

Sterling turned back. His square face with its incipient jowls was looking less happy now. "I get it. You're new here. And maybe things are different back east—"

"Different set of minorities, but it's the same ugly song, Sterling."

"Look, this could have ended in tears. Those rich assholes just complained. Somebody else might have been a tad more … proactive. Defended their God-given right to exercise their equally God-given Second Amendment right to defend their big-ass castle. Then some kid ends up dead.

Some homeowner gets indicted, and we end up on the news. Not to mention all the fucking paperwork. This was a win/win for the good guys. Meaning us. Come on, I want that coffee. Maybe some pie, too, since we gotta work Thanksgiving weekend. I can at least have some damn pumpkin pie."

Richard wasn't listening; he was frowning down at a thin ribbon of darkness winding snakelike through the sparkle of lights. As he watched, another section went dark.

He gripped Sterling's arm and pointed down into the valley. "What do you think that is?"

Sterling shrugged. "Eh, some kind of power outage."

"They go out in grids, not like *that*." Richard moved quickly to the patrol car and slid behind the wheel.

"I'm not getting my damn coffee, am I?" Sterling grumbled as he pulled the seatbelt across his chest and paunch.

✦ ✦ ✦

THEY DROVE INTO the darkness near the big shopping centers. Richard was on the radio with Delores in dispatch.

"… PNM's computers report no outages." Her voice sounded tinny over the speaker.

The plastic of the handheld mike smelled faintly of hamburgers. Richard wrinkled his nose against the stale odor, pulled the mic away from his face, and decided he'd add Lysol to his kit. His head snapped to the side when Sterling abruptly said, "Okay, let's go."

"You must really want that coffee," Richard muttered before clicking back on the radio. "Well, I have a news flash for the PNM computers. It's dark as sin out here. Everything is out—streetlights, traffic lights, neon signs; the buildings are all dark."

Dolores clicked off presumably to check again with the power company. Richard glanced over at his partner, a little surprised by Sterling's continuing silence. Usually, the older man would be bitching about eggheads, companies, politicians. Richard was surprised to see his eyes flicking from side to side nervously. Richard pulled into the parking lot of a big office building. Bringing the car to a stop seemed to break Sterling's reticence.

"Why are we messing with this?" Sterling demanded. "There are no crimes being committed that I can see. And we don't work for the fucking electric company, so let's just *go!*"

Richard was startled by the older man's vehemence, but before he could respond, Dolores's voice returned even more staticky than before. "They … ill say th … 's no out …"

"Perhaps they should try looking out a window," Richard said sweetly. He broke off abruptly and peered through the breath-frosted front windshield. He felt stupid saying it, but he said it anyway. "And now my headlights are starting to fade."

"Having … say … ag … cutting …" And then she was gone.

The headlights failed, the engine coughed, and the car shuddered as it died. Richard tried the key, and nothing happened. He clicked futilely on the radio. It was dead as well. Richard became aware of Sterling's rapidly escalating breaths. The man was practically panting and sweat bathed his face despite the growing chill in the car. Terror was evident on his face.

Puzzled and concerned, Richard put a hand on Sterling's shoulder, felt him flinch. "Hey, easy, relax. It's okay."

"No! No, it's not. We gotta get out of here. We're not supposed to be here!"

"Hey, chill, you're sounding a little …" He searched for a softer word than what he really wanted to say, which was nuts. "… overwrought. Let's just take a look around and then we'll leave. Assuming the car will start."

The hinges on the car door creaked as he pushed it open. He stepped out and took a three-sixty look. His breath puffed in white streamers. It seemed that every streetlight within a five-block radius was out. Grabbing the radio off the seat he clipped it onto his belt.

He keyed his shoulder mic. "Hi, Dolores, we're leaving the vehicle and taking a look around."

A burst of static made him jerk his head away. Faintly he heard Dolores ask, "Wha … care …"

He made a guess at what she'd said. "Right now there's nothing here but dark. We'll be careful, but if we don't check back in ten, send backup."

There was another sharp burst of static obliterating her next words. The microphone crackled on his left shoulder and then died. Sterling was climbing out of the car as he pulled his cell phone out of his pocket.

"I'm callin' for a tow. We gotta get out of here." His shoulders were hunched as if he expected a blow. He stared down at his phone, then gave Richard a panicked look. "It's … it's dead."

Richard retrieved his phone. It too had died.

"Still think I'm *overwrought*," Sterling said spitefully. "This is some unnatural shit. We gotta go."

"How? The car is dead." Richard shot back.

"We got *feet* don't we?" Sterling began to quickly walk away.

"Seriously? You're going to leave me hanging out here alone?"

Sterling just pulled his chin deeper into the collar of his coat and kept walking.

Thrusting his nightstick through the loop on his belt, Richard grabbed the flashlight and headed off down the sidewalk. The weight of his belt festooned with radio, cuffs, stick, and pistol left him feeling awkward. There was the sound of hurried footsteps and then Sterling was at his side.

"The Lord is my shepherd; I shall not want."

Richard shot the older man an incredulous look. Richard was religious, and the 23rd Psalm was lovely, but this really didn't seem like the time, or that it was warranted. He flashed the beam from the flashlight from side to side. Spindly trees encased in concrete seemed to jump toward him as the light caught them. The landscaping was professional modern, sand grass and chamisa bushes thrusting through the gravel-filled verges between the sidewalks and the tree coffins.

"He makes me lie down in green pastures. He leads me beside still waters."

As if Sterling's *Sterling's murmuring the Psalm wasn't irritating enough, it* had *to be one of these modern, ugly translations,* Richard thought. As he walked, a carpet of dry leaves whispered around his shoes and crackled underfoot, releasing a rich musty smell that raised childhood memories of lit fireplaces and warm cider. The light of his flashlight danced and glittered in the windows. Everything seemed fine at the Uptown Center building and at the small strip mall which held the bank, offices, and a couple of low-end restaurants. They were cheap and convenient which meant he'd eaten in both of them.

"He restores my soul. He leads me … something … something … even though I walk—"

Richard stopped so the crunch of the leaves wouldn't be the predominant sound and hissed at Sterling, "Could you please hush for just one moment?" Sterling glared but complied.

To the south, Richard could hear the occasional whine of tires and rumble of the motors of cars and trucks traveling on I-40. Otherwise, there was the leaden quiet that precedes a snowstorm. Richard crossed the street toward the twin buildings which housed the APS Service Center with Sterling trailing reluctantly behind him.

An icy wind came sighing down from Tijeras Canyon. Richard pulled his coat closer around his body. The beam from his heavy, black, cop's flashlight washed across the empty parking lot as they walked toward the buildings. The click of the metal toe taps on their heavy shoes echoed off the glass, steel, and concrete looming in front of the two men.

Richard paused, blinked, trying to focus, and realized that the light from the flashlight was dying. A sharp slap of the body of the light against his gloved palm produced no result. The light continued to fade with each step they took toward the building. A few moments later it died.

Sterling's recitation of the Psalm became even more frenzied. "Even though I walk through the valley of death."

Valley of the shadow of death, Richard's mind corrected, but he was starting to understand why Sterling seemed so rattled. It was inexplicable, a feeling more than a conscious thought, but Richard found himself thumbing up the holster guard and loosening the Heckler and Koch pistol where it rested at his side. Immediately he felt like a fool. He had only fired the weapon at the range. Never drawn it in the two two years he had served on the force. His rational mind argued with primal fear, but he couldn't quite lift his hand from the pistol's grip.

A sharp cry of pain came from deep between the buildings.

CHAPTER TWO

HERE BE MONSTERS

RICHARD TURNED ON his body camera only to discover that, like the radio and the car, it too was dead. Dropping the useless flashlight, Richard drew his gun as he ran down the incline between the two buildings. Then he realized Sterling wasn't following. He ran back and grabbed the man by the arm.

"*Now* we've got a crime. Come on!"

"I can't! I can't!" It emerged as a whimper that ended in a sob. Richard saw the sparkle of tears running down the man's lined face. Baffled, Richard gave his partner a hard shake. "What is *wrong* with you? Snap out of it."

He spun Sterling around so he was in front and gave the older man a shove. The driveway was steep, and inertia took over, sending Sterling stumbling down the incline. Richard leaped to his side.

Now he could hear harsh breaths and the sound of blows connecting with flesh. Richard's eyes adjusted to the gloom, and he saw three hulking figures surrounding a smaller figure who was fighting hard, throwing kicks and punches that seemed to have no effect on the attackers.

He dropped into the approved two-handed-grip horse stance and drew down on the assailants. "Police! Back off!"

There was no reaction from the three attackers. Sterling was rooted at his side, seemingly incapable of doing anything.

For an instant Richard dithered. With his camera off he was uncomfortable just shooting any of the assailants, and while he was a decent shot, there was a not insignificant chance he would hit the victim, as all four people kept moving and shifting.

In the face of so many questionable police shootings nationwide, the department had given tentative approval to the use of the warning shot. They tended to make perps run away which was why many cops didn't like the concept. Richard *wanted* these guys to run away.

He raised the pistol over his head and snapped off a shot into the air while yelling, "Police! This is your final warning."

There was something odd in the feel of the gun in his hands. The kick wasn't as strong as normal nor the report as loud. The muzzle flash did allow him to get a look at the victim of the attack.

It was a girl. Late teens at the most; long hair swirled about her face. Sweat glistened on her skin, and her features were twisted with pain and terror. A pocket on her leather coat was torn loose. All he could tell about her attackers was that they were enormous and dressed in something dark and formfitting. They were as unimpressed with the gunshot as they had been with his shrill command.

The girl ducked under a ponderous roundhouse blow from one of her attackers. There was no more time for warnings. With his palms so wet with sweat Richard was grateful he had on gloves to help steady his hold on the pistol. He was breathing in sharp, shallow pants. He forced himself to hold his breath, took careful aim at the back of one of the muggers, and fired. Once again, the recoil felt off. There was a gout of … something from the man's back. Blood? It was hard to tell in the darkness. He knew the bullet had hit, but the man seemed completely unaffected, even unaware.

Richard rushed forward and fired again, a quick double tap, only this time nothing happened. Richard's attention was distracted from his target to his pistol. Worried that the bullets were lodged in the chamber or barrel of the pistol he tossed the gun aside before it could explode in his face.

Sterling, now well behind Richard, finally took action. Richard heard the gunshot, again muted, and he registered the bullet hit the asphalt well short of any target. There wasn't even a ricochet; it was as if the bullet had no punch.

There was a hollow feeling in Richard's gut warning him that this was eerie and scary, and he ought to run the other way, but he couldn't abandon her. It was like twisting ice-covered rope to force the muscles in his legs to move. Holstering the Heckler & Koch, he managed to break into a staggering run and headed toward the girl.

"Hang on, I'm coming," Richard yelled. His voice sounded stretched and thin and more soprano than tenor. He felt something shifting under the soles of his shoes, and he realized the ground was littered with pennies.

"HELP!" she screamed. "Help me! Help … me …" She gasped down a breath and ducked beneath the encircling arms.

The eye finds patterns and the mind supplies the expected description. Since he couldn't see the bulk of clothes, his mind had provided the explanation of a formfitting jumpsuit. It wasn't until Richard launched himself onto the back of one of the attackers that his brain finally accepted the reality … they weren't wearing clothes. But now he was on the guy's back, and his brain had a whole new series of sensations to process.

There were odd bumps under Richard's knees, and he found himself sliding as if the man was greased. He gripped tighter with his right hand and punched hard at the man's temple with his left. His fist sunk three inches into the man's head, and something oozed between his fingers.

He yelled in disgust, his legs lost the battle to hang on, and he slid to the ground. Lightning shot up his spine as his tailbone connected hard with the pavement. He jumped back to his feet just as one of the other attackers came lumbering around to face Richard.

"Oh, God!" he whimpered, because what faced him wasn't a man. It was a monster.

It was constructed of mud and sticks with a featureless blank where its face should have been. Richard was not a tall man, in fact, he was quite short, so the monster loomed over him. A fist began a slow ponderous swing toward Richard's head, but ice had again encased his muscles and his mind.

Then Sterling plowed into him, tackling Richard to the ground as the fist swung through the space his head had just occupied. The *thing* was still advancing.

"When you're down you gotta roll clear to give you a chance to get to your feet. Now roll, you motherfuckers!"

The gravel voice of Sergeant Jerry Hernandez echoed through his head. Richard rolled frantically away as a fist the size of a coal scuttle smashed into the asphalt next to his head. Sterling, just climbing to his feet, was not as fast, and the creature's other hand connected, snapping his head to the side. There was a brittle *crack* and Sterling collapsed onto the asphalt.

"Sterling!" Richard scrambled on hands and knees to his partner's side. "Oh shit. Oh shit. Oh shit." He gripped the fingertip of a glove with his teeth and ripped it off. Pressed two fingers against Sterling's throat, feeling for a pulse. Mercifully there was one.

The monster got a grip on the back of Richard's coat and hoisted him into the air before flinging him aside. The air went out of him as he hit the pavement. The girl darted past one of the monstrous trio and yelled, "Penny! Do you have a penny?"

"Wha …?" he wheezed. "My partner … he needs—"

"*We* need to stay *alive*. Now *give me* a fucking *penny*!"

Richard scrambled to his feet while digging into his pants pocket. The request seemed unhinged but given what he was facing he went along with it. Pulling out a handful of change, he located a penny and lobbed it to her. She snatched it out of the air and balanced it on her outstretched palm. Richard had the sudden and unpleasant sensation that something cold and wet had been dragged across the inside of his skull. The girl stared at him with an expression that included confusion, dismay, and anger.

She shook her head, sucked in a deep breath, and called out in a strange, harsh, and guttural language. The penny began to *spin*, to *glow*, throwing out copper-colored sparks. The girl tossed it into the air where it hung spinning like a tiny firework. Richard stared at it in disbelief.

She then batted the penny toward one of their attackers. The coin struck the monster in the chest, and it was suddenly engulfed in a column of flame. Richard threw an arm over his face as the blast of heat singed his eyebrows. The other monsters reeled away from their companion as it let out an eerie keening sound. The flames died away. The creature didn't move. The girl kicked it hard, and the creature shattered.

Richard spotted the roundhouse sweeping toward the girl's head. She didn't. He wrapped his arms around her waist, and dove sideways, barking an elbow on the pavement. The rough pavement tore through his coat and shirt, and he felt blood begin to trickle down his arm. The girl was on top of him. Her hair, damp with perspiration and smelling of sweat and sandalwood, snaked across his face and mouth. He noticed, distantly, that one ear held several earrings stretching from lobe to tip.

Richard got one knee underneath him, and shoved himself upright, lifting the girl with him. It wasn't easy because she was taller than he was.

"Come on, let's get out of here!" Richard said as he moved toward Sterling. He hoped he could lift him.

"They'll just keep coming," she sobbed.

Distracted by her statement, Richard missed the massive fist coming his way. It delivered a glancing blow to his jaw, and gobbets of mud spattered against Richard's face as he was knocked backwards. He came up hard against the side of a building; there was a window to his left. He raised his uninjured elbow, smashed it against the glass, and howled in pain. It always looked so effortless in the movies; the glass broke, the hero leaped through. In fact, the glass remained firmly in place and the hero's elbow hurt like hell. Richard yanked out his nightstick and swung hard. This time the glass shattered.

"Come on!"

He felt the words ripping along his throat, and he beckoned frantically to her. She darted between the two remaining monsters and ran to him. He was going to boost her through, but she braced a foot high on his thigh, the heel grinding into the muscle, grabbed his shoulder, and climbed him like a stepladder. He heard her land inside. Which left him and Sterling outside. With the monsters.

Moving like a broken-field runner, Richard ran back to Sterling. Grunting with effort he hoisted the man into a fireman's carry. Years of gymnastics in high school and college had left him with excellent upper body strength, but he was only five feet four inches tall, and Sterling was an ungainly load across his shoulder.

He staggered back to the window and shoved Sterling through. He knew moving him was a risk but leaving him outside with the monsters seemed a greater one. Fortunately, the girl helped lift Sterling over the edges of broken glass on the bottom edge of the window and onto the floor of the office.

Richard grabbed the windowsill. The broken glass cut into his palms, particularly the one without a glove. He gritted his teeth against the pain, planted a toe of his heavy shoe against the wall, and boosted into a handstand flip. He landed on his feet in the office and felt the jar from his shins to the top of his head. It had been a long time since he'd done any serious gymnastics. His back was already awash with pain from the effort of carrying and lifting Sterling.

"Ow, ow, ow, ow, ow," he groaned as he surveyed their surroundings.

It was some kind of nondescript office space. Computers on metal desks, chairs on casters, and office cubicles formed from carpeted panels. Briefly he wondered why the alarms weren't working, then then decided it was all part of the nightmare in which he found himself.

"You should have left him," the girl snapped.

"With the monsters?" His voice had spiraled up.

"They will follow. It's *me* they want to kill. And you if you get in the way."

And, indeed, at that moment sausage-sized fingers gripped the windowsill, dripping mud from their blunt tips onto the industrial carpet. The first monster hauled itself through.

"Penny!" the girl screamed. Richard dug into his pants pocket; grateful he'd mindlessly returned the change to said pocket. The girl frantically sorted through and emerged with three more pennies.

The second monster was now through the window.

The girl huddled over the pennies cupped in the palm of her hands. She muttered in that strange language again. The pennies began to spin and burn. She tossed one into the air and batted it at the attacker. Flames exploded around the monster. The girl tottered. Richard got an arm around her, and realized they were propping each other up. Then technology decided to work. The automatic sprinkler system kicked to life and doused the flames.

"Oh … damn," Richard said. The monsters advanced.

The girl lifted her head. Water ran out of her hair and across her skin. Richard ran forward and headbutted the lead creature. If his fist had been gross, this was disgusting, and he didn't shift the monster by an inch. He lifted his head, shaking mud from his hair, and saw a fist. It connected, snapping his head around. His cheek felt like he was chewing ground glass and his neck became a column of pain. He went staggering across the room, hit the wall, and fell down.

The girl held up a penny and began to chant, but she was trembling, forcing the words past chattering teeth. A small section of mud slid off the thigh of a monster, carried in water from the sprinklers. A thin thread of hope formed. Richard scanned the walls and spotted the glass fire box with its extinguisher and coiled fire hose about ten feet to his left.

It was like moving through wet concrete, but Richard got to his feet. He tried to run and managed a shuffle. Still, it carried him to the fire box. He moaned, clenched his teeth, and broke the glass with his less-sore elbow. Icy water ran through his hair and dripped off the end of his nose. The monsters were a foot from the girl.

He uncoiled the fire hose, turned the spigot, and nearly lost his footing as high-pressure water gushed from the nozzle. Holding hard with both hands, he brought the stream of water onto the chest of one of the monsters. Despite the lack of a mouth, a high-pitched howl emanated from the creature, weird and inhuman. Mud went washing down its chest, carrying twigs and branches with it.

Richard aimed the water at the other creature. It also

produced the horrible cry. He alternated the water back and forth between them. Rivulets of filthy water sluiced around their feet as they melted. He had a wild image of the scene at the witch's castle in *The Wizard of* Oz and couldn't believe he was doing this. Eventually all that remained was a floor awash with brown water and floating sticks.

Abruptly the alarms began to howl and some of the computers sprang to life and began an automatic reboot. Outside the streetlights snapped back on. Richard began laughing hysterically. Behind him he could hear the girl's choking sobs.

A dark figure lunged through the window. The laughter died as his air choked off in fear and Richard brought the fire hose to bear. The shock of the water elicited a long string of curses in several languages, only three of which Richard recognized. He pulled the hose aside and stared at the face lifting cautiously back over the windowsill. Water plastered the man's long hair to his skull and dripped from his beard. Judging from the patched and dirty coat and the layers of sweaters, it was some homeless guy in search of a quick profit.

"Forget it, buddy. There are going to be no free computers tonight," Richard croaked, his throat raw from exertion and yelling. Water squelched between the soles of his feet and his shoes and lapped around his ankles. He was losing sensation in his toes. Now that he had stopped exerting himself, he felt the sweat trickling down his back and chest like rivulets of ice. He managed to turn the spigot, and the gusher of water died to a trickle.

"Yeah, like half of them are even going to work after

getting a shower. And how the hell did you even get in here?" the homeless man asked. The voice was youthful, and he spoke in a normal tone of voice. Richard couldn't understand why he was able to hear the man clearly over the din of the alarms. "You should not have been able to walk in darkness …"

The words were oddly ominous, and a clattering filled Richard's ears as his teeth began to chatter. He remembered Sterling's frantic prayers.

Yea though I walk through the valley of the shadow of death.

He was back in Sunday school at the strict Lutheran church his family attended. At six years old the words were parroted, meaningless and incomprehensible. Today he was twenty-seven and he was deathly afraid.

The man looked closely at Richard. "Oh." He drew out the word. "I see what you are."

Richard's breath stopped in his throat and his gut clenched down tight. Instinctively Richard wrapped his arms across his chest and belly in defense against this body blow. It was a secret carefully kept, which haunted his nights. It had sent him fleeing from the East Coast to this nondescript city in a poor and obscure state and into a new career away from the judgmental and censorious eyes of his father, and now this man had perceived it.

Another sound joined the yammering of the alarms. Police sirens wailing in the distance. The bum was breaking off the shards of glass sticking up from the frame like jagged teeth in a steel jaw. He ran a hand across the casement to verify it was clear, then leaned his elbows companionably on the windowsill like a neighbor talking across a narrow tenement street.

"Now we have a decision to make," the man said. "I was sent here for her." A jerk of the chin toward the girl who knelt in the water sobbing softly. "But then I find you, and you're not supposed to be here. I could take her, but I think she'll be safer with you. They can't see her when she's with you."

The sirens were close now. Headlights and light bars danced white, red, and amber through the windows as police cars came wheeling into the parking lot.

"What are you talking about?" Richard asked.

"I'll get back to you with that explanation, but right now I've gotta go before your brethren arrive. Remember, don't leave her. She's only safe with you."

The man spun away from the window. Richard lunged after him.

"Hey. Wait. What do you *mean*?" He was yelling after the man's retreating back as he ran up the alley. His coats ballooned around his body, giving the effect of wings. "You mean I have to … take … her … home?"

Richard turned back to survey the rescued girl. Her clothes were drenched, her black hair plastered to her cheeks. Despite the bruises and the blood-coated split lip she was the most beautiful woman Richard had ever seen. She had pale, pale skin and winged eyebrows over green eyes with epicanthic folds.

"I need you to stay quiet. Follow my lead. Okay?" The girl nodded. Richard looked around the room and spotted a copper glow. A penny. Still spinning. Still on fire. He picked it up prepared to feel heat, but it was cool to the touch. It was just a feather-like tickle against the palm of his hand. He slipped it into his pocket.

He couldn't do much about the mud and the sticks. They would have to remain, but in a state where a body found in the trunk of a car, hands tied behind the back, with with six bullet holes had been ruled a suicide, Richard didn't think anyone would inquire too closely. There were reasons he'd selected New Mexico to begin his career with the police; this was one of them.

The alarms cut off. Someone had reached the control box. The abrupt cessation of sound was almost painful. Flashlight beams were playing across the walls of the buildings outside.

Richard heard a voice yelling, "Officer down! Officer down!"

Richard pulled off his badge and held it out. The other hand he held prudently over his head. He then scrambled awkwardly through the broken window. A gun and flashlight were thrust in his face.

"Freeze … oh," the cop said.

CHAPTER THREE

IN THE DARK

THE HECKLER & Koch and Sterling's Glock rested in the center of Lieutenant Damon Weber's desk. It was unfortunate that Weber was on duty tonight because he was smart and conscientious. Richard looked up briefly, met the older man's piercing, brown-eyed gaze, and looked away again. The ice pack pressed against his bruised jaw was providing some relief, but it still hurt to talk, and his neck was a column of pain.

The battered old PC on the desk sent up a dull hum, and the blast of tepid air from the heat register ruffled the edges of the paper piles which were stacked on every available flat surface.

Richard continued with his report. "I observed three … men beating up the lady."

Richard hoped the Lou hadn't noticed the minute hesitation. He was surprised at himself for even mentally using the cop shorthand for lieutenant. Perhaps after two years he was starting to feel like an actual policeman. Although if he gave an accurate account of the night's events, he'd be packed off for a psych evaluation and quietly separated from the force. Weber cleared his throat and Richard hurriedly continued.

"I ordered them to stop. They didn't, so I fired a warning

shot."

Somebody was heating a tamale in the microwave and the smoke and bitter smell of the red chile had him salivating. Too many hours and too much exertion had left him limp and empty. At least he'd been allowed to change out of his soaked uniform and into street clothes before he faced Weber's gimlet stare. So now he was just scared, hurting, tired, and hungry instead of scared, hurting, tired, hungry, *cold and wet.*

"And that didn't produce asses and elbows?" Weber asked and rubbed his fingers over the deep acne scars running along his jaw line.

Richard had noticed the lieutenant did that a lot. He wondered if the older man was embarrassed by the blemishes. He shouldn't be. Damon was a handsome man. Richard forced himself back to the moment.

"No, sir. Since I felt the victim was in imminent danger, I shot at one of them."

"And?"

It was hard because it was going to look bad and send him back to the range for many more hours of practice, but he had no choice but to lie. Richard swallowed. "I … missed. I then advanced, fired again, but the gun jammed. I got us into the building. And then the cavalry arrived."

"And the perps?"

"They … ran."

"All three of them?" Richard nodded. He was nervous at the sharp tone of inquiry in the lieutenant's voice.

"Our guys only spotted *one* person fleeing the scene," Weber said.

"Maybe they split up," Richard offered. It sounded lame even to him.

There was a long silence as the two policemen regarded one another. Beyond the frosted glass door, phones rang, and men's voices rumbled like the basso stops on a powerful organ. Occasionally a woman's flutelike tones would add a counterpoint to the bass.

Weber laid a hand briefly across both pistols. "We're gonna keep your weapons pending an investigation. You got a spare?"

"Yes, sir, at home."

Weber laced his hands behind his head and stretched out his back. "So, what was this? Mugging? Attempted rape?" he asked.

"I don't know."

Weber stood and gathered up a file. "Well, let's go find out. Girl was identified as Rhiana Davinovitch." *So that's her name*, Richard thought. There hadn't been time during the struggle, and after they had been in different cars when they were taken to APD headquarters. "Driver's license gives a home address in Van Nuys, California, but she's got a student ID from UNM."

"Sir," Richard said before Weber could reach the door of the office. "What's the word on Sterling?"

"In a coma. Skull fracture. They're prepping him for surgery."

Guilt washed through him. "I shouldn't have moved him. If I'd realized they were going to follow us and leave him alone—"

Weber laid a hand on his shoulder. Richard fought the

urge to lean into the touch. "You didn't abandon your partner. It was the right call." Weber shook his head. "But the guy who hit him must have been fucking King Kong to do that much damage."

Richard again found himself unable to meet the lieutenant's eyes.

✧ ✧ ✧

AT THE FOOT of the mountains a man paced the confines of his elegant office. Occasionally, he glanced out of the large windows facing to the west. The lights of the city were a jeweled carpet across the valley. He checked his watch. Sighed. Regretfully, he could only conclude that Cross had failed. The girl was dead.

He returned to his desk, a massive affair constructed of granite and filled with swirling colors. Another gift from this amazing planet filled with so many wonders. He had lived in many places, on many worlds, but none had possessed the clear skies of New Mexico, and the state's lack of moisture and low scrubby trees did little to obscure the view. It was a foolish whimsy, but in these early years of the twenty-first century he wanted to be able to see into the distance since he didn't seem able to see into the future. He had thought mankind would be so much further ahead. Instead, they seemed to be sliding back into—

The hum of the elevator broke into his thoughts. He couldn't help himself. He left the office and stood waiting in the outer office for the elevator door to open. The polished stainless steel threw back his reflection. He stood over six feet tall and was was well over three hundred pounds, with ebony black skin. His features were an amalgamation of the features of all the human races. Cross stepped out. The hairs of his mustache and beard glittered where his breath had condensed and frozen in the frigid air. He was alone.

"She's dead," the waiting man said heavily.

Cross shook his head. "Nope."

"Then where is she?"

"There was a cop in the mix. The name on the tag was Oort. Funny name," Cross said as he walked into the private office and over to the untouched dinner tray sitting on an inlaid onyx table near the floor-to-ceiling bookcases. He settled into a chair and began to eat.

"What did you do with the Hunters?" the man asked as he followed after him.

"I didn't have to do anything. By the time I got there, the baby sorceress and the cop had taken care of them, though it left a big fucking mess."

That was not good news. It was best that humanity was not aware of the shadow war that was going on all around them.

"At least Grenier will think she's dead," Cross mumbled around a mouthful.

"No," Kenntnis corrected. "He'll know his constructs were destroyed. He won't assume success." Kenntnis fell silent, weighing the options.

Smacking and slurping filled the silence. His concentration broken, Kenntnis glared at Cross. Even after all these years in human form, the Old One still hadn't grasped the most basic of manners.

"Can you locate her?" the man asked as he pushed aside several files on the desk. The covers were embossed with LUMINA ENTERPRISES, A. Kenntnis, President. He leaned back against the desk. The polished granite was slick and cool beneath his palms.

"No problemo. She's like a damn flare, throwing off magic in every direction. I think I could find her even if she was in another state."

"So where is she?" Kenntnis asked, clinging to his fast-vanishing patience.

"I left her with the cop."

"And why would you do that?"

"Were you not listening? He was undeterred by The Dark. He's the one who finished off two of the hunters," Cross mumbled around a mouthful of cold mac and cheese. "The cop's one of the empty ones," Cross added as he moved to the enormous espresso machine on a bookshelf and drew a cup of coffee.

Kenntnis blinked slowly, absorbing what had just been said. "You. Found. A. Paladin. And those weren't the first words out of your mouth?" he almost shouted.

"No, because it's not particularly relevant," Cross said. He blew hard across the coffee. Steam bent and danced under the assault. "Seriously, what are you gonna do? Arm him with the sword? It ain't 800 AD anymore." The creature paused, considering. "Although he might be willing to use it on me." There was a hopeful note in the final words. "You should *totally* recruit him."

Kenntnis ignored him. "You have to go get the girl." Swinging behind his desk, he pulled the computer out of sleep mode. "I'll check out this Oort." He waved dismissal at Cross. "Go."

"Okay, might cause a fuss, busting into a cop shop like that—"

"Don't be obtuse. Find the appropriate moment."

Cross heaved a long-suffering sigh and headed out of the office, muttering, "It's fucking cold out there, but you don't care that I'm gonna be squatting behind some dumpster or hiding in the bushes ..." The complaints were cut off with the closing of the elevator doors.

Kenntnis turned back to his computer. He would investigate the background of this potential Paladin before he made contact. But the arrival of one at just this critical juncture, and the symbolism of the policeman's shield, wasn't lost on Kenntnis. Though it represented a level of coincidence which made him decidedly uncomfortable. Fate was not normally a player in Kenntnis's plans.

In fact, she was usually a downright bitch.

✧   ✧   ✧

THE GIRL WAS waiting in an interrogation room. There was a can of Coke and an open bag of potato chips in front of her. She was swallowed by the shirt and pants provided by Lucile, one of the dispatchers, who had had a change of clothes in her locker. Lucile was a lush lady, and her oversized clothes made the girl look even younger, like a child playing dress-up.

She's such a baby, Richard thought. *I wonder how old she is?* His next thought was one of worry because she hadn't heard his version of the events. How widely would their stories diverge?

Weber took a chair across from her. Richard remained standing just behind his left shoulder.

"Hi, Miss Davinovitch. I'm Lieutenant Damon Weber, and this here is Officer Richard Oort. Even though you've met, I'm betting you didn't have time for any introductions."

Her eyes flew up to meet Richard's and she blurted, "Like the Oort Cloud." Her voice was low with a husky catch at the end of the words. Richard wondered if she sounded like that normally or if it was the residue of a night of screaming.

"Yes." Richard smiled at her. "You must know astronomy."

She gave a one-sided shrug. "I'm a physics major."

Weber cleared his throat. "So, could you tell us how this started?"

"I … I left my dorm room and went to get a burrito at the Taco Bell. These guys started following me."

"Which Taco Bell?" Weber asked.

"The … the one on Monte Vista, near UNM."

Weber frowned and rubbed at his jaw. "You were a hell of a long away from campus. That's gotta be five, maybe six miles."

"I was scared, and I ran."

"And they kept following you?"

"Yes, sir."

"Why didn't you call for help? Kids your age, you always have a cell phone."

"It … it wasn't working."

Weber looked back over his shoulder at Richard. "Delores reported that your radio went on the fritz."

"And my phone was dead, too," Richard said cautiously.

"It must have been a dead zone," Rhiana offered a bit breathlessly.

"Must have been one hell of a dead zone." Silence held for several seconds. "Okay, you and Officer Oort were inside a flooded office building, but there were also a lot of sticks and mud. You know what that was about?"

Rhiana stared desperately at Richard. He cleared his throat. "Couldn't say, sir. It was like that when we got inside. Well, not the mud. That was from the sprinklers sprinklers going off. But the dirt and sticks."

"Fire hose had also been deployed," Weber said as he stared at Richard in a most disconcerting way. Richard just shrugged. "Okay, let's table that for a minute. Can you describe your assailants?"

"Big."

"Anglo, Hispanic, Black?"

"I … I couldn't tell. It was dark. And they were wearing masks," she added hurriedly. "You know those ones you pull on."

"Balaclavas?" Weber suggested.

"Yeah, those."

Richard received another piercing look. "You didn't mention that."

"Must have slipped my mind."

"Hmmm." Weber pushed back his chair. "Well, all right then. We'll let you know if we catch these guys. We'll need you to testify. I'll get somebody to take you back to your dorm."

"Could … could Officer Oort take me?" Rhiana asked as she jumped to her feet.

Richard flushed as Weber tried to hide a grin. "We'll get a policewoman to take you," Weber said.

"Oh, I'd hate to be any more of a bother." She pulled out her cell phone. "I'll call my roommate and have her pick me up."

"Are you sure?"

"Yeah, that would be better."

Richard opened the door and stepped aside for the girl to pass. As he started to leave, Weber leaned down from his six feet until his lips were level with Richard's ear, and with a leer whispered, "And another one bites the dust."

"With respect, sir, go to Hell," Richard muttered.

Weber snorted, but grabbed Richard's arm before he could walk away, no longer smiling. "I got an officer in the hospital who might not make it, and a strong feeling that I'm being treated like a damn mushroom."

"Sir?"

"You know, kept in the dark and fed with shit. If I find out you're slinging shit along with that girl … let's just say you're going to rue the day."

"Yes, sir."

"By the way, *you* look like shit. Go home."

"I'm not off shift for another couple of hours. I could get my report—"

"Go the fuck home."

"Yes, sir."

✧   ✧   ✧

LUCILE BUSTLED OVER; her arms filled with a bulging white plastic garbage bag. "I got your clothes, honey. They're still soaked so I put 'em in a bag. Just keep my things until tomorrow. Rich can bring them back."

"Richard," Richard corrected reflexively, knowing he wouldn't be heeded but needing to try anyway. Rhiana accepted the sack.

"Thank you."

"You're welcome. We're just glad you're okay. It just gets worse and worse out there."

The girl's face was bleak as she said, "Yes … yes, it does." She clutched the plastic bundle to her chest. She looked very lost and very young.

"Do you want me to wait with you until your roommate comes?" he asked.

"No, that's okay." She glanced up at him through her long lashes. "Thank you. For saving me."

He smiled at her and noticed that she blushed. "It's my job."

He turned away only to hear her say softly, "Are you really going to pretend it didn't happen?"

He hunched his shoulders and kept walking. He could almost feel her eyes boring into his back. Unbidden, the memory of the bum's final words came came to him. *"… Remember, don't leave her. She's only safe with you."*

✦ ✦ ✦

THE ELEVATOR REACHED the ground floor with an anemic *ding.* The subtle jar caused Richard's teeth to clack lightly together, and a white-hot poker jabbed up from his battered jaw to emerge somewhere over his right eye. He pushed wearily off the side of the elevator. Normally he took the stairs, but every part of his body was making itself known, and not in a good way.

He hobbled toward his used blue Volvo. It was 3:00 AM and a bitter wind was whipping through the office buildings of downtown Albuquerque. He was unlocking the door when a shadowy figure stepped out from between two parked cars. Richard yelped in alarm, then recognized Rhiana.

"Ms. Davinovitch. I thought someone was picking you up."

"Rhiana, call me Rhiana, and … and I want to go with *you.*"

"It's not appropriate for me to take you, and I want to go by the hospital and check on my partner." Richard paused and studied that piquant face. "You didn't call your roommate, did you?" She looked contrite and shook her head. "I'll call you a cab." He started to fish out his phone.

"He told you to stay with me," she said.

"Well, yes, but if we're talking about the same he, *he,* was a bum."

"He's not a bum," the girl answered.

"Okay, then what is he?"

"I don't know … exactly. Maybe a familiar," she said. The final word emerged as a question. They stood in silence. Richard in frustration. Rhiana with the tentative air of a wistful child.

"Why would he say that? That you're only safe with me?" Richard asked.

"I don't know. Maybe because you could walk in the darkness."

Richard rolled his eyes and snorted. "Yeah, that's me. Just a little ray of sunshine."

"This isn't funny. It's serious."

"Then tell me what the hell that even *means*?" He didn't often use profanity. His father had quoted Spencer Kimball's *"Profanity is the effort of a feeble brain to express itself forcibly"* ad nauseam until swear words almost felt like they choked him, but Richard was tired, hurting, and situation seemed ripe for an expletive.

"It's what happens when there's that much magic—"

"Magic?" Scorn edged both syllables of the word.

"Well, what's *your* explanation?" Rhiana demanded and gave him a withering look. "You saw me enchant the pennies."

Almost without volition, Richard's hand reached into the pocket of his trousers, and he pulled out the spinning, glowing penny. "There are these smart people in the world called scientists. They'll be able to figure this out."

"I *know*, I'm one of them … or I'm going to be one of them, but no, they *won't* figure this out because it's fucking magic." She gestured at the penny. Richard returned it to his pocket. "Magic doesn't obey the rules in our world. It screws up stuff like lights and phones and—"

"Guns?" Richard suggested.

"I guess." She frowned. "Though I'm not sure why. A gun fires because of basic mechanics." She waved her hands agitatedly in the air over her head. "Anyway, those things created the darkness and inside it people were scared, really scared, so the people inside the dark wouldn't help me and people outside couldn't come in. But you did. You weren't scared."

"Oh, trust me, I was scared."

They once again fell silent. The girl was starting to shiver, and her voice shook as she asked, "So are you?"

"So am I *what*?"

"Going to pretend like none of it happened?"

"I haven't decided yet." Richard's breath emerged as a white plume as if the fears, doubts, and questions he didn't dare to ask were seeking release.

They locked stares. Richard broke first, disquieted as much by the sooty lashes framing her beautiful eyes as by the lurking terror in their green depths. Taillights of a returning cop car flared red they pulled into the lot, braked, and parked. The officers climbed out and pulled a perp out of the backseat. Richard clocked the questioning and curious looks from Krohn and Leggett.

Richard yanked open the door of his car. "Get in." Rhiana scrambled to obey. He started the engine and music from the local classical station filled the car. Richard snapped it off.

"So, what were those things that were attacking you?" Richard asked.

"I don't know. Not exactly. They were sort of like golems, but ..." Her voice trailed away, and she shrugged.

"Is there anything that you *do* know?" Richard demanded in frustration.

"I know that whoever created them is going to find a way to kill me if you don't let me come home with you."

Richard's hands clenched on the steering wheel, and he

resisted the urge to beat his head against it. He couldn't believe he was going to do this.

"All right, but not a *word* to my boss. I'd like to keep my job."

"Okay, I won't—"

"*And.* You're going to answer some questions."

"Thank you! Thank you! I promise, I'll tell you everything."

CHAPTER FOUR

MAGIC CAN DO STUFF

THEY HADN'T TALKED during the thirty-minute drive from downtown to Apartment Row out on Montgomery Boulevard. Her face throbbed in time to the beating of her heart and exhaustion dragged at every limb. Rhiana rested her head against the back of the seat and let the music pouring from the radio lull her. It was something soft and classical. She didn't know anything about that kind of music.

The jouncing of the car passing over a speed bump woke her, unsettled, from a sleep she hadn't intended to take. As they pulled into the parking lot of an apartment complex, Rhiana noted it was one of the nicer units nestled close to the foothills and built in a pseudo-Spanish style with tiled roofs and bright stucco on the walls.

She waited by the car as the policeman opened the trunk and removed a shotgun. She noted the bulletproof vest with its ceramic inserts lying on the floor of the trunk. *That won't help him against what's coming,* she thought.

Nausea took her as the fear returned. The slamming of the trunk brought her back. Oort was indicating the way with a gesture of his long, slender hand, allowing her to go first. Was it manners or did he want to keep that shotgun at her back? She started up the path from the parking lot.

He had a ground-floor unit. He unlocked the door and stepped aside for her to enter. The cheap carpet was the usual apartment beige, but everything else was unexpected. The room was dominated by a grand piano set near the sliding glass doors leading onto the minuscule patio. There was a metal and white leather sofa of a modern design arranged in front of a small television, an armchair, a glass coffee table with a few books scattered on the top. There was no dining table. It appeared he ate at the tiny counter that separated the kitchen from the living room.

A Bose stereo system sat against one wall. On the other wall was a tall bookcase. It was filled with books and sheet music, CDs, a signed baseball, and a NY Yankees World Series mug. On one shelf in a modern, silver Nambe frame was a family photo. A stern-looking man with gray hair and amazing dark blue eyes looked out. Next to him stood two young women—one with light brown hair, the other with dark blond—both attractive without being beautiful. In front of the older man stood a slender and delicately beautiful older woman with white-blonde hair and gray eyes. The man had his hand on her shoulder, but it looked more controlling than affectionate. Rhiana didn't have to ask if this was Oort's mother. Her features were etched in his face. The cop was also in the photo, but he wasn't looking at the camera. His gaze was on his father's face with an inscrutable expression.

There were a few paintings on the wall. All abstract. All icy cool in shades of white, gray, and pale blues. Everything was excruciatingly neat. The only evidence of use was an open book of music on the piano's stand.

She couldn't help but compare it with her family's home,

cluttered with piles of old newspapers and *People* magazines, reeking of dog pee which had permeated the cheap carpet, and filled with the competing noise of four televisions in four rooms all tuned to different channels. It made her feel awkward and low-class. She felt the embarrassment transform to resentment against the cop.

Oort propped the shotgun against the wall near the front door. He crossed the room. He had an economical way of moving and an upright posture. Rhiana realized it was not the erect stance of military service but more reminiscent of dancers or gymnasts. He twitched shut the curtains over the sliding glass door.

"Are you hungry?" he asked.

The reminder had saliva bursting across her tongue and her stomach clenching. She nodded. The interior of the refrigerator was as neat as the rest of the apartment, and equally as spare. Milk, eggs, a carton of plain yogurt, and various kinds of fresh fruit and vegetables in the crisper drawers.

"I drink a yogurt shake in the mornings," Oort said. "I also have oatmeal, if that sounds more appealing."

"Oatmeal," Rhiana said. She expected the usual micro-waveable packet, but instead he took down a package of steel-cut Scottish oats from a cabinet. While the oatmeal cooked, he dumped yogurt, honey, fruit, wheat germ, protein, and milk into a blender and whipped the mixture to a froth.

The oatmeal was set before her on the counter along with the milk, honey, and a package of extremely tiny raisins. Rhiana surreptitiously turned the package to read the label.

Zante Currants. So that's what currants looked like. She had read about them, but they certainly hadn't been a staple in the Davinovitch household.

An experimental taste of the oats revealed a far richer, nuttier flavor than conventional oatmeal. The local New Mexico mesquite honey had an almost bitter aftertaste, but it was still delicious. The policeman stood in the kitchen, his shoulders propped against the front of the refrigerator, and sipped his drink. There was a frown between his pale brows. Finally, he reached into his pocket and deposited the penny on the counter.

It sat spinning and glowing. Rhiana's throat was suddenly too tight to swallow. She set down her spoon and met the icy blue eyes of her host.

"Now I need to have a few questions answered," he said in his soft tenor. His expression was worried and vulnerable.

"O …" Her voice broke. Rhiana coughed and tried again. "Okay."

"You want to explain this?" He indicated the penny.

"It's a focusing device that can carry a spell." At his raised eyebrow she added, "A magic spell. People use different objects to focus—"

"Wands?" The word carried more derision than being an actual question.

"Only poseurs. Real magic users use things that are readily available and that you're likely to carry—a set of keys, glasses, a pen. Pennies are what work for me."

"You're going to be in a tough place when they phase them out." She shot him an annoyed look. She hated being mocked. "So, what did you do to it?" he asked.

"Activated it so it could carry a spell for me." She saw no point in holding back. He was her only hope for staying alive.

"Well, that clears things right up."

"It's hard to explain if you don't have the ability. And you don't because I can't feed … *read*," she amended quickly, "anything off you." She gave him a quick look, but he didn't seem to have caught the slip.

"And that language you were speaking. I didn't recognize it, and I speak quite a few."

"It was Enochian. The language before there was language. Stuff the angels spoke." She felt her breath growing short and added breathlessly, "And demons." Furrows formed in the oatmeal and filled with milk as she dragged her spoon through her cereal.

"Well, that sounds cheery. And those … monsters, they're magical, too?" Oort asked.

Rhiana shook her head. "They were created by magic, but they're not magical. They were just sticks and mud animated by magic." She worried this was too much information, but his expression was still attentive.

"And they were sent to kill you?"

"Yes," Rhiana said.

"A gun would have been easier," Oort said. "And I'm gathering that if there hadn't been any … magic … around, a gun would have worked just fine."

"But guns need someone to shoot them, and people and guns can be traced. You can't trace mud and sticks."

"And who created and sent these things?" he asked.

"I'm not sure. Maybe the man who's been funding us. Maybe the group, but I didn't think they had the power for something like this."

"Does this man who's funding you have a name?"

"I don't know it. Josh never let any of the rest of us deal with him."

"I need this Josh's last name."

"Delay."

Oort wrote it down on a pad on the counter. "And what was the funding *for*?"

This was getting dangerously close to the heart of the matter. "You know, how magic can be used to … do … stuff."

"What kind of *stuff*?"

"You know, like power source … stuff."

"And why do they want to kill you?"

And now they were to it. The million-dollar question. If she answered, it would slam her ass in jail and remove her from the protection of this man. In jail she would die, and she didn't want to die.

Rhiana slid off the barstool and walked into the living room, playing for time and seeking inspiration. "It's complicated," she said slowly as her gaze flew across the books on the shelves, the books on the coffee table. One was open. Gilt-edged pages glinted, and she realized from the minute type and the almost translucent pages that it was a Bible. Suddenly the other titles on the shelves snapped into focus. Works by Aquinas and Augustine set alongside an array of forensic books and psychology texts.

She whirled to face the policeman. "It's because I wanted to leave the coven." It wasn't a lie. She had, just not for the reasons this man would assume.

"Coven? That implies there were more people involved than just this Josh fellow. Who are they?"

"Deb Rangold, Steve Douglas, and Naomi Parson."

"All right," he said. Oort laid a hand on the edge of the oatmeal bowl. "Are you finished?"

"Yes, thanks."

He picked up the bowl and his glass and moved to the sink. They were quickly rinsed and deposited in the dishwasher. Rhiana drifted back toward the kitchen.

"You're not denying it. Pretending it didn't happen. Telling me you don't believe in magic," she said as the cop dried his hands.

He glanced at the glowing, spinning penny. He then opened the freezer and pulled out a couple of cold packs. He tossed one to Rhiana. She instinctively caught it. He laid his against his jaw and sucked in a quick gasp.

"For the moment I'm going to accept your explanation … until I have a better one," he said.

Rhiana laid the cold pack against the side of her head where one of the monster's fists had connected. Her gasp echoed his. They stood staring at each other across the breakfast bar.

"So, what do we do now?" Rhiana asked.

"Sleep," came the reply.

The memory of Josh's pawing hands and how he always managed to press his crotch against her when they were working filled her mouth with a sour taste. Granted this man's slim body was a vast improvement over Josh's pendulous belly, but …

"You take the bed," he said. She looked into his handsome face and realized he had sensed her dismay. "I'll be sleeping on the couch."

He disappeared into the bedroom. Rhiana moved to the front door, cracked it open, and peeked outside. She then did the same at the patio doors and gave a sigh of relief. Oort returned carrying a pillow and a blanket.

"I put out clean towels and a washcloth for you. If you want, I can change the sheets—"

Tears pricked hot and moist against her eyelids and hung on her lashes. Rhiana shook her head. "No, that's okay, thank you."

As she started for the bedroom, he added, "And in case you're worried, the door locks."

She looked back and wondered what fate had placed her in such gentle hands. She found a small and nervous smile curving her lips. "I don't think I'm going to need that."

✧　✧　✧

WEBER HUNG UP the phone. The hospital wouldn't tell him much apart from the fact Sterling was now in surgery. His shift was almost over, but he couldn't shake the feeling that the young officer hadn't told him everything. Most officers went through their entire careers and never fired their weapon except on the range. He could understand Oort missing his shot. It was one thing to fire at a target. It was quite another to shoot a human being. But Sterling was a veteran of the force. He had almost put in his full twenty. So why the fuck didn't *he* fire?

He remembered Oort saying his gun jammed after his

second shot. Weber opened the chamber to clear the round, but there was no evidence that a jam had happened. He disassembled and examined both weapons and couldn't find anything wrong. A small indoor range had been included in the basement of the new APD building. Weber reassembled the guns and headed down.

Grabbing a set of earmuffs and a silhouette target from the desk, he stopped at the first bay. He set up the target and sent it sliding along its track to the back wall, settled the muffs over his ears, and fired Oort's gun. Nothing happened. He picked up Sterling's and pulled the trigger. Again nothing. There was nothing to indicate that the striker hadn't hit the bullets in either gun. He tried one more time with both weapons with the same result.

Once he was in the elevator, he checked his watch. 07:00 A.M. If he knew Angela, she was probably already at the morgue. He pulled out his phone, then hesitated. Ultimately, he gave a shrug and dialed her number. Angela was a friend, and he knew he could count on her discretion.

"Hey, lady, you got time to meet me at the lab? Got something I want you to check out."

"Sure, it was a slow night. Only had one customer."

"Great. See you in thirty?"

"You got it."

✧   ✧   ✧

THE TWO HOURS of sleep hadn't been near enough. Richard took his hand off the wheel to rub at his gritty eyes. He had listened at the bedroom door and heard nothing, so he had decided to risk leaving. He *had* to check on Sterling. Mercifully, the ambulance crew had taken the injured man to the nearest hospital rather than UNMH where most trauma patients were treated. Kaseman was not that far from his apartment. With luck he'd be back within an hour before Rhiana even knew he was gone. He also was counting on the hope that whoever wanted the girl dead not making another attempt in broad daylight.

It had been four years since his hospitalization, but the smells of rubbing alcohol, bedpans, and overcooked food and the sounds of suffering had his stomach fluttering with nausea. At the nurse's station Richard learned that Sterling had been moved out of the ICU a few hours ago and was directed to his hospital room. Richard's oldest sister, Amelia, was a physician, so he didn't waste time asking questions about his partner's condition which he knew would not be answered.

Locating the room, he knocked softly, then pushed open the door. Sarah Cotrell, Sterling's fiancée, was seated in a chair at the bedside and looked up as Richard entered. She was a heavy-set woman on the shady side of forty whose choice in clothing, more appropriate for a twenty-year-old, and bouffant hair gave her a blowsy look. She sat aside the tattered *People* magazine she had been reading.

"Jesus, you look almost as bad as him. Did you sleep in those clothes?" she asked.

"'Fraid so," Richard said as he studied his partner. Sterling's head was swathed in bandages and his skin looked like gray putty. Guilt stabbed at Richard. He laid a hand on Sarah's shoulder and gave it a squeeze. "How are you holding up?"

"Better than him," she said, jerking her head toward the comatose man in the bed.

Guilt stabbed him in the gut. "I'm so sorry, if he hadn't pushed me out of the way—"

"For God's sake, *don't*. I know cops. My last husband was a cop. You'd think I'd know better than to sign up again—but I didn't, so—you would have done the same. You've all gotta play the hero and prove you're more macho than the next guy."

Richard glanced down at his slight frame. "Well, nobody's ever said *that* about me before. But in Sterling's case it's true, at least the hero part."

Sarah looked back at Sterling and her eyes softened. "Big jerk." She turned back to Richard. "You catch the guys yet?"

Richard hesitated, hating to lie but knowing he had no choice. He shook his head. "We're working on it."

"Well, when you do, tell 'em Sarah says to burn in Hell."

"Will do. You'll call me if there's any change?" Richard asked.

Her throat worked and she finally settled with giving a quick nod. Richard squeezed her shoulder once more and left.

✦ ✦ ✦

HER DREAMS WERE filled with burning people running down cavernous streets. Her horror was tempered by the tingle of power arcing along her nerve endings. Twisting shadows pushed through mirrors. Her legs cramped, sending pain shooting through her muscles as she tried to run from their advance. Rhiana awoke with a gasp and had to reorient herself in the strange room.

The apartment was quiet apart from the ticking of the chrome-and-glass clock on the wall. The interior mechanisms were visible, the hands rotating in front of the main wheel and the escape wheel.

Pushing her hair off her face, Rhiana called softly, "Officer? Richard?" When there was no response, she tumbled out of bed and quickly dressed, wrinkling her nose a bit at the sour smell of sweat that permeated her clothes.

It was as she had feared. The apartment was empty. The man had left her alone after *everything* she had told him. Tears prickled at the edge of her eyes. Terror and anger warred within her. She spotted a handwritten note, the cursive script sweeping and elegant, propped up on the kitchen counter.

Gone to check on my partner. Will be back soon. Help yourself to anything in the refrigerator.

Richard.

The doorbell rang. Rhiana whimpered, the note falling from nerveless fingers. Creeping to the door, she looked through the peephole. The man, familiar, creature, from last night was *standing outside.* He seemed to sense her gaze and gave her a grin that seemed more predatory than friendly.

Rhiana staggered back with a gasp, ran to the doors leading to the patio, and tried to yank them open. Realized there was a security guard in the track. She pulled it out, opened the door, and rushed out. There was a hibachi, a recliner, and a small side table next to it. There was also a gate. She pulled it open and raced out into the garden area around the now-covered swimming pool.

The man was waiting for her. Rhiana's hand darted into her pocket, but he was cat quick and caught her wrists in both hands.

"Oh, no, sweetheart, you're not going to try to whammy me. But you *are* going to get to where you were supposed to be last night."

He leaned forward and for one wild and panicked moment Rhiana thought he was going to kiss her. His lips pursed and she felt his breath wash across her face. It had a sharp, metallic scent, and she spiraled down into darkness.

CHAPTER FIVE

A TRAIL OF BREADCRUMBS

THE INTERNET WAS a wonderful tool, particularly for someone with Kenntnis's skills. While Officer Oort might have an unpublished number and a fake name attached to his address, all the real information was easily discovered. Not that Cross needed the address to find the girl. As he said, she was a magical flare in the world of the mundane. He glanced at his watch. Cross should be back soon.

The chair creaked under his bulk as Kenntnis leaned back and stared at the large monitor that held the particulars of a man's life.

Richard Noel Oort, twenty-seven, born Christmas Day (Kenntnis assumed that was the source of the middle name) in Newport, Rhode Island. His father, Robert, was a federal court judge. Two older sisters, Amelia, thirty-four, a surgeon. Pamela, thirty-one, a lawyer. Mother a homemaker. The youngest Oort had obtained his undergraduate degree at Cornell, majoring in music with a minor in psychology. He had been on the gymnastic team, joined the fencing club, the ski club. In his youth he and his father periodically entered yacht races and finished modestly well.

He did a year of graduate studies at the Rome Conservatory, focusing on piano and voice. Kenntnis located a few YouTube videos. One was a vocal recital at Cornell. The boy had a soaring lyric tenor as he performed Tonio's aria "Ah! mes amis, quel jour de fête!" from Donizetti's comic opera *The Daughter of the Regiment*. Another was a piano recital in Rome. Oort's voice was very good, but his skill at the keyboard was at a professional level.

After that single year Oort had returned home and joined a Wall Street brokerage firm and lasted seven months. There was no record of him for six months after leaving the firm, until he turned up at the police academy in Albuquerque, New Mexico. He was unmarried, and he carried a staggering amount of credit card debt, much of it incurred buying clothes and art.

Kenntnis was still working on the missing six months, but either way it was a strange background for a beat cop in an undistinguished city in the poorest state in the Union.

Kenntnis looked out through the west-facing window. The telephone line below his office sagged under the weight of the birds waiting to intercept his every call. Technology was his ally, and all of his staff knew to use cell phones for mundane business and sat phones bouncing off the private satellite he had paid SpaceX to place into orbit for the calls that *really* mattered.

Kenntnis shook his head over the Luddism of his foes. There were still landlines in the building, and it amused him to have his staff periodically make calls describing investments and actions that would have Grenier and his ilk chasing their tails. He couldn't understand why the Old Ones and their human factotums continued to rely almost totally on magic rather than wiretaps, shotgun mikes, and all the other panoply of modern snooping technologies. Kenntnis would have thought Grenier would be shrewder. After all, the man ran a giant televangelist network that broadcast all over the planet. Kenntnis could only assume it was something psychological, and he fervently hoped it would continue.

Kenntnis then gave a rueful smile; of course, he had an Old One standing guard, watching for any magical attack, and doing his bidding. As if the thought had summoned him, Cross came waltzing into the office.

"Got her tucked away all nice and cozy upstairs."

"Excellent."

He rested his palms on the desk and pushed to his feet. Stretching, he took a final glance back at the computer. His people were careful, but hacks were always possible. There was a chance that his internet search had been detected and now Oort was in as much danger as the girl. Hopefully the other machinations he had set in motion would soon have the policeman under his protection as well.

✧   ✧   ✧

RHIANA PUSHED PAST the fog that had enveloped her brain and opened her eyes. While her eyelids might be working, the rest of her body felt leaden. Memory returned, the bearded man's arms closing like a vise around her body, his breath across her face. That was like a jolt of electricity through her, and she sat up abruptly, then stared in confusion at her surroundings.

She was lying on a large leather couch in an elegant living room. A Persian rug in shades of blue, white, and gold rested on the polished wood floor. In the center of the room there was a fireplace that seemed to be floating, attached to the ceiling only by its chimney. A gas fire flickered cozily. Floor-to-ceiling bookcases were on two walls, filled with books. Fresh-cut flowers in crystal vases were dotted about the room. On various side tables were scattered objects that looked expensive as well as beautiful. A carved horse in white jade, a long knife whose hilt was set with precious gems, several jars that looked Egyptian, an illuminated manuscript open to an exquisite picture of the Virgin receiving the glad tidings from an angel. The track lighting made the gold paint glow. In one corner of the room stood a triangular-shaped harp, its wooden frame decorated with Celtic knots in gold leaf.

As had happened at Richard's apartment, Rhiana suddenly had the discomforting sense of standing in two places at once, for her mind's eye had overlaid the living room of her family's home in Van Nuys. There were no bookcases, no art, just one wall dominated by a big-screen TV that they couldn't really afford, the stuffing protruding from the arms of the sofa sleeper where the dogs had chewed off the upholstery, the smell of cooking grease and an overflowing garbage can.

The large double doors at the south end of the room swung open. Rhiana had a brief glimpse of a small anteroom with a parquet marble floor and the gleam of an elevator door. A man entered. He was an imposing figure, tall and broad with ebony black skin. Epicanthic folds made Rhiana wonder if he had an Asian parent. His eyes, fixed on her, were black, and for an instant she thought she saw a flicker of silver, like stars in a night sky, deep in that midnight darkness.

As he walked past the harp, it thrummed softly, releasing a series of ascending notes. Rhiana's eyes widened. This had to be another magic user.

"Where am I? Who are you? What do you want? Why am I here?"

He raised a hand as if to stem her rapid-fire words.

"How do you do? I'm Kenntnis. This is my home, and I brought you here to keep you safe, Ms. Davinovitch."

Rhiana scrambled to her feet and rushed to place the couch between herself and Kenntnis. "Kidnapping me doesn't make me feel very damn safe!"

"I apologize, but you eluded us last night. Cross was reluctant to steal you from a police officer, so we had to wait for him to leave."

"Yeah, that asshole. If I see him again—"

"Oh, I expect you will. I've left a rather large trail of breadcrumbs for him to follow. I'm sure you must be hungry. My chef has prepared a meal for us. Shall we continue our discussions over the breakfast cups? I think I can teach you techniques that will keep you safe and hidden from those who wish to harm you."

✧　✧　✧

RICHARD PUSHED OPEN the front door to the apartment and stepped as quietly as possible in case Rhiana was still asleep, then froze when he saw the track guard flung into the center of the living room. He looked around, but there seemed to be no sign of a struggle, and nothing had been taken. The television and Bose player were still in place. The door to the bedroom was open but the room was empty, the bed rumpled and unmade.

Richard sighed. Despite her fervent desire to stay with him, it seemed that Rhiana had decided to leave. It was something of a relief. He had risked a lot by bringing her to his home, and now he could put the events of last night behind him.

He turned away and his eye was caught by the spinning, sparking penny still spinning and sparking on the kitchen counter. *Or not.* The presence of the damn thing made it impossible for him to push it all aside. A new thought intruded; why hadn't Rhiana used the front door when she left? Slipping out the back implied fear or that she perceived a threat. Well, it was too late now; she was gone.

In the meantime, he had names to investigate; *turn over to the Lou*, he amended. He was just a beat cop, a patrolman. It would probably fall to the detectives to follow up on these leads. And, honestly, if a cop hadn't been badly injured probably no investigation would occur, but he had to figure out a plausible explanation for *how* he got the names. Mentioning he had taken the girl home and she'd slept in his bed was *not* a good idea.

He longed to crawl into bed and sleep for another few hours, but he wasn't sure his mind would relax enough to allow for that. Instead, he took a shower, put on fresh clothes, grabbed up the penny, and left. The were some things that he could investigate that didn't need to involve the detectives of the APD.

❖   ❖   ❖

ANGELA ARMANDARIZ WAS humming along to the pounding beat of Lady Gaga recommending that *after he's been hooked, I'll play the one that's on his heart.* She had the Bose player cranked up so she could hear over the whining of the bone saw that was opening the chest of the morgue's current resident. Bits of bone and viscous blood spattered her apron and face shield. Suddenly the music cut off.

Pissed, she snapped off the saw and turned, pushing up her shield to see Officer Richard Oort standing by the player.

"Rude much?" Angela snapped.

He registered her tone and expression, and she watched his Adam's apple work as he gulped. "Sorry. I didn't want to scream at you."

He sounded so contrite, and the comment was so incongruous to how her day *usually* went that she found herself smiling.

"Well, that would be a switch. And why should you be different from everybody else? *Angela, have you run that DNA? Angela, is my bullet analysis back yet? Angela, where's the autopsy report?*" she said in a mocking sing song. "So, what can I do for *you,* Officer Oort?"

He frowned. "How ...?" Because the car coat he was wearing covered up his name tag.

"Oh, I've heard *all* about *you.*" *What they didn't tell me was how fucking handsome you are,* she thought as she studied the ice blue eyes, almost white-blond hair, and chiseled features. "The weirdo from back East with the fancy education and the daddy who's a federal court judge and who nobody can figure out why in hell he's a cop. In Albuquerque." She paused and gave him a one-sided smile. "So why are you a cop? In Albuquerque?"

"You don't think to serve and protect is enough of a reason?" The soft tenor voice had one of those achingly proper East Coast accents.

"I think altruists are like unicorns. Some guys become cops because they like to drive fast, shoot off guns, and beat up people. For others it's a family tradition, for most it's just a job." She gave him a demanding look. "So, what's your reason?"

"Personal. And private," he said firmly.

That surprised her, and she narrowed her eyes. Despite her diminutive size she was used to getting her way. "Okay. So, what do you need, Officer Oort?"

He reached into his coat pocket and pulled out something that sparked and glowed in the palm of his hand. She squinted to see it was a penny. "Explain this." His voice was tense.

She ripped off her gloves, and stepped up to him, noting he was not that much taller than her. It was a rather pleasant change. Angela reached out with a foreigner and gently touched the penny.

"It's not hot," she said.

"No."

"Does it keep spinning even when you're not holding it?"

"Yes."

She lifted the coin off his hand and balanced it on her own palm where it kept spinning. She gave a delighted laugh. "Hmmm, that tickles." She glanced up at him and gave him a teasing smile. "Good thing you kept it in your coat pocket and not your pants pocket. That could have been … *exciting*." She watched the blush rise in his cheeks, and his eyes dropped to the floor. She laughed. "God, you're adorable."

She walked over to one of the long metal tables that held a large microscope and began to inspect the penny.

"So where did you come by this thing?"

"It didn't start out life like that, if that's what you meant," he said as he joined her. "I watched someone take an ordinary, everyday penny and turn it into *that*. I want to know how."

"Does it do anything other than put on a light show?" Angela asked.

"Yes. When this person threw it at… at something it burst into flames and set it… on fire."

Angela snatched the penny off the microscope's stage and rushed to the backdoor of the morgue. She stepped out into the alley.

Richard plunged after her. "Wait! What are you—"

"Experiment. Basis of all scientific advancement. Otherwise known as *I wonder what shit will happen if I do* this?" She grinned at him and threw the penny at the dumpster in the alley, aware of his wince and the tension in his shoulders at the action.

It hit with a faint *clink* then fell to the pavement where it continued to serenely spin and spark. Next to her Oort released a held breath and relaxed. "Hmmm, the explody part clearly isn't integral to the penny itself." She picked it up and frowned down at it as it rested on her palm.

"Do you have *any* reasonable explanation?" It emerged as a bit of a pleading whine.

"Not a one. My *abeulo* used to go into the mountains ostensibly to wrestle demons. We all thought it was just an excuse to get away from grandma and drink a little Cuervo in peace, but I'm starting to rethink that stance." She looked up at him. "May I keep this? Run a few tests?" She found herself suddenly thinking about the two pistols Damon had brought her earlier that morning. She and the boys in the criminalistics lab had inspected them and found nothing wrong. They were now checking to see if it had been a bad batch of ammo.

"That's what I was hoping you'd say … Preferably one that doesn't involve setting the morgue on fire, or your grandfather … or demons."

There was something in his voice that had her eyeing him curiously. He turned and started to walk away. Angela called after him, "You didn't happen to have a misfire issue recently?" His shoulders stiffened.

"Why do you ask?"

Interesting. "No reason, just thought I'd heard something about that."

✧   ✧   ✧

WHAT A CHARMING *little dynamo,* Richard thought with a faint huff of laughter as he left the morgue. He couldn't deny the obvious pleasure it gave him to be taller than someone. Shaking back his sleeve Richard checked his watch, surprised to discover it was only 9:30 AM, and then he realized it was still only Sunday. After everything that had happened it felt like more than a day should have passed. If he hurried, he could make the 10:00 AM service at Prospect Christian Reformed.

As he settled behind the wheel of his car, Richard reflected that the inexplicable events of last night had him desperate for the solace of prayer that Sterling might recover and the comfort of a sung hymn. He hoped that Greg was playing today and not Sloan. The elderly choirmaster was not a good organist, and those blaring wrong notes always set Richard's teeth on edge and spoiled his pleasure in singing. Embarrassed at his own vanity and disrespect toward Sloan, Richard gave himself a mental shake as he turned on the engine.

And perhaps during the sermon he could figure out how to get the information he'd gleaned from Rhiana into the hands of his bosses.

"In other words, you're going to pray on how to come up with a good lie," he muttered out loud as he jammed the car in gear.

✧　✧　✧

"OH, GOOD, YOU'RE still here."

Damon Weber looked up from his brown study at the sound of Captain Ortiz's voice. Barrel-chested, his temples nicely frosted with gray, with a square jaw sporting a conquistador's spade beard and mustache, he looked like a recruiting poster for the APD.

"What's up, Enrique?" Weber asked.

The captain stepped deeper into the office and closed the door. "So, what's the story on this Oort kid?"

Too goddamn handsome, was Weber's first thought, but he didn't say that. "Conscientious, works hard, little—make that a lot—uptight, bit of a rule-monger." He flashed a quick grin. "His reports are always spelled right."

"That's always important," Ortiz said piously then laughed and shook his head.

"So, what's this about?" Weber asked.

"Well, he's about to be made detective."

"What the hell?" Weber couldn't control the reaction. "He's only been out of the academy for two goddamn years,"

"Apparently some rich fuck named Kenntnis leaned on the mayor who leaned on the commissioner who leaned on the Chief who leaned on *me* to move Oort out of uniform." The two men contemplated each other for a long moment. "Oh, and the Chief thinks it would be *appropriate* if Oort works on finding the fuckers who put Sterling in the hospital."

"I can't think of anything *less* appropriate," Weber growled.

"Great, I'm sure the Chief will be real happy to hear your opinion."

"Fuck you."

Enrique flashed him a grin as he opened the door. "Love you too, bro."

CHAPTER SIX

THERE IS A WAR BEING FOUGHT

WHEN RICHARD EMERGED from the church, he turned his phone his phone back on, and found a voicemail from Captain Ortiz and a text message from Damon Weber, both ordering him back to headquarters. There was a jolt of fear in his stomach like the ones he felt when his father had summoned him into the judge's study, and he wondered if his transgression with Rhiana had been discovered.

✧   ✧   ✧

"ARE YOU READY to learn some control?" Kenntnis asked. They had finished breakfast and returned to the living room.

"Will it keep me safe?"

"That's the goal," the man said. He beckoned her over to the sofa. Rhiana sat down warily at one end, Kenntnis sat at the other. "Cross says you're a veritable flare of magic energy."

"Is that unusual?" Rhiana asked.

"Very. Almost all humans have a touch of magic. It was laid down in your genes by the Old Ones." He paused and quirked an eyebrow at her. "I take it I don't have to explain Old Ones?"

Rhiana couldn't disguise the shudder that ran through her as the memory of the coiling and nauseating colors that filled every reflective surface in the trailer and the way they had sometimes coalesced into terrifying and horrifying faces returned.

"No," she breathed.

"Anyway, they seeded magic into human DNA and RNA so they could always keep a foothold in this multiverse and, more importantly, so they could feed. But you have an extraordinary amount of magic. I've never met a human with so much, and I've met a lot of humans." For an instant his eyes seemed ancient and very distant. It was quickly shaken off, and he resumed, "But fortunately you *also* have a scientific aptitude." Kenntnis frowned. "Which is also quite unusual. People in the sciences tend to have very little magic. Still, that will help us now, so we'll worry about the why later."

"It doesn't seem like you like magic."

"I don't. I fight it."

Rhiana folded her arms across her chest. "So, you must really dislike me."

"You can't help what you are, and you could be very useful to us if you were willing to help. That's why I sent Cross out after you the other night."

"So, you'd use magic to fight magic?"

"I'll use anything," he said grimly. Kenntnis clapped his hands together. "So, let's get you protected. Do you read music?"

"No."

"Hmm, that's too bad. Breaking a song down to its mathematical components is an easy way to do this."

Rhiana moved to a table and inspected a collection of netsuke. "I don't really like music." She turned back to find Kenntnis regarding her quizzically. "What?"

"That's a trait of the Old Ones. Interesting."

It felt like criticism. Rhiana felt herself flush. "Look, could you give me the big outline on how this works?"

"Oh, yeah, sorry, that might help. Emotion is the tool of magic. Tamp it down and you start to blind them. Go to the most rational and logical of the sciences—"

"Math," Rhiana interrupted.

"Right, and you disappear. None of their spells can locate you."

"But they can still see me?"

"Oh, yes. Light enters through the pupil, strikes the retina, travels down the optic nerve to the brain, and voila, sight. The natural laws of the universe continue to function."

"So, I just keep a mathematical formula running through my mind?"

"Exactly. Or a mental chess game. At first it will be a strain, but eventually you'll have either of them running subconsciously. And we'll keep a little Bach playing, just to help you along."

Rhiana stood up and stepped closer to the fireplace. She rubbed her hands together, hearing the rasp of chapped skin. "Could I actually *become* invisible?"

"Average people wouldn't be able to see you, but the folks who want to kill you would spot you in an instant. It would also take a tremendous amount of energy, and while you're under my protection you don't get to feed."

"If you want me to do magic, I've got to draw power from somewhere."

"Use yourself."

"I had to do that last night. It sucked."

"Tough. That's the deal." Kenntnis paused and gave her a shrewd look. "You tried to use Officer Oort, didn't you?"

Rhiana swallowed hard, then forced herself to face him. "Yeah, but I couldn't get *anything*."

"He's an Empty One. He can't be used in that way. But, I reiterate, no feeding."

The confidence with which the order was issued pissed her off. Rhiana set her hands on her hips and glared at Kenntnis.

"And if I do?"

"The world can do with a little less magic."

She had to force herself not to retreat. "So, you'd kill me." She shook her head, disgusted. "I thought you were supposed to be the fucking good guy."

"First, I never said anything about killing you, but there is a way to prevent someone from using magic and I won't hesitate to use it if it becomes necessary." He paused and stared intently at her. "And I *am* the fucking good guy."

Rhiana turned away petulantly and gave him her shoulder. "Yeah, right."

His hand on her shoulder was gentle. "Rhiana, you've touched what waits on the other side of the barrier. Last night they tried to kill you. Our enemies want the monsters in this world. I don't. Doesn't that make me the good guy?"

Rhiana remembered again the grayed-out mirrors and dulled stainless steel surfaces surfaces in the trailer where they had built the device. Remembered the guttural, eerie whispers all around as she worked. Shudders shook her, and Kenntnis was at her side with a comforting hand once more on her shoulder.

"I'm sorry. I'm putting too much pressure on you. Today just let me teach you how to stay safe. Later we'll talk about the future."

✧   ✧   ✧

"Hey, Oort, the captain wants to see you," the desk sergeant said as Richard arrived at APD headquarters.

"I … I know. I got his message. Do you know what this is about, Julie?"

"Probably your promotion," she said and there was no hiding the jealousy and resentment edging the words.

"What?"

"You shouldn't keep the captain waiting," she said, and turned her back on him.

Richard ducked his head and walked into the bullpen. Conversations stopped, then resumed, and the hostile stares seemed to have actual weight striking against his skin. He was a beat cop. He'd been in the captain's office once—when he had been welcomed onto the force. He forced himself to walk briskly to the frosted-glass door. Then his nerve failed, and he tapped tentatively on the glass beneath the stenciled name.

"Come in," Captain Ortiz called through the door. Richard entered and closed the door behind him, to the disappointment of the watchers in the squad room.

"So, congratulations are in order, Oort," said Ortiz.

"I don't understand, sir," Richard stammered, and felt himself blushing. "I've only been on the force two—"

"Look, somebody pulled a string. You're not the first and you won't be the last." Ortiz slid a gold badge across the desk to Richard. "We're workin' on finding a desk for you." Ortiz stood and held out his hand. Richard shook it. "And hang the uniform in the closet. You're only going to need it now for funerals and disasters."

Richard walked blindly out of the office and straight into Lieutenant Weber's broad chest. Blushing furiously, Richard jumped back.

✧   ✧   ✧

THE BRIGHT COLOR in the younger man's cheeks intensified the ice blue of his eyes. The blush also intensified Weber's firm belief the kid was somehow behind this sudden promotion.

"In my office," Weber ordered. Richard followed him in and closed the door at Weber's waved command. "So, tell me about this Kenntnis guy? Is he some kind of friend of your daddy's?"

"I … I don't know who that is."

That the man would lie to him drove his anger even higher and pushed aside other roiling emotions. "Cut the crap, Oort. Some reclusive billionaire—"

"In Albuquerque?"

The incredulous tone intensified Weber's glare, and for an instant a flash of fear crossed the handsome face. There was a subtle trembling in the slender, long-fingered hands. Oort quickly clasped them behind his back.

"You don't have to sound so fucking surprised," Weber growled. "Anyway, he's the guy who decided that Officer Richard Oort just had to become Detective Richard Oort. So, I repeat, what's the connection?"

"There isn't one. I've never heard of this man, and as for my father being behind this ..." Richard almost snorted, settled instead for shaking his head. "The Right Honorable Judge Judge Robert Oort would be more inclined to lobby for me to be *fired*. Not promoted." Richard hesitated, licked his lips. "So, how is this going to play with them?" He jerked his head toward the bullpen.

"What do you think? They already think you're an entitled, arrogant little prick. I'd say it's going to play like a turd in a punch bowl."

"Would it help if I refused? Or would that look even more entitled and arrogant?" Richard asked. Vulnerability trembled on the words.

Weber shot him a frustrated, what-the-hell-do-you-think look and gave a disbelieving headshake. "No, you're just fucked either way." Weber grabbed up the message he'd taken earlier that morning. "And this angel you claim you don't know—"

"I don't."

"He also left a message that he has information about last night's events." Oort looked numb as he accepted the message slip. He seemed frozen in place. "You should probably go talk to him," Weber said in a tone so patient he knew it was coming across as condescending.

Once again bright blood rushed into Oort's cheeks. He lifted his eyes to meet Weber's. "This … this doesn't feel right."

Weber gave him a withering look. "Gee, ya think?"

✧   ✧   ✧

HIS SECRETARY'S VOICE came over the intercom. "Detective Oort is here to see you, sir."

Kenntnis turned away from his rapt study of the Three Sisters volcano cones at the edge of the Rio Grande Rift Valley, and a snowcapped Mount Taylor some eighty miles farther to the west.

"Send him in."

The massive carved wood and frosted glass panel of the door swung open. Kenntnis had to lower his eyes to locate his visitor. He was a small man, Kenntnis estimated no more than five foot four or five, and slim. The camel overcoat over a blue cashmere sweater gave bulk to his slender frame. Perfectly tailored gray pants broke on his instep, and cufflinks glinted on the cuffs of the shirt worn beneath the sweater. Kenntnis now understood the level of debt. The clothing was all designer quality.

He transferred his attention to Oort's face. The policeman flushed under Kenntnis's intense scrutiny. Despite the bruise blooming across the right cheek, it was a face of almost unearthly beauty, and beauty was the right word despite the gender. This was simply the handsomest man Kenntnis had ever seen. Silver-gilt hair combed neatly back. Pale white skin so translucent that he could see the blue veins at Oort's temples. High cheekbones narrowing to a pointed chin, and unique eyes. The interior of the irises was ice blue, but haloed by a blue so dark that it seemed almost purple. The surface expression was polite and a bit aloof, but deeper there was a sweetness and a vulnerability in those eyes, and Kenntnis wondered again at the odd career choice.

"Detective Oort, so pleased to meet you." Kenntnis rose from behind his desk and extended his hand.

It was taken in a firm grip, the pale skin seeming even whiter against the ebony of Kenntnis's skin, but quickly released, almost an avoidance of physical contact. Kenntnis took note of those hands,—long and slender with tapering fingers ending in buffed and manicured nails. The young man wore one piece of jewelry, an elaborate gold signet ring on the little finger of the right hand. It looked old.

The blue-eyed gaze roved around the office, noting the collection of glass in the lighted cabinet, the eighteenth-century French clock, and the Reynolds hanging over the fireplace.

"It seems I have *you* to thank for the new title," Oort said. He gave Kenntnis a level stare. "My question is *why*?" The tone was level, carrying an achingly monied East Coast accent, but there was a thread of anger lacing the edges.

"It was the easiest way to get you here, and you will need the investigative freedom a detective's title will give you," Kenntnis said.

"Again, why?"

Kenntnis indicated the chair in front of his desk. "This is going to require some explanation. Please."

Oort sank down warily into the chair. Kenntnis sat on the

corner of the desk in front of the young man. The wariness intensified, keeping the policeman perched tensely on the edge of the chair. They regarded each other. The hum of the computer, the ticking of the antique clock, and the man's breath all seemed loud.

"A few years ago, I would have played the charade," Kenntnis began conversationally. "I would have set up a new company, formed a security force, wooed you with enough money so you would come to work for me—"

"You would have failed."

"Really?"

"I'm a police officer. I don't want any other career." There was something in the tone that made Kenntnis think this was part of a long-running discussion. Kenntnis wondered with whom?

"All right. Well, at least allow me to describe the work we do here at Lumina. It might interest you."

The man's eyes narrowed. "I'm listening."

The response pleased Kenntnis. Not the annoying and meaningless *I don't understand,* or the nervous babble of a man off-balance.

"I need to give you a little lecture now. Please bear with me," Kenntnis said. He drew in a deep breath and mentally looked over what he needed to impart. It loomed vast and unwieldy, an ocean of information in the era of the sound bite and two-minute segments on cable news.

"There's a war being fought, much older than the 'war on terrorism' or our current adventures worldwide but tied to them in a dark and fundamental way. And I use that word, fundamental, quite deliberately, as you will see. This ancient war is being waged for the spirit of humanity. I don't use the word 'soul' because it's too loaded, too charged, and it's one of *their* words. If *my* side wins, mankind literally inherits the stars. If *they* win, gateways between the multiverses will be fully opened again and the earth and all of her seven billion inhabitants will enter a new Dark Age with all the attendant ignorance, superstition, suffering, and death."

He stared into Oort's eyes trying to read the reaction, but there was nothing to read, and he made no response. The man clearly understood the power of silence.

"Our weapons are science, technology, rational thought," Kenntnis continued. "Their weapons are superstition, religion, and … magic. You encountered a touch of it last night." Oort stirred in his chair. Kenntnis anticipated the question. "No, it's not common for it to be used so overtly or openly in this modern world. Which either means they are very close to opening the gates and allowing a flood of Old Ones back into the world, or there is a power-drunk child wielding the power. Neither of which is good news." Kenntnis paused to encourage comment or reaction. All he got were two words, thin and tight with tension.

"And what or who are these Old Ones when they're at home?" Oort asked.

"Every dark myth and monster you can think of." Kenntnis paused, then said it. "And *every* god you can name."

That got a reaction. Oort stiffened. *He's not making the mistake of thinking that I'm only talking about safe, ancient pagan gods.*

"I think you should know … I'm a person of faith."

Kenntnis hesitated, weighing what to say. "We can negotiate about that later."

"It's not subject to negotiation."

"I think it might be when you understand things a bit better."

They had both leaned in until they were only inches apart. A whiff of aftershave reached Kenntnis, spicy and rich.

Oort tried to cover his growing nervousness by finally leaning back in the chair, feigning composure. "Go on."

"Let me explain a bit about magic. It bends, warps, and twists natural law, and that takes enormous power. Power as in will, not in the physics sense of mass and energy. The Old Ones and the humans who serve them feed on human emotion. The more powerful the emotion, the deeper they can reach into our minds. Dark and negative emotions are easier to evoke than joy. Humans are utterly unique in what brings them joy. There's nothing unique in how they experience grief, pain, fear, and death.

"We're at a crossroad here, Richard," Kenntnis continued. "We're on the verge of sharing technology, medicine, and science worldwide, and if that happens it will forever kill the chance for the magic to return. But there are forces at work, human and otherwise, who tell us that it's too much information, that there is some knowledge that man was not meant to know—the origins of the universe, or the secrets of human evolution, brain function, genetic engineering. They argue that the exploration of these questions undermines our values.

"They can no longer argue that science is the work of the devil, so they offer us junk science—global warming is natural, vaccines cause autism, condoms don't prevent disease, birth control is a sin but destroying the environment through overpopulation isn't, homosexuality is an offense against God and nature rather than a naturally occurring trait."

There was a small twitch in the young man's cheek at that. Kenntnis filed it away as he continued, "Creation science and intelligent design rather than evolution and Big Bang theory. We even have fools who once again believe that the Earth is flat." Kenntnis shook his head, depressed by the dismal litany. "We're raising a generation of truculent devout dunces inhabiting the wealthiest country on earth, with the most powerful army on earth. It's a recipe for disaster for us, and a banquet of death for our foes."

CHAPTER SEVEN

A Genetic Freak

Long, slender hands clutched at the arms of the chair and the policeman was on his feet. His agitated flight took him across the room, well away from Kenntnis. Oort ended up with his back against the window.

"What happened last night?" Oort demanded.

"Our opponents tried to kill a girl. And I owe you, my thanks. The girl you saved is vitally important. To all our efforts."

"Yeah, well, don't thank me yet. I seem to have lost track of her, and stop assuming we're united in any way," Oort snapped, but instead of sounding firm he only ended up sounding young, very young. Kenntnis debated if this was the moment to reveal that Rhiana was upstairs. Before he could decide, Richard spoke again.

"What makes this girl so important or dangerous that someone would want to kill her? Aside from the fact she can make pennies light up and spin and make sheets of flame?" he added wryly.

"You don't think that's enough?" asked Kenntnis, his sense of the absurd and ironic momentarily overcoming his good sense and very real worry. He managed to offend his guest.

Oort cloaked himself in dignity "Every tenet of my world has been thrown into question. I don't need flippant quips from you. So, either answer my question, or I'm going to get started investigating what little information I did get from the girl."

"I'm sorry," Kenntnis said sincerely. "Sometimes you just have to see the absurd in all this or you'd lose your mind. Would you like some coffee?" Kenntnis asked, partly out of politeness and partly because he needed to marshal his thoughts.

"No, thank you. I don't drink coffee," came the reply.

Kenntnis regarded his guest quizzically. "You really are in the wrong business."

"So many people have said."

It was meant to be neutral, even lightly ironic, but Kenntnis heard the resentment just below the surface of the words. Kenntnis suspected it was not so many people as *one* particular person. He again wondered, who?

Leaving the desk, Kenntnis crossed to the south wall and opened the hidden cabinet doors on the polished slate. Tucked away in the cabinet was an elaborate espresso machine. The body was a gleaming iridescent red tricked out in brass. "Well, I do drink coffee," Kenntnis tossed back over his shoulder to the policeman.

Oort joined him. A small smile played at the cop's mouth. "I'd venture that's an understatement. This looks like an altar."

Over the grinding beans Kenntnis asked, "So where was I?"

"Ms. Davinovitch."

Kenntnis poured the grounds into the porta filter and tamped them down with the weighted metal tamp. He screwed it into place and set a tiny cup underneath. The espresso machine began to hiss like a disgruntled dragon as he pulled a shot.

"Ms. Davinovitch is a physics major at the university—"

"Yes, I know. Are we approaching the point of all this?" Richard demanded.

Kenntnis resumed, unruffled, and enjoyed the young man's irritation at his interruption having no effect. "She's also at that age where one searches for spiritual meaning. She fell in with a group promising enlightenment, a way to touch the hem of God." He couldn't control the tinge of disgust that edged the final word or his lips twisting into a sneer. "And a return of magic into the world."

Kenntnis cocked an eyebrow at Oort. "Sounds lovely, doesn't it? Unfortunately, they never realize until it's far too late that all of it is fueled by pain, despair, and death. At any rate, given that some current physics theories *sound* like magic it probably wasn't a big step for our young lady." The thick, dark liquid ceased falling into the cup. Kenntnis placed a cube of raw sugar between his teeth and drew in a sip of coffee.

Once it melted, he continued. "My opponents trawl for people like this. Most are harmless, though they add to the general silliness in the world, but some, like Rhiana, have real power that can be tapped."

Kenntnis moved to his desk and keyed the intercom. "Jeannette, please bring Ms. Davinovitch to my office."

"Wait! What? She's here?" Oort stuttered.

Kenntnis forestalled any further outburst with an up-raised hand. "Please, it will be more productive if we wait for Rhiana."

A few moments later Jeannette pushed open the doors, and Rhiana walked in. She checked when she saw Richard. He rushed to her.

"Rhiana, are you all right?"

The look she bestowed on him was withering. "Yeah, no thanks to *you*. Why did you leave and not tell me?"

"I'm sorry." He paused to glare at Kenntnis. "I see now that was a mistake on my part."

"Yeah, you weren't there, so he could grab me."

Richard whirled on Kenntnis. "Tell me why I shouldn't arrest you right now for kidnapping and attempted murder?" the young cop demanded.

"Not *him*," Rhiana said impatiently. "The other guy ... from last night."

"The bum?" He turned back to Kenntnis. "He works for you?"

"In a manner of speaking. We're ... associates with somewhat shared goals. As to your other accusation, I didn't send the hunters after Ms. Davinovitch, and while my method of bringing her here was perhaps less than ideal—"

"Real master of understatement, aren't you?" Richard sneered.

Kenntnis continued, "This is where she needs to be if she's to be kept safe, and if we are to thwart what I believe is an attempt to construct a nuclear bomb."

The reactions were immediate. Both of the young people blanched, but Kenntnis suspected for different reasons.

Richard snatched out his cell phone, but Kenntnis caught him by the wrist before he could dial. The bones beneath Kenntnis's fingers were fragile, and he could feel the man's pulse racing.

"What in God's name are you doing?" Richard demanded. "We've got to call …"

"The police?" Kenntnis interrupted. "I'm talking to them."

"The Feds, the FBI. This needs to go way higher than me and the APD."

"Just hear me out. At the moment we've pulled their fangs because they don't have actual fissionable material. Rhiana was going to be their bang."

"I don't understand," Oort said.

"Rhiana possesses enormous magical aptitude. Properly fed and nurtured she would have the power to manipulate matter, but you play with that at your peril. Eventually there would have been a catastrophe. Of course, Rhiana wouldn't have survived, and I think once she fully gasped both the plan and the likely outcome she ran." Kenntnis looked at the girl. He hoped it had been the thought of thousands, if not millions, burning in nuclear fire that had driven her to flee and not just self-preservation. "At that point it was safer to kill her and hope they could locate another with Rhiana's level of power." He tried to soften the brutal recitation with a smile. "But fortunately, we have you." He turned his gaze to Richard. "And even *more* fortunate, I now have *you*."

It was as Kenntnis had expected. Oort was bright, aware of subtleties, and he hadn't missed the emphasis. Neither had the girl.

"So, what is he?" she asked.

"A genetic freak, a human utterly devoid of magic."

CROSS, KEEPING WATCH out in the street, saw it coming. A silver-gray feather against the deep blue New Mexico sky, it arched toward the building. Birds blew skyward with a clapping of wings. There was no time to enter the building, take the elevator, and issue the warning. Cross pulled a knife and plunged it into his palm. Blood streamed toward the sidewalk, but never hit. It dissolved into red swirls and vanished. Only then did Cross run for the door of the building.

KENNTNIS'S WORDS FELL like a blow. Once again, he had come up lacking. *You're a disappointment to the family ... I get you a job and then you quit ... A policeman ...? Do you really think you've got the grit for this? You've been very sheltered. What a waste of education.*

The big man sensed Richard's distress. His large hand was warm and heavy on his shoulder. "No. Lacking magic is a good thing. Almost unique." Kenntnis broke off abruptly, his head snapping around to stare at his desk.

Richard followed Kenntnis's gaze, and his eyes widened when saw that the bowl of the ornamental fountain was steaming, and the ceramic sides of the bowl flashed as swirling opalescent colors chased each other around the rim.

Kenntnis flung himself at the desk. Richard was close behind. The water that had been burbling from the pump hung frozen in space and the liquid in the bowl showed an image of the stone and glass exterior of the building in which they currently stood.

It also showed something about to break like a gray wave over the building.

Kenntnis grabbed Richard and Rhiana and propelled them through the door of the office and into the waiting room.

"Doors! Alarm! Take cover," Kenntnis ordered the older woman behind the desk. Without question or panic she hit two buttons on the desk and then dropped beneath it. An alarm began shrilling.

Kenntnis threw both Richard and Rhiana to the floor, covering them with his body. As the weight fell onto Richard, forcing the air out of his lungs and pressing his face into the marble floor, a yammering panic filled his head. He began to struggle desperately and violently. Kenntnis grunted as a fist found flesh.

"Be still! This will be over—"

The rest of the sentence vanished in the shattering explosion.

Numbing silence filled his head. For an instant Richard feared he had gone deaf. Slowly sound penetrated. It consisted of frightened queries, sobs of pain and terror from elsewhere on the floor. Breath also returned as Kenntnis rolled away.

Richard heard Kenntnis order, "Call emergency services!" Richard slowly pushed to his knees and then to his feet. He offered a hand to Rhiana. Once she was up, Richard walked slowly to the office door and pulled it open. The metal slats from the shutters lay like twisted silver crepe paper across the floor of the office. A few slats were embedded in the wood of the door along with splinters of glass from the windows. It looked like a madman's version of modern art. The upholstery on the sofa and desk chair was shredded and stuffing peeked pale and white through the rents. If they had been in the room, they would have been flayed.

Richard became aware of Kenntnis at his side. He glanced up at the older man. "Thank you."

"*De nada.*"

Richard glanced over at Rhiana. She stood with her back pressed defensively against a wall of the outer office.

"Is this a continuation of the fun from last night?" Richard asked.

Kenntnis didn't really answer. Instead, he seemed to be talking to himself. "What are they planning that they would be so overt?" His frowning focus was turned inward. He gave himself a shake, a tectonic movement of those massive shoulders. "I need to see to my employees. Fortunately, Cross got the warning to us in time ..." His voice trailed away.

"What do you want us to do?" Richard asked.

"Wait." Kenntnis threw back over his shoulder as he stepped onto the elevator.

✧   ✧   ✧

THROUGH THE BROKEN glass of the front doors Richard

watched Kenntnis climb into the back of an ambulance with the receptionist from the ground floor. She was the most severely injured and he wanted to accompany her to the hospital. The polished granite top of the horseshoe-shaped desk was spattered with blood. Richard shivered and tried to blame it on the icy wind whistling through the broken doors. Light from the ambulance splashed across the stainless steel and black marble walls, and the wail of the siren faded as it drove swiftly away.

Glass littered the floor of the lobby and crunched underfoot as Rhiana joined him. She came so close that her arm pressed lightly against his shoulder. Exhaustion clogged Richard's head, making his thoughts sluggish and disjointed. Though he longed to collapse onto one of the couches down in the main lobby, there was work to be done. It was time he and the girl had a come-to-Jesus conversation.

"So, tell me where to find this bomb," Richard said.

Rhiana jerked back from him, but not too far. "We were building it in a trailer down in South Valley. Josh put around that it was a meth lab, so nobody bothered us."

Which says a lot about Albuquerque, thought Richard. "And you never thought to call the police?"

Rhiana trudged over to a couch and crumbled as if her body had lost its skeleton. "By the time I figured out that this wasn't your typical coven, they had me locked up."

"Let's go," Richard ordered.

"You're taking me back? What if they're still there?"

It was a good question. Richard knew he should ask for backup, but the entire situation was crazy. He could imagine the conversation with either Weber or Ortiz. *"Hi, Captain,*

Lieutenant, so there might be this coven, you know that thing witches do, down in South Valley and they were building a nuclear bomb, but they didn't actually have the material that would make it explode. Instead, this girl was going to power the bomb with … magic." Yeah, that conversation was *not* going to happen.

"We'll just do some reconnaissance and then call for help," he said, and taking her arm he tugged her out into the parking lot and over to his car. He pulled the shotgun out of the trunk and propped it up between the center console and the passenger seat.

Richard had started to pull away when his peripheral vision caught a glimpse of the backdoor swinging open and a ragged figure jumping in. Richard slammed on the brakes and heard an aggrieved *"Ow"* from behind him. Twisting around, he stared into the dark eyes of the homeless man. He was nursing his nose with both hands.

"Excuse me!" The last pieces of Richard's patience frayed and snapped. "Get out of my car."

"You might need my help. And Kenntnis told me to keep an eye on you two adorable kids," he smirked.

"You better not be seriously thinking about saying yes. He fucking kidnapped me," Rhiana yelped.

"Yeah, and I'd be a lot more sympathetic if you hadn't *lied* to me," Richard shot back.

"I … I didn't lie. I just didn't… tell you… everything."

"That's called lying by omission and it's still a lie."

"Look, I get why you haven't called for backup. This is some seriously crazy shit you've gotten involved with, but it's also stupid to go there alone with only *her* for backup." The man's lips curled into a predatory smile. "And trust me, I'm some serious fucking backup." Richard sat dithering. "You're wasting time," said Homeless.

And indeed, driving did seem more profitable than continuing to argue.

✧　✧　✧

THEY FLEW SOUTH on the freeway, the westering sun a bright glare through the windows. The barrel of the shotgun was cold and bumped uncomfortably against Rhiana's knee as they bounced over New Mexico's famously bad roads. She glanced over at the driver. Oort's skin was white and taut over his cheekbones and blue shadows hung beneath his eyes. She sensed she didn't look much better. Neither of them had had much sleep. Tense and bored, Rhiana switched on the radio. Classical music poured out of the speakers. She tried several different channels, but they were all tuned to the same boring station.

"Don't you have any real music?" she complained.

"This is real music," Richard responded. His eyes flicked up to the rearview mirror and he glanced at the homeless man. "So, do you have a name?"

"Cross."

"Cross what?"

"Just Cross."

Rhiana snorted. "Like Prince, huh?"

Cross grinned at her. "Sort of."

"So Kenntnis said I'd stumbled into a war," Richard said.

"Yep. Between science and rationality on one side, and

religion, superstition, and magic on the other. We're on the science side, by the way."

"Sounds like they've got you outnumbered."

Cross shrugged. "They win some. We win some."

"By using magic."

"When you're in a war you use any and everything to win."

"Because that *never* turns out badly," Richard muttered.

Once they reached Belen, she guided Oort past the two prisons, across the railroad tracks, and down a narrow dirt road. Trailers sat on dusty one-acre lots.

Often the area around the trailers was dotted with dead cars on blocks, broken washing machines, and various kinds of farm equipment. Mixed-breed dogs, most of them chained in front of peeling doghouses, sent up an ululating chorus as they bounced across the washboard surface of the road.

"If anybody's still there they sure as hell know we're coming now," Cross remarked from the backseat.

Oort's mouth tightened into a thin line, and his grip on the steering wheel turned his knuckles white. At first Rhiana thought he was angry at the homeless man. Then she realized he was scared. She was, too. She had spent days afraid, locked in that trailer, watching the faces in the mirrors.

It loomed up ahead of them now, unique from its fellows in the total absence of yard clutter. There were no cars parked out front. She sagged with relief. It seemed that Josh and the others had decamped. Oort parked on the side of the road next to a drooping barbwire fence. Taking the shotgun, he climbed out. His hands opened and closed around the butt of the shotgun as he eyed the seemingly empty trailer.

He then moved to the back of his car, opened the trunk, and pulled out the bulletproof vest. Cross looked on approvingly.

"You're a cautious guy. That's good. You might live a bit longer. Paladin's normally got a short life span."

Richard's head snapped around, dislodging a lock of hair that fell into his right eye. "What the hell did you just call me?" He then sighed and pushed back the errant lock. "Never mind, I don't want to know. You two stay with the car." He tossed his cell phone to Rhiana. "If something happens call for help."

"If something happens, I'm going to run," she said.

"That's okay, too. Just call at some point so maybe I can get some help," said Richard as he stripped off the overcoat and jacket and shrugged into the vest. He pulled his badge out of his coat pocket and clipped it onto his belt. He looked down at the ground for a moment and drew in a slow breath, as if he were trying to gather his nerve.

Rhiana and Cross watched as Oort made his way quickly toward the trailer. He was careful to stay out of the line of sight from the windows and the front door. Cross started after him.

"Hey, wait," hissed Rhiana. "He said to stay here."

Cross looked back over his shoulder at her. "It's incredibly liberating when you can't be killed."

"Yeah, well, *I* can be killed," she hissed as he walked away.

CHAPTER EIGHT

WE BROKE YOUR HOMELESS GUY

ORT REACHED THE side of the trailer. There were three steps leading up to the front door. Rhiana watched as Richard stood well off to the side of them and stretched out an arm, but he was too short to reach the door. He reversed his hold on the shotgun and pounded on the door with the wooden butt.

"Police! Open up!"

The only response was the door swinging open under the first blow, and the cop nearly losing his grip on the barrel of the shotgun at the unexpected removal of resistance.

Cross appeared in the doorway and peered down at Richard. "They've cleared out, but you've got to see what our baby sorceress has done. You've got some serious mojo, girl," the homeless man called out to Rhiana.

Embarrassed, she hustled over to join the men.

"I thought I told you to stay with the car," Richard said angrily.

"I ignored you," said Cross.

The blunt challenge seemed to fluster him. Richard opened and closed his mouth a few times, then said weakly, "Well, this is a potential crime scene so don't touch anything."

"Her fingerprints are probably all over the place," Cross pointed out. "And I don't have fingerprints."

"Of course you do. Everybody does," Richard said. Rhiana followed him up the stairs and into the trailer. "Unless you've burned them off with acid or something."

Cross thrust out his hand, palm up. Richard inspected the tips of his fingers while Rhiana peered over his shoulder. The palms were smooth but with an old scar in the center of one and a fresh wound on the other. The fingertips were as smooth as a mannequin's. Richard didn't just drop the other man's hand. He threw it away and took a couple of steps back.

He jerked his head toward Cross's hands. "Those are stigmata."

"This one is," said Cross, pointing at the old wound. "This one was me and a knife 'bout an hour ago."

"What caused the other one?" Rhiana asked. Her family were holiday Catholics, not particularly religious, but she knew about stigmata and found this whole thing really creepy.

Cross laid a hand on his chest. "Look, kiddies, this meat envelope I'm wearing … this is a construct. How it looks depends on what folks are focusing on. Fingerprints have never been a big part of the vision, but stigmata …" He gave a thumbs up. "Very big with the religious crowd." He sighed. "It's a drag. Also, the bleeding-heart thing. That's an even *bigger* drag."

"I don't understand," said Richard.

"Of course, you don't, but this is a bad time for explanations," said Cross. "How about we save it until after we've looked for clues." He made quote marks in the air as he said the final word.

It seemed sensible, so they searched. They found some cut electronic wire, and a soldering gun which had fallen behind the battered green couch in the living room. There was a stack of DVDs next to the old fifteen-inch television and the Blu-ray player. There was food in the refrigerator, and Richard pointed at the half-filled pot of coffee sitting on its stand in the maker. The group had forgotten to turn it off and the smell of scorched coffee hung in the air.

"They left in a hurry," said Richard as he turned off the coffee maker with the tip of a pen from his coat pocket.

They checked the first bedroom and found the bed rumpled and unmade, a few clothes in the closet and a suitcase fallen open on the floor. Shirts and pants hung like tongues over the sides of the open bag. The mirror over the dresser currently had a gray sheen instead of the twisting colors that presaged the arrival of *them*. Rhiana jerked her gaze away; afraid it would draw their attention.

The second bedroom was much the same except that daylight was pouring in through the open bathroom door. They stood in the doorway and stared at the back wall of the trailer. A portion of it had crumbled into fluffy ash. The portion that remained was crisscrossed with fine gray lines like a spider's web.

"Like I said—major mojo," said Cross.

Oort's blue eyes locked on her. "You did this?" he asked.

"I had to get out." There was the faint smell of an unpumped septic system overlaid with the tropical fruit smell of an overturned bottle of shampoo. It caught in the back of

Rhiana's throat and her stomach heaved. She swallowed hard.

"What did you do?" he whispered.

"I deconstructed the molecular structure."

"Could you do this to anything?" he pressed, concern and a touch of fear etched on his face.

"With enough time and enough energy to draw on." Rhiana caught a glimpse of herself in the medicine cabinet mirror, distorted by the silvering of the mirror. Dark circles hung beneath her eyes and her hair trailed in rattails over her shoulders. She jerked her gaze away. *They might still be there.* She pulled her thoughts away from the mirrors and faced Richard. "Of … of course there's a size limit. I couldn't bring down a building … At least I don't think so."

"Well, don't test it," said Richard. He led them back to the living room. As they walked Cross bumped his shoulder against hers and asked quietly, "How did you draw the power without them noticing?"

"Naomi and Deb were so scared they weren't noticing much," said Rhiana in an undertone. She didn't want the policeman to hear and realize that she'd tried to feed on him.

Richard held out his hand and Rhiana realized he wanted his phone. She returned it and he set it on the scratched end table. Next, he removed a handkerchief from his pocket, picked up the phone receiver, and with the tip of a pen dialed in *69. He listened, then hung up the phone and typed the number into his iPhone. He took a slow turn, carefully inspecting the living room. He squatted on his heels and inspected the rectangular impression in the bilious green carpet.

"We need evidence techs," he said. "And I need a plausible story to get them."

"Our employer will get you whatever you need," said Cross.

"*My* employer is the Albuquerque Police Department." He turned to Rhiana. "So, the other people involved in this, how did you all get together?" Richard asked.

"There was a notice in the Sub at UNM." She glared when Cross rolled his eyes.

"You were all students?"

"Me and Deb and Naomi and Steve were. But not Josh, and I'm not entirely certain that was his real name."

"Another reason we need evidence techs. It doesn't look like any of you were wearing gloves, and this place hasn't been wiped."

"Yeah, and I can't wait to see what your police techs are going to make of the magically disintegrated wall," said Cross. "You really ought to keep this in the family, so to speak." Rhiana could tell from Richard's expression that he hadn't considered this aspect. "Are you going to call the number?" Cross continued.

"No, I'm going to find out who it belongs to first."

There was an aggressive pounding on the front door and all of them jumped. "Hey!" a voice yelled from outside. "We told you *pendejos* to get the fuck out of here. What are you doing back?" The accent was the lilting cadence of a New Mexico Spanish speaker.

"I'm a police officer," Richard called. "Please open the door and show yourself."

The door swung open. Standing on the top step was a

smooth-faced young man with sleek black hair and deep brown eyes. In one hand he held a statue of the Virgin of Guadalupe and in the other a .357 Magnum. In the dirt yard behind him were a number of Hispanic males ranging in age from the mid-teens to a man who looked to be in his eighties, if not older. They were all armed.

"I'm going to show you my ID. Okay?" Richard said.

The young man nodded tense and tight. Richard reached slowly down to his belt and unclipped his badge, holding it up high so as many as possible could see it.

"It's okay, he's not one of them. He's a cop," the young man called back to the crowd. They surged forward to the foot of the steps.

"What happened here?" Richard asked.

The answers battered at them. *Bunch of gringo assholes doing black magic. Strange lights. Weird noises.*

The young man who led the group concluded, "We could have handled them cooking meth, but this shit …"

The oldest male moved forward, the others giving way before him with the lightest touch from his parchment-thin hand. "My grandfather used to go into the mountains and wrestle demons—"

Richard threw up his hands. "Is this like a *thing* in New Mexico?" They all stared at him for a moment. "Sorry," he mumbled. "I just had somebody else tell me about her grand—Never mind. Go ahead."

"I saw La Llorona, the Weeping Lady, walking the other night." The old man stared at Rhiana with cataract-clouded eyes. Rhiana shifted sideways until she stood behind Cross and Richard and hoped she wouldn't be recognized.

Cross cast her a sardonic look, and muttered out of the side of his mouth, "Hey, you've been upgraded from sorceress to demon."

"Shut up."

"So, we came over this morning and told the *brujos* to get out," said the young man.

"So, they left because of your request?" Richard asked.

"No, sir, they were already packing. We just didn't let them finish."

Two spots of color blossomed in Richard's cheeks. "Then you saw what they were driving?"

"Oh, yeah, couple of minivans."

"Brand new," offered a heavyset man.

"All tricked out, too," said a teenager enviously.

Out came the phone again and within minutes Richard had detailed descriptions of both vans, including the temporary tags.

"Look, we need to make sure this place is secure, and nothing gets touched." The policeman gave the neighbors a sweet and sincere smile. "But there's this big hole in the back wall, so I was wondering if you would keep an eye on things until I can get some evidence techs out here."

"Like those guys on those *CSI* shows?" said the young man with the shotgun.

"Exactly like that."

"Cool. Yeah, we'll watch it."

"We wouldn't touch anything anyway," said the old man with a warning frown to the assembly. "Get yourself cursed."

"Great. Thanks so much." Richard checked his watch. "We've got to go."

✧ ✧ ✧

THEY PILED BACK into the Volvo. "Can you drop me back at the office?" Cross asked as they pulled back onto paved road and headed for the freeway.

"Sure."

"What about me?" Rhiana asked.

"You can stay with us," said Cross.

"Uh … no thanks, I almost got killed at your office," Rhiana said.

"Relax. They were gunning for *him*." Cross jerked his head toward Richard. "Not you."

"Me? Why?" Richard blurted, feeling his breath grow short.

"Because of what you are. You'll give us a real edge in the coming fight."

"I don't recall volunteering."

"You were drafted. You're special and we need you. For however long you're around."

Richard ignored the disturbing tag line. "You said I'm special, is that supposed to flatter me?"

"Not really. It's nothing you did. Like Kenntnis said, you're just a genetic freak. But a useful one. Maybe."

They were back on the freeway heading north. The tires thrummed on the asphalt and the headlights formed a necklace of light stretching south. Ahead of them taillights glowed red.

"What the hell is your boss's game?" Richard asked.

"Let's see, he endows universities, funds scientific research, supports Doctors without Borders, puts computers in grade schools, donates money to the United Nations Fund for Population Activities, works on climate change, denuclearization, clean water projects, vaccinations … How long you want me to go on?"

Richard glanced back over his shoulder at the homeless man. "Until you get to the *point*. He does all these things, but what's the ultimate goal?"

"You got something against charity?"

"Of course not, but he was talking to me about a secret war and those things don't tend to go together." Judging from Cross's expression reflected in the rearview mirror he was losing patience with Richard. "So I can only assume all the good works are to support an agenda. Which he wants me to join, but—"

"Look, pretty boy, he's using his fortune to try and keep you monkeys from going the way of every other sentient race in the galaxy. Me, I'm along for the ride 'cause I want to *die*."

"You said you couldn't be killed," Rhiana yelped.

"Which is why the dying thing is kinda hard. But Paladin Boy here could do it once Kenntnis gives him the sword." He shoved a forefinger into Richard's shoulder. Richard didn't react, he was trying to process the *sentient race* and *galaxy* and *not being able to die*, and *sword*.

Richard finally got his throat to work again. "Explain. Now. Please." Each word was carefully enunciated as he hung onto the ragged edge of control.

"Okay, but you're going to need a history lesson, and it goes back thousands and thousands of years."

It wasn't like him; the ostentatious lifting of the arm, shaking back the cuff and looking at the watch face, but

Richard was nearing the end of his frayed and exhausted patience. "Can we do this in the next twenty minutes? Maybe just the Cliffs Notes?"

"Okay, asshole, I'm gonna give it to you straight," said Cross. "Guess who's riding in the backseat of your fucking boring mommy car?"

Richard felt his jaw clench and he shook his head. "I am too tired for these kinds of games."

An annoyed huff came from the backseat. "Fine. Jesus Christ."

It sounded like Cross was reacting to something on the road, and Richard's head snapped to the side mirrors, checked the rearview mirror. "What? What's wrong?"

Cross was looking exasperated and surly. "No, that's me. I'm Jesus Christ."

Rhiana slid her gaze over to meet Richard's eyes. He suspected that his expression was mirrored on her face. She pressed her lips together, but a bubble of laughter escaped. It broke the policeman's control and then they were both whooping with laughter.

For Richard it was the release of almost twenty-four hours of confusion, grief, pain, and tension. The curtain had been pulled back and the Great and Powerful Oz had been revealed to be a poor deluded head case. The world began to settle back into normal patterns. Somewhere there were logical explanations for the earlier events, and like the homeless man they would be discovered and understood.

"God damn it, I'm not kidding." His tone suddenly shifted, and he sounded almost frightened. "*Ah, fuck,*" Cross whimpered.

Richard felt the laugh die in his throat because guttural gasps were coming from the backseat. Neck muscles twanging, Richard snapped his head around. Cross was arched as if he was trying to touch his feet with the back of his head. Blood suffused his face, turning it almost black. Foam speckled his lips. Richard jerked the wheel and with a squeal of tires sent them careening across three lanes of traffic. Horns blared. It was too dark to see the fingers being thrown, but he could imagine. They came to a halt on the shoulder. Richard tossed his cell phone to Rhiana.

"Call 911," he ordered as he jumped out.

He had the back door open and pulled Cross out of the car and laid him down on the cold pavement. The seizures were continuing. Richard laid his head on Cross's chest. He wasn't breathing. The man's neck was so rigid Richard had to struggle to position Cross's head for CPR. Richard feared the man's teeth were too tightly clenched to open and that proved to be the case. As he pinched the hinge of the jaws, trying to force them open, a weird witch light rose like fog from the man's body. Richard's eardrums suddenly hurt as if pressure had suddenly been lost in an airplane's cabin. He realized the cause was a sound at the upper limit of human hearing, but powerful enough to be felt.

Richard recoiled as Cross's body began to shake; there was the disorienting vision of multiple faces strobing across the core face. It was like watching an animation artist riffle page of a drawing, causing it to flicker and dance. The sound became unbearable. Richard clapped his hands over his ears and fell back. From the corner of his eye, he could see Rhiana doubled over in pain, the cell phone falling from her nerveless fingers.

Cross's body flew into multiple shards of prismatic light and scattered in all directions. Richard stared at the empty pavement where moments before a man ... no, where *something* had lain.

✧   ✧   ✧

"WE ... UH ... We broke your homeless guy," Richard said, the words emerging in a breathless rush.

They stood before him, looking like Hansel and Gretel when they discovered the birds had eaten all the breadcrumbs. Their hands were almost touching. Kenntnis suspected that if he growled, they'd be holding hands.

The building echoed to the sounds of hammering and power saws as contractors began the repairs. "Let's go in the conference room," Kenntnis shouted over the din. The door fell shut behind them and the sound abruptly cut off.

A wave of his hand over the wall switch brought up the lights and started the ornamental fountain on the stone bar at the far end of the room. Richard and Rhiana looked like they could use some relaxation. Kenntnis settled into the large chair at the far end of the hexagonal table. He waved the couple toward chairs. They didn't take him up on the implied invitation.

"He said he couldn't die, so I don't think he's dead, but he's just ... gone," Rhiana said.

They both looked absurdly young and so painfully tired and confused that Kenntnis realized they couldn't handle a full explanation.

"Look, you two didn't cause this. He'll be all right and he'll make his way back to us over the next few days." It was a calculated risk. As long as Cross was splintered there was a chance that one of the less benign fractals would make its way to Richard, but Kenntnis feared if a full understanding of Cross was presented, he'd lose the policeman. And he *needed* him.

"What happened to him?" Richard asked.

"He was attacked. He'll recover. He's tougher than he looks."

Rhiana swayed and caught herself by pressing a hand on the table. Richard's arm went around her waist to steady her, but he didn't look much better. His cheekbones were prominent blades and his eyes had sunk into hollows.

Kenntnis stood and came toward them. "Look, I have a private suite in the building. Why don't you both stay and get some rest?"

Richard shook his head. "I've got to report what we found at the trailer."

"What did you learn?" Kenntnis asked. He listened as the cop laid out the information.

"I've got a good description of the vehicles they left in, and partial information on the temporary tags. I need to get a BOLO out on the vans, and we've got the neighbors watching the trailer, but we need evidence techs."

"On what grounds will you ask for this BOLO, and what will you tell the technicians you send?" Richard's mouth open and closed several times. "That a bomb was being constructed there? There's no evidence to support that. And that wall, that's going to raise some interesting questions."

"Well … well, what did you tell the police about the attack on your building?" Richard demanded.

"I didn't involve the police."

"What!"

"I waved them off. Told them it was a gas leak explosion. I'll have to endure a series of inspections from the gas company and my insurance rates will probably increase, but that's far better than telling them about a magical spell that sent metal feathers flying through the windows to rend and cut and then dissolved into nothing once the spell was complete. Or worse, let them decide it was a terrorist attack of some kind. No, we'll handle all of this ourselves. So see, you really do have a chance to rest and begin your investigations in the morning. You might discover something that will give you grounds to ask for your BOLO. If you are unwilling to stay here, then then please go home. And rest."

The young man's shoulders slumped. "Okay."

"I'll go with you," Rhiana piped up.

Exhaustion was probably the cause, but Oort's patience snapped. "Am I stuck with you for life?" he demanded. Rhiana shrank in on herself. The policeman didn't miss it and was clearly embarrassed. He pressed a hand to his forehead as if trying to suffocate the anger or hold back a headache. Or perhaps it was both. "I'm sorry. I just need some time to myself. Some time to … think."

Kenntnis moved to Rhiana's side and laid a gentling hand on her shoulder. "You're magically opaque when you're with him, but you need to learn to do it on your own. He can't always be with you, and he might die." Now it was Richard's turn to flinch. "Let me continue with your lessons."

Rhiana sagged as if the slight pressure from his hand had leeched all the strength from her.

"You'll keep her safe?" Richard demanded.

"I swear it."

CHAPTER NINE

DESPERATE TO HAVE MEANING

THE HALLWAY OF the dorm carried the clashing scents of shampoo, perfume, last night's marijuana. Someone had also microwaved some pizza rolls for breakfast. Richard felt the protein shake he'd eaten for breakfast do a slow roll in his gut.

The door to the room finally opened to reveal a young woman dressed only in a T-shirt and bikini underwear. Her hair was tousled, and it appeared his knock had awakened her. Richard kept his eyes carefully focused on her face as he showed her his badge.

"Seriously, narcs at eight in the morning," she said over a yawn.

"No, I'm … uh, a detective. I'm looking for Deborah Rangold. Is she here?"

"Nope, haven't seen her in about a week." The girl scratched her scalp making her tumbled curls even more disordered.

"And that didn't concern you? I mean, she is your roommate."

The girl gave a one-sided shrug. "I'm not her mother. And she's gotten weird anyway. I was gonna ask for a new room assignment."

"What do you mean weird?" Richard asked.

"Like she had some big cool secret. But she wasn't going to tell me because I'm not one of the *cool kids*. Not that I'd want to know. She started going all superior after she joined this stupid church." She gave a snort. "Like going to church makes you cool."

Richard pulled out his notebook and pen. "What's the name of the church?"

The girl rolled her eyes. "Like I'd pay attention. The great thing about college is my parents can't make me go any more."

✧   ✧   ✧

WEBER WAS JUST coming off shift. He gave a yawn that threatened to crack his jaw and wondered if he had the energy to hit the market before going home. The larder was getting pretty damn bare, but damn he just wanted to go to sleep. He was getting too old for this graveyard shit. *Be glad when I get back on a day rotation.*

Then right on schedule his phone rang. He grabbed it off his desk with a growl. "Weber. I'm clocking out. This better be pretty fucking important."

"It is." It was Angela, and her voice sounded … odd. "It's about those … tests you had me run."

"Okay. What'd you find?"

"You need to come down to the lab." She hung up.

Weber stared at the receiver, gave a growl that turned into a sigh.

✧　✧　✧

PROFESSOR BERNARD WAS a spare, ascetic-looking man with shoulder-length brown hair and deep brown eyes. A jutting blade of a nose divided his his face. Deep lines cut on either side of his mouth. He was making his way down the hallway of the philosophy department on a pair of metal crutches, a satchel slung across his chest. He spotted Richard waiting at the door of his office and frowned.

"My office hours are from three to four on—"

"I'm not a student."

"Well, that's a relief," Bernard said as he unlocked the door. "I'd hate to think the youth of America had decided to rebel by dressing like a Republican." The voice was dark velvet so warm and rich that it left the listener feeling breathless.

Richard dropped his gaze from those amazing brown eyes and chuckled. "You may think I'm something worse. I'm a policeman."

"Oh, God. Well, come in then."

The office was the size of a large walk-in closet and the walls lined with bookcases and books gave the sense they were teetering and about to fall inwards under the weight of paper and binding.

"This is rather eccentric," Bernard said as he studied Richard's badge. "Am I in trouble?"

"No, sir, I just wanted to ask you about a couple of your students. Steve Douglas and Naomi Parson."

Bernard closed his eyes briefly and his brow furrowed. "Ah, yes, my little lovers. Tuesdays and Thursdays 9:00 AM to

10:30 AM. They haven't been in class for the past two weeks."

"Any idea why?" Richard asked.

"They're big kids. I let them make their own choices and mistakes."

"Could you give me a sense of them?"

"Desperate to have meaning," the professor replied dismissively. He was busy shuffling papers on his desk.

"And how is that different from any other nineteen-year-old? Eventually you grow up and realize *you will never live if you are looking for the meaning of life*," Richard responded dryly.

Bernard looked up, a sheaf of papers clutched in his hand, and blinked several times. For the first time Richard felt like the man was finally seeing him. "Albert Camus. You are a *very* odd policeman. I rather thought you would say *huh*."

"So people keep saying. But you, however, are a rather typical professor. Elitism and intellectual superiority on full display," Richard said gently. "I think these kids may be in trouble; so, shall we try this again?"

"Fair enough, Detective." Richard tried to control the stop the involuntary jolt it gave him when anyone said his new title. "What is that ridiculous saying about assumptions?"

"When you assume you make an ass out of you and me. My old training officer quoted it to me way too often. But about Steve and Naomi," Richard pressed.

"My impression is that Mr. Douglas and Ms. Parson came into my class seeking answers and a support for faith, but faith shouldn't require either support or proof. If it did then it wouldn't be faith, would it? They didn't like the fact that my course deconstructs religions, shows the fundamental similarities, and traces how religions change based on human and societal development."

"The idea that man creates God in his own image?" Richard asked.

"In a nutshell, yes."

"So, I take it they didn't find meaning from you?"

"No, but they found it somewhere. The last few times they were in class they were positively argumentative, and they had the air of people who shared a great big secret that put them well up on everyone else."

"Can you be more specific?"

Bernard looked thoughtfully off into space for a moment, then nodded. "We were discussing Abraham and Isaac. They argued that rather than being a testament to faith on Abraham's part or an example of mankind moving away from the idea of a capricious, bloodthirsty god, this was an example of a man shying away from what it took to have true understanding and great power because he couldn't make the hard choice. Naomi said that sometimes sacrifice was necessary if humanity was going to take the next evolutionary step. I confess to my response being rather sarcastic. I pointed out that she might not feel so sanguine about human sacrifice if she were the sacrificee rather than the sacrificer. They walked out in a huff." Bernard's eyes darkened. "I remember they stopped at the doors, looked back at me, and laughed. At the time I was annoyed. In retrospect I realize it was all rather threatening."

"And you don't know the root of this?"

"No, sorry." Richard turned to leave when Bernard called, "If you should run across them, you can tell them they won't be passing my class."

✧   ✧   ✧

THE TWO WEAPONS were on a table—Oort's Heckler & Koch and Sterling's Glock. "There is nothing wrong with the guns—" Angela began, only to be interrupted.

"They didn't fire, so there's something fucking wrong with the guns."

Angela shot him a glare. "If you'd let me *finish*. I pulled the rounds. To see if there was something wrong with the ammunition. There was no indication there was anything wrong with the manufacture of the bullets. Then I got obsessive—"

"You're always obsessive," Weber pointed out.

Angela reached up and punched him in the bicep. "And I hope you are appropriately grateful." She felt her smile fade. "Anyway, I opened up the cartridges, and removed the chemicals for inspection."

"Factory fucked up the mix?"

"No, well, I don't see how it would be possible given what I found."

"Is the point of this on approach or still circling the airport," Weber drawled, earning himself another glare.

"I'm going to give you a little *as you know, Bob* lecture. The basic propellant for modern ammunition is—"

"Guncotton, yeah, I know that."

She was officially getting really annoyed with the typically male dismissive attitude. "Do you know the chemical formula for guncotton?" She gave him a moment to stand silent, mouth slightly agape. "Yeah, didn't think so. Guncotton, also known as nitrocellulose. The cellulose is what you might expect, and it's usually derived from wood pulp. The other part is nitric acid. Together the chemical formula is $C_6H_8O_9N_2$. In the normal operation of a pistol, the firing pin strikes the cartridge, which ignites the primer, which is lead styphnate C6HN3O8Pb, which ignites the propellant, i.e. the guncotton. Bullet fires. Okay, I'm not going to give you a chemistry lecture on how to determine the number of electrons, neutrons, etc. in an ion. I'm going to cut to the chase." Angela was nervously twisting a strand of hair around a finger, and it was so unlike her that Weber found himself staring at the motion. She sucked in a deep breath. "God, even saying this makes me cringe."

"Spit it out," Weber said.

"Okay. Somehow, the various components in both the primer and the propellant either lost or gained electrons, which rendered them inert."

"That sounds … unlikely?" Weber said hesitantly, turning it into a question.

"Yeah, no shit. And no, I have no idea how it could happen," Angela said.

Angela watched as Weber began to pace. "I knew Oort wasn't telling me everything on Saturday night."

"Did he tell you about this?" He stopped, turned, and gave her a questioning look. Angela reached into the pocket of her lab coat and removed a spinning, sparking object. Held it on her palm for his inspection. Weber's eyes widen when he realized it was a *penny*. "Oort brought this to me Sunday morning. And no, I have no fucking idea how *this* happened either."

"What the fuck is going on?" Weber breathed. Angela just shrugged. "Are you gonna report this?"

They matched stares for a moment. "Are *you*?" Angela countered.

They were back to staring and Weber had the feeling the indecision he saw on Angela's face matched his own.

"Maybe we should talk to him first. Try to get some … clarity," Weber mumbled.

Angela gathered up the pistols and handed them to Weber. "Guess you can return these, then. They'll just need new ammo."

Weber looked down at the Glock. "Not sure Sterling will ever carry his again."

✧　✧　✧

RICHARD ACCEPTED THE cup of tea. Emma Parson was in her mid-fifties. She had a round, pleasant face, but there was a shadow in her blue eyes and her gaze kept flicking over to the pictures of her daughter that adorned the mantel. The house was in a solidly middle-class neighborhood and the furniture looked like it had been sold as a set from one of those discount furniture stores.

"A policeman. My, that's a bit alarming. My daughter … she isn't in any trouble, is she?"

"That's what I'm trying to find out, Mrs. Parson. Have you talked with Naomi recently?"

"I haven't heard from her in several days. She's not answering her phone." She then added with forced brightness, "But you know how young people are, you have to give them space. The opportunity to try their wings even if they fall down and bump their noses." Emma was trying desperately to hide her concern, but it came bleeding through.

"Tell me about your daughter," Richard asked gently.

"She's passionate and always looking for a deeper meaning in life. She recently joined a new church, and she told me many of her questions had been answered."

Richard tensed at that. He set aside the tea and pulled out his notebook. "A new church. You wouldn't happen to have the name?"

"Faith in the Rock. I gather it's one of those more charismatic, fundamentalist churches. We raised her Presbyterian, but I think she was looking for more …"

"Meaning? Could you direct me to friends, anybody who might have more information? I spoke to her roommate, but she didn't seem to have much information."

"She had a new boyfriend."

"Steve Douglas."

Emma nodded. "That's the one. They met at church. Have you talked to him?"

She was looking at him so hopefully. Richard hedged. "Um … not yet."

"She had also gotten very close with a couple of other girls, Deb and a girl from out of state, Rhiana." She gave him a desperate, pleading look. "Please tell me my daughter is all right."

He couldn't bring himself to lie to her. "I don't know, but

you have my word I'll make every every effort to find her."

As he walked to his car, Richard realized he now had a reason to issue the BOLO. There were three missing students.

✧   ✧   ✧

"Yeah, I remember them. Church group," said the young salesman at Garcia Honda. He was a lean young Hispanic in a slightly shiny suit indicating long wear and insufficient funds to replace it. They stood in the glass-walled showroom surrounded by automobiles. The indulgent scent of new car filled the air.

The information that there was a religious connection was unwelcome to Richard. "Are you sure about that?"

"Well, they said they needed the vans to take folks up to a Bible study retreat in Colorado at a sister church in Colorado Springs."

"Did they happen to mention the name of the church?" Richard asked.

"Yeah, place called Faith in the Rock."

"Do you still have the check, or has it been posted?"

"They paid cash."

"Isn't that a little unusual?" Richard asked.

"Yes and no. You know churches. Some are swimming in cash. Others scraping along begging for donated junkers. This was one of those fundamentalist groups. They seem to swim. Me, I'm Catholic. The church is rich, the parishes poor."

"Is there anything else you can tell me?"

"They were gringos, no offense."

"None taken. Accents?" Richard suggested.

"Kind of Texan," said the young man. He frowned and worried at his lower lip with his teeth. "They bought three car seats from us. That was a little strange; normally people have their own if they've got kids."

Richard thanked the salesman and went outside and stood beneath the brilliant New Mexico turquoise sky. He had been kicking himself for not getting the BOLO issued sooner, but with this information he had a feeling it wouldn't have mattered. Even if they had been pulled over, the cops would learn it was a church group, they were all white, and it was likely they would have been sent on their way.

Richard assumed it was a made-up church, but just to be certain he pulled out his phone and ran a Google search. He then stared in disbelief at the website for Faith in the Rock. There was a picture with a smiling pastor in front of a utilitarian building adorned with a cross. More shocking was the small notice at the bottom of the website that the church was affiliated with the Worldwide Christian Alliance.

Richard's family was active in charitable work, so they had crossed paths with the WWCA. Because of the Oorts' Washington connections, they had even met its founder, Mark Grenier. Richard tried to recall what he could of the man.

Grenier had risen to public prominence some fifteen years before when one of his parishioners had become president. Grenier had become the presidential spiritual adviser, displacing the Graham family. He had actively and aggressively pursued the title of the "Face of American

Christianity" in the press.

Grenier led worldwide crusades bringing the Word of God to millions, and funneled millions to conservative causes. Richard was well aware of Grenier's efforts to outlaw abortion, roll back LGBTQ rights, stop funding for stem cell research, and outlaw cloning, and how WWCA lobbied against various pure science projects like the supercollider or the replacement for the aging Hubble telescope. Though the Oorts might roll their eyes over some of the more anti-intellectual attitudes taken by the extreme religious right, his father and sisters were still rock-ribbed Republicans, conservative in their attitudes, and very devout.

And now an affiliated church in Albuquerque had either knowingly or unknowingly transported a bomb to a sister church in Colorado Springs.

It all seemed to tie into the hints that had been dropped by Kenntnis, and Richard didn't at all like what that might portend.

CHAPTER TEN

MISSED AGAIN?

L EAN CUISINE HEFTED light in the hand as if the contents of the package were as cardboard as the box. Richard hooked open the crisper drawer of the refrigerator with the toe of his shoe. Fresh bok choy, peppers, and ginger flashed color and guilt at him. He would cook. While the microwave hummed, defrosting chicken, he slowly chopped up the vegetables. He was glad he was making the effort; having something to do with his hands was helping with the memory of the phone calls he'd had with Deb's and Steve's parents. Their questions had echoed Emma's and he had no good answers for any of them. While he suspected their children had been in those vans traveling to Colorado he didn't *know,* and he wasn't going to give them false hope. He had issued a BOLO for all three of the missing kids.

Then there was his last conversation with Lieutenant Weber. He really liked and admired the man, and now Weber thought he was an ass-kissing, political climber. A stab of resentment against Kenntnis jolted through his stomach. He splashed sesame oil into the wok and set it to heating while he went to the bedroom to change out of his suit.

As he hung up the jacket, he found his hand reaching out

to touch his uniform followed by a sharp pang of regret and fear. Truth was he was finding his first full day as a detective harder and more emotionally draining than fantasy had made it. As a beat cop he issued tickets, responded to wrecks, bar fights, domestic disturbances. Upsetting, sometimes sickening, but he rarely dealt with the collateral damage caused by the fight or the wreck. Now he was searching for three lost children, and their parents' desperation was like a physical blow.

He shrugged out of his shoulder rig and set the holster and pistol on top of the dresser. Pulling on a pair of sweats and a long-sleeved APD T-shirt, Richard returned to the kitchen. Passion, rage, and fear had driven him into police work. Because it was so much more than a job, he needed it to be pure, almost a sacred calling. Unfortunately, that wasn't the reality. The creeping militarization of the police and the fact that many departments had been infiltrated by white supremacists sometimes made him question his decision, but he had promised himself he would *not* honor the blue wall of silence, that he would report bad behavior on the part of his fellow officers and try to live up to the oath he'd sworn.

On my honor, I will never betray my integrity, my character, or the public trust. I will treat all individuals with dignity and respect and ensure that my actions are dedicated to ensuring the safety of my community and the preservation of human life. I will always have the courage to hold myself and others accountable for our actions. I will always maintain the highest ethical standards and uphold the values of my community, and the agency I serve.

Because at his his core, Richard still believed that the

police and the courts enabled most people to live in peace. Without the rule of law, the darkness could engulf them all. The challenge was to make that a reality for *all* people.

"I just thought the darkness was the evil living in the soul of every person," Richard muttered aloud to the kitchen. "But nooo … there have to be monsters, too."

The oil was heating in the wok; the brown rice was in the steamer. Richard selected a CD of Schubert lieder and dropped it into the Bose. The first song began, and he realized that unconsciously he had selected the song cycle known as "Death and the Maiden." He stood frozen in the kitchen, listening to the words and the music with the growing sense that Naomi Parson was dead. From there his thoughts went to another girl who had brushed death. He wondered how Rhiana was doing and decided that after dinner he would call and check on her. It was while listening to the German lyrics that something suddenly clicked for Richard.

"Kenntnis" means "knowledge" in German. The realization set the hairs on the back of his neck to prickling.

The sound of the doorbell broke through his whirling thoughts. For an instant Richard hesitated. His holstered pistol was on the dresser in the bedroom, but it seemed absurd to answer the door holding a gun. The bell rang again. A glance through the peephole revealed Cross. The hood of his sweatshirt was pulled up, and he was shivering. Richard opened the door.

"Thanks. Cold out there," the homeless man said as he brushed past.

"What happened to you?" Richard asked.

"Kenntnis didn't explain?" Richard shook his head. Cross smiled. "Hey, what's for dinner?" he asked.

"I don't recall inviting you."

"Charity begins at home." Cross was prowling around the living room. He threw back the lid on the piano and banged on the keys with a forefinger. Two strides had Richard across the room and shutting the lid. "Wow, touchy much?"

"It's hard to keep the piano in tune in this climate. It has to be handled carefully." Richard returned to the kitchen. "If you need a ride back to Kenntnis's, I can call for an Uber."

"And here I thought you'd take me yourself." Cross's voice came from close behind him.

"Look, I've had kind of a long day, and I'd like some time to myself ..." Richard popped open the door of the microwave. As the reflective surface swung past him Richard saw Cross, the cleaver upraised.

Reflexes honed in hours of gymnastic training kicked in. Richard flung himself to the side as the cleaver cut the air where his skull had been. The linoleum's polished surface turned the lunge into a slip. Richard went with it, tucked, and rolled. Using his hands, he increased momentum and flipped back onto his feet. Cross grabbed a long butcher knife from the block. Cleaver and blade wove a deadly pattern before Richard's eyes. The hood of the sweatshirt had fallen back, revealing long *golden hair* and *blue eyes*. The Cross in the car had had *brown hair* and *brown eyes*, but the features were essentially the same. What wasn't the same was the murderous intent reflected in those blue eyes.

Fear hammered in Richard's throat, cutting off breath. A trembling in the pit of his stomach threatened to spread to his legs. He had always been terrible in his hand-to-hand combat training. He wanted to turn and run for the bedroom and his weapon. He knew if he did, he'd die.

He looked frantically around the kitchen, searching for a weapon. The knife block was behind Cross. A few pots hung from a rack overhead, but but Richard needed the footstool to reach them. Cross lunged. Richard dodged and a burning brand seemed to have been laid across his ribs. Warm and sticky blood flowed down his side. His frantic dodge left him leaning against the stove. The flames on the gas burner licked at his sleeve.

Richard grabbed the wok by its handles. The hot metal seared the soft skin of his palms. Teeth gritted against the pain; Richard tipped it forward until the oil just touched the open flames of the gas burner. The oil exploded, the flames shooting past Richard's face. He whirled and flung the burning oil over Cross. The thick fair hair went up like a hay rick. The oil permeated the sweatshirt, setting it ablaze. Richard ran backwards, frantically beating out the flames licking up his sleeve, as the burning figure came after him, swinging the cleaver and thrusting with the knife.

They were in the living room now. Bits of burning material dropped onto the carpet, starting it smoldering. Richard was almost at the bedroom door. Just a few more steps and he'd have his gun. There was a stunning crash as a dark figure, surrounded by shards of glittering glass and dripping blood from a multitude of cuts, burst through the patio door.

It was Cross. The Cross Richard knew ... or so he hoped. The burning man turned to face his *doppelganger*. They both let out bone-chilling and unearthly shrieks and leaped at each other. Locked chest to chest they rocked back and forth. Flames licked at the fringes of Cross's brown hair. Blood smeared against his opponent. The cleaver bit deep into the rescuer Cross's shoulder. Richard cried out as blood fountained from the wound.

He ran into the bedroom. It required only a few seconds to have the pistol out of its holster. He thumbed off the safety as he ran and yanked back the slide, chambering a round.

The scene in the living room had changed. The flames were out. The cleaver lay discarded on the blood-stained and burned carpet. The butcher knife quivered in the wall. The attacker held in the circle of Cross's arms seemed to be *smaller*. Appreciably smaller. Richard swiped the back of his hand across his eyes. It wasn't an illusion. The anti-Cross was shrinking not only in height but in girth. Within seconds he was a wraithlike figure. Cross bent and locked his mouth over the other's. His throat worked and he *swallowed* the other Cross. Richard gasped, gagged, and vomited. Cross, singed and smeared in gore, turned to face him.

Richard's knees were shaking, the muscles in his thighs shivering with strain and terror, but his hands were rock steady as he squeezed the trigger. He was trying for a double tap, but just as in the alley on Saturday night only one bullet fired. It did hit with enough force to have Cross stagger back a step. The recoil sent agony lancing through his burned hands. Richard kept frenziedly pulling the trigger, to no avail, as Cross huffed, "Well, that's a hell of a thank you." The words were muffled and seemed distant because of the ringing in Richard's ears. "Now we're going to have the cops on us *again*. Get to Kenntnis as soon as you can. And if you see any more of me wandering around … well, try to keep them from killing you."

And he was gone, back through the shattered door. An icy wind sent the drapes billowing into the room. Richard sat down abruptly on the floor and shook with the wailing cry of cop cars rapidly approaching as a counterpoint to his chattering teeth.

✧ ✧ ✧

"MISSED AGAIN?" DRAWLED Detective Dale Snyder.

Weber, just striding back in through the shattered patio doors after talking with the evidence techs, heard the detective's sneering tone and saw Oort flinch. The young man was huddled on the couch while an EMT treated the knife wound on his side. Weber noted the defined line of his abs. Golden hair, darker than the almost white, blond hair on his head, trailed down the center of his chest disappearing into the waistband of his trousers. The young female med tech was quick and professional, but clearly enjoying the view judging from the way her eyes occasionally flicked away from her task and up to Oort's face.

Weber pulled his attention back to Snyder. "No, he didn't miss. Bullets would have embedded in the apartment wall or the patio fence. Techs didn't find 'em. So maybe get your ass in gear and see if anybody's spotted a guy leaking blood anywhere in the neighborhood." Snyder gave him a sour look, gathered up Detective Torres, and the two men left.

Weber surveyed the room. A cleaver was laying on the floor; blood sheathed the metal. There was a knife embedded in the wall, and the carpet was blackened, burned, and bloodstained. Glass cracked beneath his soles of his shoes. The baby grand piano was a bit of a surprise. Also, the music on the stand. *Mozart Complete Piano Sonatas.*

There was a demanding knock on the front door. One of the uniforms opened it to reveal a fat, balding man wearing a bathrobe over his slacks and undershirt. There were scuffed leather slippers on his bare feet. He pushed his way inside.

He opened his mouth, but before he could speak Weber cut him off.

"Who the fuck are you?"

"I'm … I'm the manager," he announced as if it were some kind of royal title. He stared at the burned and bloodstained carpet, the damaged wall, the broken patio door, and his round cheeks puffed out even more. "Officer Oort, I can assure you your damage deposit does *not* cover *this.*"

The blue eyes filled with alarm and guilt. Weber responded before Oort could. "First, that's *Detective* Oort, and he's been assaulted in his own damn home which indicates to me that your security is for *shit* and maybe you should hire some. Now get the fuck out of here," Weber roared in his best drill sergeant voice. The manager scuttled back out the door.

The EMT had frozen. She shook her head, sending her curls bobbing. "What a prick."

"Thank you, sir," Oort murmured faintly.

Weber pulled over the piano bench and sat down. "So, what happened?"

Oort's eyes slid away. "Guy broke in. I think he must

have been hopped up on something. He grabbed a knife and the cleaver while my back was turned. Cut me. I threw burning oil on him. I managed to get to my piece, and … and … I shot him."

Weber heard the tremor in the young man's voice. Twice in the past three nights he had fired his weapon at a human being and that was never an easy thing. Weber reached out and laid a hand on the smaller man's shoulder, felt Oort tense like a spooked horse. He quickly withdrew his hand.

"How many times did you fire?" Weber asked.

"Twice." The kid was staring at the pistol where it rested on the glass coffee table.

"How'd the knife end up in the wall?" Oort's eyes flicked to the knife. He wet his lips with the tip of his tongue.

"He … he threw it at me. I dodged."

The EMT had finished wrapping Oort's burned hands and turned to look at Weber. "Your officer really needs to have stitches. We should go to the hospital."

Weber nodded. Oort's head swung between them. "You can't do it?" he asked the girl.

"No, it's better if it's done at the hospital. You don't want a scar." She helped him onto his feet.

Oort looked around. "I need a shirt, coat."

Weber went into the bedroom. Noted the neatly made bed. The Bible on the bedside table. A wooden jewelry box on the dresser with brass initials on the top: RNO. He found perfectly starched and pressed dress shirts along with a number of what looked like bespoke suits in the closet. He pulled a shirt down, and grabbed a caramel-colored cashmere overcoat, and returned to the living room.

With a hiss of pain Oort shrugged into the shirt. He turned away to button it up. Weber held the overcoat as he slipped his arms in.

"You got an extra set of keys?" Weber asked.

Oort nodded. "Top kitchen drawer next to the refrigerator."

"I'll lock up for you. After we're all done here."

Oort nodded again and, arm pressed to his side, limped out with the EMT.

Weber picked up the Heckler & Koch. He glanced around at the uniforms and evidence techs. They all seemed focused on their tasks. Weber aimed the pistol at the couch, hoped he wasn't wrong about this, and pulled the trigger.

Nothing happened.

Just the *click* of the hammer striking a cartridge that had, apparently, once again somehow been *changed*.

✧ ✧ ✧

A WOUNDED COP never waits. Within moments of arriving, Richard was whisked into a curtained cubicle. The young EMT reported and turned over her notes to the ER doc, and reluctantly departed with several backward glances. Local anesthesia was injected, and his side was carefully stitched.

The burns on his hands and arm were unwrapped and inspected. "These are second-degree. They should heal up fine but keep them dry. I'll prescribe an ointment, and the bandages should be changed at least once a day."

"May I go home now?"

"I don't see why not but stop by a pharmacy and pick up

the prescription. There's an all-night Walgreens on Montgomery. I'm going to give you some gauze and tape. Wait here."

It was cold in the emergency room and somewhere nearby someone was moaning. Richard shivered and slipped back into his shirt and coat. Worry fluttered in his stomach. There was no way his credit cards could withstand repairing the apartment. Couldn't afford a lawyer to fight the expense either. He briefly wondered about asking his sister Pamela to either represent him or for a loan, then rolled his eyes at his own naïveté. There was no way she would agree—to any of it—and honestly why would anyone in New Mexico pay attention to a lawyer from Rhode Island?

But worse than the financial worries were the lies. Lies upon lies upon lies. It made his stomach ache when he considered how he had deceived his lieutenant. He liked … he *admired* Damon Weber. If the man ever found out how Richard had deceived him …

The doctor returned with the tape and gauze. Richard thanked the man and walked out, calling for an Uber. The driver was willing to stop and wait at the pharmacy while Richard filled the prescription. He gave the woman a fifty percent tip.

He didn't bother returning to the apartment. Instead, he walked to his car. He needed answers far more than he needed food *or* sleep.

CHAPTER ELEVEN

I WILL GIVE YOU THE STARS

MUFFLED IN BANDAGES, his hands felt like paws on the steering wheel. The flare from approaching headlights burned in his eyes, and there was a throbbing point of pain at the hinges of his jaw. Richard forcibly parted his teeth and tried to relax as he once again drove toward Kenntnis's building.

As he drove up the winding road toward the foothills of the Sandias, Richard saw lights only in the top floor of Kenntnis's building. He called directory assistance and got the number for Lumina Enterprises. The phone rang five times before shunting him to voicemail, where a cultured voice gave him the office hours and suggested he call back then. Richard didn't know how he was going to get in, but he was, by God, going to get in, find Kenntnis, and throttle him if he didn't start getting some answers. Preferably answers that made *sense*.

He parked in the empty lot and as he walked to the front doors, he noted that they and the west-facing windows had all been replaced. Kenntnis must have had an army of glaziers and contractors working nonstop. The front doors were locked and there was neither buzzer nor intercom. Richard turned and looked out over the city's lights. They ran down to the river, which formed a ribbon of darkness. The lights resumed on the other side, climbing high onto the sandy mesas. Far off to the west, the setting moon struck white against the snowcapped peak of Mount Taylor.

He began a circuit of the building. In the back, nestled against a dumpster, was a large cardboard box. Light leaked around the edges of a piece of cloth serving as a door, and Richard heard the low hiss of a propane lantern. Suddenly, footsteps rushed him, and an arm was thrown across his throat. Gasping, clawing at the arm, Richard kicked back, trying to connect with his assailant's shin. A violent shove from behind sent him sprawling onto the pavement. He caught himself on his hands. Even with the cushion of the bandages it hurt like hell. The fall also ripped the knees out of his slacks and skinned one knee. He somersaulted back onto his feet and whirled.

Cross clicked his tongue. "Not careful. Not careful at all," said Cross. "Don't assume you're safe here. You're not safe anywhere."

"Why? Because of you? Because of *him*?" Richard panted, jabbing a finger at the upper floors of the building.

"Because of what you are, and because *we* found you first." Cross started toward a door set in the back wall of the building. "Come on, we've been expecting you."

Pique and humiliation almost drove Richard back to his car, but he needed answers. Logic prevailed and he followed Cross into the building.

"Where's your fucking pistol?" Cross asked as they stepped into an elevator and he inserted a key. They rode the elevator to the seventh floor.

"Once again impounded. And they don't seem all that useful, anyway," Richard gritted.

"Well, not against some of us and not in every situation, but there are some ordinary fuckers working for Grenier that a bullet can still kill." Richard stiffened at the name, but before he could react, Cross continued. "And by the way, that was a real dick move to shoot me when I'd just saved your life."

The elevator sighed to a stop and the doors opened onto a marble foyer. Through an archway Richard saw flames dancing in a glass fireplace in the center of the room. He marched in, leaving Cross to hurry after him. Kenntnis sat on the leather sofa, sipping brandy, and staring into the fire.

"Get the man a drink," he ordered Cross.

"I don't drink," said Richard, biting off the words.

"You don't? Why not?" Cross asked.

"Not that it's any of your business, but I have no head for it."

Kenntnis cranked himself around to look at Richard. "And your mother spent time in rehab," said Kenntnis.

The statement was made matter-of-factly, but it unleashed a torrent of memory and emotion. His mother, tiny and fragile, kneeling in front of him with a suitcase at her side. The perfect bow of her lips curved in a smile, and her voice was light and caressing.

"You be a good boy, and do what Ellen tells you, and don't worry. Your papa is here to care for you. I'll be home so soon you won't even know I've been gone."

But even at seven he recognized fear and shame, and he saw them glistening in her gray eyes and felt them echoed in his chest. He raised his eyes to his father waiting at the front door. His father's gaze raked across him, and he just knew it was somehow his fault that Mama was going away. That had been the first time. There had been more after that.

With a snap, Richard was back in Kenntnis's palatial living room. Anger clogged his throat and left a rank taste on the back of his tongue.

"You son of a bitch. How dare you! How dare you dig at me!"

Kenntnis stood up and bore down on Richard. "Oh, stop it! Of course, I investigated you. Fully. I couldn't risk letting you close without knowing what you were. And by the way, it's nice to see that something can penetrate those perfect manners of yours. I *need* you to be angry. It's the only way you can stand up to the fear. Now sit down and let's get your questions answered."

Richard wasn't sure why he took the indicated chair. Maybe because he wasn't certain he'd survive another day without guidance and understanding in a world gone mad. Cross bent solicitously over the arm of the big chair and said, with a jerk of the head toward Kenntnis, "He's got almost anything you'd want. Fruit juice? Milk? Tea?"

"Milk," said Richard.

Cross left. Kenntnis stood, hands clasped behind his back, bouncing lightly on the balls of his feet, and stared down at Richard. "Ulcer?" he asked. Richard grimaced and nodded.

Richard looked away and around the room. He recognized a Caravaggio on one wall and a Picasso on the other. He sensed the other works of art were equally rare and valuable, but he didn't have time for a thorough look because Cross returned carrying a tray with a glass of milk, and a gigantic slice of chocolate cake and chocolate milk for himself.

"That going to hold you for a while?" Kenntnis asked the homeless man with some exasperation, and then Richard realized that Cross wasn't exactly homeless. He referred to Kenntnis as his boss and lived in a box behind Kenntnis's building.

His hand closed around the chill curve of the glass. Richard asked, "So, why doesn't he live in the building?" The question emerged almost without volition. Cross and Kenntnis looked at him.

"Because of his episodes. I don't really need all those fractals caroming around the building. And some of them aren't terribly well-disposed toward people ... and *you* in particular ... as you discovered tonight," said Kenntnis.

The milk was rich, cold, and thick across his tongue and laid down a soothing wash over Richard's burning gut. "Does everything in your universe want to kill me?" he sighed.

"In a word ... yes. Well, strictly speaking, it's not *my* universe, it's his." Kenntnis inclined his head toward Cross.

"Yeah, but you're not exactly innocent in all this," Cross mumbled around an enormous mouthful of cake. "Because once you found Richard, he became a target." Crumbs blew between his lips, littering his lap.

"So, all I have to do is get away from you two," Richard said to Kenntnis, "and I'll be fine?"

"No, you're too valuable a piece. Now you either have to play or be eliminated."

Richard's stomach twisted and the milk suddenly tasted sour. He set the glass aside on the Italian inlaid wood table at his elbow. Kenntnis rested his hand on the back of the armchair and leaned in over Richard. The smell of the older man's aftershave was bright and sharp.

"Tonight, you get answers, as many as you want."

Richard sat in silence, gazing at the unwieldy mass of confusion and questions. He couldn't get his arms around it, much less frame a coherent question.

Cross leaned forward from his seat on the couch and laid a hand on Richard's knee. He left a chocolate thumbprint on the fabric just above the torn knee. "You probably want to start with me," he said. Richard didn't answer. He just stared down at the ruin of his pants. His lips tightened in annoyance.

Kenntnis laughed. "I'll buy you a new pair. And I'll take care of the repairs at your apartment."

"I'll take you up on that. I do think you owe me."

"So why *did* you shoot me?" Cross suddenly asked.

The fear and horror returned, only slightly dulled by the passage of a few hours, "You *swallowed* somebody ... some ... thing."

"I was just stickin' the parts back together," said Cross.

"You're confusing him," Kenntnis complained. Kenntnis sat down on the coffee table directly in front of Richard and looked him in the eye. "The forces we're opposing aren't native to this world."

"So now we're going to talk about aliens?" Richard said faintly.

"Good move, boss. *Now* who's confusing him," said

Cross sarcastically to Kenntnis.

Kenntnis waved his hands back and forth as if scattering the earlier words. "Erase that. Let's start with physics. There's a theory that there are twenty-seven folded multiverses. The theory's correct—partly—there are actually twenty-three. Anyway, they're densely compacted, touching at multiple points. We're native to this universe." Kenntnis pointed at Cross. "He's not. Which is why our four-dimensional reality and the technology created to function in it can be twisted and altered in the presence of magic, also not natural to our universe, and Old Ones."

Richard realized that no one knew where he was and that he was alone with two insane people. He decided that humoring them might be safest course of action. "So, why are you here?" Richard asked Cross with a forced smile.

"Because a few million years ago one of your distant ancestors left the trees, stood upright, and began the evolutionary scrabble toward intelligence. It doesn't happen often, and when it does it attracts us like sharks to blood, or bees to flowers." Cross smacked his lips, and Richard didn't think he was tasting chocolate any longer.

"Add to that that humans are relatively unique," Kenntnis broke in. "You have this wild, almost chaotic, creativity, and also deeply rooted and very powerful emotions. You represent a source of sustenance to these creatures in the other multiverses."

"What is it, exactly, they ... you are eating?" Richard looked over at Cross.

"Emotions," Cross grunted around another mouthful.

Kenntnis shot him a look. "That's a little simplistic. It's

more complex than that. They feed off your life energy, force, however you want to say it. Emotions are the easiest way to feed, and dark emotions are the easiest of all because they're so powerful and so easy to engender."

"Yeah, early man was a scared little sucker." Cake crumbs blew onto Cross's stained T-shirt as he grinned. It was not a pleasant expression. "I was one of the watchers, and every time some chimp got spooked by lightning, or lost a kid, the fear just poured out. We would suck it in, and soon we were tearing open the peepholes. We noticed you had a tendency to distrust anything different. Once a few of us wriggled through, we helped Cro-Magnon decide Neanderthals were icky and ought to die. After that we worked on establishing religions. The bloodier the better. That got some very tasty wars rolling. With that much power we were able to turn the rips in the fabric of space-time into full-blown gates, and more and more of us arrived." Cross jerked a thumb at Kenntnis. "Then he came along and spoiled the party."

"Ho—" Richard's voice caught. He cleared his throat and tried again "How? By doing what?"

Kenntnis smoothed a hand across his hair, tugged at his upper lip. He frowned, then finally said, "By promoting rational and scientific thought, and trying to wean you off religion and superstition."

"Eating of the fruit of the tree of the knowledge of good and evil," Richard whispered.

Cross nodded. "Exactly, and he had an effect—humans began to question, and Kenntnis and his Paladins—" There was a throat clearing from Kenntnis. "The *Lumina*," Cross stressed the word, and nodded at Kenntnis in some kind of private exchange that Richard didn't understand. "Killed some of us. We were weakened, and we couldn't keep the true gates open. But we could encourage you monkeys to keep the superstition train rolling, and we could keep opening tears into this dimension, and those of us already here could keep feeding as long as you kept killing and hating."

"Since I wasn't able to eradicate gods and religion, I tried a stopgap measure," Kenntnis said. "I fostered the idea of loving and compassionate gods, hoping that would weaken them further until we could push them back out of your world."

Cross joined back in. "Religion's all about obedience and fear, and your early ones were real lip-smackers. Blood sacrifice. Good stuff. But he"—a gesture to Kenntnis—"was having an effect. Human sacrifice gave way to animal sacrifice. Polytheism was pretty damn tolerant. So, us Old Ones got together and fucked him good."

"How?" Richard asked.

"We encouraged the One Bookers," said Cross. "They've been a magnificent disaster."

"Wha … what?" stuttered Richard.

"Monotheism. The second worst idea after religion," Kenntnis said with a sigh, and he pinched the bridge of his nose as if his head pained him. "Now everybody has the *One True God* and the Old Ones have religious hatred and religious wars on which to feed. Two thousand years of crusade, jihad, auto-da-fé, inquisition, pogrom …" Kenntnis seemed to be looking across a vast distance. For the briefest instant, Richard thought he saw whirling lights in the profound darkness of Kenntnis's eyes. Then Kenntnis blinked and the lights were gone.

"Then Scripture is—" Richard began.

"Bullshit," Cross interrupted. "Well, it's not totally untrue. You humans actually wrote down some of the unbelievably horrible shit we did—killing every firstborn son. Fucking over Job, ordering you to war with your neighbors. Actually read what 'God'"—Cross provided the quotation marks with quick flicks of his fingers—"Ordered Joshua to do to Jericho. And what's really amazing is how you humans try to justify it and find some holy meaning, instead of saying, *Wow, these gods are crazy murderous psychopaths who like to watch us suffer. Why would I be all in for this shit?*" Cross seemed to be working himself up into a rage.

Kenntnis rubbed a hand over his face, and he looked unimaginably tired. "Anyway, I thought the grand march toward secular humanism was a dismal failure, and then Cross showed up—the schizophrenic god. He had been supping on human emotions, and there had been enough people who accepted and tried to live by these compassionate ideals that it began to affect this particular Old One." Kenntnis turned and stared at Cross, and reluctantly Richard did the same.

When set beside this incredible explanation Cross's constantly changing appearance began to make a degree of sense.

"So, you reflect back the vision of the faithful," Richard said slowly.

"Yeah, but it depends on which faithful. For some I'm a pretty blond Jesus, sometimes I'm black or brown. The problem was the decent believers affected me, broke me off from the rest of myself." The homeless man stopped frowning and preened a bit. "Not to be immodest, but I was the source for three world religions. I'm just the one that doesn't do hellfire and intolerance and thinks that *do unto others* thing is pretty cool."

Memories of prayers and services spun through Richard's head. There was the feeling of an emotional snap and the core from which he guided his life seemed suddenly empty. The loss overwhelmed him, and he no longer heard them talking.

Slowly he became aware of Cross's voice again. "… got me with a triple whammy. A bombing in Tel Aviv, a retaliation in Gaza, a gay bashing in America, and a massacre of Hindus in India. Guess that's actually four, but, anyway, they split me."

"That was deliberate?" Richard asked.

"Oh, yeah, my other parts wanted to get me away from you leaving you defenseless." He paused to shoot an intense look at Kenntnis. "And send fractals to kill you."

"Why?" Richard cried.

"Because your presence at my side gives me an advantage in the struggle," Kenntnis said gently.

"How did they find out about me?"

"They watch me just as I watch them."

Richard shook his head and looked at Cross. "I don't understand how you can be all these creatures—" he began.

Cross made a rude noise. "Oh, please, you said you were a believer. That means you've accepted this shit for years— Father, Son, Holy Ghost."

"But we're not talking about faith, now," Richard said. The effort to keep his voice level made his throat hurt. He fought back the rage. "I'm talking biology."

"There are examples even in this world—amoebas, atoms. His kind evolved in a different universe, under different conditions," said Kenntnis.

"Then you contain Allah and Yahveh …?" Richard began.

Cross shook his head. "Not the big ones. They split off hundreds of of years ago. And it's a damn good thing one of them, including the Big J, didn't try to come and croak you last night. If they had, you'd be dead." There was another significant look between Cross and Kenntnis. Kenntnis gave an almost imperceptible headshake. "What I try to gather up and keep pasted together are all the little Jesusi created by small but passionate nutbag Christian sects, and the little Allahs created by equally nutty Moslem sects, and the little hoped-for messiahs created by Jewish nuts. Fortunately, there are enough decent Christians, Muslims, and Jews so I'm marginally more powerful than my evil little buddies."

Richard stood and looked down at Kenntnis. "You're trying to enlist me in a war on God."

"No, I'm trying to enlist you in a war to defend this world against invading creatures who are not native to this universe and who will enslave your kind, turn this world into a living hell, and sink you in a darkness from which there is no morning."

"And what happens if you win?"

"I will give you the stars," Kenntnis said simply.

✧ ✧ ✧

THEY LEFT IT there. It was Richard himself who ended the discussion, saying he was too tired and too disturbed to properly evaluate what he'd heard. He needed time to process. Kenntnis offered a guest room and this time it was accepted. Kenntnis thought that was a pretty major victory. The policeman had so many barriers around himself. This was the first sign they were starting to break through.

The attack on his own building had shaken Kenntnis. He had to assume it was an overzealous subordinate, but if it had been Grenier himself it meant he and his masters were far too confident for Kenntnis's peace of mind. So, he set Cross patrolling inside and outside the building, watching for magic. At least they'd managed to damp down Rhiana so she didn't interfere with the task.

Kenntnis lit a candle in one of the antique silver candle-sticks in the dining room. It was an archaic gesture, considering how deeply he revered and nurtured science and technology, but there was a power in the symbolism of the flame. Shielding the fluttering tongue of fire with his hand, Kenntnis went to the bedroom where Rhiana slept.

A fall of pale peach-colored muslin hung from a hook in the ceiling and draped, tentlike, over the graceful sleigh bed. Kenntnis caught a glimpse of himself reflected and refracted in the three mirrors in the vanity. Delicate Limoges boxes dotted the polished wood surface. The Bose was set so low that the music of the Bach fugue was more an impression than any real sound. Nervous, Kenntnis checked to make certain it was still set for continuous play.

Reassured, he moved to the bed and drew back the veiling muslin. The light fell flickering over her extraordinary features. The high angles of her cheekbones narrowed down to the pointed chin. Sooty lashes swept the top of those cheekbones. In the candlelight her skin seemed luminescent. The long black hair fanned across the pillow and cascaded over her shoulders. She slept with wanton abandon, sprawled across the entire bed, one arm thrown behind her head, one foot escaping from beneath the covers.

What was she? Kenntnis wondered. It had been long since this much power had walked in human form. Tomorrow, he would begin investigating her and try to find some answers.

He left Rhiana and moved down the hall to where Richard slept. It was a simpler space with twin beds, a dresser, and a large armchair in front of a fireplace. The closet door was open and Kenntnis could see the coat, slacks, and shirt carefully hung, the shoes set neatly on the floor beneath the clothes.

Richard slept curled tightly on his side. One hand was beneath the pillow, the other clenched beneath his chin. The white-gold hair had escaped from its perfect part, forming a soft fringe across his forehead. There was a furrow between the pale brows. If he had dreams, they weren't pleasant.

A shadow on the wrist caught Kenntnis's attention. At first, he thought it was a line formed by the sheet, but then he realized there was a scar running across Richard's right wrist. Kenntnis craned to look down at the other arm. The skin was unblemished. Disturbed, Kenntnis stepped back and considered this development. *Old, but not terribly old.*

Kenntnis wondered if this was the source of the missing months. Suddenly the man seemed terribly small and frail to be the repository for Kenntnis's hopes and the bulwark against his fears.

Kenntnis started for the door. Richard's voice stopped him before he reached it. "Who are you, really? Or maybe the better question is *what are you?*"

Kenntnis turned back slowly. "Why did you try to kill yourself?"

"A piece of rope caught around my wrist during a yacht race," said Richard. His look dared Kenntnis to disagree. Kenntnis took the dare.

"And the examiners at the police academy bought that load of shit?"

"Albuquerque has a profound shortage of police," said Richard placidly.

They stared at one another in silence for a few moments.

"I need to know if you're strong enough for this. Why did you try to kill yourself?"

"I only discuss personal matters with friends," said Richard. "Who and what are you?" he repeated.

"And I only give my name to friends," answered Kenntnis. As a barb it missed its mark. Richard just smiled.

"So, I guess we'll both keep our secrets."

Kenntnis frowned, realizing he'd been trumped and hating it. Richard chuckled, a rich, musical sound, and Kenntnis realized this was the first time he'd ever heard the policeman's laugh.

"I think you're too used to getting your own way."

"You planning on teaching me humility?" asked Kenntnis.

"No, just pricking your arrogance now and then."

"Are you going to work for me?" Kenntnis demanded.

"I don't know yet," Richard replied.

"Don't take too long. Events are moving with or without you," Kenntnis warned.

CHAPTER TWELVE
PULLING STRINGS

WEBER WALKED INTO his office to find the city attorney, Hank Maldoñado waiting for him. It was barely 9:00 AM, and Weber could already feel a headache coming on.

"Oh, don't look at me like that," Hank said. Maldoñado was a good-looking Hispanic man in his late thirties with a smile that pretty much guaranteed he'd be mayor someday, and then go on to higher political office.

"Please tell me you're not here to bust my balls or my officers' balls over something."

"Trying to head off any potential ball-busting. We got a cop in a coma, no arrests, and a partner whose camera was off during the events. The mayor just wants me to make sure the city isn't going to get hit with a big personal injury lawsuit by Officer Bond's family or, worse, a wrongful death suit. If that should happen, we need to decide along with the insurance company if we're going to defend Oort since he'll clearly be a party to this."

"First, so nice of you to give a shit about Sterling. Second, Shakespeare wasn't wrong."

"Cute."

"Third, there was some kind of power outage that affected everything in the area. Sterling's camera was on the fritz, too, along with their radios. Oort protected the victim and his partner. Fourth, Sarah ain't gonna sue the city or the APD. Tell the mayor to get his panties out of a twist."

Hank huffed out a laugh and stood. "I'll let you deliver that message yourself. This Oort kid sure does seem to have a powerful angel."

"Yeah, no kidding," Weber muttered under his breath as Hank left.

His phone rang. It was the receptionist. "Damon, I got a Sergeant Vallis with the Denver PD trying to get in touch with Oort, but he's not in yet. Thought I'd pass it on to you."

"Sure, put it through." There was a click and then he was connected. "This is Lieutenant Weber. Detective Oort isn't in yet. What can I do you for?"

"Your detective had an APB out on some kids. Well, we found 'em."

✧   ✧   ✧

RICHARD AWOKE, FROWNED at the ceiling, and then remembered the events from last night and where he was. He brought up his wrist, checked his watch, and almost levitated out of bed. It was almost 10:30 AM.

In the bathroom he found a box of non-adhesive bandages, medical tape, and scissors already waiting. He wanted to return to his apartment for shower and clean clothes, but the bandages were a stark reminder that it would be significantly easier if he had another person to help replace the bandages on his hands. The shower was stocked with high-end bath products scented with sandalwood. In a drawer by the sink, he found an antique straight razor with a mother-of-pearl handle, and he found shaving soap and a brush in a Limoges cup.

Given the attention to detail he'd found in the bathroom, Richard half expected to find a change of clothes in the closet, but only his torn and dirty clothes were there. He dressed, gathered up the antibiotic ointment and bandages, and went in search of help.

The smells of freshly baked bread, ham, and coffee led him into a large, aggressively modern kitchen. Late autumn sunlight blazed through the glass and danced across the chrome and steel appliances. Flecks of what looked like opal glittered in the granite countertops. A plump, gray-haired man, a bib apron over his dress shirt and slacks, was loading the dishwasher.

A Bose player filled the room with a Bach partita, and covered chafing dishes stood on a buffet. Rhiana, her chin propped in her hand, was seated at a table set in the bay of a window, perusing a textbook.

She jumped up when he entered, ran to him, and gripped his arm. "I didn't know you were here," she blurted.

"I arrived quite late," Richard said.

"Kenntnis should have woken me up."

A discreet cough drew their attention. "Good morning, sir, I'm Franz Rohner, Mr. Kenntnis's chef. Do you prefer coffee or tea?? Cocoa is also available."

"Richard Oort, pleased to meet you. I would shake hands, but ..." Richard shrugged and glanced down at the first aid supplies he was carrying.

"I quite understand. So, a breakfast beverage?"

"The cocoa sounds good. Thank you."

"I can help you with that," Rhiana said, with a nod to the bandages and ointment.

"Thank you, I would appreciate the help." They moved to the table and Richard glanced curiously at the open page. There were a lot of mathematical formulae. The only thing he could read said:

A Bose-Einstein condensate is a gaseous superfluid phase formed by atoms cooled to temperatures very near to absolute zero. A rotating Bose-Einstein condensate could be used as a model black hold, allowing light to enter but not to escape. For a popularized version of this theory see the science fiction story "Light of Other Days", by Bob Shaw, which introduced a condensate as "slow glass."

It was a stomach-aching reminder of how his father had reacted when Richard had only managed to pull out a C in Calculus. He sat down, depositing the scissors, ointment, tape, and bandages next to a bouquet of cheerful sunflowers in an amber-colored vase.

Rhiana took his hands in hers and gently turned them palms up. There was a hiss of quickly indrawn breath. "What happened?"

"I got burned."

"How?"

"It's a long story, and I really need to get to work. How about I come by tonight after work and tell you?"

"Yeah, okay."

She opened the tube of ointment and spread it gently across the raw blisters on his palms. The tips of her fingers were cool and soft. Three of the fingernails—two on one hand, one on the other—were broken. The rest were long, perfect ovals carefully polished.

"Did you break them the other night?" he asked.

Rhiana nodded and laid a gauze pad over his palm. Her hair fell forward, brushing lightly against her cheeks. The tang of verbena wafted to his nostrils. She finished bandaging his hands, looked up at him from beneath her lashes. Her gaze was admiring, and she drew her forefingers gently down the sensitive skin on the inside of his wrists.

"Thank you," he said, and firmly removed his hands from her grip.

She shot him a disappointed look. Richard stood and crossed quickly to the line of chafing dishes. "Let's see what's available," he said, his tone far too bright and false.

He began to lift lids while Rhiana provided a running commentary. "There's pretty much everything. Including these weird little fish thingies."

"Kippers, most likely," Richard said.

Rhiana flushed, saying quickly and aggressively, "I knew that."

But Richard hadn't been a psych minor for nothing. "I'm with you; I always thought it was crazy to eat fish for breakfast," he said quickly to get them past the moment.

Franz stifled a snort of laughter. "Mr. Cross is extremely fond of them," he said as he sat the mug of cocoa on the table.

"Mr. Cross seems willing to eat anything that's not actively moving," Richard said dryly. Franz laughed again and nodded in agreement.

Richard helped himself to some eggs Benedict, a few pieces of bacon, and some fresh fruit. He returned to the small table and took the seat on the far side from Rhiana.

Rhiana shook back her hair and looked at him. "I never thanked you for saving me." Her voice throbbed with emotion, and she gazed at him with something far too close to adoration.

Oh, dear, Richard thought.

Rhiana was a baby and clearly in the throes of severe hero worship. He would never take advantage of that. Though to be fair, there was a time in his life when he might have, back when frequent, random, sometimes anonymous sex had been his addiction as he tried to ease the aching loneliness he so often felt. And it had been an addiction that had ultimately left him badly injured and very nearly ruined his life. His salvation had been finding his way into police work. Which, ironically, his family viewed as having ruined his life. *If only they knew.*

He shook off his thoughts and gave her a quick smile. "Just doing my job, ma'am," he drawled and took a sip of the cocoa. It was excellent, not too sweet and with a touch of cinnamon on the finish.

She gave a spurt of laughter and propped her chin in her hands. "So, where are you from?"

It was pretty evident that the physics text no longer had any lure. Richard gave a mental sigh and resigned himself to breakfast conversation.

"Newport, Rhode Island." He knew that most people

liked to talk about themselves, and if he asked the questions, he might be able to eat in peace. "But you're from California. I've never been there, but it sounds exciting—Hollywood, Disneyland." He bit into a piece of honeydew melon. The rich, sweet flavor exploded across his tongue. Definitely not from a local market.

Her nose wrinkled. "Trust me, Van Nuys is *not* exciting."

"And your parents? What do they do?"

"My dad's a trucker. Mom works at a school cafeteria."

"Brothers? Sisters?"

"Three brothers, two sisters. But four of us are adopted. My folks fostered a bunch of kids over the years."

"Oh." Richard paused and speared a large blackberry. He wasn't sure how to respond. *That's nice. How noble of your parents.* He settled for another question. "And how did you end up in New Mexico?"

"They gave me a full scholarship—encouraging women in science, you know. I'm the first one in my family to go to college."

"Congratulations, that's a major accomplishment." He smiled over at her, and she blushed brightly.

"That wasn't my folks' reaction. All they could focus on was how the grant only paid for tuition and books, not housing. I had to take out a loan for that. They wouldn't help at all. Well, maybe they really couldn't, but still..." She frowned at the memory. She looked up and her brow cleared. "And anyway, I don't think they understand why I want to do it. Bet you went to college." Richard nodded. She was babbling with nervousness and twisting a strand of hair between her fingers.

"Forgive me, Rhiana, I know this is impertinent, but how old are you?" She hesitated and fiddled with her napkin.

"I'm almost eighteen," she said.

"Wow."

"I skipped a couple of grades."

"I'm impressed." A glance at his watch sent him out of his chair. "I've got to go. I've got to go by the apartment for a change of clothes before I go to work."

"Okay. But you will come by tonight, right?"

"Yes, I promise."

✧　✧　✧

AS HE WALKED to his apartment, Richard reflected on how odd human beings were. He was defensive because of his family's money and social position. Rhiana was defensive for the exact opposite reason. Maybe nobody was ever content and secure, he thought as he unlocked and pushed open the door.

The stink of burned carpet caught in his throat as Richard stepped in. He then froze at the sight of the slender older man seated on the couch. Judge Robert Oort looked up over the rims of his half-moon glasses. The dark blue eyes were cool and emotionless. He set aside the book he had been reading. A year's absence made Richard aware of how his father's iron-gray hair had turned to silver. He wondered if it was him or his mother who'd caused that, or could he not feel guilty and assume it was just the passage of time?

"Sir," Richard said unable to hide his surprise.

"The manager let me in," the older man said in answer to

a question that hadn't been asked.

"But why are you …?" Richard began.

"Bryan Diggins"—Richard struggled to place the name, then remembered Diggins was the family's insurance agent— "informed me that a hospital had made an inquiry regarding your Blue Cross insurance. Your mother found out, and the only way I could calm her was to catch a red-eye flight to check on you. I went to the hospital only to find out you had never been admitted. So, I gather this was not a serious injury and your mother's perturbation was unmerited and my trip unnecessary." His eyes did drop to Richard's bandaged hands and the torn knees in his trousers.

"I'm so sorry, sir." It was stupid and inane to apologize, but that was the nature of the relationship. "I didn't know they'd contact my secondary insurance. I assumed my APD insurance would …" His voice trailed away. "Sorry," he murmured.

"So where did you go? You were clearly not here this morning."

Friends, he almost said automatically, but he caught himself. He didn't want an inquiry into the identity of those friends. "Hotel," he answered instead.

The judge checked his Rolex. "You didn't pack a bag?"

"I … I just wanted to get some sleep." Richard walked into the bedroom. His father followed.

"Well, at least you didn't go into work looking like this. I did call the APD to see if you were there."

Richard selected a coppery brown suit and a dark gold shirt. His fingers were trembling as he flicked through the dozens of ties hanging on the electric racks in the closet.

"They told me that you were no longer Officer Oort, but Detective Oort. You didn't think that deserved a phone call?"

"It … it happened very suddenly," Richard said as he pulled shoe trees out of a pair of brown loafers. He turned to face his father and found himself unable to meet the judge's intense dark blue gaze. Instead, he rushed to the dresser and pulled out clean underwear.

"So, I gathered. I talked with Captain Murphy in Newport, and he indicated that it was almost unheard of for a young officer with so little experience to be promoted to detective without strings being pulled." The judge's voice provided the interrogatory.

Richard's stomach began to ache. He forced himself to pick up the shirt and begin opening the buttons. "You'd have to ask my captain," Richard said.

"You have no idea why you were promoted and who might have pulled those strings?" his father pressed.

Richard considered the events of the past three days and the conversation he'd had last night with Kenntnis and shook his head. He also realized that his father's arrival had little to do with concern over Richard and a lot to do with soothing his wife and distrust of the mysterious patron.

"Why the interest, sir? I thought you didn't approve of my becoming a policeman."

His father sighed. "It wasn't what I'd hoped for, but you lacked the …" He paused and then resumed, "*Temperament* for law or medicine, and after your … illness you chose to quit Drew's firm rather than return. You needed to do something."

His stomach was pressed up hard against his lungs and

Richard felt as if he had only inches with which to breathe. "I was good at music, but you—"

"You told us that only one-tenth of one percent actually succeed in having a professional singing career. I didn't like those odds. And you told me yourself you weren't certain you had sufficient talent. I wanted you to have something secure to fall back on. So, I took it upon myself to get you the job with Drew."

"But now you seem to be objecting when someone makes an effort on my behalf in *this* career," Richard said, and felt the breath freeze in his chest at his father's withering look.

"I don't know who's acting on your behalf, and I want to make certain you're not doing anything that could blow back on me. I'm on the Federal bench. I must be careful, and your judgment hasn't always impressed me. I'm just concerned that you're botching this career as well."

Richard knew the force of his father's personality and will. Captain Ortiz would tell him who had made the request. He surrendered to the inevitable. "He's a businessman named Kenntnis. He owns a company called Lumina Enterprises."

"I find it disturbing that you would lie to me even by omission. I did find it to be unlikely that you could accomplish this on your own."

The nausea was increasing. If he'd just provided his father with Kenntnis's name initially he might have avoided this rebuke.

Robert Oort shook his head. "I don't understand you at all. I raised you to be better than this." Richard didn't respond. "Well, it's apparent you are determined to set your own course." The older man turned and walked to the door of the bedroom. He paused and looked back. "And next time you come to grief please *try* to keep it from your mother. I'm a great distance away and I can't be spending the time or the money to calm your mother's nerves."

Richard heard the front door fall closed. Dropping the shirt, he ran for the bathroom, hoping to reach the toilet before he vomited.

✧　✧　✧

THE RIBBING STARTED in the parking lot outside APD headquarters and continued all the way up to the bullpen. Various officers—plainclothes and uniforms—commented about the shootout at Richard's apartment the night before, and despite Weber's attempts to defend him, the predominant impression was that he couldn't hit the broadside of a barn door. After the encounter with his father, Richard was finding it hard to maintain his equilibrium, but it was fatal with cops if you reacted. Like wolves, they sensed weakness.

So, he just kept smiling, but his cheeks were burning by the time he reached his desk in its cramped corner. He pulled out his notebook and phone, indicating dismissal, and eventually the baying pack wandered away. He tried to concentrate on transferring his notes, but his thoughts returned over and over to the conversation with his father.

If only he'd told him about Kenntnis initially. There was nothing wrong with having help. Why did he need his dad to be proud of him? The judge had never been proud of anything he'd done before. It wasn't going to change now.

A shadow fell across the desk. He looked up at Lieutenant Weber. "Come into the office," Weber ordered. He looked grim and Richard had a sudden stomachache.

Curious looks followed them. Weber shut the door and remained standing at Richard's side.

"What's wrong? Did I—"

"Relax. You're not in trouble," Weber said. Instead, he handed Richard a plane ticket to Denver. Richard blinked at it in confusion.

"Those kids you had an APB out on, they're in the morgue up in Denver." Richard felt his knees fail, and Weber suddenly had a hand under his arm and was helping him into a chair.

You know how kids are, Emma Parson had said. *They all want to try their wings.*

Well, Naomi had tried, and they'd failed her. Panic and dread overtook him as Richard realized that he'd have to break the news to this mother … to all their mothers. It had him so agitated that he momentarily lost the thread of what the lieutenant was saying. By the time he could focus again, he heard Weber say, "… got caught up in a gang shooting."

"They were shot?" Surprise sent his voice up an octave.

"Yeah, that's what I just said." Weber gave him an odd look. "Next question, *why* did you have an APB out on these three individuals?"

Richard swallowed several times. He hadn't mentioned the trailer. He hadn't mentioned that Rhiana had given him the names. Panic hammered in his chest.

Weber ran a hand through his thick mat of wavy brown hair, leaving it looking like a disturbed haystack. "Also, I found out yesterday that you were at that Kenntnis guy's building when there was that *convenient* gas line explosion. Then last night someone breaks into your apartment and tries to kill you. What the fuck is going on? Who's after you? And what have you done to set them on you?" Weber asked.

"I'm not dirty." Richard forced the words through lips stiff with dread.

"Oh, shit, I know that. You're a fucking boy scout." Weber sat on the edge of the desk in front of Richard and laid a hand on his shoulder. Richard noticed a faint dusting of freckles across the back of Weber's wrist and the powerful muscles and tendons. He wondered how those hands would feel … Richard jerked his gaze away.

"It's pretty damn obvious that you're in some kind of trouble, and I wanted you to know that if I can help, I will. You're a good cop and we'd … *I'd* hate to lose you."

The support and honest concern were unexpected and terribly welcome after his earlier encounter with his father. Richard felt a glow of pleasure that this decorated officer thought well of him. It quickly faded when he looked down at the ticket clutched in his hand.

"I get the feeling all of this is connected; the girl from Saturday night, these kids, your apartment." Weber gave his shoulder a gentle shake. "*Talk* to me."

"I will. I promise. I'm … I'm trying to make sense of it, too. I can tell you this much. Rhiana … Ms. Davinovitch and these other three were all friends. I thought they might know who … why she got … attacked."

"So not a random mugging or attempted rape?" Richard shook his head. "And you know this … how?"

"I … I interviewed her after … again."

"I got a cop in a coma. Guns that don't work. A patrolman elevated to detective on the say-so of some reclusive billionaire, explanations for explosions that don't pass the smell test, and a cop who nearly got killed in his own home. I'm going to trust you … for now. Do not make me regret that decision."

"I won't, sir."

"That plane leaves at 2:00 PM. You'd better get packed. Keep the receipts for the hotel and any meals." The shift to mundane bookkeeping issues helped center Richard. "Turn 'em in when you're back. Oh, and take this." He pulled a Glock out of his desk drawer and slid it across to Richard. "Since yours keep getting impounded pending investigation. Oh, and keep some extra ammo with you," Weber added.

It was an odd remark, but time was passing so Richard headed for the door, only to pause with his hand on the doorknob.

"Do I … am I the one who tells the families about …?"

"Some cops do it themselves. Me, I call the chaplain and have him deliver the news," Weber said, trying to sound matter of fact and failing.

"I … I think I'll do that."

CHAPTER THIRTEEN
DON'T FEEL, THINK

VALLIS WAS A heavyset man in his mid-fifties. He sported ostrich cowboy boots, and a belt buckle the size of a dinner plate wedged up his sagging belly. He nursed a big bottle of water, and periodically he would sniff at an open jar of Vicks. Richard resisted the impulse to tell him that would only carry any smells deeper into his nose.

After the turbulent flight up from Albuquerque, Richard felt like Vallis looked. The plane hadn't handled the mountain updrafts terribly well. Richard took a companionable sip from his own bottle of Evian. Vallis stuck the water bottle under his arm and held out a shovel-sized hand.

"Glad you could get up here this fast. I've got the parents due to arrive in the morning, and they all want to take their kids."

"Understandable," Richard said.

"Well, this one is pretty damn cut and dried," said Vallis over his shoulder as he led Richard through the office cubicles and the big metal double doors into the morgue itself.

Vallis choked out a cough and stuffed blobs of Vicks into each nostril. Richard looked at the older man curiously. There actually wasn't much odor in the morgue. Giant exhaust fans beat out a rhythm, moving the chilly air. Richard wondered if Vallis had gotten a whiff he couldn't forget, and now his mind provided the stench whenever he was near a body. And there were a lot of bodies. Denver was a much bigger and richer city than Albuquerque, so there were three coroners at work and a couple of assistants. A body on one table had been cracked open, rib bones starkly white against the red and yellow of the viscera and muscles. There was the sound of gurgling water running constantly down the length of the steel table carrying away the waste.

An assistant spotted them. "Who you here for?" he asked.

"The kids caught up in that gang shooting," Vallis croaked out, trying to breathe through his mouth and talk at the same time.

The assistant nodded and led the way to the lockers set in the far wall. The drawers slid out with a rumble of metal on metal. Richard pulled thin surgical gloves over his bandages and twitched back the first sheet to reveal the waxy, pale face of a young man. Dark blond hair fell limply across his forehead. Richard steeled himself and pulled again until the torso could be seen. There were four wounds like tiny mouths in the dead boy's chest and stomach. Richard covered the body and moved to the next.

The girl in the next drawer had soft brown hair cut to chin length. She had a wound in the side of her neck and two in the chest. The final drawer held a zaftig brunette with more torso wounds. He felt ghoulish, but he checked the toe tag. The zaftig brunette was Naomi.

"Okay?" Vallis asked.

Richard nodded and pulled the sheet back up. The coroner's assistant rolled the brunette back into the wall. The man's hands closed around the end of the slab. There was a large bruise across the back of one hand and something snapped into focus.

"Wait!" Richard pulled the sheet back down from the first girl's body and stared at the neck wound.

"Could you get a coroner over here, please?" he asked the assistant. The man looked bored and irritated, but he nodded and walked away.

"What?" Vallis asked in an aggrieved tone.

"This bullet went in at an angle." Richard gently touched the ragged edges of the neck wound. "It had to have hit either the carotid or the jugular or maybe both. There should be a huge swelling from the hemorrhage."

Vallis bent forward, but Richard noticed that he never actually focused on the girl's throat. His eyes kept sliding away.

"Okay, so?"

"Let's see what the coroner says," Richard replied cautiously, and turned to greet the white-haired, paunchy man approaching them. He was snapping his heels down hard as if to emphasize his annoyance at the interruption.

"Yes? Adam said you had a question," said the coroner.

"More of an observation," said Richard, and he repeated what he had told Vallis.

"Obviously, it didn't hit either the vein or the artery." Impatience and superiority made each word hit like a dart.

"Could you just take a look?" Richard asked, since the coroner hadn't once glanced at the body.

The coroner's eyes slid off the body and focused on the

far wall.

"It's what I would expect from this kind of wound. We've done the autopsies."

Richard blinked at the coroner. He looked back at the smooth, unblemished body of the girl. "But … but you haven't," he said weakly.

"Are you insinuating that I and my staff haven't done our work?"

"Well, actually … yes."

The man's face turned a mottled red. "If you'll excuse me. You can find your way out." The coroner spun on his heel and walked away.

"There hasn't been an autopsy," said Richard, appealing to Vallis.

"Of course, there has," said Vallis. "Look, I gotta get back to the precinct."

He walked to the door. Richard followed, his mind whirling.

Just outside the door he caught Vallis by the arm. "Are you releasing the bodies to a mortuary?"

"Yeah, the Davis Funeral Home."

"When?" asked Richard.

Vallis looked at his watch. "Well, now that you've had a look, probably within the hour."

"Thanks," said Richard. He waited until Vallis cleared the front doors before pulling out his cell phone and placing a call to Albuquerque.

✧ ✧ ✧

RICHARD WAITED ON the sidewalk out front of the Davis Funeral Home. A redbrick building with white trim and wide bay windows with mullioned panes, it looked more like a house than a funeral parlor, as if the sting of death could be eased with colonial respectability. His breath puffed white streamers in front of his face. Frost sparkled on the sidewalk where the light of the streetlamps pooled. Occasionally he heard a car pass on the larger street behind him. He checked his watch. 11:43 PM. Armandariz's plane had been due to land at 9:20 PM. *I wonder if she's thought better of it and isn't coming after all,* he thought. *What I'm asking* is *completely out of line.* The icy air bit at the skin of his exposed wrist. Richard quickly shook the cuffs of his shirt, suit coat, and topcoat back down, and pulled up his glove. He paced a slow circle.

A car turned the corner, the headlights sweeping across the darkened facades of the buildings. The rented Prius rolled into the curb and stopped. The lights and engine died and Armandariz stepped out wrapped in a bulky white parka with a fur-trimmed hood. The pale fur set off her rich, dark skin. She had a medical bag in one hand and a Styrofoam cup in the other. The cup added its steam to their mingled breaths.

"Okay, you told me if I came, I might get some answers about the glowing, spinning penny," Armandariz said.

Richard held up a hand. "That's not exactly what I said. I said you *might* find something as intriguing as the glowing, spinning penny."

"So, I get more questions and no answers?" asked Armandariz.

"Possibly … probably. Or I misinterpreted what I saw and wasted your time and my money."

The coroner nodded, accepting his caveats. "Okay, let's do it."

Richard led her around to the back of the mortuary. Two hearses and two white limos were parked in the lot near a dumpster.

"Tacky," Armandariz opined as they walked past the limos. "They should be black."

They reached the double doors set in the center of the back wall. Richard knocked softly.

"How did you get them to agree to this?" Armandariz asked.

"I waited until the owners had gone home, and I wooed the night staff with a flash of a badge and a hint of *Silence of the Lambs*. Todd liked the idea of being part of something bigger than a night spent embalming."

"Yeah, I could see where that would enliven his evening," said Armandariz, and she blew on her exposed fingers.

The locks clicked, and one door opened. Todd looked cautiously around the parking lot, and waved them in. He was a small man, only an inch or so taller than Richard, but softly round.

"Todd, this is Dr. Armandariz. Doctor, Todd Aikens."

"So pleased to meet you," said Todd in a hushed tone as he pumped Armandariz's hand.

"We can't thank you enough for this," Richard said.

"Not at all. I knew when I saw them, I had to do something. They looked so sad." He turned and led them down the hall.

Armandariz rolled her eyes at Richard and whispered, "What they look is *dead*."

"Don't be a cynic," Richard whispered back.

The bodies, discreetly draped with sheets, were laid out on tables. On shelves lay the mortician's tools of the trade—putty, wax, jugs of bright pink and orange fluid. Richard stared at the neon colors in confusion.

"It takes a lot of pumped-in orange and pink to turn corpses back toward normal color," said Armandariz.

Richard had been expecting the reek of formaldehyde, but the room smelled of a floral air freshener. Armandariz shed the parka, pulled a long apron and a pair of surgical gloves out of her case, and donned them. Next, she set out her instruments. Richard leaned against a wall to watch.

But the Albuquerque coroner was skittish. She pulled down a sheet, then turned away to fuss with her instruments without ever looking at the corpse. She picked up a scalpel, then asked Todd about the prospects for the Broncos in the upcoming season. Richard watched closely, trying to analyze what was happening.

Armandariz flung down her scalpel. It hit the side of the table with a metallic *ting* and went bouncing away across the tile floor. Todd ran to pick it up.

"Todd, I'm really tired. You got anything with caffeine around this place?" the coroner asked.

"There's coffee in the staff breakroom," Todd answered, handing the scalpel back.

"Would you get me a cup? Black." The mortician nod-ded. As soon as he'd cleared the room Armandariz rounded on Richard. "What the fuck is wrong with me?" she demanded.

"What do you mean?" said Richard, and he made his tone as noncommittal as possible.

Armandariz glared at him. "It's going to sound crazy."

"I won't hold it against you," Richard said.

She hesitated, then blurted out, "I can't bring myself to look at these bodies, and I've *never* had a problem looking at bodies. It's like they're repelling any kind of close inspection."

Richard nodded. "I don't think that's crazy. I think it's the only explanation for why a professional coroner would fail to autopsy homicide victims."

Armandariz stared at him. Richard stepped forward and took another pair of surgical gloves out of her case. He blew in them and pulled them on, working his fingers to smooth out any wrinkles. Taking the scalpel out of her hand, he said, "Tell me what to do. I'll do it."

"So, you don't feel it?"

Richard shook his head. Armandariz glanced down at the girl's body. Her eyes started to slide away, but she forced her gaze back to the neck wound. "Make a cut here," she ordered curtly, and indicated the line with the tip of her finger. A trickle of sweat slipped from beneath the hair at her temple and ran across her cheek.

Todd returned with the coffee. Armandariz took the cup and gulped down a large mouthful. The smell of the coffee was dark and bitter, vanquishing the floral air fresheners.

The flesh parted under the knife. "Hold it open," she ordered.

Richard clenched his teeth, worked his fingers into the

cut, and spread it open. Armandariz pulled a small, powerful halogen flashlight out of her bag and inspected the interior of the wound. She stepped back with a nod and pulled off her gloves with a sharp snap.

"I'm done. You can have them," she said to Todd.

"So, what did you find?" the mortician asked with an eager glitter in his eyes.

"Sorry, Todd, you're not cleared for that," Armandariz said portentously.

Todd managed to look both disappointed and excited at the same time. "This is big, isn't it?" he whispered.

"Yep, *X-Files* big, and we couldn't have done it without you," said Armandariz. The coroner closed her case and jerked her head toward Richard and the door.

Richard paused to shake Todd's hand again. "Thank you again, and please, please, keep this entirely between us."

"You can depend on me."

Outside, Richard sucked in several lungfuls of fresh air so cold it burned his throat. "So, what did you find?" he asked, repeating Todd's question.

"They were shot postmortem, they need to be properly autopsied, and the cops need to look for somebody other than the bangers."

"I don't think they're going to," said Richard. "And here's why." He pulled rolled-up papers from the pocket of his topcoat and handed them to Armandariz. "This is a copy of the police report complete with the testimony from the only surviving gang member. Start at paragraph six."

Armandariz pulled the flashlight out of her case. The powerful beam illuminated the page to a stark white. She read quickly, then looked over at Richard and slapped the back of her hand sharply against the page.

"I want to hear this straight from this *pendejo*'s mouth."

"No," said Richard. "You answered my question. You do not want to be involved in this."

"The fuck I don't! Get your ass in the car."

Richard shook his head. "We won't be able to see him now."

"Fine. We grab a hotel, get some sleep, and see him in the morning."

"Okay, but I'll drive myself. I have my own car." Richard waved toward his rental parked across the street.

"No. You are not ditching me. The weird just keeps propagating exponentially and we need to talk about it."

"What do you mean?"

She folded her arms across her chest and glared up at him. "Not unless you agree that I can be part of this."

Richard felt his jaw slide forward, ready to fight, but then realized he needed to know what she was going to tell him. He was also secretly relieved to have someone else around to verify and document the craziness.

"Okay, just let me get my things."

Richard retrieved his overnight bag and tossed it into the trunk.

He then opened the driver's side door for the coroner. Armandariz gave him a strange look, then shook her head and got in.

✧　✧　✧

IT WAS PARTLY because she was hungry and partly because she wanted to spend more time with the enigma that was Richard Oort that Angela insisted they stop for food. She could also tell from the subtle trembling in his hands and his his skin color that that he needed calories, or he would be likely to collapse. They found a twenty-four-hour IHOP and were led by a frowning, gum-chewing teenager to a booth. Angela used the menu as a screen as she leaned across the table and said softly,

"When I was her age, I had to have my my homework done and be in bed by ten." He smiled and Angela felt dazzled. She realized this was the first time she'd seen the detective not looking stressed, confused, or grim.

"Careful, you're showing your age," he whispered back. "But I have to agree. Where are their parents?"

"And you be careful. You're about to imply that women need to stay at home and raise the kids." She shook a finger under his nose, and he sat back like a startled puppy.

"No, not at all. I was raised in that kind of home, but my parents encouraged all of us to get an education and pursue our interests," Richard said.

"And who's all of us?"

"My two sisters. One's a doctor and the other's a lawyer."

"And you didn't become an Indian chief," Angela quipped, and glanced at him from beneath her lashes to see how he would react. He chuckled.

"I've heard how you enjoy getting under people's skin." He paused and lined up his silverware. "Are you from New Mexico?" he asked.

"Yeah, I'm a rarity—an actual native—a twelfth-generation native, or thereabouts, at least on my mom's side. I'm one of the crypto-Jews of northern New Mexico."

He scanned her face as if searching for the joke. "I beg your pardon?" said Richard.

"Jews fleeing the Inquisition in Spain. Bunch of 'em fled as far as was physically possible, which was the mountains of New Mexico. They were passing as Catholics, and over the years they became assimilated, but certain eccentric rituals survived. I can remember my great-grandmother bringing out the candles on Friday evening, covering her head with her mantilla, and praying to the Virgin."

"So, are you Jewish or Catholic?"

"Neither. I flirted with converting to Judaism, but I found out it was just as shitty toward women as Catholicism, so I opted for agnosticism. It seemed a safer bet than out-and-out atheism."

She had touched some nerve. The policeman was looking grim again. Angela paused for a long sip of her coffee. "Look, if I've offended you … well, tough. Some people believe. Some don't. I don't."

"It's not that, it's … well, it's an odd echo of … well … things that are happening in my life," Richard said.

"Want to talk about it?" Angela asked, and mentally kicked herself as she watched his face close down, and he he leaned back in the booth, putting distance between them.

"No," he said, tempering it with a smile. "But I would really like to hear the information you used to bribe me into letting you tag along."

"Tag alo—" she started to yelp, when the teenager returned for their orders. Richard went with a chef salad and a glass of milk, Angela pancakes, eggs, and ham. The teenager slouched away, and Angela leaned in across the table. "Damon had me inspect both yours and Sterling's Sterling's weapons from Saturday night." She watched him tense, his eyes becoming hooded, and she realized he was hiding something about that night. "I know why your guns didn't work."

His eyes widened in surprise and his tension increased as she walked through the explanation. She had the feeling he knew *why* the atomic structure of the guncotton had been affected, but it was clear he was going to give her nothing.

"Hmm, that is very strange. Do you have any explanation for it?"

"'Fraid not. Do *you*?"

"Not a clue." She noticed he had stopped eating. He sat silent for a few moments, then in the most awkward change of subject she'd ever heard, he said, "So, as one of the rare New Mexico natives, tell me more about the state. It seems like such an odd contradiction. You've got Los Alamos and Sandia Labs on one side and your grandfather and his demons on the other."

"The Land of Enchantment also has has lots and lots of kooks." She then launched into stories about the family, the big house on Rio Grande Boulevard, the ranch outside of Taos, the horses, crawdad hunting in the irrigation ditches. Her six siblings and her parents.

He insisted on paying but didn't make it about being a gentleman. "You came up here to help me out on a case. I'll get reimbursed."

While he took a tip back to the table, Angela checked her

phone for a nearby motel. She also pondered how to find out what he was hiding, but figured she'd have a better shot if she waited until the morning. She also couldn't help but study his ass as he walked away, and the cut of his coat across his shoulders. Angela gave herself permission to feel like a teenager.

"Ready?" he asked.

"Yeah. I found a Motel Six," she said.

"Excellent."

He held the car door for her again.

RICHARD COULD HEAR the television from Angela's room next door. It stayed on for almost an hour after they checked in. He wondered if she'd be able to sleep after the three cups of coffee she'd drunk at dinner.

He had tried, but each time he closed his eyes he saw the pale, slack faces of the dead, and replayed the conversations with their families. In a few hours they would arrive in Denver to collect their children and take them home. In the morning, he would meet the sole survivor of the gun battle, a Hispanic kid who would undoubtedly be charged with felony murder, and there would be *another* grieving family to mourn the loss of a child. Whoever had actually murdered Deborah, Naomi, and Steve had a lot to answer for, and he was going to see to it that they did. Which meant he needed help. The kind no police department was equipped to provide.

He lifted his wallet out of the breast pocket of his coat

and pulled out Kenntnis's card. For a long time, he sat on the foot of the bed holding his cell phone, staring at the card, and feeling his stomach clench down into a tight, painful ball.

Kenntnis answered on the first ring, and there was no hint of sleepiness in the voice.

"Okay, I'm with you," Richard said without preamble.

"Why?" Kenntnis asked with equal directness.

"They killed those kids, at least three of them. We need to find the fourth, this Josh Delay. Perhaps you can make inquiries through less formal channels."

"All right. You need to be careful. I think this Delay is the one who threw the spell at the building. He's a pretty major sorcerer."

The incongruity of the words seemed to beat in time with his throbbing headache. Richard covered his eyes. "I can't believe I'm listening to this, much less doing it."

"Do you think it's the right thing to do?" Kenntnis asked.

"I don't know what I feel …" Richard began.

"Don't feel," Kenntnis interrupted sharply. "I want you to *think*."

"I'm human. I feel," Richard said with matching sharpness.

"That's fine, feel all you want … on your own time. With me, you think," Kenntnis replied. "You need to get back, and quickly, so I can arm you." He hung up before Richard could respond.

"Well, I hope it's going to work better than my damn gun." He threw up his hands in frustration. "Oh, to hell with it." He crawled into bed.

CHAPTER FOURTEEN

THINGS ARE WAY PAST DANGEROUS

THE INTERROGATION ROOM at the county's juvenile facility was painted a bilious shade of green. The predominant smells were disinfectant, coffee, and bacon. Angela glared at Richard.

"Damn, you had an actual change of clothes."

"Yes. What did you think I had in that bag?"

"I assumed you were like most cops and had a razor, a pair of socks, and some clean underwear."

"Sorry to disappoint."

"You just make me look bad. I hung my pantsuit up in the bathroom while I showered, and hoped," Angela said.

"It didn't work," Richard said, but he softened it with a smiled.

"Yes, I know that."

Shuffling footsteps and the rattle of metal on metal interrupted them. A guard escorted Danny Sisneros into the room. The guard removed the handcuffs but left the ankle fetters.

"Knock when you're finished," the guard said, and left.

Sisneros was a burly kid with a long scrawny neck, like a straw balancing the square head on broad, blocky shoulders. His prominent Adam's apple bobbed up and down the length of his his throat like a cartoon character. His left leg was in a cast and thrust out stiffly along the side of the table. He stared at them bleary-eyed and kept rubbing his cheeks. The scratch of skin on stubble was loud in the interrogation room.

"Is this gonna take long, man?"

"No," said Richard. "I just want to hear what happened night before last."

"I didn't shoot nobody," Danny said with some urgency.

"We know that."

"In fact, you got shot," said Angela encouragingly.

The boy's lower lip drooped in a pout. "Yeah, and somebody's gonna pay for that. Not like you think," Danny hastened to add.

He had that *oh, shit, I shouldn't have said that* look that Richard had seen far too many times on suspects' faces. Richard looked away toward the dingy pale-green walls. He didn't enjoy witnessing the general stupidity and low impulse control of most criminals. He couldn't forget how much of it was due to trauma in the womb from drug-addicted mothers, and the violence and crushing grind of poverty after they entered the world, and a system that shunted the poor and many POC into substandard schools and then into the school to prison pipeline. Richard's was not a popular view in law enforcement, which was why he mostly kept it to himself.

"Maybe we'll sue 'em," Sisneros added belligerently.

"Yeah, you hold that thought, sport," said Armandariz. "Now answer the nice policeman's questions." Richard threw Angela an exasperated look. She shrugged an apology.

"Please," he said gently.

"We were dealing … like big surprise."

Richard threw up his hand to stop the flow of words. "Have you said this before and have you seen an attorney?" He caught Angela's look of surprise out of the corner of his eye.

The kid rolled his eyes. "There was like shit all over the sidewalk, and the PD said the dope was like the *least* of my problems."

Richard sighed. "All right then, go on."

"Anyway, I was down the street about half a block on lookout. Everything seemed to be smooth. Sander had the shit and Juan had the money. Then these Anglo assholes come walking around the corner at the other end of the street. Right into the middle of the deal. Next thing I know everybody's shootin'."

"And why was that?" Richard asked. "Did the Anglos do anything to provoke it?"

"I couldn't see. Me, I think Juan decided they were cops and Sander had ratted him out, so he pulled his piece." He paused and massaged his face with his palms again. Richard waited and pinched his nose to briefly shut out the smell of scrambled eggs and old grease. "It was weird, though. Everybody else was diving for cover or running, but these dumb fucks just stood there in the middle of a gunfight gettin' hit with bullets."

Richard stood. "Thank you, Danny."

"That's it?"

"Yes, thanks."

Richard was pleased that Armandariz kept silent all the

way back to the car. Dark gray and white clouds hung heavy in the sky and there was the smell of moisture in the air. He opened the driver's door for Angela, and moved to the passenger side, but she paused, leaned her folded arms along the top of the car, and stared at Richard.

"Dead people don't walk," she said.

"I warned you not to get involved," Richard replied quietly.

"You're pretty cool about all this."

He didn't respond, just got into the car. Armandariz swallowed her annoyance and got in. Hit the ignition and set the heater on high. "Let's hope we can get to the airport before the snow hits," she said.

"I've got to pick up my car," said Richard. "Drop me back at the mortuary. I'll meet you at the airport."

✧　✧　✧

AS SHE CLIMBED the narrow steps into the Mesa plane, Angela cursed Richard mentally in English and Spanish. Despite her best efforts, he had managed to ditch her. She had waited until the absolute final call for the flight and kept ringing his cell phone every fifteen minutes only to get his voicemail. She had finally left a message; simple, short, and to the point.

"I'm in. Like it or not, I'm in."

During the short flight back to Albuquerque, she considered. She needed details on the case, and she knew enough people within the police that it shouldn't be a problem. She didn't stop at home for clean clothes but went straight to APD headquarters.

She spotted Oort's desk immediately. It had the same neat economy as the man himself. There were only two detectives in at this hour. One of them was Snyder. Angela knew his reputation from friends on the force. He was a grumbler who always felt underappreciated.

She hailed him. "Hey, Snyder."

He looked up from his newspaper. Powdered sugar from the open box of donuts coated his fingers. Angela sighed. Cops resented being stereotyped, but they were often total clichés.

"Doc," he said, and waved his coffee mug at her.

"The lab's doing tests for Oort, and he's fucked up some documents." It was absolutely the right tack to take. Snyder beamed.

"Little asshole. He's either got pictures of the chief fucking a chimp or he's fucking the chief."

"So may I look through his files?" Angela asked.

"Be my guest," Snyder said, and waved a hand grandly at Oort's desk.

Angela settled into the chair and read quickly through the handwritten notes, noting the small and precise handwriting and the distinctive lefthander's tilt. She also paid close attention to his report from Saturday night. She had read a lot of lawyers' briefs over the years; this had that same careful quality of trying not to say too much. There were notes about the Faith in the Rock church, and the Worldwide Christian Alliance, and Mark Grenier. She finally unearthed a note with only two words, carefully underlined.

Kenntnis???

Lumina?

✧   ✧   ✧

HIS FIRST IMPULSE had been to drive directly to the Faith in the Rock Church in Castle Rock, but Richard thought about it and acknowledged that he was exhausted and hungry. He checked into a Super 8 and walked to a nearby cafe for lunch. Castle Rock had become a bedroom community for both Denver and Colorado Springs, but it still maintained its charm. The downtown held nineteenth-century redbrick buildings and there was a stretch of cobblestone on a few streets. He was seated at a window table that gave him a view of the rock formation that provided the name for the town.

His waitress was a gawky girl with long, straight brown hair, a long torso, and equally long legs. She was also chatty, and she told him about the restaurant that used to be open on the top of the rock, but rattlesnakes had infested the walls and slithered out to the dismay of the diners. Despite Kenntnis's disdain for feelings, it still felt like an omen to Richard.

After returning to the hotel, Richard called the church and made an appointment with the pastor for 5:00 PM. He changed into pajamas. Like many cops, he kept a big bottle of generic aspirin close at hand. He shook out three pills and dry swallowed them. He also had a wider range of pharmacopeia available. The Xanax bottle came easily to his hand. Richard checked the expiration date. It was a few months past the date. He hadn't needed the drug in a long time. He bounced the bottle on the palm of his hand and considered. No doubt he was stressed. No doubt he needed to rest. He placed the bottle back in the overnight case and climbed into bed. It felt like a victory.

✧   ✧   ✧

ANGELA HAD NEVER paid much attention to the elegant modern building with its multiple angles placed on a knoll at the foot of the mountains. She'd seen it on her way to hike the La Luz trail up the side of the Sandia Mountains, but never given it much thought. Now it held far more significance as the headquarters of the man who had arranged for Richard's elevation to detective. Also, a building where there had been a violent explosion that had sent six people to the hospital.

She studied it closely as she wound her way up the hill and pulled into the parking lot. It reminded her of the prow of some fantastic ship preparing to sail out across the river valley far below.

There was a security guard as well as a receptionist in the lobby. The walls sent back the echoes from her heels tapping on the black-and-silver marble floor. She showed her credentials to the receptionist.

"I want to see Mr. Kenntnis."

"Who should I say is calling?" the woman asked.

"Doctor Armandariz." The woman turned aside and spoke so softly into a throat mike that Angela didn't catch a word.

Angela wandered around the lobby. Drew a hand across

the butter-soft leather upholstery on the black leather sofas and the chairs. Flipped through the assortment of magazines and newspapers, both scientific and business and not all of them American or even in English. The African American security guard watched her sleepy-eyed, but his physical stance told her he was very much awake. The perfectly coiffed young woman answered the gentle chimes of the phone. Bored, Angela wandered up to the security guard and indicated the alternating dark silver panels on the walls and the dark floor with its swirls of silver.

"You know, if Darth Vader had an office, it would be in a building like this."

"What makes you think he doesn't?" rumbled a basso voice.

Angela whirled, grasping for her scattering composure. She hadn't heard the elevator. The man who was stepping off and into the lobby was massive and African American. She hadn't expected that. Then on closer inspection she realized his face was a fascinating mix of racial types. He thrust out a hand.

"I'm Kenntnis."

"Dr. Armandariz."

"Please come upstairs to my office."

The elevator doors sighed shut. "You wouldn't know you had a gas leak explosion here two days ago," Angela said conversationally. "It was a gas leak, right?" She had to crane her head back to deliver her challenging stare, but she managed. "Seems sort of strange it only hit one side of the building."

Kenntnis's eyes narrowed. "Are you here in your official

capacity, Doctor? Though my understanding is that while you have access to and work with the CSI division, your focus is primarily that of coroner. And there was no crime committed here." He had taken a step back from her while he was speaking. The retreat seemed odd from a man so large and powerful.

"First, little creepy you were investigating me while I was loitering in your Death Star lobby. Also, I was up in Denver with Detective Oort examining the bodies of three young murder victims. Richard sure does seem to be the nexus of what we in the police business call *weird shit*. Or would if we ever saw shit as weird as this."

"You are beginning to interest and alarm me a great deal, Doctor" Kenntnis said.

"Hey, relax. I'm a good guy."

"I would feel so much better if Richard were here to vouch for that."

"So, you haven't been able to reach him, either," Angela said.

Kenntnis reached out and hit the stop button on the elevator. "What is your interest in this?"

"I think Richard's in trouble," Angela said simply.

"Why?"

"He was supposed to be on the same flight with me this morning, but I think he's still investigating in Denver, and it's never a good idea to work a high wire act solo."

"You act as if this investigation is dangerous," Kenntnis said, clearly probing.

"Considering three dead people managed to walk down a street and get shot, I think it's *way* past dangerous and into fucking surreal. Not to mention this stupid thing." She pulled the glowing penny from her pocket. "And the restructuring of guncotton on the atomic level. Now can we get this elevator moving and finish this conversation sitting down? I had three hours of sleep last night."

Suddenly Kenntnis was grinning down at her. It made her feel that shiver of joy reminiscent of when her father had praised her efforts after a track meet, or the grades arrived. Kenntnis jammed his thumb on the button and the elevator hummed back into motion.

"How did you find me?"

"Richard's notes."

"You wouldn't happen to have a copy of those, would you?"

"Hell, no." She paused and enjoyed his discomfort. "I have the originals."

This time Kenntnis laughed out loud. The elevator sighed to a stop, and they stepped into an elegant outer office. Kenntnis began flipping through the pages; his eyes scanning quickly down the lines. Suddenly he stiffened and stopped walking.

"We need to go someplace more secure," he said, and turning on his heel, he led Angela back into the elevator. It took a key override to ascend to the topmost floor.

He was walking so quickly that Angela had only an instant to react to the marble parquet floor and the intricate plaster work. As they pushed through a pair of double doors Kenntnis called out, "Rhiana, if you're doing anything unnatural, please stop."

A stunningly beautiful girl looked up, startled, as they

walked in. Angela registered the seven or eight tennis balls spinning like a green nimbus around the girl's head and shoulders before they fell onto the thick oriental carpet and went rolling in all directions.

Kenntnis glanced over at Angela. "How are you holding up?"

Angela made a rude noise. "Telekinesis? Please, that's kid stuff compared to zombies."

Kenntnis looked at her approvingly. "You'll do."

"Who is she?" the girl called Rhiana asked, and she didn't sound real happy.

"Someone Richard has pulled in on his line."

Rhiana stood up. "How do you know we can trust her?"

"Because there's no coincidence, just convergence. Work out the math," said Kenntnis shortly. He turned back to Angela. "Now, do you think Richard has gone to this church?" He slapped the file with the back of his hand.

"Maybe, but I wouldn't worry about—"

"Oh, I'm very worried," Kenntnis interrupted. He looked at Rhiana. "Do you think you're ready to confront some of the faces in the mirrors?"

The sentence was nonsense to Angela, but it had a profound impact on the girl. The pale skin grayed as the blood retreated from her face and her lips thinned to a tight line.

"He saved your life," Kenntnis said softly.

The girl shuddered and clenched her fists at her sides. She raised green and frightened eyes to Kenntnis's face. "Am I strong enough?" she asked.

"Yes. And you won't be alone. Cross and I will be there."

"And me," Angela chimed in, though she had no idea

where they were going or what she was getting into.

✧　✧　✧

THE FAITH IN the Rock Church was at the north end of Castle Rock in an industrial area. In fact, the church looked like it was housed in a converted warehouse. There were only a few cars in the enormous parking lot. Either they got a lot of worshippers, or they were really hopeful.

The lobby area held the usual array of flyers listing the times of worship. The pastor, a blow-dried young man in a light blue suit, grinned out from the front cover. He was posed seated with an open Bible resting on his knee. The air held the dusty smell of cheap paper and candle wax. A sign on the wall of a hallway read *Office*. Richard headed down the hall. His heels echoed against the bright blue linoleum floor. He reached a door. Etched on the glass was *Reverend Darryl Hines*. Richard knocked.

"Come in."

The voice was deeper and more cultured than Richard had expected. He entered and understood why the voice didn't match the picture of the man on the flyer. Mark Grenier was seated behind the broad desk. The presence of this counselor and comforter of presidents in a seedy, makeshift church in Castle Rock, Colorado, suddenly made Kenntnis's claims a great deal more credible. A cold hand seemed to brush across the back of Richard's neck. He shuddered, beginning to regret that no one knew where he was.

"Welcome. Do come in," Grenier repeated as he unfolded

the long, spare length of his body from the chair. He indicated a chair in front of the desk with an elegant turn of wrist and hand.

He was as tall as Kenntnis but lacked the bulk. Where Kenntnis's hair was black and thick, Grenier's was iron gray shading to white over the temples and it formed a close cap across his skull. His features were aquiline. He had hazel eyes, and he boasted a perfect tan achieved on a variety of expensive and exclusive golf courses.

Richard felt off-balance both from Grenier's presence and from his physical similarities to Richard's father. He retreated to rote, using it like a security blanket. Pulling out his badge in its leather holder, he held it out, saying, "I'm Detective Richard Oort of the Albuquerque Police …"

Grenier waved a hand dismissively. "Let's dispense with all this. I know who you are and why you're here. And more importantly I know *what* you are, which is why I made the trip to Colorado so I could meet with you in person." Grenier was fiddling with a pair of thin reading glasses. There was something odd about them, and then Richard noticed that the lenses weren't clear, but silvered. *Like the mirrors and reflective surfaces in the trailer.*

Richard glanced around the office, registering the surprising number of mirrors on the walls, that the top of the desk was glass, as was the top of the coffee table. He noted the same silver-graying in all the surfaces and a stab of alarm jolted through him.

Ignoring the proffered chair, Richard went to the Naugahyde sofa and sat down. It forced Grenier to cross to him and bought him a few more seconds to think. It was in

Richard's nature to wait and allow others to make the opening move. For some reason that didn't seem safe this time.

"I'm gathering from hints I've received that *you* might not be *exactly* what you seem," Richard said cautiously as Grenier sank into the chair on the other side of the coffee table.

"Heard that from Kenntnis, did you?" Grenier replied. Richard's alarm ratcheted higher, breath fluttering in his chest and a trembling settling into his gut at the dropping of the name. "Has he told you what he is?" Grenier arched an eyebrow. "He also might not be *exactly what he seems.* So now you have a dilemma. Which of us will you trust?"

"No, you don't get off that easy. He made his case. Let me hear yours," said Richard.

Grenier threw back his head and laughed. "You're a cool one, aren't you?"

Richard was glad the veneer was working because he could feel his heart beating in his throat and the air didn't seem to want to reach his lungs.

"I'm sure Kenntnis has been railing against the evils and dangers of faith and religion, and feeling and magic, all while extolling the virtues of science and rationality. I'm sure he's nattered on about the stars, but never mentioned the flip side of all his wonderful technology. Somehow, he always turns a blind eye to pollution, extinction, resistive bacteria, pandemics, not to mention rush hour and gridlock." Grenier paused and smiled at Richard. It was a practiced smile exuding warmth and charm, but it never reached his eyes.

"All that's true," said Richard, then added, "but why have

you opposed beneficial research such as the work with stem cells and research for the sake of pure knowledge like the supercollider or deep space telescopes?"

"My, my, we have done our homework," said Grenier, and there seemed to be a bit of an edge to the smile this time. "Because, while worthy, these things are like tiny pebbles shaken loose on a cliff's edge that will eventually lead to a catastrophic avalanche. Think about the end point of Kenntnis's position. It's sterile, cold logic, and utterly confining. The universe as clockwork and humans trapped without choice or free will. All of us just following our genetic coding. Think how horrifying."

Richard crossed his legs and straightened the crease on his pants before answering. "You've picked the wrong argument with me. I was raised in the Dutch Reformed Church, the closest thing to old-fashioned Calvinism still around. I've grown up with the idea of predestination. Free will seems a luxury to me." Richard forced himself to meet Grenier's gaze. "Shall we try another?"

Grenier surprised him by laughing, and this time it sounded genuine. "All right, let's talk about magic ..."

"Let's not," Richard interrupted. "It doesn't seem to be terribly relevant since I apparently don't have any."

Grenier leaned forward avidly, his hands closing tightly around the reading glasses. "Ah, so Kenntnis *has* told you that."

"Yes ..."

"So, he's no doubt told you other things." The man's eyes were intent, and he leaned completely across the coffee table, his hand reaching for Richard's knee.

At the edge of his vision Richard thought he caught a glimpse of putrid colors roiling turgidly through the glass tabletop and an answering flash of color in the lenses of the glasses. A stab of fear sent minute shivers through the muscles in Richard's arms and legs. He jerked his knee away from Grenier.

"Look, why don't we come to the point. What do you want from me? You wouldn't have come here yourself unless you wanted something."

Grenier stood up and stared down at Richard. "Kenntnis gave you something. We want it."

CHAPTER FIFTEEN

Aren't Those Traditionally *My* Lines?

HE ALMOST BLURTED out, *no, he hasn't,* but his usual caution reasserted itself. "Why?" he said instead.

"We need it."

"Well, *there's* a compelling argument," Richard said.

Grenier frowned at the sarcastic tone. He took the time to fold and refold the earpieces of his glasses, wipe the silvered lenses until his beatific expression was back in place. "Let's break this down into advantages and disadvantages. First, no one who's ever carried this thing lives very long, but I expect that won't mean much to you. You have the look of a man who would enjoy martyrdom. My allies will suck you dry and kill you. But before you die, I can make your life quite unpleasant." Grenier stood and strolled back over to the desk, where he picked up a thick file folder.

"I have a large, well-organized, and well-financed organization. We've dug into every aspect of your life." He paused and flipped through a few pages. "Your mother is certainly a weak reed, isn't she?" Grenier lifted his head and smiled at Richard. "And secrets … my, you have more than your fair share. Believe me when I tell you that I won't hesitate to disseminate them in the places where they will do the most harm."

Panic stopped the air in his lungs. Richard found himself gripping his wrists with either hand. He couldn't feel the scar on his right arm through the bandages and the material of his shirt and coat, but the memory of hours of pain, humiliation, and betrayal that had led to the suicide attempt crashed across his mind and swept away all rational thought.

The memory of a voice surfaced through the black memories and desperate shame. *"Face the monsters who hurt you …"*

Officer Patrick McGowan, sturdy and round as a boulder, his face seamed with wrinkles and his head crowned with a thatch of thick, white hair. He was the reason Richard had become a cop. Pat had found Richard in his apartment, leaking blood from his right wrist into the warm waters of the bathtub and trying to keep a grip on the knife handle, his hand so slippery with blood that he couldn't slash the other. Pat had been a medic in Iraq, and he'd sewn up the wrist, keeping Richard out of the hospital so no one would know he'd tried suicide. Richard asked the older man if he didn't think he needed a shrink. It was McGowan's answer—*face the monsters*—that now pushed back the fear raised by Grenier.

Four months before he'd made the statement, McGowan had found Richard dumped in an alley, taken him to the hospital, and visited him for weeks after, trying to get Richard to say who'd assaulted him. Richard never had. But a deep friendship had formed, and McGowan had continued to monitor the younger man.

As he wrapped the bandage around his wrist, McGowan had said, *"No, boy, I think rather than lie on a couch you need to make a difference. Face the monsters who hurt you, and don't let others like 'em hurt anybody else."*

Richard slowly stood, raised his head, and locked eyes with Grenier. Whatever Grenier saw there made him take a half step backward.

Grenier said hurriedly, "Look, all you have to do is give us what we want, and we'll support you in *any* and *all* of your goals. Chief of Detectives for New York? Director of the FBI? A brilliant concert career? A contract with the Met? Whatever it is you desire—"

"You could do all that?" Richard asked softly.

"Yes." Grenier stepped in closer, gripped Richard's shoulders in both hands. Richard tried to step away, but Grenier tightened his grip. "Listen to me. Our world is not so terrible …"

"The parents of Naomi and Steve and Deb wouldn't agree," said Richard.

"Ask the dead at Hiroshima if Kenntnis's path doesn't exact a price." Grenier gave an angry wave with his glasses. "You can't counter the faith of millions. Even now, you want to believe. Go back to that. Worship. Live your life. Be safe and we will give you *anything you want*. The only cost is that you turn aside and leave this unwinnable fight to others."

"Excuse me. Aren't those traditionally *my* lines?" Kenntnis's voice came rolling like distant thunder from the doorway.

Richard and Grenier whirled. Kenntnis pushed his shoulders off the doorframe where he had been lounging and strolled into the room. Cross, Rhiana, and Angela appeared from behind Kenntnis's camouflaging bulk.

"A rescue." Grenier's lips skinned back from his teeth in a parody of a smile that he turned on Richard. "Which tells me all I needed to know."

"He's throwing a spell!" Cross yelled, and he flung himself between Richard and Grenier.

Richard had the briefest glimpse of color flashing in the lenses of the reading glasses before electricity arced from the overhead light and the lamp on the desk and the electrical outlets in the walls, all heading straight at him. Cross took one bolt full in the chest, then pirouetted and threw himself this way and that to intercept the others. He lay on the floor, his clothes smoldering, and grinned thinly up at Grenier.

"Shot your wad, asshole," he growled.

"Not quite," said Grenier calmly, and reached into his coat pocket. Richard heard a woman scream in wordless warning. The barrel of the gun looked enormous at such close range.

ANGELA JERKED AT Rhiana's shrill scream, and then registered the gun leveling at Richard. *No time! No time!* her mind yammered as Richard flung himself sideways. The deafening report of the pistol crashed off the walls of the room. The impact of the bullet sent Richard tumbling into the coffee table. The top broke into a thousand glittering shards, leaving the policeman tangled in the metal frame. Cross struggled to his feet as Kenntnis rushed the gunman, but Grenier was running straight for a blank wall by a window.

Angela ran to Richard. Blood was pumping from a cut on

the side of his head. He groaned as he pushed to a sitting position. His hand was pressed against his chest, but there was no blood oozing from between his slender fingers or staining the bandages on his palm. He clutched Angela's shoulder with his free hand and used her to lever himself to his feet. She could smell sweat overlaid with the rich scent of his aftershave.

"Stop him," Kenntnis was bellowing.

Angela looked up. Grenier was clawing at the wall, and suddenly a crack appeared. Cross put on an added burst of speed. The crack lengthened and widened, and Grenier turned sideways and vanished through it. The rent disappeared, leaving a plain white gypsum wall. Cross smashed face first into it.

"Shit! Fuck! Hell! Piss!" Cross bellowed as he cupped his bleeding nose.

Angela became aware of Rhiana standing stiffly in the center of the room muttering to herself. A penny lay on the palm of her hand. It began spinning and glowing, throwing off copper-colored sparks. She threw it at the wall. It left a trail of sparks like a comet's tail.

The copper fire struck the wall, and the wall tore open again. There was no sign of the man. There was also no sign of the parking lot of the church. Instead, Angela saw a vast expanse of seething gray sand and several burning suns. *It was night in Castle Rock, Colorado,* Angela's mind provided with rare calm. Then she saw the shapes on the other side, but her mind was unable to define what her eyes perceived.

"This ain't good," said Cross in a tight, high voice.

Rhiana gasped and ran to Kenntnis's side. Kenntnis gathered Rhiana within the circle of his arm. Angela realized she was screaming. She *never* screamed.

"Sure hope you got some cunning plan," Cross said to Kenntnis, "'Cause they've seen us."

Angela clamped her teeth shut to silence herself. Kenntnis reached into the pocket of his overcoat and pulled out a strange, twisting object that looked like a piece of blown grey glass. "Richard!" he called out commandingly. Richard looked up and Kenntnis tossed the object to him. Angela had a feeling that the cop caught it more by reflex than design. Richard's fingers twined through the open curves and Angela realized that it resembled nothing so much as a Klein bottle.

"Okay, now what?" Richard called, and his voice was a tenor squeak. The shapes were moving, drawing closer.

"That is a tear in reality. An opening between the dimensions. You've got to close it."

"How?" Richard interrupted desperately.

"I'm going to tell you. Just shut up and listen." Kenntnis sucked in a deep breath. "That's a sword hilt. Draw the sword." Richard stared at the man blankly. Angela didn't blame him. She was just as befuddled.

Kenntnis set Rhiana aside and mimed drawing a sword. "Pretend your free hand is the scabbard and just draw it!"

The *things* on the other side were drawing closer.

"Boy, I sure hope my detect magic/no magic gizmo wasn't broke when we found him," muttered Cross.

Angela stared at Richard to avoid looking through the tear in the wall. His face was tight with concentration. The pale brows furrowed, and he cupped his right hand at the base of the hilt. With his left hand he swept the abstractly shaped hilt away from his right hand in a smooth gesture.

Angela's gasp was involuntary. A meter-long sword blade appeared, seeming to slide out of the palm of Richard's right hand. It was profoundly black, the blackness of deep space, but also contained whirling silver, like stars coruscating deep within the darkness. She felt, rather than heard, a deep thrumming hum as if she were leaning against the mother of all amplifiers, followed by cascading chordal overtones. Everyone in the room and the *things* on the other side of the opening froze.

"Go," Kenntnis whispered, and Richard launched himself at the opening.

A nimbus of light began to flow from the blade, wrapping it about Richard's body. He held his torso slightly hunched, and his panting breaths were loud in the silence.

"Of course. Kevlar," Angela muttered hysterically to herself. "He was wearing a vest. Clever boy."

Richard was at the opening. He hesitated, looking from side to side as if trying to figure out how to bring them together.

"Make like you're stitching," Cross yelled.

Richard lightly touched the sword's point to the floor, then with sinuous turns of the wrist he parried his way from side to side up the length of the tear. Beneath the sword the normal drywall appeared, but it was scorched and blackened. He had almost closed the rent when a bubble of coiling and pulsing colors ranging from darkest purple to bilious green pushed through the remaining gap at the top. Richard lunged and stabbed at the thing. There was a high-pitched squealing like a needle being ripped across an old-style LP, and the intruder withdrew. The gap closed.

Richard slowly turned, rested the tip of the sword on the floor, leaned on it, and stared at Kenntnis. "Does everything have to be so damned operatic with you?" he asked, trying to make it sound casual and failing completely because his voice was shaking. Kenntnis threw back his head and filled the room with his booming laugh.

Angela rushed to Richard's side, and found Cross there before her, pounding the far smaller man on the back. Cross reeked of burned material and singed hair. Angela shoved the bum away before he could drive the cop to his knees.

"Back off," she snapped. She gently pulled back the side of Richard's suit coat. "I know I normally work on the dead but let me have a look at you."

"Not now. Not yet," Kenntnis ordered. "Grenier's people will be returning, and we don't want to have to answer any awkward questions."

"Yeah," said Angela. "You're going to have enough trouble dealing with *my* awkward questions."

"I'm sorry." The strained and tearful whisper brought all their attention to Rhiana. The young girl was shivering, tears coursing down her cheeks. "I was just trying to stop him. What did I do?"

"Shhh," Kenntnis soothed, and gathered her once more in the circle of his arms. "We'll sort that out later, too."

✧   ✧   ✧

THE POWERFUL JET engines on the Gulfstream GV were a muted roar and a subtle vibration through the floor and seats of the jet. The air in the plane tasted rich and thick, heavy with oxygen, and carried none of the stink of stale coffee that one found on commercial flights. Outside the window, stars shown diamond bright against the night sky. Beneath the wings roiled and bulked heavy white and gray clouds illuminated by a westering half-moon.

Cross was seated at a small, polished mahogany conference table off to their right, a bottle of beer and a bowl of pretzels in front of him. The *object*, the hilt of the mysterious sword, was also on the table. Richard jerked his eyes away. He didn't want to think about it. *Any of it.*

Angela was treating the cut on Richard's forehead. He hissed a bit as she sprayed it with disinfectant, dabbed on Neosporin, and closed it with a butterfly bandage.

"Get out of that coat and shirt. I want to check your chest. I know you're going to be bruised. I want to make sure no ribs are cracked."

"I'm fine, really."

"OFF!" Her arms were akimbo, and she glared down at him.

Richard found himself muttering, "Yes, ma'am." And then glaring when Cross snorted in amusement.

He glanced nervously toward the front of the plane where Rhiana, curled up in one of the oversized, leather-covered seats, slept deeply, then sighed and removed his coat, tie, shirt, and the Kevlar vest. Doing so revealed the bandage covering the knife thrust from Cross's *doppelgänger*, and a spectacular eggplant-colored bruise just to the side of and slightly below his sternum.

"Jesus Christ, you're a walking disaster area!" Angela

yelped. Cross burst out laughing and even Richard couldn't help his lips pulling into a wry smile. Angela's head swung between them. "What? What's so fucking funny?"

Richard shook his head. "Nothing." His amusement didn't last long. After today's events, Richard was beginning to think both Cross and Grenier had spoken the truth when they said his life expectancy wasn't all that great.

Angela had moved to the galley and filled a baggie with ice. "Hold this on the bruise," she ordered.

"I'm cold. It's cold," Richard said, and hoped it hadn't emerged as a whine. He had a feeling it had.

"Tough," and she shoved against his chest.

It couldn't be avoided any longer. Richard grunted in pain as he stood and sat down in the chair across from Cross. He touched the hilt with a forefinger.

"So, what is it?" Richard asked Cross.

"It looks like a Klein bottle," Angela said. "I mean before it has the … pointy part." Richard wasn't sure what a Klein bottle was. To him it looked like something out of an Escher drawing.

The homeless god shook his head and held out his hands palms out. "I think we should let Himself tell you. He's the answer guy. I can tell you this. You're in exalted company to be able to draw it and use it, along with a lot of ordinary schmucks, into which category I place you."

"Gee, thanks," Richard muttered.

Angela treated Cross to one of her patented glares, and Richard was pleased to see even the homeless god looked chastened. "Like who?" she demanded.

"Hammurabi, Tiberius and Gaius Gracchus, Justinian,

Arthur—the real Arthur, the one who tried to hold back the darkness after the Romans pulled out—Charlemagne, Franklin."

Richard sat up straight. "As in Benjamin?"

"Yep."

"Why?" asked Angela.

Cross looked at Richard like a teacher encouraging a reluctant student.

"He was the last great renaissance man," said Richard slowly. "Scientist, a publisher who valued books and learning above everything, and when asked to edit Jefferson's first draft of the Declaration of Independence, he removed the word sacred from the text."

"Where did it say sacred?" Angela asked.

"We hold these truths to be sacred and undeniable," Richard quoted. "Franklin argued that our rights derived from a rational source. He changed it to read, '*We hold these truths to be self-evident.*'" For some reason this knowledge about one of America's founders gave greater credence and strength to Kenntnis's arguments.

Cross glanced at Richard. "And in between the famous guys it's mostly been poor, noble guys like you. You know, schmucks." He fell silent for a moment and shook his head. "I also now know we are really, truly fucked because I didn't think Kenntnis would arm you. I mean, it is the twenty-first century, and this is a fucking sword. I mean, Jesus wept."

"So, who carried it after Franklin?" Richard asked.

"I'm betting Darwin," Angela said.

"And you'd lose," came Kenntnis's voice. Even before takeoff in the elegantly appointed private jet he had removed himself into a small cubicle office at the back of the plane and closed the door. "No, it was no one you've ever heard of."

Richard set aside the ice pack and scrambled back into his shirt and coat.

"One of the schmucks," Cross interjected.

Kenntnis frowned at him. "Though Jonathan did cross paths with Darwin and touched him with the sword."

"You remember his name," Angela said.

Kenntnis bent his dark gaze on Richard. His stomach dropped because Kenntnis looked so very, very sad and suddenly very old.

"I remember *all* your names."

CHAPTER SIXTEEN

THE SERPENT, PROMETHEUS & LUCIFER

PUSHING ASIDE THE rush of dread, Richard pointed at the hilt and repeated his question.

"What is it?"

"A weapon that only a select few can wield." Kenntnis turned his dark-eyed gaze on Angela. "You saw what he did. Try to draw it."

She stood and picked up the hilt. For a moment she bounced it in her hand, then, drawing in a deep breath, she twined her fingers through the curves, and drew. Nothing happened. Frowning, she turned it and inspected it from all angles.

"Okay, what's the trick? Where's the release button?"

"Coded in your genes," said Kenntnis, taking the hilt from her and handing it to Richard. "Like most humans, you possess a touch of magic. Only a human born without any magic can activate the sword."

"And now your involvement with the human genome project and stem cell research makes more sense," Richard mused.

"Yes, if we could design a CRISPR to edit magic out of your DNA it would be a big help. But until we have that, I must wait for that particular confluence of genes to occur before I get a new Paladin."

"And boy, could we have used one in the twentieth century," Cross said. He ticked off on his fingers. "World War I, World War II, Stalin, Mao, Hitler, Pol Pot, Rwanda, the Uighurs in China, Trump, Putin—"

Kenntnis held up a hand. "Spare me the recitation." Cross subsided.

Kenntnis resumed. "Sometimes there will be a whole clump of you born. Other times we go for years without a single one."

"You mentioned touching Darwin," Richard said. "What does that mean?"

"If you touch a normal human with the blade of the sword it will render them incapable of performing magic. It also means the Old Ones and magic users can't feed on that individual. And it has many other uses. As you saw today, it can repair the tears in reality caused by the injudicious use of magic by humans, and the judicious efforts by the Old Ones. When it's drawn it makes people in the immediate vicinity sane. Unfortunately, its effect can't cover the entire world."

"Okay." Angela gave the gesture for "time out."

"He"—she pointed at Cross—"says you're"—she pointed at Kenntnis—"the answer guy. Well, I need some. I've been pretty cool with this so far, but now I really need to know what the fuck is going on."

"Richard first. He's more important than you," said Kenntnis. It was rude and arrogant and put Richard in the spotlight, and he wanted to hit Kenntnis.

"Because he can use this thingy?" asked Angela.

"Precisely."

Richard raised up the hilt. "So, this was why you wanted me to work for you?"

"Partly."

"And what am I supposed to do? Go through the world touching everyone with this thing?"

"A daunting if not impossible task, and enlightenment can't be handed out like a magic pill."

"Meaning what?" Angela broke in.

"People must develop a conscience. As late as the nineteenth century, slavery was accepted. One hundred years ago women were property all over the world. Today only some of you are freed. African Americans won the right to vote a scant fifty years ago. Since we can't go throughout the world removing magic from every living human, we have to work to help people give up the violence associated with bone-searing hatreds: racial, religious, political, and ethnic. Until that happens the Old Ones will continue to thrive."

The two humans present and awake sat silent, and Richard wondered if the prospect of a tolerant humanity was so remote as to be hopeless. He stirred and looked up at Kenntnis.

"So, you've told me how it affects humans. What does it do to …" He had a hard time forming the words. "To magical creatures."

"It's deadly."

"So that thing I stabbed?"

"You killed it."

Richard looked at Cross. "So, I could kill him?" Cross sat up and looked hopeful.

"Yes." Kenntnis held up a restraining hand. "But I'm not

certain if it would kill his splinters, too, and if it didn't, they would be free to operate. And the most compelling reason to deny him that release ... we need Cross and his abilities on our side." The homeless god slumped back down in his seat looking glum.

The rumble of the engines changed cadence and tone. Kenntnis glanced out the window, then back. "Sounds like we're beginning our descent. If you'll excuse me, Doctor Armandariz, I need to speak to Richard in private. Bring the sword," he ordered.

Richard followed him into the private office. The door closed and the hum of the engines faded to mere vibration, indicating the extent of the soundproofing. It was a confining space made too small by the presence of a desk and three chairs and the lavatory. There was an array of office equipment and three phones cluttering the desk. The screen of a laptop computer glowed in the dim lighting.

Kenntnis settled into the chair behind the desk, the springs creaking under his bulk. "Rhiana is your backup, so you're going to have to be careful using the sword around her. We need her ... for now."

"Okay, that seems pretty self-evident. So why bring me in here to tell me that?" Richard asked.

"Cross and I are having a difference of opinion regarding Rhiana. Based on what I witnessed today, I believe she's not completely human. The safest course would be to neutralize her, but I think she can be controlled and guided and will be useful to us."

"What do you mean she's not human?" Richard asked, and felt crazy for even saying the words.

"There is no way a normal human could have opened a tear between the dimensions with such ease. I've been doing some checking on Rhiana, and discovered she was an abandoned baby in the California foster care system. Her birth mother had gone mad and was committed. Eventually Rhiana was adopted, but it's all completely consistent with her being a changeling."

Richard started edging toward the office door. "This is … is … ludicrous."

"You need to remember your legends, Richard, and remember that they're all based on fact," Kenntnis said. "In the Bible they talk of the sons of God coming down and lying with the daughters of men. In the Middle Ages, it was stolen away by elves; today, we've got alien abductions."

"Would you stop lecturing!" Richard snapped. "Rhiana is a living girl—not an abstract."

The slap of Kenntnis's hands on the desktop was like a gunshot as the man reared to his feet. "You're *all* abstracts to me. You have to be. I've known so many of you, and I can't allow myself to care for any of you. Or at least not much." Kenntnis's voice softened to a bass rumble and for the first time since meeting the man, Richard sensed emotion behind the words.

Richard concluded the thought. "Because you've watched so many of us die." Kenntnis nodded.

The door to the office opened and Cross entered. "You're discussing *her*, aren't you?" he accused. Richard followed Kenntnis's lead and remained silent. "Well, I'm warning you both I want something done about her. She can't be trusted. Nobody knows better than me what she's capable of doing."

"So, just kill her because she *might* do something?" Richard asked. Disgust was a bad taste across the back of his tongue. "I've never liked this doctrine of preemption, not nationally and not personally."

"Who said anything about killing her?" Cross replied. "Just use the damn sword on her. Neutralize her."

Richard pulled the hilt out of his coat pocket and turned it slowly in his hands. "But this thing kills magical creatures."

Cross shrugged. "She's only half magic. She'll probably survive."

"And what happens if half of her nature is destroyed?" Growing anger had Richard's voice rising in level and pitch.

"My guess is that it would be similar to a lobotomy," said Kenntnis smoothly.

Cross glared at him. "Whose side are you on?"

"Humanity's," said Kenntnis.

Moving slowly and deliberately, Richard returned the sword hilt to his pocket. "That's too esoteric for me. I'll be on Rhiana's side." He looked at Cross. "If you won't work with her then we'll send her away."

Kenntnis shook his head. "No, she's far too dangerous and valuable an asset. If she's not our piece, she'll be someone else's. She must not fall into Grenier's hands again."

"She's a girl. Not a piece. And I won't harm her … or allow anyone else to," Richard added, stressing the final words.

"And how are you going to stop me?" Cross's normally open and pleasant expression was twisted.

"I'll go to Grenier."

"Then I'll kill you," blustered Cross.

"No, you won't," said Richard. He was oddly calm, but he'd realized this was chess and he saw the endgame. "You need me, and if you start the killing, you're just giving strength to your enemies. You'll end up consumed by one of your counterparts, and you'll never achieve the peace you're seeking. So, let's accept the stalemate, and not give Rhiana any reason to turn against us."

"You're not in charge here," said Cross.

"Yes, I am. I have to be." Richard seated himself in the chair opposite Kenntnis. "Now it's my turn to give a little lecture." Resting his arms on the desk, he leaned in on Kenntnis. "You honor, almost worship, the scientific method, but you've lost sight of its most important element. Doubt is the key to everything you profess to represent; the ability to say *I don't know*, and the strength to examine and question every conclusion. But ever since I've met you, you've been claiming you can give me all the answers, and when that happens you've lost touch with humility, and that makes you no different from your opponents."

"You ballsy little bastard," Cross whispered.

Kenntnis didn't respond, he just stared at Richard. Richard forced himself to meet that dark gaze. It wasn't easy. The force of Kenntnis's personality was a physical presence in the room, making Richard feel even smaller than usual.

"You present a utopian outcome for your path, but there are dangers on your path as well," Richard continued.

"I'm listening." The voice rumbled out deep and dark as the eyes.

"You can end up with profoundly secular and profoundly evil regimes—"

"No, no, Richard." Kenntnis shook his finger at him. "You don't get to trot out the old 'intellect without humanity' argument. It's been used by reactionaries since Hume to frighten people into obeying religious authorities. Which is not to say that your argument isn't valid. I bear watching as much as any living being. Just be intellectually honest and say what you mean."

"All right." Richard slowly stood and looked down at Kenntnis. "I will not harm Rhiana. No matter how justified the end." He paused and drew in a breath. The explosion of air into his lungs made Richard realize he had been holding his breath.

Cross blew out a breath, startlingly loud in the silent room. Kenntnis shook his head. "Why couldn't you have just been an ignorant flatfoot?"

Richard allowed himself a small smile. "And just done what I was told?"

The briefest of answering smiles touched Kenntnis's lips. "No, that's Grenier's way. All right, I accept your terms."

Richard walked to the door, then paused and looked back. "By the way, I know who you are, or at least some of the names we humans have used for you." Kenntnis raised an inquiring eyebrow.

"You're the Serpent, and Prometheus, and Lucifer."

"I've always liked Prometheus the best," Kenntnis mused.

"And you need to remember that we're the good guys," Cross added truculently.

"And I'm here to keep you good," Richard said softly.

✦　✦　✦

"ISN'T IT A little late?" Rhiana asked as Kenntnis deposited the standing rib roast in the center of the dining room table. Mashed potatoes were piped around the edge of the platter, vegetable whitecaps breaking against the dark sides of the roast. Cross and Franz followed with a basket of popovers, a bowl of green beans, and a gravy boat.

The rich smell of fresh ground black pepper and beef juices hit Angela's nose and saliva erupted in her mouth. "Food is good," she said. "Keeps the strength up. Calms jittery nerves."

"You're my kind of woman," said Cross as he seated himself and stuffed a napkin into the collar of his dirty flannel shirt.

"You shouldn't have let Richard leave," Rhiana directed at Kenntnis. Her tone was aggrieved and accusing.

"Short of sitting on him, I don't know how I was supposed to stop him," Kenntnis replied mildly.

"He might be in danger," Rhiana persisted.

Got a major crush developing here, Angela thought, but she knew from the faint twinge of pique that she was also in danger. Not wanting that much self-analysis, she turned her attention to the room. She studied the art gracing the dark wood-paneled walls, the ethereal crystal chandelier looking like a frozen waterfall, the deep glow of carved and polished wood in the table, chairs, and buffet.

Kenntnis opened a bottle of Merlot and filled their glasses. He then raised his. "To the Lumina."

"About damn time we have it back in full operation," grunted Cross.

Angela tapped the rim of her glass against Cross's, and a

pure ringing tone hung in the silence. Rhiana held out her glass toward the homeless god, but Cross ignored it, focusing on his plate.

So, I wonder what's up his ass? Angela thought.

The candles on the table sprang to life, their fire dancing in the crystal and reflecting in the polished wood of the tabletop. Angela jumped. Kenntnis and Cross looked at Rhiana. She looked back, and her posture yelled defiance.

"I'm still here," Rhiana said.

"We're not likely to forget about you," grunted Cross, and the tone wasn't friendly.

"Don't do parlor tricks," Kenntnis ordered. "It takes energy, and it puts a pinprick hole in the universe. Do magic when I tell you to."

"So, I can keep using magic?" Rhiana asked.

"Yes, of course."

"But I thought magic was baaad." Angela put a long drawl on the final word and was pleased to see Kenntnis flash her a look of annoyance.

Her *abuela* had always told her the way she liked to poke people was perverse, but she couldn't help herself. Even with a man who possessed this much presence and, she suspected, power, she couldn't rein in her unruly tongue.

"There are no perfect or totally harmless choices here. We're playing to win," Kenntnis replied.

"So, the ends justify the means?" Angela asked and gave Kenntnis a limpid and innocent look.

The big man looked even more annoyed, and Cross gave a bark of laughter that sent popover crumbs spewing across the table. "He's already had this conversation once tonight."

"With Richard?" Rhiana asked eagerly.

Kenntnis didn't reply. Instead, he picked up a carving knife and a sharpener. Steel rasped against stone. He cut into the roast, parting the seared exterior. Blood flowed and red meat showed against the bone. Angela saw Rhiana staring with repellent fascination.

"Vegetarian?" she asked the younger woman. Rhiana nodded.

Cross reached across the table and speared a slice of beef. Angela watched the blood drip onto the white damask tablecloth and had a sudden flash of Richard's blood.

"I'll take a burnt end," Angela said firmly, and held out her plate to Kenntnis.

Kenntnis sent down her plate, and filled Rhiana's with potatoes, green beans, and a popover. Angela broke open the hot popover, filled the hollow interior with a large pat of butter, and took a bite. It was heavenly.

Rhiana took a few tiny bites then threw down her fork. "I still don't think you should have let Richard leave," she repeated.

"He needed a break from all of us."

"From you, maybe," Rhiana muttered at her plate.

Angela cast a covert glance at Rhiana's flawless profile. The line of Richard's jaw was suddenly foremost in her mind. *Why couldn't this have been like a perfect television sitcom with a perfect set of couples? Instead, we've got a monster, an enigma, a man, and two women. Lovely.*

She took a bite of roast and decided to pull the attention away from Richard. "I have a question," she said. Kenntnis and Cross looked at her. "Why did Grenier resort to a gun?

Why not continue to use magic?"

"Because I took the magical blast and he didn't have enough juice for another one," Cross answered.

"But based on the universe according to you"—Angela shot Kenntnis a quick ironic smile—"Couldn't he have used our fear to recharge?"

"He did; it's how he got through the wall," said Kenntnis. "But a death spell takes real power. He got it by killing those college kids."

"You're not suggesting that every time someone goes postal these guys are behind it?" Angela asked.

"No, but they certainly take advantage when it does happen," Kenntnis replied dryly.

Aside from the smacking as Cross wolfed food, they ate in silence for a few minutes.

Angela found she didn't like the privacy of her own head right now. She framed another question. "So, in the lexicon of mythic monsters what's Grenier? Or is he just a person?"

"He's a person," Kenntnis answered.

"Yeah, he's been carrying water for one of my splinters for years," Cross grunted, and crammed a popover into his mouth.

"Why? Why him and not another preacher?" Angela asked.

"Access," said Kenntnis shortly. "He hooked up with a governor who became president, and then he was in. Given the rightward tilt of recent administrations he's been able to push the Old Ones' agenda."

"He's the reason they're teaching Intelligent Design instead of evolution in six states," added Cross, but the words were blurred as he continued to masticate popover. Angela watched the homeless god's throat work as he swallowed, and she was reminded of pythons and puppies. "He's also got a lot of magical juice, so it was easy for him to learn the skills."

"Are all your … splinters hostile to each other?" Angela asked. "Could we do a little divide and conquer action?"

"Use your brain, girl," Cross muttered. "As long as they can get Christians and Muslims, and Jews and Muslims, and Muslims and Hindus, and Protestants and Catholics killing each other they're in hog heaven. I'm the only wart in their ointment."

"So why don't they just kill you?" Angela asked sweetly. "And don't call me 'girl.'"

"They're not certain what that would do to the other fragments," said Kenntnis, stepping in as if he sensed she and Cross were about to spat.

"How do angels fit into all this?" Rhiana asked.

"Ah, angels." Kenntnis shook his head. "It was a fallback position for some of the late arrivals. People like our friend here," he indicated Cross, "had taken most of the god positions, but they found a use for their tardy companions. You get to spread a lot of destruction when you're an angel."

"Or you got to until he"—Cross jerked his chin toward Kenntnis.—"Came up with the idea of guardian angels."

"I never thought of angels as bad," said Rhiana.

Angela looked at the girl. "In the Bible, the first words out of an angel's mouth were usually 'Don't be afraid. I'm not here to kill you.' Which now makes a whole lot more sense."

"Except that usually they *were* going to kill you," said

Kenntnis dryly.

Thoughts spinning, Angela leaned back in her chair. "So, is there anything sacred that is good?"

"No," Cross said brightly, and helped himself to another slice of beef.

"So, there is no God," Angela persisted, wanting to be sure she understood the full implications of the day's revelations.

Kenntnis dropped his chin to his chest and pursed his lips thoughtfully. Angela counted her heartbeats as they waited.

"I've been around a long, long time," Kenntnis said slowly. "I have yet to see any evidence of one. What I have seen is that out of the birth of the universe stars were born. Ultraviolet light from young stars heated hydrogen molecules and hydrocarbons were formed—"

"Carbon, the basis of all life," Angela whispered.

And the LORD God formed man of the dust of the ground and breathed into his nostrils the breath of life; and man became a living soul. Memories from when Angela had learned her catechism. *Could the ultraviolet light of a newly born star not substitute for the breath of life? Sulfur, phosphorous, oxygen, nitrogen, carbon, and hydrogen for the dust? Was there no way to find unity and agreement between science and religion; that faith and knowledge did not need to be incompatible?*

✧　✧　✧

EXHAUSTION DRAGGED AT his eyelids, and the various aches

and cuts in parts of his body throbbed in time to his heartbeat. Richard knew he would need to rest soon, but his apartment was still under repair.

That left the Lumina headquarters, and he couldn't face them right now. No, correct that, he couldn't face *Kenntnis*, not with what he now knew.

So, he drove aimlessly through the streets of Albuquerque. The light from the streetlamps flickered in his fogged windshield as the blast of warm air from the Volvo's heater struck cold glass.

He had thrown out the challenge to Kenntnis hoping to be denied but knowing his conclusions about the man … creature … were correct. It helped if Richard thought of him as Prometheus, but the other names remained, leaden, frightful, and horrifying—Lucifer, the Serpent, Satan.

But he saved my life. And based on what I've seen, haven't his arguments been proven?

But they would, wouldn't they? He's the Father of Lies.

The mountains served as a magnet, drawing him toward the frowning rock face iced now with new-fallen snow. The storm had entered the city, and he drove through swirling snow as he followed Central Avenue east. To the north, Kenntnis, Cross, and the women ate and talked in the elegant confines of the penthouse. He assumed they were talking about him.

Judge Robert Oort's dry voice echoed in his ears. *"Why do you think people would notice you? You have a pretty face that attracts attention, but it's fool's gold. As yet you've failed to demonstrate that there is either accomplishment or character behind it. You lack the intellectual abilities of your sisters, and you're not a woman, so you can't rely on beauty and charm the way your mother has. You'd best find some-thing to recommend you."*

But now somebody had said he was special.

Unfortunately, that somebody had admitted he was the embodiment of ancient evil.

But he he also stole fire from the gods and gave to mankind the fruit of the tree of knowledge.

Richard saw the outline of a cross dark against the shifting backdrop of snow. The building came into view, the peaked profile of a church reaching toward the sky like prayerful hands. He didn't know what denomination it might be, but right then he needed the comfort of his faith despite the demands that he forswear it. Spinning the wheel, he pulled into the parking lot. With the turn of the key the engine died. Snow tapped like fingernails against the windows and body of the car. The engine pinged as it cooled.

The snow squeaked under the leather soles of his shoes as he walked to the front doors. Letters in brass spelled out *Saint Luke's on the Mesa* over the door. Richard didn't have much hope the church would be open, so he had to scramble to keep his balance when the door swung open in response to his tug. It was unusual in these secular and uncertain times to find a church unlocked at night. Richard wanted to take it as a sign, but it seemed a pathetic reed on which to hang his faith.

CHAPTER SEVENTEEN

Inertia Still Works

THE WALL AT the end of the nave was an expanse of glass. The sloping walls to either side were vast fields of stained glass. The white of the snow beyond the front window gave a pale illumination to the interior of the church. There were tall candles on the draped altar and the scent of frankincense hung in the air. A red light burned over the altar. With the steps and railing separating the nave from the apse and the kneelers in each pew it felt like a Catholic church. Richard glanced down at the hymnals in the holders on the back of the pews and saw the *Book of Common Prayer* among them. He was in an Episcopalian church.

He wasn't a smoker, but Richard carried a lighter in case he found himself stranded during one of his long drives into the New Mexico back country. Because he had been raised in such a fiercely Protestant sect, the barrier of the railing held no power for him. He walked to the altar and lit both candles. He then bowed his head and began to pray.

Dear God, are you there? Do you exist? I don't know what to believe anymore. Is it presumptuous to ask for a sign? Help me, Dear Lord, I'm losing myself.

The wind hissed around the building, the snow pecked at the glass, and the flames on the candles shrank briefly and then elongated once more into orange-yellow flares.

"That's it?" Richard said aloud. "Your enemy is giving me wonders."

He yanked the sword hilt out of his pocket and tossed it onto the floor in front of the altar. There was the sound of a deep-throated bell as the twisted form hit the stones. For long seconds Richard heard the overtones echoing away toward the distant ceiling.

"I've only heard something similar in the baptistery in Pisa with its perfect acoustical overtones," came a deep and gravelly voice from the back of the church. Richard whirled and peered into the dimness. "This building has crappy acoustics, so I have to assume that remarkable sound was produced by whatever it was you threw on the floor." The voice was getting closer.

A stocky figure dressed in faded blue jeans but topped with a black shirt and the white collar of a priest came rolling down the aisle. The candlelight gleamed on his bald pate and reflected in the deep-set eyes.

"I'm Charlie," the man said, and thrust out his hand.

Richard shook it. "Father."

"Just Charlie," came the correction.

Now that the priest was in the pale circle of light provided by the candles, Richard could see the gray fringe of hair just above his ears and the seamed face.

"You seem to be a man in need of a conversation," said the older man.

Richard glanced back at the embroidered altar cloth. "Yeah, but God's not talking."

"Maybe he's just coming in on a different channel," the

priest said placidly. He hesitated, then said, "Look, how about coming over to the rectory for a cup of something warm?"

Richard glanced toward the altar, and as if the priest had read his mind, he added softly, "If God can't find you next door he's not much of a God, is he?"

✧ ✧ ✧

ANGELA PULLED ON her coat, left the penthouse, and punched the elevator call button. There was a distant clunk and whine as gears began to move. She leaned her shoulder against the wall. A muffling blanket of exhaustion fell across her head and neck. The elevator arrived with a sharp ding. The doors slid open, and she staggered inside. The doors were almost closed when a slender hand was thrust in. The doors bounced apart and Rhiana joined her.

The girl leaned against the wall opposite Angela. The vivid green eyes were hard, and a frown disturbed the perfect line of her brow.

"Why are you here?" she demanded.

Too many times in her life, in medical school, in police forces, in morgues, Angela had met resistance and handled it. This time she was pretty confident it was coming from more than just a protection of territory.

"Because Richard needed a coroner," she said placidly.

"You don't bring us *anything*," the girl continued. "You're just an ordinary person."

"And you don't think an ordinary person might be of help?" Angela asked, and reminded herself that Rhiana was very young, and you treat the young in the throes of a first crush tenderly.

"No," Rhiana said bluntly.

On the other hand, not too *tenderly,* Angela decided.

"Look, sweetie, Kenntnis can talk all he wants about using any tool to win," she said with a tight smile. "But let's remember what winning entails—banishing all magic from the world. So, I'd suggest you polish up your ordinary human skills in preparation for the time when you're no longer Super Witch and remember that politeness is one of them." There was a faint jar through the soles of her feet as the elevator came to rest on the ground floor.

The doors opened and Angela headed for the front doors fully expecting Rhiana to come in pursuit, but she heard no answering footfalls. She looked back. Rhiana slumped against the doors of the elevator. Tears leaked slowly from beneath her closed eyelids.

Two quick strides brought her back to the girl and she wrapped her arms around her. She expected resistance, but there was none. Rhiana slumped against her, crying harder now.

"I wanted to be *special,*" came Rhiana's muffled voice. "But nobody likes smart, and now *this* is wrong, *too.*"

Angela knew all about being smart and female in American society, and being a bright, ambitious Black/Hispanic woman in a culture where white supremacy had never been addressed.

"What happens when they take it all away from me?" Rhiana wailed.

"They can't take it *all.* You're a frigging physicist. That makes medicine look easy." Rhiana shook her head. "And you're beautiful," Angela added.

"That shouldn't matter," Rhiana sniffed.

"Well, it does, and if anyone ever told you otherwise … well, they're an idiot." Angela paused. Her joints seemed to be grinding together with weariness. "Look, there's a twenty-four-hour Carrow's just down the road. How about we get a cup of coffee and talk? I could use a crappy cup of coffee. I've spent years drinking hospital coffee or morgue coffee. Kenntnis's is just way too fancy for my plebeian tastes." Rhiana gave a watery chuckle. "That's better. Come on."

"IT FEELS LIKE my faith is shriveling," said Richard as he sat huddled at the breakfast table, hands cupped around a mug of tea.

The rectory was a 1950s crackerbox house, and it looked like neither the cabinets nor the appliances had been replaced since then. The residual smell of boiled peas and pot roast hung in the air. There was a guilty niggling at the back of Richard's mind telling him he ought to go back into the church and recover the sword. But he didn't want to face the cold … or the sword.

"Why? Because of a profound disappointment? A trage-dy?" the priest asked.

"No, because this man I'm working for … with … is shining a brutally cold light on it."

"Challenging faith with logic," Charlie said. He canted his chair onto its back legs and balanced his cup on his paunch.

"Yes."

"But you can't apply logic to faith. I've talked to you long enough to tell that you're a more sophisticated believer than that."

Richard hunched forward, dropping his eyes so he didn't have to meet the priest's gaze. "Recently the words haven't been able to drown out the hundreds ... thousands of years of atrocities."

"*Men* committed those atrocities," Charlie corrected.

"Guided by religions," countered Richard.

"Religions aren't about God," said the priest.

"So, they're only for crowd control? Setting a standard of behavior and demanding people obey under pain of Hell? God as strict daddy?"

Charlie lifted his cup and blew across the top of his coffee. "At their best. At their worst they're about influence, manipulation, and power."

Richard shook his head. "You're the strangest minister I've ever met. I actually think you could talk to Kenntnis and he would enjoy the debate."

Charlie laughed. "Yeah, my mom always said I would have made a good Jesuit."

Richard paused for a sip of tea, and as the liquid hit his stomach, he realized he was achingly hungry. "So, what do you believe?"

"That faith is transcendent, exalting. It calls you to service, worship, and duty," replied the priest, and his face was alight with fervor. "And I also think that religion is a deeply and totally personal experience."

Richard sunk his chin into the collar of his turtleneck and

tried to think how to frame the questions. But it always came back to the same question. *Did God exist?* A real God, not these masqueraders. He stared at the stains on the heavy wooden table.

"It seems like you come from a more dogmatic tradition," Charlie said.

"Meaning what?" asked Richard a bit defensively.

Charlie tapped his chest. "I teach and have always believed that Jesus wasn't kidding when he said the kingdom of God is within you. Other sects have a more arm's length relationship. I think every human is capable of Godlike behavior, so if you believe in yourself you believe in God."

"So, by celebrating humanity …" Richard said slowly.

"You celebrate God," Charlie finished.

"So, it's all about people."

"Yes, ultimately … or at least it is for me," said Charlie simply.

"*Very* like Kenntnis." Richard stood and carried his mug with the dregs of his tea over to the sink. He turned, resting his hands and back against the counter. "So, you set no rules?"

"Only one," Charlie said. "Do unto others as you would have others do unto you. Everything else is pretty much just noise." They regarded each other for a long time. "This man who has you questioning your faith, what does he say?" Charlie asked gently.

Richard sighed and took a drink of tea. "That it's all about people. But, unlike you, he demands that I reject God."

"And that would be a mortal sin."

✧   ✧   ✧

THE CARROW'S WAS noisy and lively from the invasion of a post-high-school-football-game crowd. A large corner booth was bursting with four enormous young men whose necks were wider than their heads. Acne bloomed across their cheeks and chins. Wedged between them like slender white aspens growing among boulders were the cheerleaders, still dressed in their perky little gold-and-white uniforms and showing a lot of skin and goose bumps.

The rest of the room was filled with exuberant fans, and at a far corner a couple of young male shitkickers were trying to set the brims of each other's straw cowboy hats on fire with lighters. The waitresses looked harried and the manager, a kid just a few years older than his customers, kept setting his hand on the phone as if trying to decide whether or not to call for help.

Rhiana and Angela sat next to a broad window that gave them an uninspiring view of the cars flowing past on Montgomery Boulevard. Rhiana couldn't help it; her lip curled as she regarded the chattering teenagers running between cliques at various tables with tosses of long hair and tugs at the waistbands of absurdly baggy jeans.

"Oh, come on," came the coroner's voice. "You aren't *that* far removed. You're what, eighteen? Nineteen?"

"Eighteen … almost. And I only went to one football game in high school."

Angela shook open the paper napkin and placed it in her lap with a flourish. "Sounds like a traumatic experience."

"Do you always have to make fun of me?" Rhiana asked

tightly. The older woman glanced up at her quickly and looked abashed.

"I'm really not. It's just my manner. I come across glib and aggressive even when I don't mean to. It was a survival technique in the family and in medical school. So, what happened at the football game?"

"I took a book," said Rhiana shortly, and glared at a pimply boy whose lank hair hung well into his eyes. "The popular kids grabbed it and tore all the pages out."

"You realize, of course, that we are twin sisters separated by almost two decades and nine hundred miles. I was the kind of geek who took a book to a ball game, too." Angela smiled to remove any sting.

A waitress arrived. They both ordered coffee and handed back the menus. The roar of conversation created an odd dissonance with the music leaking from the stereo speakers. The smell of frying hamburgers filled the room, adding to Rhiana's nausea.

Angela played with her utensils for a few seconds, then she rushed into speech. "So, according to Kenntnis I've got a little bit of magic. And after watching you in action it made me wonder … well, if you could teach me how to do what you do. I'm really curious."

"As an experiment?" Rhiana asked.

"Yes … maybe … no. For a lot of reasons," the older woman confessed.

"It can't be tested. I've tried. Remember, I was a scientist before I became a, well, a witch for lack of a better term," said Rhiana.

"Kenntnis called you a sorceress. I think that fits you

better," said Angela, and in answer to Rhiana's questioning look, she elaborated. "I've got two visions of witches. One formed at an early age from watching *The Wizard of Oz* every year, and the other from the pagan communities that were around during college. You don't fit into either category."

"I don't think Kenntnis would like it if I teach you," Rhiana said slowly.

"Do you see me asking his permission?" came the quick response.

"It could be dangerous," said Rhiana.

"We'll hide behind Richard," said Angela. Their eyes met as they considered the diminutive stature of the policeman and they both started laughing.

✧   ✧   ✧

TO BE A musician it helped to have good hearing. Richard's was exceptional, so even over the whistle of the teakettle and the east winds howling through Tijeras Canyon he heard the crunch of tires on snow and the snick of a car door closing. He checked his watch—a few minutes past midnight.

"Do you often get people this late?" he asked Charlie.

Holding a tea bag in each hand, the priest turned and looked at him. "Huh?"

"Somebody's just pulled into the parking lot," said Richard as he crossed to the window and barely lifted a curtain to look out.

A couple of darkly clad figures were hurrying toward the main door of the church, and Richard realized with a sick lurch in the pit of his stomach that he should have gone back after the sword. He'd wanted a physical break from Kenntnis's world and tossing away the sword seemed like the best way to accomplish that. Now it just seemed stupid.

Charlie had brought them over to the house through the door in the sacristy. It wasn't immediately evident from the parking lot. "Stay here," Richard threw back at the priest as he ran out the kitchen door. He nipped across the snow-covered gravel of the southwestern style landscaping toward the side of the church.

The wind had the snow blowing horizontal. The fat, wet flakes of earlier in the evening had become ice pellets that stung the exposed skin of his face. He reached the door and slipped into the robing room beyond.

THE PARKING LOT of the Carrow's had become a skating rink. The snow was now covered with a thin coating of ice. Angela and Rhiana linked arms to help balance each other and headed for Angela's robin's-egg-blue Thunderbird.

Rhiana felt Angela stiffen and she looked up from her feet. The older woman was staring at a man seated on the hood of one of the parked cars. The man lifted a hand and waved, but all his attention was focused on Rhiana. She had the impression of a narrow face with upswept eyebrows. A gust of wind carried a squall of snow. When it passed the man had vanished.

✧　✧　✧

ONCE INSIDE, HE heard the creak and clunk of the heavy front doors opening and closing. Carefully, Richard opened the hidden door of the sacristy and looked out. Two men were hurrying up the aisle toward the altar. Allowing the door to softly close, he pressed his back against the wall, tried to slow his breathing, and dithered. *Gun? Phone? Gun? Phone?* He knew he should call for backup, but fear was filling his stomach. He didn't want the intruders—or maybe they were also just people seeking solace as he had been? *Don't be stupid!* he raged at himself. He didn't want them to hear him. He cautiously opened the door and peered out.

The altar was directly across from him, perhaps ten feet away. The sword hilt lay on the concrete floor in front of it. The candles he had lit were still burning. Richard blinked, wondering if exhaustion was causing the room beyond to dim. Then he realized the flames on the altar candles were sinking. They dwindled to tiny sparks and were extinguished. Richard glanced down at his right wrist, the luminous dial on his watch was also going dark. But the darkness wasn't complete. A nimbus of white light hovered around the sword hilt as if a swirl of stars surrounded it.

Knowing from his experience with Rhiana and the faux Cross that his pistol was now useless, Richard holstered the Glock. The smaller of the two men was pushing through the gate at the railing, hand outstretched for the hilt. Fear was forgotten. Richard flung himself out the door running full out. It was going to be close. Memories of summer days, the ping of a metal bat on a ball, home plate shimmering before him in the heat haze, inspired him. Richard threw himself into a dive and went sliding across the floor. The other man's fingers scraped across the back of his coat. Richard swept up the hilt, tucked and rolled to his feet. The moment his hand closed around the hilt the swirl of lights spread to encompass his body.

The man Richard had beaten out for the sword stood staring at him. His panting breaths were loud in the cavernous room. He was skinny and angular and not much older than Richard. Brown hair flopped into his eyes. The eyes froze Richard in his tracks. They were flat and utterly void of expression. Blackboard dark and just as daunting. The man's pants were shabby and despite the cold he wore only a nylon windbreaker.

The other man was younger, burlier, with a large belly that sagged over the waistband of his trousers. He seemed to be in charge. He wore an expensive ski parka and fancy hiking boots. Swinging loosely in his right hand was a riding crop. It was so incongruous that for an instant Richard's attention was distracted from the skinny man.

The metallic rattle of a butterfly knife opening and the glint of light on the blade were his only warning. Richard sprang back, sucking in his gut as the tip caught on the material of his sweater, slicing it. He felt the sharp sting as it cut across his abdomen, followed by the warm rush of blood.

Spinning, Richard swept his hand away from the hilt, summoning the blade. There was that deafening series of chordal overtones that filled the church as if ten thousand organs were playing. The spin brought him around 360 degrees to face his assailant. Grimly, Richard gestured with the thirty-inch blade of the sword against the six-inch blade of the butterfly knife.

"Set it down and back away," he ordered. Richard kept his eyes locked on Skinny's eyes. Fencing had taught him that the eyes telegraphed the physical.

Not surprisingly, the skinny man didn't respond. The burly one suddenly swept his crop through the air, crying out in a strange language. But Richard had heard it before. It was the language that Rhiana had used in the alley. Fire arced from the end of the crop heading toward Richard. He didn't have a lot of options. The knife-wielding thug blocked one direction and the heavy stone altar the other possible avenues for retreat.

Richard braced for searing pain and instinctively held the sword across his chest. The fire was yanked off its trajectory and sucked into the black, black blade, the embedded stars seeming to flare as the magical fire was consumed. Richard might have been spared the fire, but the knife man had seen his opportunity and he took it.

He rushed Richard, knife held low and ready, the point angled up for a thrust directly into the heart. Muscles do learn and remember. Those drills in hand-to-hand combat paid off. Richard pivoted to the side to offer a smaller target to his attacker and pushed the knife hand away. The man spun, trying to once again reach Richard, but the wet soles of his shoes slipped on the polished concrete, and he crashed into him. They both fell back against the altar. Richard's head rang and spun as the back of his skull connected with the stone lip of the altar.

Fingers closed around Richard's left wrist. The bones ground together under the unrelenting pressure. Fighting back nausea and the throbbing in his head, Richard headbutted his opponent in the face. Blood from the man's broken nose spattered warm and sticky across him. Struggling desperately, Richard flung himself from side to side trying to dislodge the man. Panic yammered in his head as he heard the approaching footfalls of the second man.

A new sound entered the equation; the harsh rasping slide of a pump shotgun being cocked. "Church or no, if you don't back off, I'll blow a hole through you," came Charlie's bass growl.

The skinny man rolled quickly off Richard, trying to find cover. "No, stupid, it won't fire," yelled the burly young man at his associate.

"Charlie, it won't work," Richard yelled at the same time.

But it's hard to believe something so outlandish, and Charlie squeezed the trigger anyway. Skinny's chest sunk in as if anticipating the pellets, and of course nothing happened.

With a braying laugh Skinny threw himself toward Richard. There was a blur of motion as the wooden grip of the shotgun swept past Richard's face and smashed into the side of Skinny's head. The impact drove the attacker sideways into the altar. He sank down onto the floor moaning, one hand nursing his head, the other his ribs. The butterfly knife lay forgotten. Richard kicked it aside.

"Yeah, but inertia sure as hell works," grunted the priest.

Richard vaulted over the railing. The other man ran backward, the crop outstretched as if warding him off. The edge of the sword cut through the crop, severing it. But that wasn't the extent of the damage. The leather twisted, writhed, and liquefied. A foul choking smell filled Richard's nose.

With a sob of fear the man whirled and bolted for the

door. Richard raced after him, each step sending a jar of pain through the back of his head. *If you touch a normal human, it will render him or her incapable of performing magic,* Kenntnis's words filled his mind. They were at the door, the man scrabbling at the handle. Richard adjusted his grip and laid the flat of the blade across the sorcerer's back. The tearing scream echoed around the church. His arms thrust behind his back, hands clawing at the area where the sword had rested.

Charlie lumbered down the aisle. "Stop it! What are you doing to him!"

The man sank onto his knees and vomited. The smell of bile now joined the smell of incense, sweat, and the sludge that remained of the riding crop.

"Call the police," Richard said, pulling out his cell phone, but then he realized that the flames on the candles had not returned, and his phone was dark and inert. "Oh, dear," Richard whispered.

There was a whisper of sound from the altar.

CHAPTER EIGHTEEN

NO OMNIPOTENCE. NO OMNISCIENCE. NO OMNIPRESENCE

THE BONES IN his neck cracked and the muscles stretched taut as Richard whipped his head around. At the same time the priest gave a gasping moan. Behind him the front doors creaked, and a blast of cold air whistled down the length of the church. He looked back. The burly man tottered out the door, but there was nothing Richard could do to prevent the escape because the spare, suffering figure on the cross was coiling, stretching, climbing down. A bare foot touched the top of the altar. Charlie crossed himself and sank to his knees. The inert form of the knife-wielding thug still huddled at the base of the altar. God didn't spare him a glance.

God lifted his head and looked at Richard. And the eyes captured him. A golden brown—like sunlight on amber. They were soft and warm and loving. Richard stood rooted, unable to turn away.

"So, you do not totally deny me, Richard," said his God.

That this day, even in this night, before the cock crow twice, thou shalt deny me thrice. The words so often read and repeated suddenly had power. Guilt and fear tore at him.

"There is still time before you are lost to me forever." The voice was dark velvet, low and deep and plaintive.

Richard sucked in a shuddering breath and found it breaking on a barely suppressed sob.

"Richard. My child. My son." Now the figure was draped in a gleaming white robe. The Lord stretched out his hand. The smell of lilies caressed the air, but too sweet and too cloying.

The point of the sword dropped to the floor. The echoing chime rang through the church, but now it sounded dissonant, creating a painful pressure deep within his ears. Richard's control broke and the sobs came. He dropped to his knees, struggling through the force of his tears.

"Be at peace. You have struggled and been tested, but not found wanting. There, there. Hush, now. Hush. I have always heard you, Richard." God approached, careful step by careful step. "When you prayed for your mother. When those men hurt you."

But like sand through one's fingers, the exaltation and comfort drained away because *Richard had never prayed for his mother*. When she had been committed, his father had brought all the children into his study and battered into them the understanding that *no one* was to know where she had gone. Friends, neighbors, and schoolmates were all told of a trip to Europe. The shame was too great to be revealed. Richard, age seven, had been terrified that if God knew about his mother's drinking and drug use, she would surely go to Hell. So, Richard never mentioned her in his prayers, fearful that if reminded, God might go looking for her, find her wanting, and *punish* her.

Richard remembered the file Grenier had perused. There

was no mystery here. No omnipotence. No omniscience. No omnipresence.

Just lies.

Springing to his feet, Richard swept up the sword and flung himself forward in a deep lunge. But the creature manipulating the wooden figure was preternaturally fast. It coiled and leaped back onto the altar before the point could connect. Its feet tangled briefly in the altar cloth, toppling the candlesticks. As it swarmed up the cross, a hoarse ululating cry gurgled from its throat.

Behind him, Richard heard Charlie give a gagging cough. There was a thud. Glancing back, Richard saw that the priest had fallen onto his side, gripping his left arm with his right hand.

It was a lousy time for a heart attack because Richard knew an attack of another kind was coming. He whirled and started running to Charlie. Even as he ran, he studied the church, trying to determine the potential source of the danger. The heavy stone altar? The wooden pews? His eyes lifted toward the sloping expanses of stained glass that formed the upper half of the walls. His heart sank. These creatures seemed to really like glass.

The cross was wreathed in a bilious green light that coalesced and lanced out toward the stained-glass windows, and Richard was horribly aware of Kenntnis' lecture that physics still worked. If the spell hit the windows they would shatter, and rainbow shards of death would rain down on him and the priest.

It was stupid, but Richard raised the sword straight over his head as if it could ward off what was coming, and then gaped as the swirling nimbus of light shot off the point of the sword and intercepted the spell. The clashing colors rippled across the glass, and it seemed like the pieces writhed and moved. Then both the swirling stars and the green light were sucked back into the sword.

Silence.

The flicker of fire danced on the walls. The extinguished candles were burning again and had ignited the altar cloth and the Bible. For an instant Richard dithered between Charlie and the flames. The altar was stone. The fire wouldn't spread. As for the Bible … Richard turned his back and ran toward Charlie.

Dropping the sword, Richard gripped Charlie by the shoulders and rolled him onto his back. The priest's lips were cold and slack. Richard drew in a singer's breath, deep and full, and sent the air into the priest's lungs. The taste of the tea Charlie had been drinking lingered on his lips and in his mouth. Richard did chest compression with one hand as he groped for his cell phone. Eventually he managed to dial 911 and call out their location.

His head was swimming by the time the ambulance arrived.

Oddly, Lieutenant Weber was with the EMTs.

✧   ✧   ✧

IT WAS HARD to hear the ambulance's siren over the whine of the wind. Weber and Richard, standing in the parking lot of the church, watched the red glow of its taillights dwindle as it went racing down Central toward hospital row bearing the priest and the perp. Oort's muscles were contracting from the violence of his shivers. He had his arms tightly wrapped around his body, and Weber could hear the chattering of his teeth. Damon dropped an arm over Richard's shoulders and drew him in close and was startled when Richard twisted aside and put three feet between them.

Damon gave him a searching look, but then just said simply, "Let's go back inside."

"I'd rather not," Richard said.

"Did that sound like a request? I need a statement from you and I'm not going do it out here freezing my damn ass off." Weber watched the internal struggle followed by a tense nod.

As they walked up the steps Weber glanced up at the pendulous snow clouds that seemed to be pierced by the peaked roof of the church and the cross atop it.

Weber pulled open the door and they stepped inside, carefully skirting the pool of vomit. Evidence techs were busily securing the scene. Richard stood frozen like a frightened horse, gripping the edge of the last pew; Weber strolled around the church while he pulled on his gloves. A tech held out the shotgun that already had an evidence tag hanging from it. He examined the stock, sticky now with blood and hair.

"Who did the head-cracking?" he called back to Richard.

"Charlie … the priest."

"Hmm," Weber grunted. "Tough priest."

He handed the shotgun back to the tech, who placed it in an evidence bag. Shoving his hands deep into the pockets of his sheepskin coat, he stared down at the tech who was applying fingerprint powder to the discarded butterfly knife. He frowned as he spotted the blood staining the blade.

He turned and glared down the length of the nave at Oort. "Should there have been *three* patients in that ambulance?" he asked.

Richard gaped at him then shook his head. "No, I'm fine, it was just a scratch."

Weber walked back to him. "Let me have a look."

"It's nothing, really," Richard remonstrated, trying to turn away, but Weber was taller and stronger. He pushed the slighter man into the pew, pushed open his coat, and pulled up the hem of the torn and bloodstained sweater. As his fingers brushed against the skin of Oort's abdomen the blond gave a faint gasp.

It was indeed only a scratch, but Weber's inspection revealed the deep brushing on Richard's chest. Weber's brows drew together in a sharp frown. The blue eyes, vulnerable and filled with fear, were raised to meet his. Weber drew his fingertips across the bruise. Richard sucked in another quick breath.

"This is the kind of bruising you get when a bullet hits body armor." Richard remained silent. "Did you get shot?" Weber demanded. His tone was harsh, ugly, and Oort shrank back. He gave Weber another frightened, vulnerable look, then finally nodded. "Who the fuck shot you? Did this happen in Colorado? And why the hell didn't you report it?"

Richard shrugged, nodded, and shrugged again.

"What the *fuck* is going on with you?" Weber bellowed. All the evidence techs froze, and the quiet murmur of conversation ceased.

"Shit," he muttered, then waved at the techs and called out, "Carry on." Weber threw back his head and gave it a despairing shake. Which for the first time pulled his focus to the windows that marched along the top half of the walls of the nave. *That can't be right,* he thought, because the stained glass now seemed to have been designed courtesy of Hieronymus Bosch or Salvador Dali. In one frame a palm tree sprouted from Joseph's ear. In another there was simply a jumble of eyes. An icy tendril ran down his back and he looked over at Oort. The younger man had followed his gaze and was now staring in horror at the jumbled windows.

Weber leaned in close and hissed in Richard's ear, "Okay. That's it. Now you are fucking going to tell me what the fuck is going on! Is your apartment still all fucked up?" Richard nodded. Weber grabbed him by the upper arm, dragged him out of the pew. "You're coming home with me. And do not fucking argue with me!" Gripping Richard's upper arm, Weber began marching the smaller man toward the door.

Richard balked. "I have to write up a report."

"You'll write it in the morning, and didn't I tell you not to fucking argue?"

✧   ✧   ✧

NEEDLES OF HOT water washed through his hair and across his body, digging into each cut, scrape, and bruise. The water swirling around his bare feet and gurgling down the drain was rust colored with blood. Richard hoped that most of it was Skinny's washing off his face and out of his hair. He stayed in the shower until the water ran clean. Richard rubbed himself dry with Weber's thin and faded towels and leaned into the medicine cabinet mirror. Pale gold bristle ghosted across his jaw and upper lip. He wished he could shave.

The older officer had left a bathrobe flung across the foot of the bed. It was a typical man's robe meant to reach mid-calf. On Richard it nearly brushed the floor. He rubbed his cheek against the soft collar and breathed in the smell of coffee and cigarette smoke. Pausing for a moment, Richard regarded the unmade bed. It was rumpled temptation. He hurriedly left the bedroom.

Weber waited in the living room of the furnished apartment, feet up on the scarred and cluttered coffee table, body slouched on the ugly brown couch. Smoke from his cigarette floated around his head, a murderous halo. Hotel-room art hung on a couple of the walls. There was a big-screen TV on the far wall. An armchair was overflowing with coats, including Richard's cashmere overcoat. Richard gathered them up and set them on the small dinette table. From that vantage point he could see into the narrow kitchen. The surfaces of the counters were covered with take-out Chinese and pizza boxes.

"Separated or divorced?" *Or single,* his mind provided, but he thought that option was unlikely.

"Separated," Weber replied. "Why I haven't bought any dishes. Keep thinking I'll be going home soon." He flicked ash into an ashtray and sighed, took a long drag on his cigarette. "You ever been married?"

Richard shook his head. He seated himself in the armchair and watched his lieutenant crush out the cigarette in an overflowing ashtray.

"Don't. At least not until you retire from the force. Thought maybe third time would be the charm but …" His voice trailed away.

"I … I don't mean to be rude, but do you have anything to eat?" Richard asked, shifting his focus from one hunger to another. "I haven't had anything since …" He thought about it. "Well, since yesterday morning."

Weber shook out another cigarette, jammed it into his mouth, and strode into the kitchen.

The interior of the refrigerator yawned empty before them. There were a few bottles of Corona, a carton of cottage cheese, and a plain white plastic container. Weber popped the lid off the cottage cheese and surveyed the green lumps inside. He tossed it onto the counter and pulled out the white plastic tub.

"I know this will be okay. Nothing could live in this."

From a lower cabinet he pulled out a bag of tortilla chips and shoved them into Richard's chest. Snagging a beer, he led them back into the living room and set everything on the coffee table. The lid came off the container, revealing a dark red salsa.

Richard took a chip and cautiously dipped in one corner. As the salsa passed beneath his nose the acrid, smoky scent of chile set his eyes watering. The bite, modest though it was, had the edges of his tongue burning, caught in the back of his throat, and exploded in his gut. He could almost feel his ulcer cringing, but he didn't care what it might do to his stomach; his hunger was too great.

Richard mopped sweat off his brow, and Weber grinned

that sadistic New Mexican's grin that translated to *we may be poor and eccentric, but our chile is kick-ass.*

Silence once more stretched between them. "So, I'm waiting for my explanation," Weber finally said.

"And what does that mean … exactly?" Richard hoped it would buy him a little time to think about how he was ultimately going to answer.

What it bought him was Weber's face thrust pugnaciously into his. A gust of warm, alcohol-laden breath gusted across his skin.

"Do not treat me like a fucking mushroom or so help me God I will go straight to the captain."

Blue eyes and brown met and held. Richard broke first. He studied the faint line of acne scars peppered around Weber's eyes, the square chin losing some of its definition to incipient jowl, the straight brows now drawn together in a deep frown. Not a handsome face, but honest and totally reassuring.

"It's … it's complicated."

"I'll cope."

"It will sound crazy."

"I can handle that, too."

Richard got up and walked over to his overcoat, reached into the pocket, and touched the hilt of the sword. For a long moment he reviewed the past three days, the people he'd met, the information he'd received, and this object he'd been given. He wondered how he would explain it to Kenntnis, especially since the decision he'd just reached was based on nothing more than gut feeling.

Richard turned back to Weber and tried to form his expression into one of cool confidence. "So, how do you feel about ancient and secret societies?"

WEBER HAD INSISTED he take the bed while the older man slept on the couch. Despite the warm blankets, a decent mattress, and pillows to clutch, Richard's sleep had been torn with nightmares. Over and over, he awoke from the memory of that figure writhing and then descending from the cross.

Exhaustion formed grit in his eyes as Richard criss-crossed the snow-blanketed streets of Albuquerque. Weber had been sent to the Lumina offices to receive a lecture on the-world-according-to-Kenntnis, while Richard went to APD headquarters to collect the jacket on the man they'd arrested last night, who turned out to be Doug Andresson.

Realizing he was almost faint from hunger, Richard paused at Golden Fried Chicken for a breakfast burrito, which he ate in the parking lot of UNMH hospital. The rich flavors of green chile, cheese, bacon, eggs, and potatoes exploded in his mouth, and he almost moaned in pleasure even though he knew his ulcer was going to make itself known in short order.

While he ate, he read Andresson's rap sheet. It detailed numerous B&Es, a few armed robberies, violent assaults against girlfriends, random bar fights, and a carjacking. The record extended across Arizona, Colorado, and Texas, with most of the crimes centered in his home state of Texas.

Crumpling the foil, still warm from the burrito and redolent of green chile, Richard spared a moment to wonder where Kenntnis had gotten in the lecture, and how Weber was reacting. He then gathered up the file and headed into the hospital.

He ended up sharing the elevator with a slender Hispanic male nurse and his elderly charge. Slumped in a wheelchair, the old man's every inhale was a sonorous wheeze and every exhale a whimper. Richard couldn't bear to look at the age-spotted skin, the rheumy eyes, and the sliver of saliva coursing down the corner of the old man's mouth. He wondered if he had family. If they visited him. If there was any life beyond the hospital or if this was his final stay.

He stared at the doors until a prickling made him aware of close scrutiny. He looked over and met the eyes of the nurse over the wispy white hair of the old man. The nurse's skin was a pale olive with touches of rose in the cheeks. Jet-black hair sprang thickly back from a sharp widow's peak. The interest and invitation were bold fire in the nurse's dark brown eyes. The breath caught in Richard's throat, and he looked quickly away. The elevator shuddered to a stop, and he stepped out. He looked back quickly at the young man who gave him a regretful shrug. The doors closed, leaving Richard still staring at the scuffed white metal.

He wished he could explain this sudden return of desire. Was it because he had come dangerously close to death twice in the past week? Because of the adoration in a beautiful girl's eyes? His lieutenant's obvious concern for him? *Or maybe I'm finally over it,* he thought as he walked along the ward looking for Andresson's room. What he couldn't determine was if that was a good thing or a bad thing. Sex had been his vice and ultimately his downfall.

The room was easy to find. It was the only one with a uniformed policeman seated outside the door. Nodding to the guard, Richard put Rhiana and attractive male nurses and APD lieutenants out of his mind and asked, "Is he alone?"

"Yeah," grunted the uniform. "Docs did rounds 'bout an hour ago. You know, if he was to fall out of bed while you were talkin' to him ... well, let's just say I wouldn't notice."

Richard gave the young man a small smile. Cops took an extremely dim view of perps who attacked cops, much less priests, so the remark was not unexpected, though it made Richard cringe. It had becoming increasingly apparent over the past few years that far too many people who shouldn't be police had become police.

Maybe Weber is right. Maybe I am too much of a boy scout to do this job, he thought as he entered the hospital room.

The head of the bed was elevated so Andresson could have a better angle on the television that hung high on the wall. It was several morning news anchors mugging for the camera. One hand was cuffed to the railing of the hospital bed. Andresson muted the sound with his free hand, but otherwise lay unnaturally still. The unblinking shark eyes watched as Richard approached to within a few feet of the bed. Andresson's head was bandaged.

Like any good predator, he noted the stiffness of Richard's walk and how still he kept his torso. A slow smile lifted Andresson's lips. It was a disturbing expression, exposing both teeth and gums.

"Got ya, didn't I?" It was less a question than a statement of pleasure.

"Not as well as I got you," Richard responded, and nodded toward the door and the guard.

"Yeah, well." Andresson shrugged. "They always let me out." Richard took another step toward the bed, then felt a prickling down the back of his neck because Andresson's muscles had tightened as if in preparation for a move. Acutely aware of the pistol beneath his right armpit and the hilt of the sword resting in the holster at the small of his back, and of Andresson's penchant for physical violence, he took three steps back.

There was a flare of disappointment deep in those flat eyes, and Andresson relaxed back against the pillows. He dug between his teeth with a fingernail. "I want a lawyer."

"This isn't a formal interrogation." Richard pulled the hilt out of the holster and held it up. "You were after this, weren't you? How do you even know about it?"

"And I should talk to you why?"

"Because your buddy ran out on you, leaving you to take the rap, and believe me, assault on a police officer is just a tad more serious than your previous felonies."

The man's eyes narrowed. "You don't have Fat Boy?" Richard shook his head. "Shit."

"Does … er, Fat Boy have an actual name?" Richard asked.

"Yeah, Josh Delay," Andresson said in an exaggerated prissy voice. He then stared intently at Richard, assessing every aspect of his looks and clothing. "They told me that you and me are alike. I sure as fuck don't see it."

A thrill of cold horror shot down his back, and Richard wanted to deny the possibility. But it made sense. The issue was magic—whether you had it or not. There was no moral imperative that said only *good* people lacked the touch of magic. It was up to the cosmic dice roll of genetics. The question was whether Richard and Andresson had rolled craps.

"Why didn't you come after *me*? Why did you go into the church?"

"Fat Boy did something with his prissy little riding crop and said the thing we were going after was in the church. He was real pleased. Said you were a dumb motherfucker."

Richard mentally acknowledged the truth of Delay's remark, and after another look into those empty emotionless eyes, he made a fervent promise that he would never, ever, ever, let the sword out of his sight or out of his reach again.

"Who hired you?"

"Fat Boy."

It was disappointing, but not unexpected. Grenier was too smart to have his fingerprints on this.

"And to do what ... exactly?"

"Get ahold of that weird thing, and then to go work for them. They wanted me bad, cop. They still do."

"And how do you know that?"

The only answer was again a fulsome display of those teeth and gums. "We're done talking." Andresson turned back on the sound and focused on the television.

This was information that Kenntnis needed to hear.

There were still two more stops before Richard could return to Lumina.

Charlie was in intensive care up on the third floor. They wouldn't let him in to see the priest and they didn't want to give him any information either, but Richard showed them his badge and explained that Charlie had saved his life last night. That broke the bureaucratic barriers, and a sympathetic nurse told him the priest was recovering after a triple bypass, and so far, the prognosis looked good.

Richard left with an ache in his throat and his soul, heading to yet another hospital to check on Sterling. It seemed everyone around him came to grief. It made his heart clench with concern for Weber, Angela, and Rhiana.

CHAPTER NINETEEN

T HE RECEPTIONIST IN the lobby gave him a wave. The African American security guard nodded a hello, and Richard realized that he'd become a fixture at Lumina. He wasn't entirely certain how he felt about that, but he knew one thing. If these people were going to be so accepting of him, he needed to know their names.

He reversed course, walked to the receptionist, and held out his hand. "Hi, I'm Richard Oort."

She had a nice smile, flawless ebony skin, and a set of elaborate corn rows forming sharp geometric patterns across her skull.

"Paulette," she said.

"Nice to meet you."

"Same here."

He repeated the process with the guard, whose name was Joseph, and whose stance looked military and whose handshake was crushing. There were scars across his knuckles and his nose had been broken several times, but the eyes were kind and determined. He'd fought, but it clearly hadn't been for the sake of fighting.

Richard decided to start in the office. It didn't seem like Kenntnis welcomed people into his penthouse until he'd gotten their measure, and Richard knew he'd thrown a large and unwelcome curve ball at the industrialist when he'd shown up with another recruit for the Lumina.

The final hiss of the espresso machine accompanied Richard's entrance. Kenntnis garnished the coffee with foam and handed it to Weber. Angela stared critically at the lieutenant's poleaxed expression and said, "I think he needs a dollop of something a hell of a lot stronger than milk."

Kenntnis pulled open low cabinet drawers and held up a bottle of Irish whisky for Weber's consideration. The cop nodded vigorously. Kenntnis poured a shot into the coffee. Weber took a grateful sip.

"Can I make you something?" Kenntnis asked Richard.

"Tea, please."

"Milk?"

"Yes, please."

Weber lifted his face out of the soup-bowl-sized cup and stared at Richard. The expression was hard to interpret, and Richard got that sick feeling that he'd lost a friendship before it had even had a chance to form. Or maybe he was just being paranoid.

"I want to see this magic thingamajigger," Weber stated.

"It's not magic," Kenntnis corrected.

"Then what is it?" Richard asked. "I confess to being a little fuzzy on the details, since it certainly seems like magic to me."

"Arthur C. Clarke wasn't wrong when he wrote '*Any sufficiently advanced technology is indistinguishable from magic.*'"

"Evocative, but not exactly illuminating," Richard drawled.

Kenntnis gave him an amused glance. "It's a little piece of the Big Bang."

"Meaning what?" Angela asked.

"Magic violates natural law. This device restores order."

"It didn't do a very good job on the windows of the church," Richard snapped.

"I didn't say it did it *perfectly*. Quantum mechanics and chaos theory are, well … chaotic," Kenntnis said sharply.

Weber held up a hand. "Look, first I had Angela gabbling at me about chemistry and ions and electrons and shit. Now, I got you going on about … well, all that shit. Just show me the damn thing."

Richard reached under his coat to the holster at the small of his back and pulled out the hilt. Before meeting Andresson he might have just tossed it over, but now he carefully carried it to Weber and handed it to the older man.

Frowning, the lieutenant turned it in his hands. "You said this thing was a sword?"

"Richard," Kenntnis said.

Richard took back the hilt, drew his hand away. The blade appeared. Once again, he felt, more than heard, a sound that seemed to reverberate in every cell of his body. Angela clasped her arms across her stomach and bent forward, collapsing at the intensity.

Coffee spilled into his crotch as Weber jumped. *"Shit!"* Richard wasn't sure which had elicited the yell—the sword or the hot coffee. Weber's brown eyes were blown wide as he stared up at Richard while mopping frantically at his trousers. "So, all this shit they've been telling me … it's true?"

"Sadly, yes," Richard said quietly.

"And why the fuck didn't you show me this thing last night? If you had, I might not have come here thinking you needed a psych evaluation."

Richard glanced at Kenntnis and gave a shrug. "I didn't think I had the right until you'd talked with Kenntnis."

Weber looked to the big man. "And the kid here is the only person in the world who can use this magical, Big Bang thingamajig?"

"No," Kenntnis answered. "It's a genetic anomaly, and, while it's quite quite rare, there are other people in the world like Richard. Fortunately, I found him first and, equally fortunate he's a good person."

Richard felt the blood rush to his face. Angela elbowed him in the ribs and hit him right on the cut inflicted by the faux Cross. He gasped with pain, and her hands lifted to cover her mouth.

"Oh, shit, sorry. That hurting thing … I keep forgetting about that. Probably because all my customers are dead." She gave him her imp's grin, her teeth flashing brightly in her dark face. He smiled back.

"So let me see, stabbed twice, gunshot to the chest." Weber looked again at Kenntnis, and he was no longer smiling. "Doesn't sound like your interest in Richard has been all that great … for *Richard*."

Kenntnis shrugged. "Unavoidable. Also, necessary."

Richard gave a wan smile. "Hey, he got me a promotion." His feeble attempt at humor did not have the hoped-for effect; Richard could see Weber was still preparing to go ballistic. He hoped maybe a change of subject would.

"So, that kid who was in the church … I visited him in

the hospital this morning, and he's like me." Richard told them the little he had learned from Andresson.

Kenntnis began to pace. "We have to make certain that he doesn't end up with Grenier," Kenntnis said, and his tone was grim. "If they had the sword, they could destroy Cross and that would be … well, a terrible setback for us."

"Who's Cross?" Weber asked plaintively.

"Another member of the Lumina," Kenntnis answered.

"You know that thing about how magic is bad, and we don't use magic?" Angela asked. "Well, there are two big exceptions. Cross is one and our resident sorceress is another."

"Shhh. Don't confuse him any more than necessary." Kenntnis glared at her, then turned his attention to Weber, who was blotting at the front of his pants. "So how do you feel about all this? Do you want to be part of it, or do you want to return to your own world?"

"Like I could pretend I hadn't heard any of this or seen those church windows." Weber sighed and scrubbed a hand across his face. "What is it you want from me?"

"Guard Richard. Keep him safe. Keep the sword safe."

✧   ✧   ✧

ANGELA'S SQUAWK KEPT Weber from answering. "Hey," she said. "What about me? I'm in this, too. I can keep an eye on Richard, too."

Damon stood and walked over to stand between Richard and Angela. At six feet he'd always considered himself to be pretty average, but looking down at the two much smaller people, he felt like King Kong. He also knew Angela's temper, and in an effort to tone things down a notch, he said, "Yeah, but without me, you two look like the Munchkin Brigade. Or maybe Jawas." Richard's mouth opened in indignation. Angela glared up at Weber and stretched up to punch him in the arm. His grin widened and he rubbed at his bicep. "Hell of right hook there."

"If you're done, children, may we call this settled?" Kenntnis huffed.

"Sure, but what do we do now … in addition to watching out for Richard?" Weber asked, dropping a hand on the younger man's shoulder. Once again Richard slipped from beneath his hand.

"Go back to work. Do your jobs. There are other evils in the world that you can combat until we're ready to move," was Kenntnis's answer.

Weber felt a wash of relief; a chance to return to a world he understood, push this aside, at least for the moment, seemed like a great idea. Of course, Angela was not having it.

"Excuse me. Grenier is waltzing around free after killing those three kids and trying to kill Richard. Aren't we going to do anything about *that*?" Angela demanded.

Kenntnis didn't answer; instead, he strolled back over to the espresso machine and poured in a carafe of water. While it heated, he tossed tea leaves into a pot. The delicate china teapot looked small in his massive hand.

Weber spoke up. "And what exactly did you have in mind?" he asked the diminutive coroner.

Kenntnis looked up and for an instant Weber thought he saw a flash of weary respect as their eyes met two parents dealing with recalcitrant kids. "A newspaper reported that Grenier was at a ladies' Bible study class at the same hour he was supposedly attacking Richard in Colorado Springs," Kenntnis said. "We can't prove he wasn't."

Richard looked up from where he had been turning the hilt over and over in his hands. "I think Delay was also involved in killing those kids. He seemed to have a lot of power. I did use the sword on him last night, so I presume that means he's neutralized?" Richard said uncertainly.

Kenntnis gave an affirming nod.

Angela whirled on Richard. "And I suppose that's enough payback for committing murder?"

Weber watched as Richard seemed to shrink in on himself and shame washed across that chiseled face. He bit back the flare of anger he felt toward Angela. The kid had been through hell and a half the past few days, and Damon wasn't sure he was strong enough to carry the weight of all that had happened. Then he watched Richard's back straighten and his jaw set.

"It does us no good to bring a charge we cannot prove. It could make it even more difficult to bring him to justice next time." Damon was impressed the young man's tone remained so even and level.

"Richard is correct. There *is* going to be a next time and, trust me, it is going to be worse," Kenntnis said. "And when you strike at the king, you best not miss," he added grimly.

Weber found Kenntnis's final words ominous, but of course Angela never knew when to climb down. It was both infuriating and wonderful. Because of that tenacity they had often brought people to justice when a less dedicated person might have stopped looking for the necessary evidence.

"Well, for a world-spanning secret organization we're pretty damn wimpy," she sniffed.

"*They're* the world-spanning evil secret society," Kenntnis said as he filled the pot with boiling water. "We're rebuilding." He gave the three of them one of his half-mocking smiles. "We've we've been waiting on reinforcements. Which have now arrived."

"What exactly does striking at the king actually mean?" Damon asked. "I'm a police officer. If you're planning on sending Richard to Virginia to assault this Grenier guy with that … thing, then this conversation's gonna take a turn for the worse and real quick."

"No, no, I have no intention of risking my Paladin."

"Paladin?" Weber grinned and allowed his eyes to sweep across Richard. Blood rushed into Richard's face. Weber couldn't control the chuckle.

Angela and Kenntnis were staring at each other. Angela broke first. She turned away with an irritated and dismissive shrug of her shoulder. "So, I guess we don't do squat."

"We don't move directly against Grenier, no. We interfere with some of his smaller operations, while we look for ways to strike at him directly."

"What small operations?" Weber asked.

Kenntnis set aside the teapot, moved to his desk, and gathered up a fistful of newspaper and magazine clippings and computer printouts. He plucked one at random. "There are plans to build a prayerful subdivision in California. That one really has me worried." He riffled through the papers and selected another. "A minister in Clovis is planning a major book burning." He looked up at their blank faces. "The pattern people walk as they advance toward a fire at a book burning is an elaborate power rune. It weakens the fabric of space and time and starts to open a gate. The Old Ones loved the Nazis. Hitler was involved in an occult circle in Vienna in his youth. Most of his lieutenants dabbled with magic. Himmler aggressively revived the worship of the old Teutonic gods with the SS. Odin made a big comeback during the forties," Kenntnis sighed.

"Odin?" Weber said faintly, and he found himself wishing that Richard Oort had decided to become a police officer in any other city but Albuquerque …

For a lot of reasons …

✧　✧　✧

THE IMPORT OF Kenntnis's words were a jolt to his gut, and a sharp memory surfaced. It had been his first year at the conservatory in Rome. Robert had brought over the rest of the family for a visit, and they had all gone on a family ski trip to Switzerland. Perhaps it had been Richard's fault; five months with Italians had had an effect and his father had spoken long and harshly regarding Richard's levity and lack of decorum. It hadn't helped when Pamela took up with the French ski instructor. Robert cut short their time in Innsbruck and decreed that the family would take a trip to Dachau and Auschwitz as a reminder of the true state of man's nature. A shiver shook him as Richard remembered: the cold and damp of that plain in Poland; the heaps of rubble, remnants of the ovens; the warehouse filled with the luggage of the dead, name tags still in place, awaiting pickup from a generation vanished in smoke.

"It was a massive blood sacrifice, wasn't it?" he forced out through a dry and constricted throat.

Kenntnis pivoted and nodded at him. "Correct."

Angela walked over and planted herself in front of Kenntnis. "So now I'm even *less* inclined to go slow."

Kenntnis fanned the clippings and printouts in front of her face. "These are just the American sources and I've only had staff on the task for a day. Where would you like to start, Ms. Armandariz?"

"With fucking Grenier who *tried to kill Richard*!"

With a sound like a road grader over gravel, Weber cleared his throat, breaking Richard's spiraling thoughts. "Yeah, so, well … okay, we're up against Nazis and televangelists, and Islamic extremists, and on our side, we've got …" Weber looked around the room, nodding his head as he made a point of counting. "Four of us?"

The doors flew open and Rhiana, hair tumbling around her face, rushed in.

"Actually six, and here is the fifth," said Kenntnis.

"Oh, I feel *so* much better now," muttered Weber as Rhiana ran to Richard's side.

Her skin was cool and soft as she grabbed his hand and pressed her cheek against his. Her hair brushed across his lips, and he smelled vanilla and almond.

"Where were you last night? Why didn't you come back? I was so worried."

"I'm fine," Richard soothed. "Do you remember Lieutenant Weber?" He half turned to indicate his boss and gently slipped his hand free.

"Oh, yes, hi."

"The girl from the other night," Weber said. He looked at Kenntnis. "Should I be surprised?"

"No, there is no coincidence, just convergence," Kenntnis responded.

"He says that a lot," Angela said. "I think it's supposed to make us feel better."

"Didn't work," Weber said. "So, who's the sixth member of our Scooby gang?"

"An associate of mine, Cross, but he is presently … indisposed."

Rhiana looked up. "Did he shatter again?"

"Shatter?" Weber repeated plaintively.

Kenntnis looked at the older cop and waved a dismissive hand. "You don't want to hear about him yet. I've given you quite enough to chew on."

"I still can't believe we're just going to lie low, do nothing," Angela muttered, clearly preparing to resume the argument.

Richard crossed to her and placed his hands on her shoulders. "Kenntnis is right," he said. "We're not ready to take on Grenier."

There was no warning. Suddenly Angela's face was pressed against Richard's chest, wetting his shirt with her tears. "I'm afraid they're going to kill you," came the muffled, tear-choked words.

He laid his cheek on the top of her head, feeling the crisp spring of her dark curls against his skin. "Won't happen. I've got you … all of you, watching my back." He swept them all with a look and a smile that froze and shattered when he met the blazing fury in Rhiana's gaze. Only the ire wasn't directed it at *him*, it was focused squarely on Angela.

Angela stepped out of his embrace and rubbed furiously at her cheeks. "Shit, I'm sorry. I'm tired. I get weepy and stupid when I'm tired. I need to go home."

"I'll take you."

"I can give you a lift."

Richard and Weber stopped and looked at each other. Rhiana whirled and walked out of the office. Angela watched the younger woman go, then looked back at the two men.

"Probably better drive myself … and make sure that she knows that."

She hurried out, and Richard suspected that she was going to try and catch Rhiana. He hoped she succeeded and that she would be able to smooth over the clash of hormones and attraction. It was a hell of a situation. He wasn't a fool. He could see what was happening. *Can't they all sense that I'm broken, irretrievably broken—*

Kenntnis's voice interrupted his reverie. "It is imperative that we keep control of her, so you must do whatever is necessary to achieve that. It shouldn't be difficult since you saved her life, and gratitude has become attraction. As for Ms. Armandariz, while I am grateful for the aid, she has rendered us, she is of far less importance than Rhiana."

Richard stiffened. "We really are just chess pieces to you, aren't we?" He could hear throbbing in his voice the echo of three hundred years of outraged Yankee ancestors. Kenntnis's response was one raised eyebrow. "I know exactly what you're suggesting, and the answer is no. I will not use

Rhiana's … feelings for me to manipulate her."

"Not to mention she's underage," Weber muttered.

Kenntnis stared at Richard, exasperated. "I really, really wish you were an ignorant flatfoot."

"Hey," said Weber. "Watch it."

"Apologies," Kenntnis threw to Weber. "How about this? A more typical male."

✦　✦　✦

"A more typical male."

The words haunted him as Richard unlocked the apartment door. He braced himself for the smell of smoke and burnt carpet, but the apartment smelled fresh and clean. He stepped inside to find the carpet replaced with something far thicker and nicer than the almost industrial beige carpet that was standard in the apartments. The patio doors had been replaced; the wall patched and repainted. It seemed that Kenntnis hadn't been kidding when he said he would handle the repairs.

There was a note on the closet door in his bedroom.

Have taken your clothes to be laundered to deal with any lingering smoke. We noticed you like Zegna suits. We used one of yours as a template. Hope these "suit" until yours come back from the dry cleaners.

Paulette

Richard opened the sliding mirrored door to reveal a deep blue pinstripe and a delicate gray window-paned suit.

There were dress shirts and two appropriate ties. It was incredibly thoughtful. It was also rather creepy, as if his life and choices were no longer his own.

He gave a longing look toward his bed. Found himself remembering the scent of Weber as he rested his cheek on a pillow.

I wish you were … a more typical male.

So do I, Richard thought wearily as he forced himself to stand.

CHAPTER TWENTY

GUN, GUN, GUN!

ANGELA TURNED AWAY from the electron microscope when Richard entered. It had been two days since she had joined what she secretly (she had a feeling Kenntnis would *not* be amused) called the Supernatural Scooby Gang.

She smiled. He continued to frown. "Shouldn't you be at work?" he asked.

"I took a few days off. Had a theory I wanted to test. I told Kenntnis about it and ..." She gestured at the lab. "Voila! A state-of-the-art laboratory all for me. I mean seriously, how much money does this guy have?"

"Apparently, a great deal," Richard said. His blue eyes flicked about the room studying all the equipment. "So why did you need me?"

"Don't look so put upon. But it's not just you. I need Rhiana, too."

Angela glanced at the time on her phone. *Damn the girl.* She'd hoped her bright, inconsequential chatter the other night had helped defuse the situation. She couldn't blame the girl for developing a crush; hell, she was thirty-six and dangerously close to being smitten, too. She typed in a quick text. A few seconds later an answering text arrived.

On my way.

"She's coming," Angela said, and noted the way his shoulders tensed beneath his cashmere sweater.

The door to the lab swung open and Rhiana slouched in. She was dressed in leggings, ankle boots, and a baggy sweatshirt with Einstein's general theory of relativity emblazoned across it and the quote, *"Everything should be made as simple as possible, but not simpler—A. Einstein."* And she was still gorgeous, damn it.

Angela rubbed her hands together. "Okay." She turned to Richard. "Have you got your pistol?"

"Yes." His tone was so questioning as to be suspicious.

"And the ... thing?" She couldn't bring herself to say sword. It still felt so ridiculous.

"Yes."

"Okay, so we've established that when ..." She once again found herself hesitating, unable to believe she was actually going to say this. Angela cleared her throat. "When magic happens, shit starts going screwy at the atomic level. I want to see if having that thing drawn *before* magic starts happening will prevent the atomic particles from being affected."

Rhiana perked up, curiosity replacing the sulky expression. "You mean that it might keep a bubble of reality around Richard?"

"Exactly. So, I want Richard Richard to draw the thing." Angela turned to Rhiana. "And then after that you'll do some magic."

The girl frowned. "I thought Kenntnis didn't want me doing magic unless he or Cross said it was okay."

"Well, Kenntnis isn't here—"

"Where is he?" Richard asked.

"Jeannette said he's out of town on business," Angela replied airily. "And he did say I could feel free to conduct any experiments I wanted, so …" She drew out the last word. "So, let's do it."

Richard and Rhiana exchanged glances, then Richard muttered, "It would be nice if I could rely on my weapon, my *real* weapon, again." And he drew the sword as Rhiana readied a penny.

After they finished, Angela stripped the ammunition from the clip, and handed it back to Richard. "It'll take me a while to analyze the guncotton. I'll let you know what I find."

"There's an easier test," Richard said, and raised an eyebrow.

"Duh, of course."

They all went tumbling out the back door, ducked past Cross's box and into the boulders at the foot of the mountain. Richard picked a place where the rounds would bury themselves in the dirt, in case the gun did fire.

"I just hope we don't bring down the cops on us," Richard muttered out of the side of his mouth as he chambered a round. "Of course, it *is* New Mexico, so we'll probably be fine."

"Hey!" Angela yelped.

Richard gave her an amused look. "Come on, this is the state where people celebrate *Easter* by shooting off guns."

"Okay, you've got a point," Angela reluctantly admitted. She then instructed Rhiana to cover her ears, she did the same, and Richard drew the sword and fired three times just to be sure. The gun worked perfectly.

"I wonder if just the presence of the hilt is enough to keep things from getting messed up?" Richard mused.

"Let's try it," Angela said.

Once again Rhiana readied a penny and cast a spell that had a sunflower grow out of one of the granite boulders. This time the pistol failed to fire.

Rhiana glanced at her phone, muttered about needing to get to class, and left.

"Well, that's a bummer," Angela said.

"I'll just need to make sure I have this thing with me at all times, and draw it the minute things get… hinky," Richard said as they headed back to the building. "And practice shooting with one hand."

"I'd still rely more on the sword if you're facing magical baddies," Angela said. "You said it was the sword that sucked the spell in the church, I mean the second church."

"Good point."

He held the door for her, and Angela gathered her nerve, asking casually, "Do you ski?"

"Yes. Why?"

"Well, despite climate change it's been a great fall and Taos is open. Maybe when you next have a break we can go."

"All right. Sounds fun."

IT WAS STRANGE to be back in school. Kenntnis had insisted, pointing out that sorceress didn't constitute an acceptable career choice, and Rhiana had acquiesced because it was tough to refuse when the man provided her with room and board, bought her a car, and had paid off her student loan. The corner of a textbook gouged her shoulder. Rhiana shifted the backpack and admitted that she didn't actually mind that much. She loved the play of numbers. They almost had weight and mass, like crystals of jet, all sharp-edged and glittering.

The sandstone paving the quad shone golden in the setting sunlight. Rhiana cut through the Student Union building. The scent of coffee and hamburgers elicited a growl from her stomach. She wished she didn't have this late class, but Kenntnis always had a dinner waiting when she returned to the penthouse. She fought back the impulse to get a snack, but decided she'd better stop at the bathroom before class.

Her fingers ached and tingled as the warm water flowed across her cold hands. She pulled free a paper towel and rubbed vigorously, feeling the rough paper catch on hangnails. She needed to get a manicure.

She dug through her backpack for a hairbrush and lipstick. The brush scratched and massaged her scalp and tugged free minute tangles as she swept it down through the mass of her hair. Maybe Richard preferred short hair like Angela's? Maybe she should drop by his apartment? He hadn't come around for the past three days. Rhiana tried to think of anything she might have done or said the last time they met that would have kept him away.

Then abruptly her frowning image shifted, and what stared back at her was *her*, but a Rhiana dressed in a gown shivering and glittering with diamonds and silver thread. Her hair floated as if blown by an unseen breeze and jewels sparkled in the black tresses. Her lips were redder, her eyes greener, the blush in her cheeks as rich and vibrant as a rose petal. The brush fell clattering into the sink. Rhiana gripped the edges of the counter so tightly that her knuckles went white and gazed and gazed at the vision. She was scared but mesmerized.

The image of a perfect Rhiana shivered and dissolved into component colors. The colors swirled and surged through the glass. She had seen this before, but what coalesced from the colors was not the nightmare creatures from the trailer. It was an achingly handsome face, golden-skinned and green-eyed, and very familiar. It was the face of the man from the Carrow's parking lot. He smiled warmly and fondly at her and lifting a hand he beckoned to her.

Rhiana stumbled back. The glass of the mirror silvered and went dark, offering no reflection. She fled, forgetting both brush and backpack.

An ache in her throat and a sharp stitch in her side pulled her out of her run and down to a walk just in front of the doors of the library. She gulped down air, bending over her knees until her heart stopped racing. Her first instinct was to run to the car and rush to Kenntnis to seek help. But she'd left her backpack, which that held held her books, and those physics texts cost the Earth. And the stranger wasn't like the monsters even if he had come out of a mirror like they did. And she'd seen him before and nothing bad had happened. Maybe it would be okay?

Straightening, she pushed back her hair, feeling the moisture from the sweat that hugged her hairline. She started back toward the Student Union building and froze as the man flowed out of the shadows of the courtyard. He held her backpack. Against his preternatural beauty and inhuman grace, the canvas bag looked as incongruous as a cigar in an angel's mouth.

"You forgot this," he said, and his voice was low but with an overtone of bells carrying the soft words farther than a natural voice could carry.

Rhiana took it numbly. His smile enfolded her. "We need to have a talk some time. I can give you the answers to *all* of your questions." He stepped back into the shadows and was gone.

THINGS STILL FELT surreal when Richard got into work. His first few days as a detective had been spent in Denver. Then had come the events at the church, but perhaps now a normal schedule would begin. The only downside was detectives didn't tend to have permanent partners, they got assigned on a rotating basis. Which meant at some point he was going to have to spend some time working with Snyder. The thought had Richard's gut clenching with anxiety.

As if he'd read Richard's mind, Snyder gave Richard a smirk that also seemed somehow threatening. Snyder wasn't alone, three other detectives surrounded his desk, and they gave Richard a look that promised ... *well, nothing good,* Richard concluded.

Richard veered away from his desk and went into Damon's office. He had meant to get directly into his concerns that he was going to face hazing or worse, but Weber's drawn face stopped him.

"Have you been getting any sleep since … well, you know?" Richard asked quietly.

"Some. Bourbon is a great relaxer," Weber grunted.

Xanax, thought Richard, but he didn't say it.

"But after talking with your Lumina buddy … I'm not sure I'm ever gonna sleep soundly again."

"I understand." Richard took a breath and plunged in. "On a more mundane topic," Richard said, "you're not going to try pairing me with Snyder, at least not right away, are you?"

"Yeah, I'm really stupid about personnel and can't tell when people rub each other the wrong way. No, of course not."

"Sorry. I wish I could work with you—"

"Not happening." Weber was suddenly the lieutenant and Richard's superior officer. "I don't do that much street work anymore. Also, it would make your situation here even worse, and we're partnered, sort of, on this … other thing. That's enough. That has to be enough," Weber repeated, his tone harsh. "Oh, and you're with Torres for the next week."

"Yes, sir," Richard whispered and backed himself out of the office.

Joe Torres was waiting, literally tapping his foot as he scrolled through his phone with one hand. "You finally done brownnosing?" he growled.

"Sorry. I just had something …" It was pointless to say more. Especially since Torres had already turned his back and was striding toward the elevators. Chastened, Richard followed.

They emerged into the parking lot and Richard blinked in the bright late-November sun. The sunlight glittered on the gold tinsel of the Christmas stars that hung on wires stretching across Grand Avenue. Richard shook his head. Thanksgiving was barely past, and here were Christmas decorations already. Sometimes he thought Americans were a very unserious people.

"Would you like me to drive?" Richard offered.

"Hell, no. We'll take my truck."

"Okay."

"And seriously, what the fuck kind of cop drives a fucking Volvo?" Torres added as they walked to the big Ford 4x4 pickup.

"A safe one?" Richard suggested.

Torres whirled back on him. "Don't fuckin' push it. So, you got some sugar daddy to push you up the ladder. Well, we're gonna be in *my* territory today. You keep your fuckin' mouth shut."

"Could you at least read me in on what we're doing?" Richard asked as he placed a foot on the running board, grabbed the panic handle, and pulled himself into the tall truck.

"Shooting at an impromptu party over on Edith Boulevard last night. We need to try to find witnesses."

✦   ✦   ✦

THEY SPENT THE day on it without notable success, and it was adding to the other cop's general outrage at the world. It was now past 4:00 PM, and the cold winter afternoon was rapidly fading as they turned down the short street. On the north it dead-ended into the brown berm of the irrigation ditch. On the south the street T-boned into Cherokee Road and the graffiti-covered walls of an out-of-business indoor archery range.

Someone had been very hopeful or lured by low rents, thought Richard as he studied the chipped and faded sign. This section of the North Valley was known for its dingy pawnshops and rundown bars, not high-end hobbies.

He glanced over at Torres's profile. The sun through the car windows gave the Hispanic's skin the color and consistency of polished mahogany. Thick black hair sprang up and away from his forehead and made his bushy eyebrows look like escapees from his skull—particularly when he was frowning, and he'd been frowning ever since their little exchange in the parking lot hours before.

Richard tried to keep focused, but it had been a long, boring day. He felt like the ventriloquist's dummy, standing mute on front porches and in a succession of living rooms while Torres asked questions. His thoughts kept drifting to Weber; had he been wrong to bring the lieutenant into Lumina? And should try to get Angela *out* of Lumina?? He didn't want to endanger anyone else.

The truck rolled to a stop. Richard looked up at the house that was to be their final stop of the day. It shared half the lot with its neighbor, and both were so small they had the quality of dollhouses. Richard was relieved that this house didn't have any dogs. Most of their stops this day had involved dogs. Lots and lots of dogs.

They climbed out. The house next door had a blasted

brown wasteland for a front yard, the boundary delineated by a six-foot-tall chain link fence. Suddenly, three large dogs of indeterminate breed and varying colors came flying around the corner of the neighboring house and flung themselves against the chain link, which twanged and rattled under the assault. Richard couldn't control the flinch. Unfortunately, Torres caught it, snorted, and rolled his eyes.

The older detective walked up to the front door of their target. This house had as little vegetation as its neighbor, but no fence—and no dogs. There was a flicker of movement from the dingy drapes in the front window. All the endless stops this day had been routine, but this time Richard had a surge of disquiet as he watched Torres plowing doggedly up to the front door.

"Maybe you shouldn't just walk right up ..." Richard began. Torres raised his hand to pound on the door.

"Look, *pendejo*, when you do something to fucking deserve your fucking promotion"—he half turned to look at Richard—"then maybe you can tell me how to do police work."

His fist hammered sharply twice, then the door flew open.

Richard was smarting under the unfair attack, but then he saw the glint of sun on metal and all conscious thought ceased.

"GUN! GUN! GUN!" Richard shouted, and then found himself looking down the barrel of his own gun that he couldn't recall drawing. The rough rubber on the grip rasped across his sweat-slick palm.

Torres, his face twisted into a rictus of terror, tried to

jump sideways. There was a simultaneous roar of a .357 Magnum and the sharp report from Richard's pistol. The shooter jerked as Richard's bullet took him in the forehead. The man's head snapped back, and his arms raised like an evangelical praising God. That lifting hand meant the round from the perp's Magnum had parted Torres's hair and torn across the scalp instead of blowing the policeman's face off.

Torres lay on the ground, hands clasped over his head, blood seeping between his fingers. He was cussing, but sobs of pain and fear punctuated the profanity.

For Richard, there was an instant where exhilaration washed up like a fierce heat, followed closely by horror. All the human-shaped targets in the world hadn't prepared him for the reality and finality of *this*.

He had *shot* a man. In the *head*. That man was *dead*.

A new thought intruded; maybe he wasn't dead, and Torres was helpless on his back in the dirt while Richard's gun hung limply at his side. Training reasserted itself. Rushing up the two small, discolored concrete steps, Richard drew down on the perp. The Magnum's butt rested in the man's open hand. Richard kicked it away and finally really looked at his handiwork.

There was a neat hole just above the man's left eyebrow and very little blood. The smell of blood and evacuated bowels hung over the body. Richard's stomach heaved and before he could control the reaction he turned aside and vomited. Acid burned his throat, and the foul sour taste coated his tongue.

Did this man lying at his feet have a wife? Children? Parents? A man killed by a white officer, who was probably rightly viewed as a carpetbagger to New Mexico natives.

Fuck your navel-gazing bullshit! There's an officer down! Get control of yourself!

Wiping the back of his hand across his mouth, Richard whirled, jumped off the stoop, and knelt beside Torres. The other cop's curses had faded to mumbles, and there were tears in his eyes. Richard pulled Torres's hands away, terrified that he'd see brain, but there was only a long, bleeding gouge.

"Hang on. I don't think it's too bad." The words tumbled and rattled out as he grabbed his radio and called out the codes for *shots fired* and *officer down*. It was only about four minutes from his call when he heard a converging symphony of sirens drawing ever closer.

DINNER WAS OVER. Rhiana had eaten in solitary splendor in the dining room. Kenntnis was away and Cross refused to tell her where the head of Lumina had gone, when he would return, or what he was doing. The homeless god had then taken a plate down to his shelter in the alley. He said it was because it seemed likely he would shatter again before the night was over, but Rhiana suspected it was more his desire to not be around her.

Rhiana returned to her room and reached into her backpack to pull out her books and start on her homework. The tips of her fingers met the soft brush of velvet in among the physics texts. Frightened, she jumped up and grabbed a penny. Holding it at the ready she grasped the backpack by its bottom and upended it onto the bed. Among the books was a velvet-covered scrapbook. Rhiana flipped back the front cover with her toe.

On the front page in flowing script was her name—*Rhiana.* Inside were pictures of her, from babyhood through high school graduation. From the angles and distance, they seemed to have been captured with a telephoto lens. Playing on the swings at the park near their house. In her little pink tutu at the dance recital when she was five. Digging in the wet sand at the beach at Zuma when she was eleven. The final picture was her high school graduation. Hundreds of pictures detailing a life. *Her life.*

Should she be alarmed? Was it creepy … or flattering?

She turned another page to find every clipping from every LA newspaper that had ever mentioned her, from the *LA Times* to the local Van Nuys neighborhood rag: pitching for the girls' softball team, winning the state science fair, receiving the physics scholarship. Every tiny victory carefully recorded. Nothing like it had ever been kept in the Davinovitch household.

Rhiana hugged it to her chest.

RICHARD SAT LIMPLY in a convenient wheelchair in the emergency room of UNMH. At first, he had frantically paced as beyond the curtained cubicle a doctor and two nurses worked on Torres. Then the adrenaline crash hit, and Richard had collapsed into the wheelchair.

I killed a man today. I killed a man today. I killed a man today.

The doors from the emergency waiting room burst open and Weber strode in. He spotted Richard, and Richard leaned into the warm hand that landed on his shoulder. He caught himself, he hoped before Weber noticed, and pulling back he sat up straighter.

"Where's Torres?" Weber asked.

With a jerk of the head Richard indicated the curtained cubicle. "There, sir."

"You okay?"

"Yes, sir. Just …"

"We'll talk about it." Weber walked through the curtain and the doctor's outraged squawk became a low murmur of conversation. Moments later Weber emerged and joined Richard.

"You're going to need to talk to IAD, and you'll be on administrative leave again for a few days until the investigation is over." He smiled at Richard's look of alarm. "Relax, it looks like a totally righteous shoot. Joe said you saved his life out there." Richard couldn't respond. He just swallowed hard and nodded. "If you need to talk to somebody, we've got shrinks available." Richard nodded again. "And don't think you need to be a macho asshole," the lieutenant added. "This is no easy thing. Do you feel up to writing your report?"

Richard gathered his scattered wits. "Yes, sir."

Back at APD headquarters, Weber kept his hand on Richard's shoulder all the way into the building, and all the way up the elevator. The touch had been comforting at the hospital, but now it felt more like the bigger man was trying to press Richard through the floor like a tent peg. Richard realized that Weber was nervous. *About the squad room's reaction? Will they blame me that Joe got shot?*

They stepped through the doors of the bullpen and a raucous cheer went up. Richard found his hand grabbed and pumped, his shoulders buffeted, shouts of congratulations, queries about the shooting, questions about Torres.

He was pretty certain he never managed a coherent sentence. Even Snyder grinned at him and yelled something about "Deadeye Dick." To Richard's horror, the phrase went rocketing around the room.

Next to him, Weber had relaxed. Richard looked up at him and found that while the brown eyes held worry there was also pride. Richard smiled shyly up at him.

Maybe he had finally been accepted.

CHAPTER TWENTY-ONE
THEY KEEP THE MONSTERS AT BAY

THE CLOUDS SEEMED to balance on the tops of New York's skyscrapers. They spat rain down the glass-and-concrete structures and onto the hundreds of jostling umbrellas in the streets below. Water dripped off the brim of Kenntnis's homburg. The crowds parted before him and closed back in a few feet behind him. It had been a long time since he'd mingled so openly among vast numbers of humans, and he was still having the same effect. The trees were millennia behind them, but humans still had an animal's sense when something was different, powerful, and potentially dangerous. Individually, humans seemed to handle him better now, but get a lot of them together and the monkey troop returned.

Despite being only 3:30 PM, the lowering cloud cover made it dark. Light from the store windows illuminated the wares on display and formed pools of gold on the wet sidewalks. He wished he could have had Cross with him, but when he'd left, the creature was shattered. The constant assaults on his Old One ally were evidence that Grenier was planning something big. That meant Richard became even more critical and that Kenntnis had to resolve the mystery of the missing months. He had to know if they hid something damaging for Lumina.

Up ahead, Kenntnis spotted the neon sign for City Sushi. Briefly, Kenntnis longed for another time and eras long past when a private detective would have wanted to meet at Katz's, and Kenntnis could have ordered a bowl of matzo ball soup with a matzo the size of a softball floating among the nuggets of meat, tangled masses of noodles, onions, and carrots, and a sandwich piled high with chicken liver and pastrami. But no, Rosenblum had picked sushi, and sushi always left Kenntnis feeling hungry.

The private detective waited for him at a table. Kenntnis was grateful; with his bulk, the washitsu rooms were pure torture. Rosenblum was a medium-sized man with brown hair and brown eyes and a forgettable face. His attire suggested a low-level accountant or salesman and was as unremarkable as his face. In front of him was a celadon tray, its lovely green color obscured by the large amount of sushi. Kenntnis guessed sushi left Rosenblum hungry, too. A bottle of sake sat in a pot of steaming water.

"Hope you don't mind. I didn't wait. I was hungry," Rosenblum mumbled around a bite of squid as Kenntnis slid into the chair across from him.

"No problem. I could use some fuel myself." He lifted a finger and the waitress, an exquisite Japanese girl, tripped lightly over. The silk of her kimono rustled as she moved.

"I'll have a bowl of beef udon soup." *At least it had noodles.* The girl bowed and pattered away. Kenntnis stared across at Rosenblum. "Okay, what have you got?"

Rosenblum fished out a reporter's thin notebook and flipped it open. "So, nobody at the hospital would talk—no big surprise there. I tracked down the EMTs who brought him into the hospital. One of them was willing to talk." Rosenblum glanced up, his brown eyes bright. "But it cost you three bills. Somebody else had already been there ahead of us and had established the base price."

Grenier, thought Kenntnis, and gave voice to the next thought. "And is there anything here that's going to hurt us?"

"Depends on what you're using this Oort for. If you're planning on running him for Congress, as a Republican … well, in the present climate you're gonna have a problem." The detective gave a one-sided shrug. "Otherwise, not really."

✧   ✧   ✧

"Ow! SHIT, SHIT, shit, shit," Rhiana muttered as the power arced from the Tarot cards, blistering her fingertips.

"Those would be the ones." Cross nodded with approval and picked up the Tarot deck. Kenntnis was still out of town, but they were under standing orders to patrol for incursions whenever the shattered god was in one piece. Since they had to limit the search in some way, absent any specific instructions from Kenntnis, the pair trawled through occult, New Age, and religious stores whenever Rhiana wasn't in class. This was the first time they'd gotten a hit.

Rhiana, sucking on her burned fingers, glared at him. The shop was in a converted house just off Central Avenue in the University area. Heavy curtains blocked out the winter sun. Light was provided by horn lanterns wired for electricity. Incense hung heavy and cloying in the overheated air. The dominant feature was cases and cases of books on the occult, but there was also a section for magical paraphernalia—crystals, athames, Tarot decks, incense burners, and jewelry.

They went up to the counter to pay for the cards. The owner of the Crystal Eye Mystic Book Store was a heavyset young woman dressed in jeans and a baggy sweatshirt. Tumbling curls of exquisitely beautiful auburn hair framed her pale, bloated face. She had the sulky expression of one who's been disappointed by life.

Rhiana wondered if the girl blessed or cursed her one beauty? Would it have been easier to simply be plain and have no expectations? Or had the hair led her to need to be special, to be magic?

"You ever use this deck?" Cross asked, casually wagging the cards in the air.

"Yeah, I test them all out. See which ones really spark for me. They're all different, you know. Some manufacturers are just hacks. There's no pride in the work, it's just about money. These cards seemed to really be keyed in."

"Cool," said Cross.

Out on the sidewalk Cross shoved the Tarot deck into Rhiana's coat pocket and looked back at the building. "That gal's got some mojo. We need to get her neutralized without getting Richard arrested for assault. Otherwise, she's just going to keep on powering decks without realizing she's doing it." He started to walk away. Rhiana got in front of him.

"Since you see magic, would it have strained you to give me a heads-up? Or was it just more fun to let me get burned?" Her voice shook with anger.

Cross stared down at her. His eyes had gone completely

black, and looked anything but human. Rhiana forced herself to hold the stare. "You needed the reminder."

Rhiana took two running steps and caught up. "Reminder of *what*?" The homeless god didn't answer. "You just wanted to see me get hurt. You don't like me, do you?"

Cross stopped so abruptly that Rhiana, unable to react quickly enough, walked on for several feet. She swung back and met the brunt of the blunt and brutal answer.

"No. I don't."

"Why? What have I ever done to you?"

"I know what you are," he said cryptically, and walked on.

Rhiana stared hard at his back, fingered the pennies in her pocket, swallowed the ache in her throat, and prayed for him to shatter into a thousand pieces and *never* get back together again.

✧   ✧   ✧

RICHARD WAS IN the zone, fingers flying across the keys of the piano. Next to him, Susanna, her face tight with concentration and the effort of holding the violin tucked beneath her chin, attacked the strings with her bow hard enough to make her muscles flex and flare. A strand of long blonde hair was caught in her lips. Bob Figge nodded his gray crew-cut head, keeping the count as he sawed away at the strings of his cello. Lee Titelbaum played his viola with a gentle smile. Even the most passionate music failed to pierce his superior calm. Mozart's piano quartet in E Flat swirled in the narrow confines of Richard's apartment, undaunted by poor acoustics. It thrummed in his chest, filling him with a wild joy. The quartet danced toward the climax, four bodies and four minds linked by music.

The phone rang.

The perfect blending of sound faltered. "No," Richard shouted. "Let it go to voicemail!"

They recaptured the connection. Ignored the dissonance of the blaring telephone. The final chords wound into a perfect resolution. Richard lifted his hands from the keyboard of the Bösendorfer. Susanna pulled the hair out of her her mouth and laughed from sheer exuberance. Figge frowned and tapped his bow on the page, resting on his music stand. Lee gave his soft, superior smile as he wiped his hands with a perfectly starched handkerchief.

"Come on, Bob," Richard said encouragingly. "That was *good.*"

"The best we've ever played it," Susanna added.

Titelbaum pulled a pocket watch out of his vest pocket, snapped it open, and checked the time. "8:30 PM. Can we risk another?"

With a regretful headshake Richard closed the cover on the piano. "Better not. I don't need a noise complaint. I barely got to stay here, what with the fire and all."

Also, he was returning to duty in the morning now that he had been cleared in the shooting. His union rep had warned him he might get hit with a civil suit, but because the shooting had been so clearly justified, the city would likely represent him, saving him from having to hire his own lawyer.

Figge looked around the apartment. "You'd never know

anything happened."

"Yes," said Richard, suppressing a flare of discomfort at the army of workers Kenntnis had unleashed.

"Besides, we've got snackies," caroled Susanna in her little girl's voice, and she headed into the kitchen.

Over tea and coffee and pastries from a local French bakery, they discussed their lives, books they were reading, and movies they had seen. Titelbaum taught at the law school. Figge taught history at a local high school. Susanna worked at an upscale jewelry store and kept auditioning for the New Mexico Symphony Orchestra. The general rule was that you auditioned five times before you got hired. Richard hoped she'd make it.

They were disparate people brought together through a love of music, but they never managed to socialize outside of their bimonthly jam sessions. Titelbaum had a wife and two small children. Figge was a dedicated bachelor who liked his privacy. Susanna spent her time working, practicing, and caring for her elderly parents. And Richard was a cop. *And the Paladin, whatever the heck that actually means.*

As Richard shut the door behind them a little after 9:00 PM, he mused that he knew a lot of people, but seemed to have few friends.

And whose fault is that? You're the one avoiding intimacy.

For a brief instant, a kaleidoscope of faces whirled through his mind—Rhiana, Angela, and Weber, and faces from his past—Victor, Brett, Blythe, Alex, Rachel, Sal, Mario …

Richard shook his head to dispel the visions and the physical reaction and the sudden wave of utter loneliness.

The red message light blinked on the phone. He called voicemail and, phone tucked beneath his chin, started loading the plates and cups into the dishwasher.

At first there was just the sound of soft, desperate breathing. Then his mother's voice began to speak. "Richard ... I can't lose you ..." He had to strain to hear, her voice was so soft and broken. "You must be good. I can't lose you to Hell." Hysteria edged the words. There were more of the panting breaths punctuated with barely audible sobs like whimpers.

The call ended and the blank voice of the voicemail server began. "Press seven to ..."

Richard didn't bother to delete the message. He started dialing home, and then abruptly stopped. It was 11:30 PM in Rhode Island. His parents would be asleep by now. It didn't take much to imagine his father's anger if Richard woke them. And a call would betray his mother. He would phone tomorrow after Robert left for work.

✧ ✧ ✧

SERGEANT PATRICK MCGOWAN leaned on the bar drinking a beer, shoveling peanuts into his mouth, and watching the Patriots game on the TV hung over the bar. Kenntnis studied the man. The broad shoulders bled down into a wide, spreading waist. Judging by those shoulders, the man had been an athlete in his youth. Now a shock of gray hair crowned his head, and the backs of his hands were ridged with veins and discolored by age spots. Kenntnis moved to the bar and ordered a single malt scotch. McGowan's face was pugnacious, but the brown eyes belied the thrust of the jaw; they were soft and kind.

"Sergeant McGowan?"

"Who wants to know?" the man growled. There was a lilt to the words. Kenntnis guessed an Irish grandmother who had lived long enough to bequeath the music of her native land to her children and grandchildren.

In answer to the question Kenntnis slid over his business card. McGowan studied it with care but made no effort to pick it up. He then gave Kenntnis an equally long look before pushing the card back. "I'm not retired yet, and when I do, I'm stayin' here." A Puck's grin pulled at the full mouth. "I'll not be running away from the snow. I'll shovel the white shit and outlive all them pansy asses who ran away to Florida."

"I don't doubt it, sir, but I'm not, in fact, here to offer you a job or sell you a condo in the sunbelt. I'm seeking some information about—" Kenntnis broke off as McGowan came off the stool. McGowan's big hands clenched and unclenched at his sides, and they were nose to nose, for Kenntnis had not retreated.

"I sent that *other* bastard about his business, and I'll send you about yours, too."

"I'm not here to do any harm to Richard. In fact, he works for me in a—"

Again, he was interrupted as McGowan roared, "Like Hell he does. He's a policeman in Albuquerque!" The bartender, face tight with concern, edged toward them. "Back off, Todd, I'll not be needing your help."

"If you would let me finish, I was going to add—in a manner of speaking," Kenntnis said. "And Richard's made detective, by the way."

That broke through the anger. The old cop frowned and rubbed at his head in confusion. "Now why the devil wouldn't the boy tell me?"

"Because I helped him get the promotion," Kenntnis answered. "And therefore, it's tainted and he's ashamed. Not that he'd brag anyway, it doesn't seem to be in his nature."

McGowan stepped back to the barstool and sat down. "Okay, you actually seem to know the kid, unlike that other bastard."

"I assume you didn't tell the other … er, bastard anything?"

"Damn right I didn't."

"Good, because unlike me, he *does* intend to do Richard an injury." Kenntnis paused for a sip of scotch.

"What is it you're digging for?" McGowan asked after a few swallows of beer.

"Take a drive with me," Kenntnis said. "I'd feel better in a less public venue."

Out on the rain-slick sidewalk, McGowan pushed back his hat and gave a soundless whistle at the sight of the stretch limo parked in front of the bar. The driver opened the back door for them.

"Just drive around until I tell you otherwise," Kenntnis said, and hit the button to roll up the dividing window. "Drink?"

"Please. You got one of those single malts in there?" Kenntnis poured out a liberal shot and handed over the cut crystal glass. The cop took a sip and rolled it around in his mouth for a long moment before swallowing. He gusted out a sigh, then shook his head. "Who the fuck are you?"

"A really rich guy who has Richard's best interests at heart. I learned from the EMT that Richard was … injured. Others also have this information. I expect they will use it, and …" He paused, wondering how to phrase this diplomatically. He gave up and just said it. "I'm concerned about Richard's reaction."

"Then you don't know him as well as you think, mister. He's small and pretty, and you could break him with one hand, but you'll never *break* him, if you get what I'm sayin'. He has a will of steel."

"He tried to commit suicide."

"That was before he had the calling."

"Police work, you mean?"

"Aye."

"You make it sound like a religious vocation."

"It is for the good ones. They keep the monsters at bay."

Kenntnis smiled. *How little you know,* he thought. "I think you're one of the good ones, Sergeant, and that you taught Richard a great deal."

"Well, I tried, and it must have took because he was able to stand up to the old bastard."

"And who might that be?"

"His father. Right old bastard, on the one hand talking about what low-lives cops were, and on the other tearing Richard down saying as how he wasn't tough enough to take it." McGowan drained the scotch in a long swallow. "Richard will never be pushed to try suicide again. You can take that to the bank."

"And I assume you won't tell me how you came to meet Richard or the reason for the suicide attempt."

"Nope, not my story to tell." McGowan glanced at the window. "You can let me off here." Kenntnis tapped on the glass and indicated the curb with a jerk of his chin. The car glided to a stop. "Thanks for the scotch." He leaned back in the open door. "When you see the kid remind him that God don't make mistakes. However, you're made it was all part of His plan."

Kenntnis didn't respond to that, just nodded, and leaned back. Events were definitely moving, but since he was already on the East Coast, he decided he would take the time to visit the Lumina physics facility up in Rochester. He knew that Cross was training Rhiana to control her powers, and Richard was … well, he now felt more confident that Richard was doing just fine.

AN OVERFULL BLADDER sent Rhiana out of the study carrel on the seventh floor of the UNM library tower and into the cramped bathroom. As she was washing her hands, she felt that coiling pressure, and her gaze jerked up to the mirror over the sink. The man … the Old One was looking out at her.

"You've been spying on me!" Rhiana pushed the outrage, hoping that her secret pleasure over the scrapbook didn't show.

The man smiled fondly. "Since the moment of your birth."

"Why?"

"You're very special to me … to us."

Rhiana scuttled back a few feet. "You're with *them*," she accused.

"I might say the same of you."

"What do you want?"

"Nothing very fearsome. To take you to dinner. To get to know you. That's all."

"No!" She fled toward the door.

"You know how you used to think you were special?" he called after her. "Well, you are, Rhiana. More special than you know. I can tell you why. Contact me when you're ready to learn the truth."

✧　✧　✧

AS HE DROVE to work, a strong wind through Tijeras Canyon buffeted the car. The endless rings as he called home to Newport sounded hollow and distant, as if underlining the fact he had traveled so far from home. He pushed aside the fanciful thought. The voicemail system picked up.

"Hi, Mama, got your message. What are you up to? Call me on my cell. Love you."

Despite his overcoat and gloves, Richard shivered and kicked the heat higher. *Maybe I did abandon her. Maybe I should have tried Rhode Island's various police forces instead of moving so far away.*

The lack of an answer was really starting to worry him. He had tried her at 5:30 AM when he got up. He had tried to reach her again as he left the gym at the complex, and now this call. He gave a nervous little hum, then asked Siri to call call his sister Amelia. He didn't think there was much hope of reaching her. His eldest sister was a surgeon at Mass General, but he preferred to start with her. Pamela was a defense attorney in Newport, and she viewed Richard's new career choice with disapproval. In fact, she'd made him feel as if he'd joined the Brownshirts. They hadn't talked much in the past few years.

His musings were broken when, surprisingly, Amelia picked up her phone.

"Richard, what a surprise." Her voice was deep, and husky and she had a habit of interrupting her words with hesitations that should have been annoying but ended up endearing and fascinating.

"Sorry I haven't called for a while. Things have been … well, a little hectic out here."

"Papa said you got a promotion."

"Yes."

"Congratulations."

"Thanks."

"We missed you at Thanksgiving."

"I just couldn't leave. I'll come at Christmas, at least I'm going to try. How are Brent and Paul?"

"They're fine. Paul wants to take up hockey. We're negotiating."

"Which means he'll be picking a different sport," said Richard, and couldn't help smiling. His eldest sister was formidable and would be more than a match for an eight-year-old's tantrums.

"What is that noise? I can hardly hear you."

"I'm driving into work and the wind is really howling."

"So, what's up?"

"Have you talked to Mama recently?"

"Early last week, Monday, I think. Why?"

"How did she seem to you?" Richard carefully asked.

"A little hyper, but I'd rather have her bouncing than depressed." Richard agreed with the sentiment. When depression hit, Alannis Oort tended to dull the pain with alcohol and pills. It was one of many reasons why Richard tried to keep his Valium and Xanax bottles closed. "Is something wrong?" Amelia asked.

"I don't know. She left a message for me last night, and she seemed very agitated and upset. She was crying and talking about … well, about me going to Hell. I keep calling, but I haven't been able to reach her."

"Oh, dear. She's been very active at church chairing some fundraising committees. Maybe it's been too much for her."

"You need to tell Papa," Richard said.

"You tell him. She's calling you."

"I'd feel like I was betraying her."

"Oh, Richard, don't start. Papa isn't the enemy. She isn't easy."

"And he doesn't help."

"Look, let's not have an argument. I've got rounds in five minutes. Was there anything else?" Amelia asked.

"No, I was just worried."

"If you don't want to talk to Papa, then talk to Pamela. At least she's in Newport."

"Yeah, okay. See you at Christmas."

"Take care, Richard, love you."

"Love you, too."

"She's been very active at church …"

Worried thoughts chased one another through his head. They had attended that church Richard's entire life.

Not every church was evil.

They had been created to foster Kenntnis's vision of a loving God.

Some still served that mission.

Cross was proof of that.

There was absolutely nothing to indicate Grenier was behind his mother's erratic behavior. *Nothing.*

CHAPTER TWENTY-TWO
Sometimes Feelings Matter

THREE DAYS LATER Richard once again lacked a partner. Torres was still on sick leave, and McCracken, whom he had been working with, had come down with a stomach bug. Figuring it was a good time to finish off reports, Richard settled in at his desk and started swiftly typing. On his left Snyder was laboriously hunting and pecking as he also wrote a report. Snyder caught Richard's gaze and glared. Richard quickly looked back at his screen. It seemed the detente he'd enjoyed was, at least with this coworker, at an end.

A large, warm hand clapped onto his shoulder as a folder slapped onto the desk next to him.

"Nice work," said Weber.

"You complimenting his typing skills or his detective skills?" Snyder snarked.

Weber glared. Richard ignored the other man and instead enjoyed the surge of pride he felt at Weber's words.

"It wasn't precisely complex. Once his mother realized he was in more danger from the victim's friends than from us, she told me where to find him."

"Didn't hurt that you speak Spanish," Weber said. Snyder muttered something under his breath. Weber rounded on him. "You got something you want to share with the class,

Snyder?"

"Just remarking that he dresses well, too, and has such a big vocabulary."

The overly sweet, singsong quality of his voice had Richard blushing. Weber's face suffused with blood. He looked on the verge of a stroke.

"What the fuck is your problem, Snyder?"

Richard laid a hand on the older man's wrist, a feather touch, begging him not to make it worse. Weber shut his mouth, took a few deep breaths.

Richard examined his options. Having Weber fight his battles would be the worst, but letting Synder's remark pass without reaction wouldn't be much better. Sometimes you had to hit back before a bully would stop. Richard had learned that painful lesson on a succession of playgrounds and in various locker rooms. His small size and handsome face had made him an irresistible target.

"Always happy to serve as an inspiration." He gave Snyder a thin smile. "Just let me know if you want me to teach you about … well, actually, almost anything."

Hitting the print button, Richard rolled back his chair. The hilt of the sword dug into his back, a reminder of the two worlds he now inhabited. Standing, he walked over to the communal printer. Weber joined him.

"Showing some teeth, little man. About damn time, but what's gotten into you?"

Richard considered mentioning his worries about his mother, but then reminded himself this was his boss, not a friend. He shook his head. "Sorry, I shouldn't have let him get to me. It won't happen again."

Ortiz came out of his office, head craning as he looked across the squad room. His gaze fell on Richard.

"Oort, where's McCracken?"

"Out sick today, sir."

"Well, grab Snyder and—"

"I can ride with him," Weber interrupted.

Richard nearly snapped his neck so quickly did he look over at Weber. Then felt his heart sink when Ortiz said, "Snyder's free."

"Nah, let me go with him. I could use a break from paperwork," Weber said. "What have we got?"

"Missing kid. Maybe a snatch. Down at the McDonald's on Isleta."

✧　✧　✧

THE SLOWLY SPINNING lights on a couple of patrol cars marked the location, which was good, because the McDonald's was missing the usual golden arches. It had been designed to meet zoning regulations requiring architectural sensitivity to historical style. That meant it looked like a runaway pueblo set among the rundown stucco and metal buildings to either side. One held a custom body shop specializing in turning your ride into a primo lowrider. The howl of tortured metal echoed over the traffic noise from Isleta Boulevard. On the other side was a check-cashing service.

"I hate those places," Richard muttered as they climbed out of the car. "They're a racket designed to prey on the poor."

"You really are a unicorn," Weber said, eyeing the smaller man.

Richard bristled. "What does that mean?"

"A liberal cop."

"My family is Republican," came the huffy response.

Weber stopped, put his hands on his hips, and gazed down at the younger man. "Who'd you vote for last election?"

"None of your business."

"Yeah, liberal."

"I presume you're a Republican," Richard said, and while his tone was neutral the aquiline nose wrinkled a bit.

"None of your business," Weber shot back with a grin, then transferred his attention to the playground.

In the parking lot the odor of grease, fries, and that peculiar, boiled meat smell of McDonald's burgers was strong enough to defeat the blast of exhaust from the passing cars. Weber's belly gave a soft growl.

The uniforms were gathered in the outdoor play area, and cultural sensitivity hadn't extended to there. It held the usual garishly colored plastic and metal maze. It squatted on a high platform supported by thick steel pipes that could double as a jungle gym. Green, red, blue, orange, and purple plastic tubes punctuated with globes snaked down from the central body, creating the impression that a psychedelic octopus had washed up to die incongruously in the New Mexico desert.

There were three round concrete tables with benches. Underfoot, the dirt was covered with rubberized outdoor carpet. The playground was surrounded by a high wrought iron fence with mesh wire between the posts. Hamburger wrappers and squeezed ketchup packets had blown up against the western side. It had all the charm of an exercise yard in a prison. There was a gate set in the fence. Weber and Richard chose to enter through that rather than walk through the restaurant. Curious faces peered through the windows facing out on the playground with expressions of mingled fear and excitement.

Everyone loves a tragedy as long as it's not theirs, Damon thought.

A distraught young Hispanic woman dressed in a shabby sweat suit slumped on a concrete bench at one of the tables. She had a Madonna's face atop a deep-bosomed, wide-hipped body. The rich brown tones of her skin were blotched red from crying.

"I'm telling you I was here the whole time! I didn't go away. I wouldn't leave Miguel! Why don't you listen to me?" And she went off in a torrent of Spanish.

"Do I want a translation?" Weber asked.

"No," said Richard.

They walked up and flashed their shields. One of the uniforms joined them. He was a heavyset Anglo man whose buzz cut suggested that cop was a second career and the first had been the military. His name tag read KOPEK. He hitched up his belt and glanced back at the young woman. The look wasn't kind.

"What have we got?" Damon asked.

The uniform flipped open his notebook. "Miguel Rodriquez, age three. Wearing a Dallas Cowboys sweatshirt, jeans, and tennis shoes. He was out here playin' in the maze.

She …" Another disgusted glance. "Says he went in and never came out. I think she went inside to pack on another Quarter Pounder with fries and some creep grabbed the kid."

Perhaps it was the sniping from Snyder that had reduced his tolerance, but Weber was startled when Richard lost his usual polite reserve and snapped scornfully, "Why, thank you for that thoughtful and helpful insight."

Damon laid a quelling hand on Richard's shoulder. "What's her name?"

"Sophia Rodriquez," the uniform answered.

"What's the word on the dad? Any chance this is a custody snatch?" Weber asked.

"Unwed mother, big surprise," Kopek grunted.

"Do we know for certain he's *not* in the maze?" Richard asked.

"You hear a kid cryin' in there? If he was stuck, we'd fuckin' know it. It's been an hour and a half since he's gone missing, according to the mother."

"So, in fact, you haven't checked," Richard demanded. The younger man was at his most haughty, and Kopek responded just as Damon expected.

"You want to go crawl through it and check, Detective? 'Course you're about the right size," Kopek grunted, thrusting out his chin and chest, daring Richard to react.

Weber sighed and interposed himself between the two men. "Okay, we'll take it from here." They walked away toward the woman.

"What a …"

Damon watched as Richard struggled with himself. "Oh, go ahead, say it."

"Prick. Racist prick," Richard added breathily as if saying such things was shocking, if not wicked.

"Agreed, but remember those guys are usually first on the scene. You want them working *with* you, not *against* you."

"I know, I know," Richard said. They reached the young mother. Sophia Rodriquez's hands were tightly clenched. Weber clocked the tatters of a tear- and snot-soaked napkin in her hand. Richard hadn't missed it either; he pulled out a handkerchief and gave it to her. Damon noticed it was monogrammed. On the table behind her were the half-eaten remains of a Happy Meal. It was poignant and depressing.

"Do we need an Amber alert?" Richard asked Weber quietly.

"Too early to tell. Let's ask a few questions first."

The woman's dark eyes darted back and forth between them. "He's here! I swear he's here. I *didn't* leave him. I didn't!"

Weber held up his hands and patted the air in a soothing gesture. "Okay, okay, ma'am. We understand you didn't leave the playground."

"That's right," Rodriquez said. She relaxed a bit with the indication that she might actually be believed.

"But maybe you got distracted … you talked to some-body, or you were focusing on your food, and you took your eye off him for a few minutes," Weber suggested gently.

"No! He wanted me to watch him climb inside. Last week he was scared, and some other kids made fun of him. So this time he was going to do it." Her voice had the musical cadences of her distant Spanish ancestors. "He was real proud when he went in. He turned around and smiled and waved to me. I told him how brave he was." Her voice caught on a sob. "I watched his little feet as he climbed farther up." She mopped at the sudden stream of tears with the handkerchief. Throwing back her mane of black hair, she cleared her throat and continued. "So, I waited. I thought I'd see him in some of those little window things." She indicated the gray plastic portholes and one large bulge set in the side of the squat body of the maze as if the octopus were in the process of ingesting a bathyscaphe. "But I never saw him. I waited for a while, and then I went over and called. He didn't answer, and he didn't come out, and that's the truth."

Weber glanced over at Richard and raised his eyebrows. When you're a cop you get an instinct when somebody is laying a story on you. This didn't sound like a story. The problem was it didn't make any damn sense.

"And no one's been in?" Richard asked.

"Well, I won't fit." She laid her hands self-consciously on her wide hips. "But one of the clerks, she's a little thing, she went in."

Richard shot a glare at Kopek. "Would have been nice of him to *mention* that."

Damon just stared down at him, allowing his expression to drive home the lesson. Weber could see that it stung, but Richard muttered, "Okay, point taken."

"Go, find her and talk to her," Damon ordered. Richard went.

INSIDE THE RESTAURANT, curiosity had a few people edging

closer but most stayed away. He was an Anglo cop, and in this neighborhood their experiences with Anglo cops probably hadn't been great. He called out, "Which one of you went in the maze?" A tiny Hispanic girl in her late teens raised her hand. She was behind the service counter and wore the McDonald's uniform. Richard took her over to one of the preformed, bolted-down tables and they sat. There was a blot of ketchup on the table. He used a napkin to wipe it clean and then leaned forward, resting his arms on the table.

"Could you tell me what happened?"

"Well, this lady comes in and she's all excited, yelling about how her little boy is lost in the maze. The manager, he tells her how a lot of kids like to tease their moms, but she's not having any of it. She's yellin' louder and wavin' her hands around, so he sends me out to look."

"And?" Richard prompted.

"He wasn't in there, and I went through the whole thing. There was this funny crack in the plastic in one place. Told the boss it's probably going to need to be replaced."

Depressed, he walked back out to the playground. Sophia Rodriquez seemed so sincere, and he hated to think his instincts were that far wrong.

Weber was continuing his questioning, taking different angles, but no matter what he tried the story stayed the same. Richard waited for a natural break, then pulled his boss aside and repeated the clerk's story.

"So that's it, then." Weber flipped closed his notebook. "Now we call the Amber alert."

"Let me check in the maze." Richard started toward it. Weber's hand fell hard on his shoulder, stopping him cold.

"No." He jerked his head toward the uniforms. "Now, you can bet Kopek has been busy bragging to his partner about how he put the gold shield in his place, and since we're a small department everybody knows you're the new kid. After the crack Kopek made—"

Crack, Richard thought, and he lost the thread of what Weber was saying.

"… be all over APD by shift change, and you can't afford to get humiliated … again." Weber realized Richard hadn't been listening. He registered Richard's tension. "What?"

Frowning, Richard scanned the maze. "I don't know, this just feels … like something out of Kenntnis's world."

"You got anything more than a *feeling*?"

Richard shook his head, frustrated that Weber sounded so much like Kenntnis. It made him feel gauche and young and inexperienced. He could accept the inexperienced, but not all three, and whatever Kenntnis might say, sometimes feelings mattered.

"Okay," Richard finally said, and knew he sounded churlish.

They returned to Rodriquez. "Ma'am," Weber said, "we're going to need a picture of Miguel. We'll get it up on the TV."

"Why? He's in *there*!" Her voice rose and she pointed a shaking hand at the maze.

Weber put a hand under her arm. "Come on now. These gentlemen are going to take you downtown and you're going to give us all the particulars."

Hands flailing, she beat at Weber's chest and face. "No, *no*, he'll hear me. He'll come back to me."

"Ma'am; *ma'am*." Richard caught one of her hands, only to be shoved aside as Kopek and his partner ran over and grabbed the distraught woman.

"Go easy, guys, she didn't hurt me, and she's upset," Weber said.

All the fight went out of Rodriquez and her knees buckled. Her shrieking sobs accompanied the trio across the parking lot to the squad car.

Weber sighed. "Let's get started. This is about to become a very long day."

But Richard took one more look back at the maze before hurrying after Weber.

✧   ✧   ✧

IT WAS AFTER 9:00 PM before Richard left headquarters. There had been a lot of calls, but none of them the right call. Miguel Rodriquez remained missing. Sophia's extended family turned up at 6:00 PM and took her back to her parents' home. There they would hold vigil. Neighbors would come with food. Possibly the priest. This was a community that rallied to any crisis or catastrophe. In his time with APD Richard had walked into many such vigils, where tall votive candles, their glass holders imprinted with an image of the Virgin of Guadalupe, flickered in front of pictures of the Savior of the Bleeding Heart. Now that bleeding heart had a whole different meaning for Richard, and he shuddered as he stepped into the parking lot.

He found himself driving past the entrance to his apartment complex and continuing up Montgomery to Lumina.

But Kenntnis wasn't there—still out of town on business. Rhiana was at class.

"Would you like to wait in Mr. Kenntnis's private quarters until she gets back?" Joseph asked as they stood in the black marble lobby.

"No, thanks." He stood dithering. His stomach felt hollow. He never had eaten lunch. He considered finding dinner, but quickly rejected the idea. Even a brief thought about food nauseated him. He couldn't forget the round face of Miguel Rodriquez, age three, thirty-four pounds, black hair, brown eyes. Where was he? What were they missing?

He intended to head to his car but found himself walking behind the building instead. Golden light spilled out from the cardboard box. Cross was in and intact. He was sitting on a blanket-covered mattress on the ground, eating Beluga caviar out of a can. The tiny glistening black beads shivered on the tines of the fork and a few spilled, catching on his lower lip and beard. His tongue darted out to lick them up.

"Good evening," Richard said.

"Hey, hi." Cross held up the can. "Want some? I love the stuff."

"No, thank you."

"Yeah, I know, it's better with the chopped egg and onion and little crackers, but it's just fine this way, too. Come on in."

Richard stepped into the box. Cross indicated the wooden spool that had once carried cable. Richard sat down. "I'm sorry to bother you, but if you're not too busy, I was wondering if you would come with me and check something out."

"Let me check my calendar and see if I'm available." He stared down into the smooth palm of one hand. "You're in luck." Richard flushed and Cross laughed. "You are the funniest little guy," the homeless god said. He tossed the nearly empty caviar can out the crude doorway, wiped his hands down his dirty jeans, and stood up. "So, where we going?"

✧   ✧   ✧

SINCE IT WAS a weeknight, the McDonald's closed at 10:00 PM. They waited in the parking lot of the thrift store across the street, watching the night crew scrubbing down the floor and the tables. Finally, the last trash can was emptied, and the lights turned out. The taillights of the clerks' cars went off north and south on Isleta. Two of three had a taillight either busted out or burned out. Richard wondered if there was a special assembly plant where they made cars intended for the state. *"Yeah, Fred, that one's going to New Mexico, so bust out a headlight and make sure the turn signals don't work."* He immediately felt guilty for his whimsical little thought, because the truth was that most of the citizens of New Mexico were poor. They kept their cars running, but there wasn't usually anything left for elective repairs.

They gave it a few more minutes just in case someone had forgotten something and returned. Then Cross and Richard left the Volvo and ran across Isleta. There were small bouquets of flowers resting against the fence. Votive candles flickered among them. Yellow ribbons had been twined through the bars. Richard tried the gate, but it was locked.

Richard eyed the eight-foot-high fence. He backed up and trotted forward, testing the distance he would need. Cross tapped him on the shoulder as he passed, and, twining his fingers together, offered his hands. Richard shrugged, placed his foot in the cupped hands, and Cross boosted. Richard caught the narrow strut at the top and swung over. Since he thought he might like to sire children someday, he cautiously lowered himself onto the top rail with a leg on either side. He reached down, offering his hand. Cross scrambled up to join him. They dropped down inside. Richard didn't even need to cue the homeless god.

Cross warily circled the maze. "Oh, that is uuuugly."

Richard heard a crunch of gravel beneath a shoe. He whirled, drawing his pistol, panic setting his heart to pounding, his his pulse drumming in his ears. A dark form loomed behind the iron bars of the fence.

CHAPTER TWENTY-THREE
I Didn't Want It To Be True

"Whoa, whoa, watch where you point that thing," Weber yelped.

"Damon," breathed Richard. He sounded relieved. Damon also realized that for the first time Richard had called him by his first name. Weber pulled himself back to the moment when Richard asked, "Why are you here?"

"I went by your place. Didn't find you home. Thought you might come back here because you can't seem to let anything go. You know you're breaking and entering."

Cross came up and stood by Richard's shoulder. "If this is the new guy you brought in, I don't think much of your choice," he said.

"Yeah, and who the fuck are you?" Weber asked.

"He's Cross," said Richard quickly, before the Old One could launch into his Jesus lecture. "He sees magic."

"And there is a great big steaming pile of it right there," Cross said, pointing at the maze.

"I'm coming in," Weber said.

A few minutes later they all stood staring at the maze.

"It's a bad tear," Cross said. "But it's inside. They've got a glamour on this thing to hide it, but I can see it glowing through the joints. That was actually cleverer than we usually manage. Usually when we see an opening, we just go balls to the wall. The mind behind this one is subtle." He looked down at Richard. "So, hop to it."

"Hop to what?" asked Weber.

"Only one of us can close it, bucko, and you ain't him."

"Cross, I think the little boy went through. Into that other dimension. I've got to try and find him," Richard said.

"No, you get in there and you close it. The kid is toast."

"We don't know that. They feed on pain and fear and despair. Wouldn't they want to keep him alive?"

"It's been a long damn time on this side, and you don't know how long on the other."

Weber held up a hand. "Time out."

Cross threw him an impatient glance. "This is an opening into another universe. Time is a dimension. Natural law operates differently in different universes." He bent a dark gaze back on Richard. Weber realized that the man's pupils had vanished. The eyes were like fragments of obsidian. Weber couldn't control his shudder. "And many of the folded dimensions are inimical to your little fleshy life."

Richard shrugged out of his suit coat. "Still, I've got to try. I'll only be a step into their world. I can step back."

"I'll go with him," Weber said. He unbuckled his belt and pulled it off. "Give me yours," he ordered Richard. He hooked them together. "We'll loop it around your waist. I'll keep the other end."

"Okay. Good." Richard slipped off his shoulder rig.

"You don't want to keep your piece?" Weber asked.

"I don't want to get snagged on anything, and if this is something … unnatural, I don't think a gun is going to help."

Weber shrugged, then nodded and took off his coat and unclipped his holster from his belt.

"How come a bunch more kids didn't disappear?" Weber asked as Richard pulled the hilt out of its holster.

"It takes a lot of power to keep one of these dimensional tears open. They come and go," Cross answered.

"So, what if it's not there now?" Weber pressed.

"Richard will find it," Cross replied.

"How?" Richard drew the sword. Weber pressed a hand against his chest as the sound battered at him. "Jesus. I'm never going to get used to that," he gasped.

"Because of *that*." Cross thrust a finger at the sword.

Weber shifted from foot to foot as he watched Richard's profile as the younger man studied the maze. He suddenly did not want Richard to go into that thing. "Maybe if he just cuts it open from out here …" he suggested.

"The kid's not gonna fall out like candy out of a piñata," grunted Cross.

"I could hope," Weber muttered.

"Yeah, fuck that. Hope is just as god damn useless as prayer," Cross said.

"Let's do this," Richard ordered.

SQUARING HIS SHOULDERS, he took a breath and climbed into the maze. He could hear Weber scrambling up behind him. There were little blue plastic wedges to serve as handholds and footrests snaking up and away. Despite his slenderness, Richard had broad shoulders from the years of gymnastics.

He hoped he would fit, and he wondered if there was any chance of Weber making it deeper into the maze. But as they climbed the tube expanded. *Like a throat widening to accommodate a big bite. Puppies and pythons,* Richard thought, and shuddered.

They continued up. Richard blinked and realized the glittering spots swirling before his eyes were caused by the aura off the sword. "I think we're getting close," he whispered.

He cleared the tube and was in the central core of the maze. Against one wall was what had looked like the gray plastic diving bell from outside. From this side it pulsed and shivered. Searing cold like a rhythmic exhalation swept across them. Weber stared at it and Richard watched the older man's Adam's apple work as he swallowed and swallowed.

"Oh, shit," he croaked.

"Can you handle this?" Richard asked.

Weber gave an abrupt nod. "Let's get you tethered." He looped the belt around Richard's waist. It took Weber several tries as the dreadful cold stiffened the older man's fingers. Richard understood, it was becoming hard to feel the curves and coils of the hilt. Richard brought his hands up to his mouth and breathed hard across the fingers. Weber grabbed his hands and almost bumped into the blade. Richard yanked it aside.

"Careful."

"It's okay, I'm beginning to think this 'no magic' thing is the right choice and I should have you bop me with that thing."

"Yes, probably, but the effects seem to be pretty extreme on a body," Richard replied, remembering Delay's agony. "And right now, I *need* you."

"Fair enough. So, set that thing aside, and give me your hands," Weber said. He took Richard's hands between his and briskly chafed them. His skin was rough. It was an endemic problem in New Mexico, and almost nothing had ever felt quite so comforting.

Richard pulled his hands away. "Thanks. Let's do it." Picking up the hilt, he managed to draw he blade again.

Holding the sword diagonally across his body, the blade resting lightly in the palm of his right hand, he drew in a long breath, held it, and stepped through the rip in reality. The belt tugged against his belly but held.

Instantly his eyes flowed water from the bite of bitter cold. He could feel the moisture freezing on his cheeks. The glittering aura around the sword vanished, perhaps because there was no longer magic to react against. On this side of the barrier, it wasn't magic, this was reality. The sword was a sliver of silver and ebony in the gloom.

The light was strange. He could make out shapes but no details. The impression was as if mountains of stone had turned to regard him; a soft and shivering little flesh creature. Only one thing stood out. A flash of white from a Cowboys sweatshirt. Miguel's round fat belly strained against the ice-coated fabric. He seemed prematurely gray from the frost icing his hair. His eyes were open and staring where he lay on the ice-coated rocks.

I'm going to join him, Richard realized when his legs buckled under the implacable hatred of the watchers and the bitter cold. He collapsed onto his knees. Only the belt kept him from falling full length. The yank of the belt forced the breath out of him. He couldn't help gulping in a lungful of air. It was so cold it hurt.

Then Weber was there, wrapping his arms around Richard's chest and pulling him to his feet. Weber's eyes scanned the unseen sky and occasionally he flinched, hunching toward the ground. Richard understood. The sky was falling. Soon the monstrous forms would crush them. They were coming. Soon they would reach them.

Richard staggered forward and twisted his free hand in the back of the sweatshirt. His shoulder joint popped from the strain, but he heaved the child up and clasped him against his chest. He turned back to Weber and the opening. One foot, another, but the intense cold coupled with the weight of the child and his growing fear sapped his strength. He fell again and was suddenly being dragged across the icy rocks by the belt.

Weber, jaw set with effort, was reeling them in hand over hand. Richard hugged Miguel tighter. Weber heaved Richard up, holding both Richard and Miguel in a bear hug. He dug in his back foot and threw himself backward through the opening. There was a high-pitched keening, a cry of rage.

"Jesus God, Jesus God," Weber mumbled as they were lying were lying on the floor of the maze. Richard felt the older man's breath puffing against his ear. It smelled of cigarettes and beer and was wonderful. But there was no time. A gray bulge, trailing tendrils of icy mist as it reacted with the warmer air of Earth, loomed over them. It licked toward them like a questing tongue.

Richard swung the sword up. Weber grunted when Richard's heel dug into his thigh as Richard pushed himself upright. The point of the sword sank deep into the center of the bubble. It shrank back, undulating like a jellyfish. He pursued and swept the sword in an arc on the edge of the bubble. *Close!*

Then it was just plastic again, but perhaps because of the extremes to which it had been subjected, or perhaps because of the touch of the sword, it blew out, raining shards across the playground. A pair of hands grabbed the edge of the platform and Cross's face came into view as he chinned himself up.

"Well, I'll be dipped in shit and fried for a hush puppy, you did it," said the homeless god. Richard glanced back. Weber was bent over the boy, administering CPR.

"I don't know. Have we?" he asked faintly as he shivered.

Weber gave him a wan grin and a thumbs-up.

✧   ✧   ✧

THE AMBULANCE HAD pulled away, rushing the child to the hospital. Weber was worried the little boy would not make a full recovery, but one of the EMTs had been more hopeful, talking about something called *infant drowning syndrome* where children immersed in extremely cold water had survived without any harm, maybe the little boy who had been out in the December cold for so many hours would be lucky.

Honestly, it had mostly been a buzz in Damon's ears as he tried to process what he had witnessed and experienced.

The captain's big SUV pulled up and Ortiz climbed out. As he crossed to them, his gaze flicked across the damaged maze.

"Well?" the captain demanded.

Damon glanced down at Richard, whose arms were wrapped tightly about his body. Shudders shook his slender frame, but whether from cold or nerves Damon wasn't sure. *Probably both.* He had a sudden urge to drop an arm over Oort's shoulder and pull him close to his side. He thrust it aside—now was the time for him to bring the bullshit since it was clear Richard wasn't able to.

He heard himself as if from a distance—*angry locals busted up the maze ... Oort got a tip ... called ... we walked a search pattern ...*

" ... found the kid ten blocks away." Ortiz continued to stare at him. Weber cleared his throat. "Sooo, want us to—"

"Good work, both of you," Ortiz said abruptly. Weber knew the political calculation the captain had made; he knew it was bullshit but the outcome was good and the APD looked great, so Ortiz wasn't going to look too closely ... or at all. "I've got Child Protective Services meeting him at the hospital," Ortiz said.

That pulled Richard out of his blue study; he looked at Ortiz in dismay. "Why, sir? He's got a mother."

"Yeah, and she left him alone and then lied to the police about it. They'll keep an eye on her. If she knows they're watching, she'll be more careful going forward. She'll know if she screws up again, she loses the kid," Ortiz said.

Weber shot him a warning look and Richard folded his lips together.

Ortiz pulled out a stick of gum, unwrapped it, and stuffed it into his mouth. The overly sweet smell of Juicy Fruit floated in the air. The wrapper fell to the sidewalk. "Look, you two, go home, sleep in. Come in at noon. You can write your report then."

Eventually they were alone except for the occasionally passing car on Isleta. Weber frowned down at the cracked and stained sidewalk and the wadded-up piece of foil.

"How awful. She did everything right, but she'll be branded unfit." Richard's voice was hoarse with fatigue.

"She got her son back. It's not perfect, but it's probably better than any of us had any right to hope for."

Richard put a hand on Weber's shoulder. "Thank you."

He felt himself blush. "I was just brawn."

"Brave brawn, and quick-thinking brawn. You didn't have to come through that tear. But I'm so glad you did; I could never have gotten him out without you."

"I didn't want it to be true," Weber confessed.

"Neither did I," Richard replied softly.

CHAPTER TWENTY-FOUR

Is Sex Ever Simple?

R HIANA HAD FINISHED her last final. As she walked across the campus toward the bus stop that would take her up to student parking, she watched the flow of students. It was finals week but also Christmas break was coming, so the expressions ranged from tension and depression, to manic joy. There were couples seated on the edge of the now-dry fountain holding hands and gazing into each other's eyes. She felt a stab of loneliness. Boys had always wanted her for her looks. But then they hadn't wanted her when they found out how smart she was. She had a visceral memory of the boy in her calculus class.

They'd flirted, started what she thought would be a friendly competition, taken a bet about who would get the better grade on the first test. When she'd gotten back her test, she had turned around in her chair in the lecture hall to flaunt her A plus to find him staring at a D. He had called her a fucking cunt and stormed out.

Her family had called to tell her that if she wanted to come home over Christmas break, they couldn't really afford to buy her a plane ticket since they were helping Scott buy his food truck. She could probably ask Kenntnis for the money, but he was still out of town. If he didn't get back in time, she was looking at spending Christmas rattling around the penthouse with only him and Cross for company, and Cross treated her like shit. As for Richard, it had been days and days since she'd seen him. She'd read in the paper about the shooting, about finding the lost child. She had just wanted to call and congratulate him, but Jeannette wouldn't give her Richard's cell phone number without asking him first, and the receptionist either hadn't asked or he'd refused to allow Rhiana to have it.

The only person who seemed to give a shit about her was … *not a person*. No, she couldn't go there. She was a person and she needed somebody to … she just needed somebody.

✧　✧　✧

FOG SHROUDED THE winding canyon road up to the Taos ski basin, floated in ghost tendrils around the white trunks of the bare aspens, and swathed the blue-green needles of the towering ponderosa pines. Along the side of the road a mountain stream frothed and bubbled between its icy edges. Angela drove the snow-packed road with nonchalant ease.

They had chatted on the long drive up from Albuquerque, and Angela had informed him with ghoulish glee that the Taos ski resort was where the US Olympic ski team had once trained before climate change made the snow fall inconsistent. Point being there were a number of black diamond runs on the mountain.

Now, three hours later, they were approaching their destination. Richard gazed silently out the front window, wondering if they were going to drive back tonight or if Angela would insist on staying in Taos. And if they stayed, they would have to discuss sleeping arrangements. He dreaded that conversation. *Maybe she'd be okay with driving home,* he thought.

Richard sensed her gaze and looked over. Her eyes played slowly and languidly across his face and came to rest on his crotch and thighs encased in the skintight ski pants, and he knew, with a sinking heart, that a return to Albuquerque was probably not likely. Blushing, he waved toward the road.

"It's pretty windy. Maybe it would be better if you watched the road?"

"Am I scaring you?" she challenged, and he knew she wasn't talking about her driving.

"Should I be worried?"

"Absolutely."

Yes, they were going to have *the conversation.* Unless he could forestall it. And maybe he didn't want to. Desire had reentered his life. In the past month he had found himself looking and noticing and reacting, without the touch of that icy fear that had gripped him for the past few years. He stole a glance at her profile. The short upper lip and the uptilted nose and the riot of dark curls. She wasn't a raving beauty like Rhiana, but it wasn't about physical looks. She was whip smart, warm, and funny and direct and honest. She was his friend. *You could do far worse for your first attempt at intimacy again,* he reminded himself.

Then there was his own self-confidence. Acceptance within the APD had provided a sense of deep satisfaction. He was experiencing admiration, respect, and friendship, and he liked it—a lot.

Another curve and a steep climb and they broke through the fog bank. Sunlight glittered on the new snow. The needles of the pines were frosted white. Amazing views of distant snowcapped peaks distracted him from his self-congratulatory musings.

He smiled at her. "I'm glad you suggested this."

"So am I. It gives me a chance to see you in ski pants." She then laughed at his expression. "It's so much fun to make you blush."

"You're a terrible woman," Richard said with a smile, and Angela laughed.

They pulled into the parking lot. Above them, nestled in the arms of the mountains, was a cluster of buildings. A couple of lodges, a beautiful condo and spa facility under construction, shops, and restaurants, and above them all loomed the sheer white face of the mountain.

"Holy hell," Richard said.

Angela grinned. "Oh, that's one of the easier runs."

Two lifts were in view, the chairs trembling and swaying as they made their way up the mountain. There were a few hardy souls, dark silhouettes against the white mountain, riding the lift up to the runs, but it was a weekday, and the crowds were thin.

They plowed through the snow to the back doors of the SUV, the snow squeaking and crunching beneath their feet. Richard pulled out their skis and boots and before long the shuttle came by, an open trailer pulled behind a snow cat, and they were driven up to the base of the lift. Soon they were booted and waiting for the chair to grind and whine toward them. It caught him behind the knees and with a swoop and a sway they were on their way up the mountain.

Angela shifted on the narrow seat to face him. "Richard, we have to talk." She drew in a quick, deep breath. "Okay, here goes. I like you. I want to spend time with you, really get to know you."

"Aren't we doing that?" he asked, nervousness fluttering in his stomach.

"Oh, hell, there's no graceful way to say this so I'm just going to say it. I want to have sex with you." Lust and panic were equally balanced, and he felt like he couldn't breathe. When he didn't respond she gave him a wry look and added, "You know, fuck?" He couldn't find his voice. When he still didn't speak, she rolled her eyes and looked away. "Oh fuck, I really fucked this up. I'm sorry. Forget I ever said—"

He grabbed her flapping hand. "No, no, this is on *me*. I just … I can't …"

"It's my age, right? I'm too old for you. Or there's somebody else?"

"No, no, no, *you're* not the problem, and there isn't anybody else. I'm the problem." He hesitated and allowed his gaze gaze to drift across her trim body, felt again that lick of arousal. "Or I have been," he concluded slowly.

"Does that mean the problem has been resolved?" she asked.

"Maybe. I don't know."

"You want to test out the theory?"

He hesitated for a moment, then pulled off his glove and laid his hand against the side of her face. Her skin was soft and warm beneath his palm. It seemed that desire and embarrassment had trumped wind chill. He leaned in and pressed his lips on hers. It began chastely, but years of abstinence had taken its toll. Arousal shot straight down into his cock. Richard couldn't control it, a sound somewhere between a whimper and a groan escaped. Cupping her face between his hands, he kissed her long and deeply. She responded fiercely.

And then she closed her teeth on his lower lip.

Blackness danced before his eyes and his nostrils were filled with the phantom smell of sweat and sperm, all overlaid with the musty smell of Kouros aftershave. The ghostly taste of blood from his brutally bitten lip filled his mouth. Fear swept away passion. Richard jerked back, his eyes snapped open, and reality returned. Only the fact that the ground was thirty feet below kept him in the chairlift.

"Are you all right?"

His mind churned for some explanation, some plausible lie. "I … I was afraid we were getting close to the top."

"Yeah, I guess we are." With her tumbled curls and crooked little grin, she looked like a particularly endearing and naughty elf. "So, hold that erection 'til later!" He gave her a wan smile in answer.

She grabbed her poles, and they both made it off the chairlift without mishap. Angela grabbed his face and planted a hard kiss on him. She skied off, throwing over her shoulder, "See you at the bottom."

Richard watched her small form leaning into each turn as she flew down the mountain. Richard dug in his poles and pushed off in a spray of new powder. So much for confidence. He'd opened this particular Pandora's box, and he couldn't back out now. If he tried and failed, she would never believe it had nothing to do with her. He couldn't hurt her that way.

But you were wrong*! You can't do this!*

He tucked his poles, bent low over his skis, and raced down the mountain, trying to outrun the memories ... and the fear.

✧　✧　✧

RHIANA SELECTED THE bathroom at the Frontier Restaurant across the street from the university. It was a dive, open twenty-four hours a day, and she figured no one would notice or give a shit about a darkened mirror. The cloying smell of icing and cinnamon followed her to the back of the restaurant. The Frontier was famous for their plate-sized cinnamon rolls oozing butter.

Richard had gone skiing with Angela.

Nobody stopped to think that maybe she would have have liked to go along. Okay, so maybe she didn't know how to ski, but it would have been nice to be included. She had a moment of fantasizing about Richard teaching her to ski. Maybe wrapping his arms around her to help her up after she'd fallen. Or maybe she would have been great at it, and he'd be so impressed. But instead, she'd been ignored, forgotten yet again.

Franz was nice enough, but it wasn't like they talked about anything other than bland pleasantries. Cross either grunted at her or insulted her, and nobody would tell her where Kenntnis had gone or what he was doing.

She closed the door against the roar of conversation and carefully locked it. Was she really going to do this? She pictured Richard and Angela and the decision was made. She dropped the flow of numbers out of her thoughts.

It was as if he'd been waiting for her. The colors boiled and coalesced in the mirror, and he was there gazing fondly out at her.

"I'll have dinner with you," she said before he could speak, and she left, unwilling to take part in any planning. That would make it actual betrayal. This was just … reconnaissance. Or so she could tell herself.

✧   ✧   ✧

THEY HAD MADE run after run and Angela was beginning to think that *run* was in fact the operative word. On their frequent rides back up the mountain there had not been a repeat of the kiss, and Richard seemed to be in a brown study. Clearly, she had done something wrong.

After their final run and as they were loading the skies and boots back into her SUV, she braced him.

"Are we staying the night up here? More to the point, are we staying up here *together*?"

He shook his head, but more in confusion than as a negative. "I don't know. I used to be … a lot better at this."

They were standing so close that the white ribbons of their breaths were mingling.

"If it helps, I have no romantic illusions here. I find you attractive. I'd like to have sex. But it would be just that, sex. No expectations, no commitments."

He gave her a wan smile. "Is sex ever that simple?"

"Look, with the snow and the dark it will be at least three hours before we could get back to Albuquerque. Why don't we find a place that offers both food and beds. Eat some dinner and then decide about the bed part?"

"That sounds good."

They climbed into the car and made their way out of the box canyon. Some eight miles from the ski valley they came upon the Adobe and Stars and, amazingly, they had a vacancy. The building formed a shallow arc, crowned with snow and electric luminarias. Smoke spiraled up from chimneys, blurring the stars and the sharp points of the crescent moon. The rich and spicy smell of burning piñon perfumed the frigid night air. Angela had stayed there with a former boyfriend and knew both the quality of the food and the amenities in the rooms. She pulled into the parking lot.

"You'll like this place," she said as they walked to the front door. The owner, Sally Rogers, a comfortably plump older woman with a muted Texan accent, remembered Angela and welcomed her back. Angela noticed how the woman's eyes slid across Richard's face and checked out the blue-and-white Nordic sweater and the tight ski pants that hugged his narrow hips and strong legs.

"What's on the menu tonight?" Angela asked.

"Venison and quail in a wine sauce, corn cakes, and wilted kale."

Angela turned to Richard. "Sound good?"

"Sounds fantastic."

"And would you hold that room for us? We're going to decide after dinner if we … stay."

Sally gave her a knowing smile. "I doubt we're going to have anybody else arrive this late."

✦　✦　✦

THE GARMENT BAG hit the floor with a dull thud. The living room was dark and chill. Kenntnis flicked on a torchiere lamp and kicked up the heat. The penthouse held that silence in which no living thing breathes.

"Damn the girl. Where has she gotten to?"

He quickly unpacked his suits while waiting for Cross to come upstairs. It didn't happen and Kenntnis took the elevator to the ground floor and out the back door. There was the sweet rotten smell of garbage in the dumpster, and the faint hiss of a propane lantern shedding its muted light through the blanket hung over the opening in the cardboard shipping crate.

Bending almost double, Kenntnis swept aside the blanket and entered the crate. What he saw shocked him. Cross lay huddled on an old mattress, blankets clutched tightly around him. His skin was stretched so tightly across his bones that his head seemed skeletal, as if the human envelope that contained the true creature was being burned away.

Kenntnis squatted down next to the creature and laid a hand over his wrist. Cross pulled back his lips in a grotesque caricature of a smile. His gums were bleeding, staining his teeth.

"We pissed 'em off bad last night. Richard and the new guy." He coughed, spraying bloodstained spittle. "He's okay. Closed a gate. Took back a snack."

"You've got to resist," Kenntnis said.

"I'm trying, but it's beatin' me down—the breaking and the hunting, the fighting and the finding my way home."

"Do you think the girl can ward you?" Kenntnis asked.

"I doubt it, and that girl wouldn't do shit to help me."

"You haven't given her much reason to." The homeless god coughed wetly. Kenntnis held a bottle of water to the gray, emaciated lips. "Where is she?"

"Fuck if I know."

"Could you find her?" Kenntnis asked.

"If my brains were made of dynamite, I couldn't pop my eardrums right now."

Kenntnis gnawed at his lower lip. Something told him this was significant, but he didn't have enough of the pieces for it to make a picture.

He stood. "I'll bring you something to eat."

CHAPTER TWENTY-FIVE
GOT A REAL MESS NOW

THREE SOFT-FOOTED WAITERS, two women and a man, orbited their table. Rhiana choked back an urge to giggle. Maybe this was the standard of service at the Artichoke Cafe, but she had a feeling some of it had to do with her and her companion's looks. He was dressed in a black turtleneck sweater that heightened the effect of his high cheekbones and almost slanted green eyes. A lock of blue-black hair lay across his forehead. He tossed it back with a hand, and the waitress's hand shook as she poured water into Rhiana's glass.

"So, you said you'd tell me why I was ..." She hesitated, embarrassed to use the word.

"Special?" he provided. "I will, but let's not blunt the pleasure of a good appetite with business. May I order for you?" the man asked.

"I ... I'm a vegetarian."

"What a shame. I was going to order foie gras and oysters Rockefeller."

An internal struggle began. She had read about food like this in books and seen it in movies. But there was principle. He seemed to sense her dilemma. His hand closed around hers.

"I won't try to tempt you out of your beliefs but consider. You are a superior being. The bounties of this world are yours to enjoy. Or at least to try once before you reject them. Then it truly is a sacrifice, and therefore worthier."

And so it began. They shared a split of champagne with their appetizers. It was nothing like the stuff her dad sometimes brought home for New Year's. The bubbles tickled the back of her nose and the flavors exploded across her tongue.

Once she got used to the texture, the oysters prepared with spinach were delicious and the foie gras beyond description. She ate well at Kenntnis's but she had never experienced food like this. She had a salad with honey-toasted pecans and crumbled cheese while he sipped at lobster bisque. For her main course, he selected sweet and succulent king crab. There were different wines with each course. They concluded with a chocolate mousse, brandy, and coffee.

No course was rushed, providing them with plenty of opportunity to talk. He said little, using his words like keys to unlock more information from her, and she responded. Books, movies, her dreams of travel, her family, her isolation, her studies, her feelings for Richard; it all came out. Finally, she wound down, replete and oddly exhausted; she leaned back in her chair, feeling as if her skin was too small to contain both her emotions and the masses of food and liquor she'd consumed. Sensation prickled across her skin. Heat blossomed at the base of her spine. Somehow, she was feeding her power and she wasn't even trying.

She lifted her eyes and met the man's blazing green gaze.

His look seemed to pierce through to her heart. He smiled, displaying sharp narrow teeth, and Rhiana knew he sensed the power rising within her. With an autocratic gesture he dismissed the hovering waiters. They were the last people in the restaurant.

"This is what you deserve and what you will receive if you join with me … us. I hope you will. I don't wish to battle you."

"And why is that? Are you afraid you'll lose?" It was pure bravado. She could sense the magic pulsing off him like a subsonic drone.

"I would hate to hurt you. You are my daughter."

The brandy caught in the back of her throat and her gasp of shock carried the hot fumes into her lungs. Coughing, she leaned over the table. Now the pictures, the care that they represented, made sense. The man came around the table and patted her on the back, and *something* merged like twining tentacles piercing her mind and soul.

And it didn't flow in only one direction. She ate his memories and recognized the kinship. Eventually the waves of pure emotion settled into images. The human woman giving herself in lust and ending in terror. Her mother's descent into drugs, drink, and degradation, all of this feeding the embryo—*her*—inside. She tasted the wild flare of suffering and death that accompanied her birth. Then the human flesh had dulled and blunted the raw power bequeathed to her by her father.

Minutes or hours passed in that communion. When Rhiana finally returned to her body and surroundings, she saw the wait staff and the maître d' collapsed on the floor.

"Are they …?" she began.

"Merely unconscious. We needed them to forge the bond," Madoc replied—for she had consumed his name among many other bits of knowledge and experience.

Some questions still remained, and she asked one. "If I'm your child, why did they … you try to kill me?"

"The golems would not have harmed you. They accomplished their purpose, which was to put you into Kenntnis's household."

"Why?"

He ignored her and instead asked, "Do you want your birthright? I rule a vast kingdom both in this world and in others. You have only to reach out and take it."

"And what do I have to do in return?"

Madoc smiled fondly at her. "You're no fool. Yes, you are my child." He paused to dab delicately at his mouth with his napkin. "But before we trust all our plans to you, we must be a little more certain where your loyalties lie."

He stood and smiled down at her. "Now open a way for me. I need to go home."

"I'm not sure I can. I'm not sure how I did it before."

"Think of what you know of physics and combine it with your magic."

Rhiana considered all that she knew, particles versus waves, uncertainty principles, strong and weak forces, string theory. As her mind closed on the competing theories, the walls of the restaurant seemed to waver, shift, and flow. She pulled out a penny and balanced it on the tip of her index finger.

"I need power."

Madoc made an expansive gesture with his arm, indicating the restaurant and its prone employees. "Feed, by all means."

And she did, watching the electrical fields surrounding their bodies dim and fade as she sucked it in, hot and vibrant. The plump waitress laying by the kitchen door gave a gasp and her breath began coming in wheezing pants. The pain of her laboring lungs and shuddering heart smashed into Rhiana, and for a wild instant she did feel as if she had burst through the confines of her body and was stretching out, massive and powerful, across the night sky.

She was aware of Madoc's mind linked to hers, guiding her through the complex designs of competing universes. She knew from his feeling of satisfaction when she had reached the correct thread.

A rent appeared in the back wall. She had only a confused image of too-bright colors, some of which she couldn't identify, and a blast of icy air, and he was gone.

Stepping over the unconscious staff, she left the restaurant.

✧　✧　✧

ANGELA SHOVED THE key into the lock on the bright blue door and they stepped into the room. A queen-size bed dominated the space. In a corner there was a kiva fireplace with logs already laid in the hearth. Eastern-facing windows framed a section of the mountains. Through a door she could see a two-person Jacuzzi and a spectacular western view of mesas.

Dinner had been lovely, but she realized he had once again enticed her into doing most of the talking. The enigma that was Richard Oort remained. She had had a margarita to start and a glass of wine with dinner. He had politely but firmly declined and drank only water with dinner.

There was a chill in the room, and she saw a brief shiver wash through him. Moving to the fireplace, she shook out a long match and snapped it across the striking service. When the match flame reached the fat wood it ignited with a burst of green and orange. Tongues of flame licked eagerly up the length of the tented logs. Within moments the dried piñon was snapping and crackling, filling the room with its perfume. She heard Richard draw in a long, shuddering breath, and the overhead light went out leaving only the light from the fire for illumination. That seemed an encouraging sign, so she stood and crossed to him.

Shadows ballooned and swayed across the whitewashed plaster walls. He looked down at her and she drank in the play of firelight across the high cheekbones, the line of his jaw, and the aquiline nose.

Reaching up, she ran her fingers through his hair. It was soft and fine. She pulled off her sweater and silk undershirt and turned around, offering him the bra clasp. After a few seconds she felt his fingers against her back. They were icy cold. The clasp sprung free, and she shrugged out of her bra. She pirouetted to face him, looking forward to his reaction. Angela knew she fell into the cute rather than beautiful category, but she also knew that her tits were dynamite and their effect on men electrifying.

Richard surveyed her body, but then his eyes drifted

away to stare at the far wall. There was a sheen of sweat on his forehead. He wet his lips with the tip of his tongue and said, "I haven't done this … well, for a while … a long while." He brought his focus back to her and forced a smile. "Just bear with me, okay?"

"Okay. And by the way I'm half naked and freezing, so could we …" She glanced toward the bed.

His teeth caught at his lower lip. Then with a jerky nod, like an inexpertly controlled puppet, he bent and began to unlace his boots. Angela quickly stripped off the rest of her clothes. The floor felt like it had been tiled with ice cubes rather than Saltillo. She hustled over to the bed, ripped back the down comforter, and plunged between the sheets. They were colder than shit, too.

Richard yanked off his sweater and silk undershirt. The fading bruise and the healing cuts were barely visible in the faint light from the fire. She admired the dips of his abs, the faint brush of hair that ran down his chest to vanish into the waistband of his ski pants. It was dark gold against his marble-white skin. He breathed out and slipped off his slacks and underwear but held his clothes in front of him.

"*Ahem*, I have seen a few penises in my time," she said, she said, and then added, "and no, they haven't *all* been on dead guys."

The laugh seemed forced, but he carefully folded the ski pants over the arm of a wicker chair. She watched the play of long, flat muscles across his shoulders, and the way his back tapered down to his narrow hips. He straightened and turned to her, and all breath stopped in her chest.

Desire roiled warm and heavy in her belly, but judging

from his lack of an erection he wasn't yet sharing her need.

Why is the First Time *always such a bitch?* she thought. A log snapped loudly as the flames reached the sap. Richard jumped like a runner at the starting blocks, causing his cock to slap against his thigh.

She smiled and lifted the covers suggestively. Richard slid into the bed. With a deep breath he rolled over, arms on either side of her body, and held himself above her. There was the barest glitter of blond stubble along his jawline. He lowered himself slowly and kissed her.

Angela relished the touch of skin against skin, and she sighed against his lips. She opened her lips, inviting him to explore deeper, and there was finally a reaction from his cock. She ran her hands down his back, gripped that muscular ass, and he gave a faint moan. But it still felt like there was something separating them like a layer of ice.

Angela looked up into that beautiful face. Richard's eyes were tightly shut. His lashes were a deep amber, and they brushed his cheeks, but the muscles of his face were so taut that his face seemed more like marble than pliant skin. He clearly wasn't going with the moment, but rather *working* at the moment.

"Here," she whispered. "Let me help."

She rolled him over so she ended sitting on his thighs. Her hands swept down his torso, feeling the ribs and the bands of muscle in his belly. She bent, gently took his cock in her mouth, and went to work. A groan broke from between his lips when she stiffened her tongue and worked the frenulum. She drew her nail down his sternum and teased his navel, sending his hips arching beneath her.

She chuckled and lifted her head from his now very stiff and erect member. Richard reached up to cup her breasts, but she caught him by the wrists and forced his arms back toward the wrought iron headboard and held him down.

A look of utter terror crossed his face, and he began to thrash wildly. Bucked to the side of the bed, Angela went sliding off onto the floor. She stared in shock as he hunched over, forehead pressed tightly to his drawn-up knees, hands clasped over his head, body shaking, breaths coming sharp and shallow.

She could barely hear his whispered litany of, "Sorry. I'm so sorry. So sorry."

"Breathe," she ordered. "I'll be right back."

Angela ran into the bathroom and began to fill the tub with hot water. She then filled a glass with water and ran back, her bare feet slapping on the tile.

"Here." She held out the glass. He accepted it and took a sip. "May I touch you?" she asked in her best (hopefully) calming Doctor Voice. He nodded. She gave his back a gentle rub, then urged him to his feet, guided him into the bathroom and into the tub. She snatched down a washcloth, the thick Egyptian cotton soft against her fingers. Carefully, she dipped it in the steaming water and squeezed it across his shoulders. His muscles were banded iron.

For a long time, she sluiced water across his neck and back, and mentally berated herself. Not nervousness, flat-out terror, and she had missed it. Missed every cue. Missed it on the lift. Missed it. Missed it. Missed it. *Because you were so focused on getting past that first coitus so you could get down to the lovemaking that can only happen when a lover's abilities are known. Well, congratulations, you've got a real mess on your hands now.*

Eventually the shivers subsided, and his breathing slowed. The water was cooling and her fingers puckering and wrinkling. Richard hadn't looked at her once, but now he said, "I didn't think ... I thought I could ... It's not you. It's me." His voice broke. "I'm so sorry."

Knees screaming in protest, Angela levered herself to her feet, using the cold porcelain side of the tub for balance. She pulled down a huge, fluffy bath sheet and held it out to him. He climbed out, sluicing water, and she wrapped the towel around him.

"Look, before you try this again you've got to set the ground rules, so your partner doesn't hit ... well, whatever button I hit." Placing her hands on his shoulders she guided him back toward the bed. He froze in place.

"No. I'll ... I'll sit in the chair." The leather on the woven Spanish basket chair creaked under his weight. Angela pulled the down comforter off the bed and wrapped him in it.

She began throwing on her clothes. "I'm going to go downstairs and get you a brandy—"

"No, please don't. Alcohol ... alcohol always gets me ... got me ... into trouble."

"Buddy, you are already in trouble." And she cursed her smart mouth because it had the same effect as if she'd hit him. "Not with *me*. I meant ... oh, hell."

He flung himself out of the chair and headed for his clothes. "Look, I'll take a taxi or the bus back to Albuquerque."

"No, you will not. Richard, I'm a doctor. That means I

did a rotation in psych. It's clear you've endured some kind of trauma. You need to talk about it."

The pale head gave a violent shake of negation. "No. It will destroy me."

"I'd say it's doing that right now."

"I've been fine as long as I didn't—" He broke off abruptly. "Sorry, sorry, that makes it sound like I blame you. This is all on me."

It was hard, but she said it anyway. "Richard, as of this moment, I'm assuming that we will never make love. So, we can put all that aside. But I am still, and will always be, your friend. You can talk to me. I also think having this bed sitting here staring at us doesn't make this the best venue. So, let's get dressed and get the hell out of here."

BUT HE NEVER would talk. She ended up dropping him off around 1:00 AM at his apartment. They had exchanged not a word on the drive back from Taos. As she drove down Montgomery headed for Rio Grande and her condo, she wondered if she should tell Weber or Kenntnis. But that seemed like a betrayal. And, honestly, she was embarrassed. What would they think of her behavior, going out of her way to seduce this younger man?

Still, she had unleashed a torrent of memory and trauma, and it was her experience that people didn't easily rebury those kinds of memories. In this strange twilight world of gods and monsters, it was Richard who had to hold them at bay, and she was pretty damn sure it was going to take all his strength and concentration.

And she had just blown a hole in both of those.

CHAPTER TWENTY-SIX
A Fearful Torment Past

RICHARD OVERSLEPT, WAKING near noon, and rolled out of bed with a groan. Some of it was sore muscles from skiing after five years away from the sport, but much of it was due to the vivid and terrifying nightmares that had disturbed his rest. The figure on the cross kept coiling down, but it wore a different face, a face Richard had spent years trying to forget. In the dreams he kept trying to talk to Angela, but she kept turning her back on him. At one point in the confused and tumbled images and sounds, his father walked through. Richard had tried to follow him, to catch him and talk with him, but Robert Oort always stayed just out of reach.

He forced himself out of the apartment and went to the club for a swim. The sunlight outside the wide bay windows at the end of the pool was deceptively bright, and the sky a brilliant turquoise blue. At the end of the hour his muscles didn't hurt quite so badly, but depression still dragged at his mind and body.

The message light on the phone was blinking. Tossing his keys on the small bar, Richard called the voicemail center. While he listened to the first two messages—Rhiana and Weber—he stared into the refrigerator, but the thought of food was nauseating.

He nudged the door shut with his hip and listened while the impassive and impersonal voice on the service said, "Message three received yesterday at 7:33 AM."

We were already on the road to Taos, he thought, and the queasiness increased.

But there was no voice—just barely audible breathing, rapid and desperate. "End of message," said the computer voice. "Message four received yesterday at 9:17 AM." Again, the breathing. There were two more messages in the early afternoon. On the final one he could hear a woman crying.

Berating himself for not checking the messages last night, Richard dialed home and felt his gut clench when his father answered.

"Oort residence."

"Papa. What are you doing home?" Cringing at the inadvertent blurt, Richard closed his eyes and leaned his head against the wall.

"I might ask the same of you." Richard could hear the congestion from a cold blurring his father's voice.

"I took a personal day."

"Why?" The judgmental tone, and obvious implication that he was shirking sunk Richard's spirits even lower.

"I was involved in a shooting."

"Oh, dear God. Did you hurt anyone?" Robert Oort asked.

A flare of anger and resentment kindled in his chest. *Why doesn't he ask if I got hurt?* "Actually, I killed someone."

"Dear God," the judge repeated, but this time in a whisper.

"He was trying to kill my partner."

"So, you're in trouble?"

"No, sir. It was a righteous shoot, I just needed… needed a break."

"So, you called to tell us about your cowboy moment?" his father asked lightly, as if making a joke, but Richard knew better.

"No, I called to talk to Mama."

"She's out."

"Papa, is Mama all right? She's called me a couple of times and she seemed … upset."

"She's fine. A little tired. She's on a number of committees at church. This time of year, things get very busy."

The phone shifted in his grip because his palms were slick with sweat. Richard remembered the dossier on his mother and Grenier's threats. "Has … has anything changed at church?"

"What do you mean?"

"Is there anyone new there?"

"Well, of course there is. Our membership is growing. Don't be so foolish," his father snapped.

"I meant like a new minister."

"What is this about?"

What indeed? How could he possibly explain, and more to the point, warn his father? And warn him against what?

"Is there a new minister?"

"I don't understand why you are asking. But no. We do not have a new minister. Reverend Hoffsteader is still here."

Relief made his knees sag. "Okay. Well, tell Mama I called and that I love her."

"When are you coming to visit?"

"Christmas."

"See to it that you do."

"Yes, sir. And Papa, please keep an eye on Mama."

There was a snort that could have been assent, disgust, or goodbye, and his father hung up.

Richard drifted back into the living room and stared out at the small patio. The flat expanse of concrete looked sterile. Only a small hibachi broke the monotony. *I don't really live anywhere, or belong anywhere,* he thought. Then he remembered the admiring faces of his coworkers and he smiled wistfully, wishing he could go back to work.

He was pouring out a glass of milk when the realization hit. *It doesn't need to be a new minister. Anyone would do. A new member of the congregation who showed an interest in her.*

Richard knew his mother was lonely. That had been the hardest part of leaving. Robert and Pamela's disdain over his new career choice and Amelia's disinterest had made it easy, but his mother's brittle cheerfulness, the books she had bought about New Mexico so she would know what it was like where he was going, and how he'd have such a wonderful adventure and come home a real cowboy—he knew it hid a bruised heart.

And suddenly Angela's face was before him. He dropped his face into his hands.

I hurt everyone I care about.

✧　✧　✧

HE TRIED THE piano, but the notes hadn't been sufficient to

stop the constant play and replay of the disastrous events in Taos. Richard kept searching for that one action that would have made it all turn out differently. A total waste of time, but he couldn't help it.

Finally, in desperation, he turned to the vocal repertoire. He chose Schubert. *Litanei auf das Fest Allersellen,* an *andante lied* to commemorate All Souls' Day. The keys depressed softly beneath his fingers and his foot working the pedal was like a second, slower heartbeat. He played the three notes of the introduction, and he began to sing.

The music wove a net of sound, filling the room and resonating in his chest and head with the shiver of overtones. Long breaths took air deep into his lungs. The strength of his diaphragm forced those breaths back out, carrying on them the glowing notes. He sang in German, but his mind provided the translation.

✧   ✧   ✧

Rest in peace, all souls who, a fearful torment past

and sweet dream over, sated with life, scarcely born,

have departed from the world:

Rest in peace, all souls

And those who never smiled at the sun

but under the moon lay awake on thorns

to see God face to face

one day in heaven's pure light:

all who have departed hence,

rest in peace, all souls.

✧　✧　✧

AS HE SANG, he mourned friendship lost and faith destroyed, an aching hunger for one word of pride, one touch of affection from a distant father. The final note died away. He bent forward, resting his forehead on the music stand. A soft knock at the door jerked him up.

He had both the sword hilt and his pistol at the ready, but it wasn't who he'd expected. Kenntnis stood outside, his bulk blotting out the light.

"May I come in?" he asked with great formality once Richard had opened the door.

Richard stepped back, holstering both weapons. "Please." As Kenntnis entered, the piano gave a soft, melodic sigh as if a wind had passed across the strings.

Kenntnis surveyed the living room, his gaze lingering on the grand piano. "So that wasn't a CD. You play and sing extremely well."

"Thank you."

"Mourning for lost innocence?" the big man asked with an eerie omniscience.

"A few days ago, I killed a man. Before that I denied my god. I think I'm entitled." *And I hurt and shamed a woman I care deeply about.* But he didn't say that. For a long moment they regarded each other, then Richard remembered his manners. "Would you like something to drink?"

"I take it the offer doesn't include coffee or liquor?"

"No, sorry. I can offer milk or water. Or I can make hot chocolate," Richard said.

"Chocolate sounds good."

While Richard busied himself in the kitchen, grating the Mexican chocolate and heating the milk, Kenntnis strolled about, studying the books on the shelves.

"*My Fifty Years in Baseball*; *Babe: The Legend Comes to Life*; *Lucky to be a Yankee*; *Five O'clock Lightning*; *Damned Yankees*; *The Mick*; *Field of Dreams*," Kenntnis read aloud, trailing his fingers along the spines of the books. "You like baseball."

"Yes."

"I'm betting the Yankees."

"Yes." Richard knew his responses were not rising to the level of conversation, but he didn't feel much like talking. He carried the chocolate into the living room and handed Kenntnis a mug.

"Some people say they're evil incarnate," Kenntnis said.

"Some people say that about *you*," Richard shot back, and Kenntnis gave his rich, rolling chuckle.

Richard settled into the armchair, giving Kenntnis the entire couch to accommodate his massive body. They sipped chocolate in silence for a few minutes, then Kenntnis said, "I came by yesterday evening."

They had been at the Adobe and Stars, Richard thought.

"I went skiing," is what he said. "I didn't get back until late. I'm sorry. Was it important? Stupid question: with you *everything* is important, right?" Richard forced a smile.

Kenntnis swirled the cup, watching the chocolate form a whirlpool, then sat it down on the glass coffee table. "I went to New York." Richard cocked his head, indicating polite interest. "I met Pat McGowan."

A constriction closed around his throat, cutting off the

air.

Richard coughed and hoped his tone was disinterested as he said, "Oh, and how is he?"

"Hurt that a young man he rescued didn't see fit to tell him about his promotion."

Richard wasn't aware of his hand moving, but he found himself tugging at his cuff to cover the scar on his right wrist. "Well … yes, but I didn't really … earn it."

"From what I hear from the chief you are earning it now, but I'm not here to bolster your ego." Standing, Kenntnis walked to the piano and softly stroked his hand across the keys, pulling out a whisper of sound. "Grenier's people have also been making inquiries."

"Pat wouldn't talk to them."

"He didn't, but others have. One of the EMTs who picked you up out of that alley and took you to the hospital. Our enemies know the nature of your injuries."

Shame roiled corrosively through his gut. Richard bent over, clutching his stomach, fighting down nausea, the ulcer feeling like it was burning through his spine. A hand cupped the nape of his neck, the fingers began to gently massage his taut muscles. Richard jerked away.

KENNTNIS STEPPED BACK quickly, and held up his hands, palms out in a placating gesture. He hated to add to the young man's stress, but the warning had to be delivered. He did wait until Richard's breathing had steadied. "They will try to find the man who hurt you."

"I … I don't think he'll talk to them," Richard said.

"Are you sure? They can be most persuasive. They use both threats and bribes."

"He has both money and status."

"And men like that often think that *much* is never *enough*." Richard didn't respond. Kenntnis sighed. "Who knows what happened to you?"

"No one. Well, Pat, sort of, but he doesn't know the specifics."

"You never told your parents?" He couldn't keep the disbelief and surprise off the words.

"No. Medical confidentiality is a wonderful thing. They just think I was mugged."

"What did you tell the police? You had clearly been raped and tortured." Kenntnis didn't miss the flinch, but Richard's voice was steady when he answered.

"I told them I was attacked on the street. That I never got a look at them."

"And they believed this farrago?"

"No, of course not." Richard glanced down at his wrists. "I had ligature marks, but they didn't push. Why should they? They have a lot of cases, and what was one faggot getting hurt by some rough trade? Probably asked for it, right?" He gave Kenntnis a smile that was more a rictus of pain. "But Pat wouldn't let it go. He came and visited me almost every day while I was in the hospital and tried to get me to tell him what really happened."

"But you didn't?"

"No."

"Have you ever talked to *anyone* about this?" Kenntnis

asked. Richard shook his head. "And this man … he's walking free?" Richard nodded. The vulnerability on the boy's face cut through the layers of callus Kenntnis had built over eons. He knelt in front of Richard, and took his chin in his hand, gently lifting Richard's head up until their eyes met.

"Why are you protecting him?"

The blue eyes widened in shock, and Kenntnis realized no one had ever asked the question.

"Because he was … is … a close friend of my father's." Richard ran a hand through his hair. "And I worked for him. I was stupid. I asked for it."

"Really? You wanted to get raped and beaten? You trusted this man. He was a family friend. How does his crime reflect on you?" Kenntnis asked.

"Because I'm unnatural," Richard whispered. There was no response from Kenntnis, forcing him to elaborate. "I sleep with men as well as women. I craved sex," he burst out, his cheeks flaming with shame and disgust.

"Sex is a good thing, Richard; it's a life force. We serve and defend life. And homosexuality is natural. It's religion that's made it evil."

"*He* was evil," Richard choked out.

"Yes, because he's a sadist. Not because he found you desirable." Kenntnis paused, then asked, "How did you come to work for this man?"

"My father."

"Aaahh." Silence hung between them. Kenntnis made a "go on" gesture.

"I had done one year in Rome, but my father wasn't willing to pay for any more college. He quoted first Corinthians

13:11—"

"Time to put away childish things," Kenntnis said softly.

Richard nodded. "Exactly. So, I came back to the States. I wanted to stay in New York, to be close to the musical scene. I worked at Macy's and gave piano lessons and went to auditions. But I was just drifting, and I was twenty-three years old. Past time I took responsibility and amounted to something."

"I take it that's a quote?"

Richard held up a hand, forestalling any further remark by Kenntnis. "Please don't say anything. He's my father."

"Which doesn't mean you're required to like him." Richard's head jerked up at that, his lips parting in a shocked O of surprise. "You can honor him and respect him, maybe even love him, and still know he's a bastard. But let's stay on this other man. What does he do?"

"He owns a boutique investment company."

Kenntnis shook his head. "Does your father not know you at *all*?"

That drew a small smile and a faint chuckle from the boy. "I know, it was ludicrous. I was Drew's assistant, and he was very good to me even though I showed little aptitude. It didn't take long for me to read the signals."

"Go on," Kenntnis ordered.

"I went to his bed. He was far more experienced than I was, and his tastes were—" He searched for the word. "Eclectic? Exotic? Sometimes he scared me, hurt me, and sometimes it made the pleasure even more intense, but he always apologized, and was always so complimentary and admiring of me afterward. He gave me lovely things. He made me feel good about myself … special." Kenntnis's eyes flicked around the room. "No, I don't have any of them anymore. Well, only one … as a … reminder." Richard paused for a shuddering breath. A thin line of sweat had begun to crawl down his cheek. He brushed it away.

"One night he invited me to dinner with a couple of 'special' clients. Men whose money he was hoping to manage. One was another American. The other Russian, I think, maybe Ukrainian, I don't know for certain. Just that he was one of those Russian gangster billionaires. Deep in Putin's circle of cronies. We ate, but there was a lot of alcohol." Richard raised his eyes to meet Kenntnis's. "I don't drink, not anymore. Partly because of my mother, but also because every time I drank, I'd wake up in somebody's bed, not remembering how I got there … sometimes not even remembering who they were. And then this … happened." He fell silent for a long minute.

Kenntnis gave his shoulder a squeeze. "Go on."

Richard drew in a shuddering breath. "We finished dessert and Drew shoved me into the arms of the Russian, indicated the bedroom. That's when I realized … realized. I balked, pulled back, and got free. Drew caught me, dug his fingers into my arm, hanging onto me. The Russian was *pissed*. Upshot was that the party broke up and Drew didn't make the deal."

Richard began to shake. Kenntnis pulled Richard onto his feet and walked him up and down the length of the room. Back and forth, never stopping.

"How did you get the bone breaks?" Kenntnis pressed.

"Drew was angry, really angry. He slapped me, ripped

open my shirt. I punched him." Richard looked down at his left hand and flexed it a few times.

"I take it you never learned to box," Kenntnis said in a matter-of-fact tone.

Richard shook his head. "Not until the academy. I'm still not very good at hand-to-hand." He fell silent.

"That's the hand. What about the rest?"

"That really set Drew off. He slugged me, hard. I went down. He started kicking me, dragged me into the bedroom …"

"I know from the EMT that your wrists and ankles were raw and torn. Was it rope or metal? How did he bind you?" Kenntnis's tone was clinical and matter of fact.

"C-c-cord." The sweat rolling off his brow stung his eyes. Richard dashed a hand across them. He quit walking. Stood shivering.

Kenntnis gave Richard a gentle shake. "Finish it."

✧ ✧ ✧

KENNTNIS GRIPPED HIS shoulder, gave it a squeeze. The memories hung like an abstract painting—impressions but no details. Richard feared if he made them coherent, they would tear him apart. *Haven't they been doing that for years? Haunting his nights. Denying him the comfort of a human touch.* The simple act of acknowledgement brought them all into focus. No longer the scattered images of nightmares, or memories he refused to face, or the panic that buried him like an avalanche whenever he felt confined, or someone touched his lips.

He remembered it all.

The taste of blood from his badly bitten lips, the smell of sex and sweat, the taste of Drew's semen mingled with vomit, the pain from the cuts and burns, the blood trickling down his legs, the screams.

Richard hadn't realized he had said it all aloud until he looked up and saw the look of horror and sorrow on Kenntnis's face. The panic was gone, if not the shame. Richard sighed, surprised by his almost matter-of-fact tone as he finished. "Eventually Drew calmed down, maybe the alcohol began to wear off. He bundled me up and dumped me in an alley. Like I was garbage."

Kenntnis pulled him against his shoulder. The soft nap of cashmere caressed Richard's cheek. There was the sharp, rich scent of sandalwood. Everything combined to break his rigid control. The sob burst from him, a cry of grief and despair. Kenntnis made no sound, offered no platitudes. He simply held Richard as Richard wept as he had never wept since that night of terror, pain, and betrayal. Eventually the paroxysms eased, and finally Kenntnis spoke.

"You are not garbage. You were not stupid. You did not ask for it. You trusted and cared for this man. He used you and betrayed you. That is his shame, not yours." Richard's hair had fallen forward over his forehead. Kenntnis brushed it back softly.

Richard looked up to meet Kenntnis's gaze, searching for any sign of disgust or contempt. He saw only affection and concern. Richard ran his hands across his face. They came away wet from tears.

"I ask again, why did you protect him?"

He drew in a shaky breath. "I didn't do it for him. I did to protect my father. While Drew untied me, he reminded me how bad it would be if any of this came out. That the scandal would blow back on Dad, and that my dad would disown me. He added that shame was a great silencer."

"And death's an even better one," Kenntnis said quietly. "Is that why you tried to commit suicide?"

"There were a lot of reasons," Richard said as he pulled away and went to sit on the piano bench.

"And Pat kept your attempt quiet."

"Yes. He checked up on me even after I got out of the hospital. He found me that day." Richard pulled back the sleeve of his sweater and studied the narrow white scar. "While he sewed me up, he made me realize that dying let my assaulter win. He told me to face the monsters."

The corner of Kenntnis's mouth quirked up in an impish half smile. "Little did you know …"

Suddenly Richard found himself chuckling. Kenntnis joined in.

"But why a policeman?" Kenntnis asked after they'd regained control. "Gratitude? Admiration for McGowan?"

"That was probably some of it, but I wanted to protect people. I didn't want anyone to get hurt the way I had been hurt." Richard glanced up shyly at Kenntnis. "Sorry, that probably sounds really corny."

"Yes, but it's also admirable. You told me you kept something this Drew gave you. Show it to me."

Richard went into the bedroom and opened the jewelry box on his dresser. The gold Rolex with its shattered crystal glinted among the cufflinks and tie tacks. He returned and handed the broken watch to Kenntnis.

"This. I was wearing it that night. I broke it in the struggle. I kept it to remind me."

Kenntnis pocketed the watch. "And now it's time to forget."

"No, it's inspiration for me, a goad."

"I think it's been more of a scourge. Let it go. McGowan's right. You've found your calling. Nothing will ever break you again."

"He said that?" Richard asked, absurdly pleased.

"Yes, he did." Placing his hands on Richard's shoulders, he guided him over to the piano. "Now, play something for me."

"What would you like?"

"Something more cheerful than that dismal Schubert."

Richard riffled through the stacks of music and pulled out a Mozart sonata. "Will Grenier use this to hurt me?" Richard asked as he set the music on the stand and settled onto the bench.

"First, it's a new day. There is no shame in being gay or bi or trans or whatever you are. You're free to love who you want, marry who you love."

"My family … my father won't see it that way. And I've already disappointed him … so much."

Kenntnis didn't have to voice the question for Richard to hear it—*Why do you care?*

Because just once *I'd like him to be proud of me,* he thought, but he didn't say that aloud.

CHAPTER TWENTY-SEVEN
THINGS CAN ALWAYS GET WORSE

ANGELA LOOKED UP from her take-out container of egg foo yung. Richard stood in the doorway. It was déjà vu. He had looked just this hesitant and lost the first time she'd seen him. *God, had it only been a month ago?* Of course, then he'd worn a uniform, and looked a little like a boy dressed up for Halloween. Today he wore a beautiful gray Prince of Wales windowpane suit and was gorgeous. The knowledge she had hurt him and potentially wrecked whatever they might have become, or even their friendship, tightened Angela's throat.

"You got more dead people for me?" she asked, keeping her tone friendly but professional.

"No, I have this for you." He pulled a bouquet of seven perfect white roses from behind his back. "Will you accept them and my apology?"

"You have nothing to apologize for. If anyone should be apologizing—"

He held up a restraining hand. "No. I should have been honest with you. About … my … issues."

He walked behind her overladen desk, bent down, kissed her chastely on the cheek, and laid the roses in her arms. Unlike so many florist and hot house roses, these had fragrance.

"Has the situation changed?" she asked.

"Maybe. I don't know yet, but I wouldn't mind if we stepped back, took a breath, and maybe tried again." He hastened to add, "As long as we go a little slow."

"I can do slow." She stood. "Why don't we start with friendship first." Angela offered her hand. "Hello, I'm Angela Armandariz. How do you do?"

He gave her that heartbreaking smile and shook her hand. "Richard Oort, so pleased to meet you." He moved aside a stack of papers, perched his hip on the corner of her desk, and conversationally asked, "So what's new in your life?"

"A stabbing from one of the homeless shelters and, according to the fire department, a gas leak that laid out every person in the Artichoke Cafe. One girl had an undiagnosed heart condition and it killed her."

"You sound dubious."

"I didn't find any evidence of carbon monoxide in her blood work."

"What's the staff's story?" Richard asked.

"They were down to the last table of the night. A man and a young woman. Then they don't remember anything until one of them woke up and smelled smoke in the kitchen."

"The cook was down, too?"

"Chef, please, this was the Artichoke Cafe. And yes, he was unconscious, too. A pot had started to scorch."

"What about the customers?"

"They left. Without paying, according to the driver of the

meat wagon." Angela sighed and dug out another bite of foo yung. "That seemed to piss him off more than anything else. I swear I don't know where they find these people."

"Well, it's not like they have to be sensitive to their passengers," Richard said. "I've got to get back to work. Would you like to have dinner tomorrow night?" he asked with shy formality.

"Yes, I would very much like that."

"I'll pick you up at 7:00 PM."

✧   ✧   ✧

Assistant District Attorney Jennifer Salisbury was waiting by his desk when Richard arrived at headquarters. She was an elegant woman in her mid-thirties. He was surprised to see her. Normally the lawyers in the DA's office sent for cops.

"Hi," Richard said.

"Hi. You don't need to be at the Grand Jury hearing on Thursday."

"Which one is that for?" Richard asked, only half listening as he flipped through the phone message slips on his desk.

"Andresson."

That got his attention. The papers fell from between his fingers and scattered like pink leaves across his desk. "Why? What's happened?"

"He's been extradited to Texas. Amarillo. Some B&E rap."

"We've got him on attempted murder of a police officer.

What is this horseshit?"

Jennifer held up her hands. "Hey, don't yell at me. I didn't know about it until today."

"I'm sorry." Richard ran a hand through his hair. "Look, could you call the DA in Texas and at least try to keep them from pleading this out?"

"Sure," Jennifer said.

✧　✧　✧

THE HEAT FROM the pizza warmed the palm of Rhiana's hand, reminding her that she should have worn gloves. She shifted nervously from foot to foot and stared at the apartment door. Finally, she reached up and knocked. Richard answered. He wore a heavy robe and was towel-drying his hair.

"Rhiana."

"Hi," she said brightly. "It's Friday and I thought, hey, I'll pick up a pie and a movie, and catch up. I haven't seen you in days and days." She closed her eyes briefly, cursing herself for sounding whiny.

"I … I apologize. Things have been … hectic."

"They said on the news that you were on leave or something."

He had the grace to blush. "Well, yes, I have been, but I'm back at work now, and I've had a lot on my mind, and—"

"Yeah, I guess you would. I mean shooting somebody … that must be weird."

"Yes," he said shortly.

"Look, me and the pizza are turning to ice," Rhiana said, forcing the words past the growing lump in her throat.

"I'm sorry. Come in."

She followed him into the apartment. The room no longer looked like a showroom. Music was scattered across the piano. A dirty mug rested on the coffee table among a tumble of pages from the *New York Times*. Rhiana set the pizza down on the breakfast bar.

"I wish you'd called me," Richard said, sounding hesitant and embarrassed. "I … I have plans tonight. I would have been free tomorrow."

Suspicion tightened her voice. "Who are you … what are you doing?"

He looked up at her, and Rhiana watched him stiffen and withdraw. "I'm inclined to say that that is none of your business, but perhaps it's time we talked." He tossed aside the towel. "I'm going to dinner with Angela."

"Why her and not me?" Rhiana cried.

"You're making too much of this," Richard said. "We're not dating."

She flung herself away, pacing the room. "What would you call it?"

"Spending time with a friend."

"I could be a friend."

"I don't think you want to be 'friends,'" Richard said, and his dry tone provided the quotation marks.

"It could start that way, couldn't it? I mean, and then become … more."

"I'm too old for you, Rhi, and frankly I've got too much baggage that you don't need to deal with." His tone was warm and gentle, and it gave her hope.

"Oh, that's just silly. I'm going to be eighteen soon."

"Which still makes you underage."

"Angela's old. A lot older than you. Why doesn't she feel weird about it?"

"Because we're not dating. We're just friends."

"Yeah, right. You didn't want to tell me what you were doing tonight. That means you're dating."

"No, we're not. And you need to leave now." Richard handed her the pizza box and walked to the door.

Rhiana dropped the pizza onto the floor and jammed a hand into her pocket. "I could …"

His expression went from embarrassment to ice and fury. "Don't even think about it." His tone reminded her of her dad's, her human dad, when she'd wanted to go out on a school night. not the breathtaking creature who had treated her with such care and reverence. She suddenly felt grubby and stupid and young, and she hated him for it. "You know a purely magic spell won't work on me."

"You're scared I'll try, and maybe succeed."

"No. What scares me is that you'd actually consider using your power like this. Love can't be coerced. You should know that." He kept his tone level, reasonable, like an adult remonstrating with a turbulent child. Her cheeks flamed with embarrassment and fury.

"Who said anything about *loving* you? From what I've overheard from Cross and Kenntnis you can't even get your *dad* to love you."

As she stalked to the door, she saw his cheeks flare with color, and he seemed to shrink in on himself. She had hit a nerve and she took a bitter joy in hurting him.

✧   ✧   ✧

THEY HAD THE cozy corner booth at Graze, one of Albuquerque's more upscale restaurants, which offered a selection of "American tapas." Since they offered half glasses of wine, Angela sampled a red or a white, depending upon the dish. Richard, as usual, drank water and one of the fancy bottled teas.

"So, Weber goes into the cell with a turkey baster and starts sampling the air all around the perp. The man is becoming more and more agitated, and finally he asks what Weber's doing. So, Damon tells him that he's taking samples of the gentleman's pheromones and he's going to compare them with samples he took at the house."

Richard had a musical little chuckle, and Angela enjoyed listening to it. "So, what happened?" she asked.

"What you'd expect. The perp immediately confessed to the burglaries."

"If you think that's good, get Weber to tell you about the bunny suit and the two-by-four carrot sometime," Angela said.

"Bunny suit? Carrot?"

"You need to hear it from him."

Their waiter arrived and set down several plates with a flourish. "The Mediterranean grazing plate, French country pate, and tilapia in banana leaves," he announced. "Enjoy."

Angela spooned some of each entree onto her plate. She looked up to find Richard gazing with amusement at her plate, and she realized that she was ending up with well more than half. Making a rueful face, she said, "You should have taken me to the all-you-can-eat buffet at Bella Vista. You're going to go broke feeding me here."

"I'll risk it."

They ate in silence for a few minutes. Despite his amusement over Weber's antics, Angela could tell that something was bothering the young detective. Figuring it was lingering embarrassment over their disastrous night in Taos, she decided to take the issue head on.

"So, I want you to know that I'm not expecting anything from you, but I do have some advice. What you need is a good casual fuck with a total stranger."

Richard stared at her, the blood rushing to his cheeks and even to the tips of ears. Then he burst out laughing. "Angela, could we not discuss my"—he lowered his voice—"sexual dysfunction in quite such a public forum?"

"Nobody's listening," she protested.

Richard leaned in and pressed his forehead against hers. "Well, let's hope not. I'd like to keep a shred of reputation."

"Okay, so if it's not your dick, what is bothering you?"

He sighed. "Rhiana."

"Ah, you've finally noticed the crush?"

He gave her an exasperated look. "Of course, I noticed it. I just didn't realize how bad it had become."

"Ah, the agonies of a teenage crush. I vaguely remember that."

"Stop acting like you're a grandmother," Richard said with a laugh. "But since you're experienced in these matters … what do I do?"

"Ignore it. Be avuncular. She'll cry it out and get over it."

"By the way, I prefer the term *make love* rather than fu …

well, you know."

Angela shook her head and laughed.

✦ ✦ ✦

THE FIRE FROM the pennies sent shadows dancing across the scarred pine of the study carrel and across the shelves of books. One spun on the top of the computer monitor. The other two flashed on the desk to either side. Rhiana murmured power words and swept the palm of her hand across the screen. Sullen colors began to crawl through the black surface. A picture, small and remote, appeared in the center of the screen. It was Richard and Angela. Their heads, pale and dark, were close together. Plates of food lay on the table before them.

"... She'll cry it out and get over it."

"By the way, I prefer the term make love rather than fu ... well, you know."

Angela laughed.

A sob broke from Rhiana's lips, and she bent forward over the hurt in her gut.

A long hand reached over her shoulder and picked up the pennies. For the first time Rhiana noticed Madoc's nails, long and very sharp. The picture on the screen vanished and there was a sharp *pop* as the motherboard, stressed by its unnatural use, died.

"He's just a human," Madoc said softly.

"But I want him." Rhiana drew her sleeve across her face and sniffed.

"There's time." His hand played in her long hair. "Why

don't you come away with me?"

"Where?"

"Venice, Paris, London. Wherever you would like."

"I thought you meant …" She hesitated, then said, "Home."

His cat's smile caressed her. "I don't think you are quite ready to make that choice, or that journey. But I know your dreams. Allow me to make a few of them come true." He threw back his head and laughed. "Actually, I can make *all* of them come true."

✧   ✧   ✧

MONDAY MORNING. A sad, cold rain fell outside, and the room smelled of wet coats and strong coffee. The incident board was filled with new murders and assaults. Richard stood in front of it and shook his head.

"It's worse than last weekend. What is going on?" he asked Weber as the older man sauntered up to join him.

"It's just going to get worse. The holidays are hell. Disappointments, expectations, and stress. Nice lethal combinations."

Weber was holding his giant coffee mug shaped like the ass end of a horse.

"Do you think the captain is going to let me take vacation over Christmas?" Richard asked anxiously. "I put in my papers, but I haven't heard yet." Richard moved to his desk and got out his mug and a tea bag.

"You *are* the new kid."

"So don't count on it?"

"Yep."

They headed over toward the coffeepots. There was a knot of cops, both uniform and detective, hovering there. Snyder was prominent in the center. The low-voiced conversation stopped and all of them looked at him. Richard reached up and straightened a suddenly too-tight tie. He heard the single muttered word.

"Faggot."

Richard stopped. Snyder grinned nastily at him. The seconds seemed as long as hours as he faced the pack. Damon's face darkened.

"What is this shit?" Weber asked.

"Richie's *friend* came by yesterday lookin' for him," Snyder said, and batted his eyelashes.

Terror and shame fluttered in his belly and his throat felt too narrow. Richard forced himself to walk over. They all seemed so tall.

"If you have something to say, say it to my face," Richard said. Yankee pride kept his back straight and his words clipped.

"Okay. Your sweetie came by lookin' for you."

"Does this person have a name?"

"It's on your desk."

Richard could hear Kenntnis's voice urging him to do something outrageous, take control of the situation, but he couldn't. A few short days ago all these men had looked at him with admiration and friendship. Now their expressions ranged from disgust to discomfort. While being gay or lesbian was officially supported by APD, regulations couldn't overcome biases, and law enforcement law enforcement tended to be a spectacularly macho profession.

Turning on his heel, Richard went to his desk and looked down at the yellow legal pad. In large print surrounded by hearts he read *Sal Verzzi* and a telephone number. In an instant he felt the burn of sunbaked sand beneath his feet, smelled the briny scent of seaweed and ocean water, and heard the shouts of children darting like minnows in and out of the waves. Fire Island, a few months before he started working for Drew Sandringham. The young actor he had met. It began with a shot of tequila, and became a wild, passionate, and drunken weekend. They had promised to stay in touch, but a few weeks later Sal had landed the leading role on a new television drama and moved to California.

Most actors hid their proclivities, so something—or *someone*, Richard thought—had happened to lead to this betrayal.

He wanted to flee, but he forced himself to sit down, pulled the pad and phone close, and started to dial. Richard noticed that Weber stayed in the knot of detectives around the coffeepot, listening as they talked. One young detective flung out a hand and went swishing toward the copier accompanied by raucous laughter. Cheeks burning, Richard bent to his task.

Soon he was talking to the front desk clerk at the Night Lighter Inn on Central. The Night Lighter was a rundown dump on East Central Boulevard that hadn't quite sunk to catering to whores, junkies, and dealers, but it was hanging on by its fingernails. The clerk's soft voice held the lilt and song of subcontinental India, and he sounded tired as he provided the information that Sal Verzzi had checked out that morning.

A growing fury hammered in Richard's temples. It wasn't strictly proper to use his status as a police officer for private use, but he figured he might as well be hung for a sheep as a lamb. A few more calls and he'd learned that Sal Verzzi was booked on an Allegiant Air flight to LA, departing at 10:20 AM. Grabbing his overcoat and radio Richard headed for the door.

He couldn't help it. He looked over to Weber. The older man's eyes slid away, and he turned back to face the other officers. The broad expanse of his back said it all.

RICHARD FLASHED HIS badge to the TSA screeners at the security checkpoint and was waved through. Usually, he savored a stroll through the Albuquerque International Airport with its Southwestern furnishings, wood-beamed ceilings, tile floors, and leather chairs. It was a pleasant change from the usual sterile plastic and cheap carpet found in most airports. This day he stormed through.

Sal sat reading by one of the wide windows that offered a view of the towering mountains. Richard thought for a moment that the actor seemed huddled and hunched but decided that was merely wishful thinking on his part.

"Hello, Sal."

Sal gasped, jumped, and dropped his iPad. "Ri-Richard!"

"How nice to see you again, Sal. Pity you couldn't stick around to say hello *after stabbing me in the back*."

The nearly five years had brought a few changes. The

forehead shone high and white because of a receding hairline. There were a few etched lines around the wide, mobile mouth that looked more like sorrow and disappointment than dissipation. The eyes were the same, a warm golden brown. As Richard watched, tears welled up and hung on the long, dark lashes. Richard's anger faded, replaced with a weary sadness.

"They didn't tell me you were a cop," Sal whispered.

"Telling you to go to APD headquarters wasn't a clue?" Richard asked.

"They just gave me an address."

"You could have walked away once you realized."

Sal shook his head. The tears left damp streaks down his cheeks.

"What have they got on you?" Richard asked in a gentler tone as he settled into the chair next to Sal.

"Nothing." It seemed to require an effort, but Sal managed to meet Richard's eyes. "It was what they *offered*. I'm in terrible shape, Richard. I needed help desperately." Richard studied the pinched face. *AIDS?* he wondered. *Hepatitis* C?

Sal swept away the tears and canted around in the chair to face Richard. "I haven't worked in two years."

"What happened to your series?"

"Canceled after four episodes. You don't understand how tough it is out there. You're only as good as your last job and I was associated with a bomb." Resentment laced the words and flashed in his eyes. "But you've got to keep up appearances."

"What does that mean?"

"You've got to look hot. Keep the right address. Not have

an area code in the Valley. Drive a nice car. Well, it's all about to collapse on top of me. And then they turned up and offered me a series. All I had to do was pay you a visit."

Richard stood up, pity fading. "This is about a *job*!"

"What else would it be?" Sal was honestly puzzled.

"I thought you were sick, or … or something," Richard replied.

"No."

"So, you bought your life with mine. Thanks so much. And what makes you think they'll keep their promise? You're flying a cattle-car airline and staying in a fleabag motel. Doesn't look like they value your efforts much."

Sal's jaw sagged as he stared up at Richard. "You think they'll back out?"

"I think they don't need you anymore," Richard said coldly.

"I'll … I'll tell."

"Who? And tell them what?" he surged onto his feet. "That you outed a gay cop? Not exactly earthshaking. Except to the cop," Richard added bitterly.

"I'm … I'm sorry. I didn't think," Sal began …

"Yes, yes, you did. You just didn't care!"

His heel squeaked on the tile as Richard spun and walked away.

He made it all the way out to the main concourse before shame over how he'd treated Sal and dread at the prospect of returning to work overwhelmed him. He dropped onto a bench behind a tall pillar to hide from everyone and everything.

But there was no escaping his thoughts.

"Look, all you have to do is give us what we want, and we'll support you in any and all of your goals. Chief of Detectives for New York? Director of the FBI? A brilliant concert career? A contract with the Met?" Grenier's liquid baritone echoed in his memory.

He had been both cruel and sanctimonious with Sal. If Richard hadn't had the memory of Naomi, Alice, and Dan, their cold, mutilated bodies fresh in his heart and mind, he might well have been tempted by Grenier. All Sal had had was a driving need and massive insecurity, and nothing to temper the *wanting*.

Richard's thoughts moved on to his own situation, and he sat studying his options. *Quit and try to go to a new city and a new police force?*

How long before they locate another lover and send him in to wreck everything? Or got Snyder to make a few calls to his new job?

Try going back to music?

Work for Lumina?

But once again he would have been given *a job.*

Give up police work?

Simply thinking about it brought him even lower. The grief he felt at giving up this profession was far more profound than his dread at facing his fellow officers. Richard thought about the cases waiting on his desk.

The dead were beyond his help, but their memory could be honored by bringing their killers to justice. Their loved ones would find some small measure of comfort, and other potential victims would be protected. It was good work, honorable work, and he didn't need the approbation of his peers to accomplish it. He was good at this—

He was surprised and startled by the ringing of his cell phone.

"Hello?" Richard cautiously.

"Give us the sword and all of this stops," came Grenier's voice.

Richard came to his feet. "You son of a bitch."

"Is that a no?"

"Is this the best you got? Because it wasn't enough," Richard shouted.

"Oh, dear Richard, do remember … things can always get worse."

CHAPTER TWENTY-EIGHT
It's Always About Him

"*J*UST BRING BARE *necessities. I'll rig you out when we arrive.*" Rhiana smiled with anticipation, remembering Madoc's instructions as she tossed a couple of sweatshirts and another pair of pants into the duffel bag.

"You're traveling light," Kenntnis's voice came from the doorway.

"Well, I've got stuff at home," Rhiana replied, and focused on zipping up her makeup bag while she uttered the lie. She didn't think Kenntnis had any abilities greater than those of a perceptive human to detect a lie, but she didn't want to test the theory.

Looking up, she glanced around the room and wondered if she would ever inhabit it again. It was beautiful, with peach-colored curtains draping the sleigh bed, and elegant carving on the dressing table and chest of drawers, but it wasn't hers. She had been a beggar, and now that she knew she belonged somewhere she didn't want to live on anyone's charity any longer. Maybe Madoc would let her come home this time.

Kenntnis entered the room and began picking up items randomly. From the mantelpiece—an eighteenth-century couple in Meissen white porcelain. From the table by the deep armchair in front of the fireplace—a Limoge box. From the bedside table—the Diana Gabaldon novel she was reading. Everything seemed small in his wide, powerful hands.

"I'm worried about you," he finally said. "These assaults on Cross are a preparation for something. I don't want you to be on the receiving end of … well, whatever they throw at us."

"I'll be fine. You've taught me how to hide and ward myself," Rhiana said, zipping the duffel shut. "And I haven't seen my family for months." She slung the duffel onto her shoulder and started for the door.

"You haven't seemed all that fond of them." Kenntnis's voice was dry. And maybe a little suspicious? Rhiana shook that off as nerves on her part.

"You can change your mind about things … people," she said.

"True." Kenntnis surprised Rhiana by pulling her into a hug. "Just be careful. I've grown quite fond of my 'roomie.'"

Rhiana felt doubt assail her. The phone on the bedside table rang. Rhiana answered, listened, and handed it to Kenntnis.

"It's for you."

Rhiana could faintly hear the words from Kenntnis's secretary. "Mr. Kenntnis, Detective Oort is in your office. He's saying it's urgent."

"Tell him I'll be right down." Kenntnis hung up the phone and pointed at Rhiana. "Don't leave. We're not quite done yet."

"I have a plane to catch. I can't wait."

"And I have to go talk to Richard."

"It's always going to be about him first, isn't it?" Rhiana asked.

"For obvious reasons—yes."

She watched him walk out and threw a surreptitious finger at his broad back. Fuck 'em. Tomorrow she'd be in Venice.

✧　✧　✧

KENNTNIS SAT BEHIND his desk and listened while Richard poured out the story. The young cop paced the room, flinging himself back and forth until he suddenly dropped into the armchair, as if the recitation had exhausted him.

"This wasn't entirely unexpected," Kenntnis said.

"I know, but it just seems so … petty. Why not just kill me and take the damn thing?"

"Because they don't leave fingerprints, metaphorically speaking. They sent golems after Rhiana; they used the gang members to 'kill' the college kids. And killing a cop brings down a hornet's nest of problems."

"Do they actually think this will work?" Richard was up and pacing again.

"Probably not, but it's going to take a toll on you emotionally, and they might get lucky, and you'll fold. Remember they didn't manage to talk to McGowan. They think you're a fragile weakling. Grenier doesn't know he's just going to stiffen your backbone with this."

"Fragile." Richard covered his mouth with a hand. "Oh, God, they're going to go after my mother! I've got to get back to Rhode Island. Find out who's behind it and stop them." He flung himself at the door. "You've got to arrange it with the chief."

"Wait. Wait. Wait. I can't have Rhiana gone, and you gone, with Cross to all intents and purposes incapacitated."

"Excuse me, how did you manage before?"

"Hid. Moved. Had Cross. Richard, they're planning something. Let's not play into their hands, shall we?"

"This is my family!"

"Yes, and the Lumina is more important."

"You have one day to fix this and then I'm gone." The door fell shut behind Richard. Kenntnis dropped his head into his hands, and wished humans could get past emotionalism.

✧   ✧   ✧

ANGELA STOOD IN the driveway, leaned on her shovel, and eyed the pile of sand. She didn't seem to have made a dint in it. Beneath her sweatshirt sweat clung to her sides, rapidly becoming a clammy chill now that she wasn't working. From her complex on Rio Grande Boulevard Angela had a great view of the Sandias. The snow powdered the rocky sides of the mountain and blushed rose as the sun sank in the west. She gave herself a few more moments to contemplate the view, then opened another bag of brown paper lunch sacks and started folding down the edges to form a narrow cuff.

The electric *farolitos* on the condo to her left seemed to mock her. She surreptitiously threw a finger at the offensive display. At least she'd convinced the young transplant couple from Boston on the other side that going electric was tacky and if they really wanted to experience a New Mexico Christmas they needed to go all natural. They, however, had ordered five dozen *farolitos* from the Valley High School Marching Band, unlike Angela, who was building each *farolito* from scratch.

Richard was supposed to have joined her after work, but he had called and begged off, saying he had to take a double shift. He'd sounded funny, but Angela hadn't pushed. She'd pushed once, and to disastrous effect. *No,* she thought as she lined up the sacks at the rim of the sand pile, *I'm going to be a model of patience and understanding.*

Soon she had several dozen sacks prepared and her hands were cramping. They looked like squat little soldiers in their neat lines. Gathering up the shovel, she dumped scoops of sand into the sacks. Next, she set a votive candle inside each one. Pressing her hands against the ache in the small of her back, Angela straightened, groaned, and sighed. This was a lot more fun with other people. She had apple cider simmering on the stove, pork tamales her *abuela* had made, and a plate of *biscochitos*, but no one to share them with.

She returned to the sacks. *These are supposed to light the way for the Christ Child to come to Earth,* she thought. *Not that I've ever been much of a believer, but it does seem pretty weird this year knowing what I know now. I sure as hell hope this isn't going to serve as runway lights for monsters.* She chuckled, trying to pretend she wasn't *really* worried, but she shivered as she remembered that *thing* seen through the wall up in Colorado Springs.

A car door slammed. Angela paid no attention until she

heard footsteps coming up the driveway. She looked up eagerly, but it was Damon Weber, not Richard, who approached. His tread was heavy, his shoulders slumped, and his broad, pockmarked face seemed to be pulled down as if gravity had proved too much for flesh and bone to resist.

"Wow, you look like shit," Angela said, but he didn't crack a smile.

Alarmed now, Angela jumped to her feet, dusting sand off the knees of her blue jeans. "What? What's wrong? What's happened?"

"I need to talk to you," Weber said. He looked strained.

"Is it Richard? Has something happened to Richard?"

He shook his head and she thought he looked embarrassed. "Not … exactly. Look, can I come in?"

"Sure. Okay."

The entrance hall had a white plaster barrel vault ceiling. Light was provided by two blue glass Mexican star lights. There was still enough light for the stained-glass window next to the front door to make a rainbow on the slate floor. Weber looked at the glass and gave a grunt of disapproval.

"You should pull that out. All some guy has to do is bust it, reach around, and the front door's unlocked."

"And then I'll shoot him," Angela said, wondering why cops always had to be so negative. "But I'm not taking out my stained-glass window."

"Okay, hope you don't live to regret it," came the comfortless reply.

She settled Weber on the sofa in the living room and ducked into the kitchen for cider, tamales, and cookies. He was standing when she returned, studying the art that graced the walls, paying particular attention to the Doug West serigraph of the blossoming apple orchards of Velarde. Underfoot was a Navajo rug in a Two Gray Hills pattern.

"Most folks hang these," Weber said with a nod to the rug. "They don't walk on them."

"Yes, but they're *rugs* and I believe in using things."

He followed her over to the sofa and accepted a mug of cider. He sat warming his palms on the glass and stared, frowning, into the yawning black depths of the kiva fireplace. Angela noticed that he chewed his hangnails, leaving bloody trails around his cuticles. She couldn't help but contrast them with Richard's perfectly manicured hands. Nibbling on a *biscochito*, Angela kicked off her boots and tucked her feet up under her. She was striving for patience, but the thought of the waiting *farolitos* kept intruding. The minutes crawled past and still he didn't speak.

"Look, I don't mean to be rude, but I've got another three dozen sacks to fill and store in the garage."

Weber shot to his feet. "How about I help you?"

"Fine, but I thought you wanted to talk."

"You hold, I'll shovel, we'll talk," he said.

Once more bundled against the cold, they went to work. The western sky glowed with a pearly light. Overhead, stars glittered in a midnight blue sky. Angela didn't turn on the garage lights, wanting to use the last of this magical twilight.

The rows of completed *farolitos* clustered about her like chicks around a hen and still Weber hadn't spoken. "So, we got two out of three. When does the talking part happen?" Angela asked brightly.

Weber's face twisted as a complex rush of emotions

passed across it. He threw the shovel violently into the sand. "He's a fag." His jaw worked as if he were biting down on an aftertaste from the words.

Angela didn't need to ask which *he* they were talking about. Dismay and anger, though at whom she couldn't say, squeezed her heart.

Weber paced, the sand grating beneath his shoes. "Christ! I had him stay at my apartment. He slept in my bed!" He ran a hand through his hair.

She forced herself to think again. "Well, unless you were in it with him"—Weber flinched—"I don't see the problem."

"I liked him. I trusted him," Weber said.

"And that's changed how, exactly?"

"Because I don't think I can work with … around the guy now. Queers just … I can't work with him."

"I don't get it. You work with Jerry," Angela said, naming the only out gay member of the APD.

"That's different."

"How?"

Weber threw his arms in the air. "I don't know. It just is." He paced in a circle, hands running through his tumbled, gray-flecked brown hair. "This doesn't bother you at all?" Weber demanded. "You've had the hots for him."

"And I expect I will continue to, though it appears I'm doomed to disappointment. On the bright side, *friend* and *ally* are also honorable titles." She gave him a significant look. "You might want to try them on." Angela paused, then added, "And this is all assuming that any of this is true."

"This guy came to headquarters. According to the guys who saw him, a real mincing pansy."

"And how do you know Grenier didn't just hire *this guy* off the street?"

"Richard's reaction," Weber replied. "He didn't deny it. He just left."

Angela bowed her head and stared at her knees. It didn't feel like a lie. It felt like a piece of the puzzle that was Richard Oort had fallen into place. They had spent some time snogging after their date, and he'd seemed willing to at least try for sex that night in Taos. Which implied he might be bi but … What the *but* encompassed she couldn't say.

"Look, I don't know if this helps, but I think he might be bisexual—"

"Bi, gay, it's all the same to me. He fucks men. I can't handle that. I need to you tell him." He turned and walked toward the street.

"Tell him what?"

He turned and walked backwards, hands up as if pushing away an invisible weight. "I'm out. Out of all of it."

"Tell him yourself!" Angela shouted after him. He spun, jammed his hands into his pockets. "Coward!" she added spitefully.

Weber's shoulders hunched as if she'd launched a blow rather than words. He increased his pace until he was almost running by the time he reached his car.

Angela sank down on what remained of the sand pile, feeling the grains shift beneath her and the cold start seeping through her jeans. The *farolitos* surrounded her like little monks in brown robes, but they had no counsel or comfort to give. Tears coursed across her cold cheeks like trails of bile, but whether they were for herself or for Richard, she couldn't say.

✧　✧　✧

AFTER THE TUMULT of the day before, Richard almost skipped his ritual stop at the hospital to inquire after Sterling, but he felt guilty, so he got off the freeway at Wyoming and stopped at Kaseman. He was now down to one hospital stop since Father Fish had been released and gone to Chicago to stay with his sister while he finished his rehab. Richard had been a bit hurt the priest had left without a word, but a moment's reflection told him why. Richard was the only other person who had witnessed that creature on the cross. If Charlie never spoke to Richard again it would be easier to assume it had been a hallucination ... or hadn't happened at all. Richard wished he could do the same.

Today when Richard walked past the nurses' station, the nurse on duty set aside a chart and hurried to intercept him. She was an older woman, her face careworn but kind, and she smelled of vanilla and chocolate, as if she'd been baking cookies before coming into work. Richard's heart seemed to beat in the pit of his stomach, and the stink of bedpans and antiseptic broke through his control. Richard gagged and the nurse gripped his hands.

"What's happened," he forced out.

"I'm so sorry, but your partner took a turn for the worse and was moved back to intensive care." The musical cadence of her Hispanic heritage softened her words. She read the question in his eyes. "Things don't look good. You should probably prepare yourself." Tears spilled over. The nurse pulled out a tissue from the box on the desk and offered it to him. Richard wiped his eyes and cleared his throat.

"Was … was there any reason to think it … the turn for the worse … wasn't … natural?"

The nurse gave him an odd look. "No, he's been in a coma and that takes a toll on a body."

"Yes, yes, of course." He turned to leave, but her voice stopped him.

"May I ask you something?"

"Yes, of course."

"You were so good, coming almost every day. I … I wondered why?"

"He saved my life."

✦   ✦   ✦

ACCORDING TO THE rotation Weber should have been on duty, but instead Lieutenant Patrisco was behind the desk. Snyder looked up from his computer. His eyes were narrowed with cruel amusement, but he didn't say a word, forcing Richard to ask, "Where's Damon?"

"Transferred to the Arroyo del Oso substation, pretty boy," Snyder said.

Richard sank into his chair. Desolation settled onto his chest, crushing his breath. There was a pile of papers on his desk. He started through them, then realized they were all gay personals and flyers about the gay and lesbian alliance of Albuquerque. He swept them all into the trash, pulled the phone close, and called the DA's office.

He was lucky. Salisbury wasn't in court. "You've got to

get Andresson back," Richard said without preamble.

"What? Who is this? Oh, Oort."

"Yes."

"Look, Detective. I've got twenty-three files on my desk. Why would I increase that by one?"

"Because it's a murder now."

"What?"

"I was at the hospital last night. I don't think … it sounds like Sterling isn't going to make it."

"Oh, shit, I'm sorry." She paused. "Look, I don't mean to seem unfeeling, but Andresson was arrested for his assault on *you* at that church. He wasn't involved in the events that injured Sterling."

But he was. Obliquely, or at least his accomplice was, and Andresson was certainly part of the conspiracy that had set the golems after Rhiana and killed three college kids. But he couldn't say any of that. Taking a deep breath, he perjured himself.

"I've had a lot of time to think about that night, and once I got a good look at Andresson … I'm certain he was one of the three."

There was a long silence from the other end of the phone. "You're sure about this?"

He ignored her dubious tone. "Yes. If you can bootstrap the driver of a getaway car into a felony murder charge you can certainly make this stick."

"Don't throw around terms you don't understand." Her tone held the dismissive tone used by many professionals when talking to someone less educated.

"My father is a federal court judge. My sister is a public

defender, but she was a prosecutor before that. Don't treat me like an idiot!" Richard found he'd slammed the flat of his hand down on the desk. A number of people in the squad room looked over at him. He moderated his tone. "Please, please, pull this man back."

"I'll try," Salisbury promised, and hung up.

Snyder smirked at Richard. "If butch don't work, you could always try crying."

Richard gave him a look of loathing. Ortiz came out of his office and beckoned to Richard, indicating his office.

"I'm pulling you off the street," the captain said.

Richard, standing in front of the desk, stared down at Ortiz, but the captain never looked up to meet his gaze.

"My solve rate is at ninety-two percent."

The office chair squeaked as Ortiz spun around and started rummaging in the credenza behind his desk. "So why not take a little break? Rest on your laurels." The captain's voice was muffled.

"Look, let's just come to the point." Richard was pleased to hear that his voice was steady. "I can work without a partner." He could feel another headache starting and he rubbed at his temples.

"That's not how we do things around here."

They were both surprised by the sharp knock on the frosted glass door. "Who is it? I'm in a meeting," Ortiz bawled.

But whoever it was didn't answer. Instead, the door opened, and Torres walked in. The crown of his head sported a bald strip where they had shaved away the hair to treat the gouge left by the bullet. There was a tiny sprouting of black fuzz, but Torres still looked like he had a racing stripe.

"Captain." He touched two fingers to his eyebrow in an almost salute.

"What do you want, Joe? I'm busy here," said Ortiz.

"This won't take long. I'll partner with Oort."

Nothing could have surprised Richard more. From the captain's expression he apparently shared the sentiment.

"Excuse me?"

"It's all over the building that you're pulling Oort off the street. That's a waste, sir. He's good. Nobody knows that better than me." Richard smiled in gratitude, but Torres didn't look at him. "So, what do you say?"

Ortiz cocked an eye over at Richard. "You okay with that?"

"Yes, sir, I'll be happy to partner with Detective Torres, but after—"

"Excuse me?"

"I really have to go home to Rhode Island. It's imperative," Richard said.

"It is, huh?"

"Yes, sir," and Richard's voice sounded small.

"Do you want to continue to have a job here?"

"Yes, sir."

"Torres comes in here and gives you a fucking gift. It's two weeks before Christmas, and you're asking to leave. Are you seeing the problem here?"

"Yes, sir."

"Good. Now get out of here and make me not regret this." Richard followed Torres out of the office and pulled the door closed behind them. Torres stared down at him.

"I'm just going to say this once. I'll work with you because I owe you, and you're a good cop, but keep your fucking hands to yourself, okay?" Torres pulled a piece of paper out of his pocket.

"Don't flatter yourself."

Torres looked up from the note. "Huh?"

"What makes you think you're cute enough to interest me?" Richard asked and gave him a bland look. Torres stared hard at him and gave a sudden single crack of laughter.

"Okay. Touché. We got a dead hooker out on the West Mesa. You coming, or are you quittin' and going to Rhode Island?"

CHAPTER TWENTY-NINE
MOTHERS & SONS, FATHERS & DAUGHTERS

RICHARD SAT IN the dark in Kenntnis's living room and gazed out at the rocks of the Sandias. The moonlight glittered off the snow. It was a motif of silver and black, and it was repeated in the sword that rested across his knees.

Kenntnis had asked him to sleep at the penthouse until Rhiana returned. With Cross basically incapacitated Kenntnis felt unprotected and exposed. Not, as he had explained, for himself, but for his employees. Richard had agreed because he still hadn't bought that plane ticket home.

If he left, he'd lose his job. And how could he go home and face the judge if he'd walked away from another job? But he had to go because they were after his mother. He was sure of it. He felt like a bug on a pin, tugged in opposing directions and therefore unable to move at all.

His thoughts skipped and jumped to the sad bundle of bone and flesh, platinum wig askew, sand from the West Mesa caked in the bloody wounds that he'd looked at earlier in the day. They had a solid lead. He and Torres would pick the guy up tomorrow. Maybe if it turned out to be a righteous bust the captain would let him leave as a reward. Richard played with that happy outcome for a few moments, then regretfully put it aside. Life didn't tend to work out that way.

Richard released the hilt and the blade vanished. He checked his watch. 1:00 AM on the East Coast. He couldn't call Amelia at this hour. He'd he'd wake the whole family, and she was in Boston. She wouldn't know how their mom was doing. His father had already dismissed his fears. Which left only one person. He pulled out his cell phone and dialed.

Pamela answered on the third ring. The husky blur of sleep softened her normally sharp consonants.

"Hello?"

"Pam, it's Richard."

He heard fumbling, the snap of a bedside lamp being switched on. "Do you know what time it is?"

"Yes, I'm sorry, but I needed to talk to you."

"Why? Do you need a lawyer?"

"No, why would you think that?" Richard felt the constriction closing down his lungs, his own tone sharpening to match hers. It had always been this way between them.

"Papa told me you shot and killed a man."

"Who was trying to kill my partner, and then probably would have shot me ... Oh, never mind. I wanted to talk to you about Mama."

"Yes, Amelia told me that you called her about Mama's latest psychodrama." That feeling of always being the outsider while his sisters discussed and dissected him returned.

"Look, Pam, could you not beat me up right now and just listen? I think Mama could be in danger ... trouble," he amended. "Could you please just ..." Richard hesitated, trying to think of something concrete to suggest. "Take her out to lunch, or go shopping with her, be there for her. Make sure she's all right. Please."

"I have a job. I'm busy, and she doesn't talk to me—"

"Because you're always so damned unsympathetic," Richard snapped.

"Yes, yes, I am, because her problems are so damn trivial!" his sister shot back.

Richard gave a hiss of frustration. "I don't even know why I bothered. I knew you'd be like this—"

"I wish you'd figured that out before you called and woke me up. I'm going back to sleep now. Goodnight."

He forced himself to release his death grip on the cell phone and shoved it back into his pocket.

Kenntnis padded into the room. The strings on the piano and the Celtic harp gave a ghost of sound as he entered the room. He settled onto the bench of the new addition to the furnishings, a Steinway grand piano. Richard knew it had been bought for him. It didn't change the resentment he felt toward Kenntnis. Richard glanced over at Kenntnis, then returned to his rapt contemplation of the boulders.

"Send Angela," Kenntnis suddenly said.

Richard cranked around in his chair. "I beg your pardon?"

"Send Angela to check on your mother."

"I haven't seen Angela since, since … people found out … well, you know, and I really don't want to have to go into another humiliating explanation about my sex life."

"You think she doesn't know? Cops are the biggest gossips in the world, at least with each other. She's the coroner and she's popular."

"What if she reacts like Weber?"

"Then you get hurt again, but I'd at least try." Kenntnis rested his hands on his knees and levered himself to his feet.

✧　　✧　　✧

THEY SAT IN a booth at the Carrow's. The median age had shifted from sixteen to sixty-five since Angela's last visit. Older women, with crimped red or silver hair, wearing gaudy silver-and-gold-trimmed fiesta skirts, sat with their husbands, who wore white shirts and black trousers and bolo ties. It was a square dance club, pausing for dinner after cutting a rug at the senior center up the street. They were a good deal more restrained than the high school football team, fans, and cheerleaders, but one old guy insisted on reeling out a call while banging on the edge of the plastic table with his spoon.

"… So, there it is. I have no idea how my father might react to you showing up. Mama would be fine." Angela noted that Richard gave the word a French pronunciation. "But I'd have someone there. I … I know it's incredibly presumptuous of me to ask—"

"Of course, I'll do it," Angela interrupted. "My dad's family is still in Philadelphia. I'll tell your folks you asked me to bring their Christmas presents by since I was coming out east anyway. If things are fine, and you are being paranoid, I'll head back. And if things look hinky then you can head home."

He touched her hand lightly and withdrew. "Thank you."

She took a sip of her coffee. "I do need to be back by

Christmas Eve, however. That's kind of a big deal for my family."

"What do you do?"

"Well, apart from eating, we go to the cemetery and place *farolitos* on the family graves. It takes a while since I've got four hundred years of dead relatives resting up there. And by the way, I don't give a shit that you're bi or gay or whatever."

He flinched at her bluntness. "I do," he said shortly.

"Why? For fuck's sake, this isn't 1950. Nobody has to be in the closet now."

His fingers writhed in his hair, disturbing the perfect part. "Angela, please, I really can't take a session of tough love, or whatever the hell you want to call this, right now."

The fact he'd used a profanity told her that he really was upset. "Fine." She stood up. "How about we meet tomorrow noon in Old Town? We'll pick out some quaint and exotic New Mexico *tchotchkes* for your family."

✧ ✧ ✧

IT SEEMED TO have become all about food. Rhiana forced herself to set down the fork and contemplate the view across the water. Not that the water could be seen. This late in the year the canals and lagoon of Venice were hidden beneath swirling white fog, and the buildings floated like pastel dreams on billows of mist. It was beyond description beautiful, but the food …

Rhiana returned to her Venetian specialty, calve's liver in a delicate wine and mushroom sauce. "I'm sorry," she said between bites. "I don't know what's wrong with me." The kerosene heaters dotted about the balcony hissed, and warmth rolled off them. The scent of brine and the faintest whiff of sewage rose off the water. Voices called from the enshrouded buildings, the sound amplified by the fog and water. The liquid Italian syllables were like music.

Madoc smiled at her and sipped his wine. "It's all about sensation. You're compensating with physical feeding instead of feeding your magic. You should feed the magic."

She had a sudden image of Cross looking at her … looking *through* her. Her appetite deserted her. Rhiana pushed away the plate. "Kenntnis would find out. Cross would sense what I'd done," she whispered. "Unless I left," she added hopefully.

"Not yet. We went to a deal of trouble to place you there."

"Why?"

"Soon," Madoc said soothingly.

Rhiana couldn't resist the food. She pulled the plate back. "Do you actually look like"—she gestured with her knife—"This?"

"No, I'm wearing a mask on a mask."

"I don't understand," Rhiana said.

There was a strange rippling as if Madoc were made of water and she found herself looking into the round face and brown eyes of a cute but ordinary-looking young man who wore blue jeans and sneakers and whose backpack rested against the legs of his chair. "This is what Kenntnis's spies see."

"He watches me?" Her voice rose in indignation.

"Of course."

"Cross can see through that." She waved her fork at him.

"Which is why we neutralized him while you and I are … getting to know one another."

"Then that shape you show me?"

"Isn't real either. I tried to make myself attractive. Your mother thought I was."

"You are. So, you wanted to be attractive to human women?"

"Yes," he answered simply.

"Why?"

"We needed a half-breed."

"Every theory suggests that aliens and humans would be sterile," Rhiana said.

"Yes, but we are masters at manipulating matter, particularly DNA. We want children, we get them."

"But you haven't done it in a long time." *Please, don't take away the specialness.* She couldn't control the pathetic little thought.

"Actually, we have, but you may be what we've been seeking."

"And what is that?"

"A melding of technological understanding and magic."

"And I'm that melding?" she asked.

"We think so. We hope so. We arranged for your scholarship to see if you truly had the aptitude."

"And sent me to UNM?" Rhiana scoffed. "Not exactly the physics capital of the world."

"No, but close to Kenntnis."

"Oh," she said, no longer feeling clever. "So, how will you know? If I'm the one?"

"When you go back, take a hard look at Kenntnis. Beyond the physical. Tell me what you see. That will answer the question of whether we've succeeded or not." Madoc reached out and stroked his hand down her cheek caressingly. "I hope you are. I want my child to be the one."

✧ ✧ ✧

THE CROWDS IN Andrew's Pueblo Pottery were shoulder to shoulder as people dashed to buy Christmas gifts. Angela wriggled through and finally found Richard in rapt contemplation of a Hopi kachina Snow Maiden, and a San Juan Pueblo Corn Maiden carved out of a delicate seashell. His hands were folded on the counter, chin resting on his hands as he studied them at eye level.

"I don't know which one she'd like better," he said as she joined him.

Angela took in a deep breath, struggled with how to say it, then settled for her usual bluntness. "Richard, I've got to go to Farmington. Some roughnecks digging a containment pit for a new natural gas well found a body dump. The coroner in San Juan can't handle this. I've been called in." The expression on his face pushed her to say more. "Look, it should only be a few days' delay. As soon as I can, I'll head east."

Richard slowly straightened and pushed the Snow Maiden toward the clerk. "I'll take her."

"Richard, she's three grand," Angela said, then stopped at his look.

✧   ✧   ✧

"YOU IMPOTENT FUCKER!"

Even Richard shrank back, and he was prepared for the roar. The suspect seemed to be trying to push his spine through the back of the wooden chair. He was a skinny man with a protuberant Adam's apple, pasty, pockmarked skin, and mud-colored eyes. Sparse hair had been carefully combed across a wide bald spot. Torres slammed his hands down on the arms of the chair, penning the man. The cop's blood-congested face was only inches from the pale, sweating face of the perp.

"You can't fuck a woman normally, so you hurt 'em and then kill 'em!" Torres allowed spit to fly from his mouth into Cobb's face.

As the saliva struck his skin Randall Cobb let out a whistling squeak. It was what they had been waiting for. Richard flung himself forward, wrapped his arms around Torres's chest and pulled the older man away from Cobb.

"Back off, back off, man!" Richard said urgently.

The broad one-way mirror gave back their reflections. The interrogation room stank with years of fear-induced sweat. The acoustic tile ceiling was a dingy white, but in one corner the tiles were stained brown as if something had died in the crawl space and bled through.

Torres roughly shook off Richard's hands and stormed out of the room. Richard pulled a starched handkerchief from his pocket, crossed to Cobb, offered the cloth. Grimacing with distaste, the man wiped the spittle from his face. But his hand was shaking.

"I apologize for that," Richard said.

"He's a barbarian. Uncouth. Uneducated." Richard looked sympathetic.

The legs of the chair scraped across the stained and scratched linoleum as Richard pulled over a chair and sat down. "Look, Mr. Cobb … Randall. May I call you Randall?" The man nodded; his gaze suspicious. "Just answer a few of our questions and you'll be out of here. I don't really think you had anything to do with this woman. I can tell you're a man of taste and refinement, and she was … well …" Richard shrugged and tried not to think about the woman's body so he could remain sympathetic. "But my partner is nervous. He needs an arrest. As long as you don't talk to him you give him a reason to suspect you." Cobb began to relax, twining the handkerchief through his fingers. There were tufts of coarse dark hair on the joints and the knuckles were enlarged. Richard swallowed his disgust and leaned in closer. "So, why don't we talk? If you talk to me, he doesn't have to come back in."

"Okay."

"So where were you Thursday night around 9:30 PM?"

The intercom came on with a hiss and click. "Detective, you have a phone call."

Richard's back teeth closed with an audible snap, for the wariness was back in Cobb's face and he'd subtly withdrawn.

"Not now," he called back.

"They said it was urgent."

Richard looked down at Cobb and gave him the most warm and charming smile he could muster. "Excuse me just one moment. I'm very sorry."

Slipping out the door, Richard found Lucile waiting. "We told you we weren't to be disturbed!" Richard snapped. Torres was hustling down the hall, his brow thunderous.

Lucile looked guilty and defensive. "They said it was a family emergency, Rich. The woman on the phone, she was crying," she added.

Torres arrived in time to hear part of Lucile's remark. "You gotta take it. Go. I'll keep him softened up."

"He's ripe now. I'm afraid we're going to overplay it," Richard fretted.

"We've already broken the mood," Torres answered. "We can only do the best we can." He went through the door into the interrogation room.

Richard heard Cobb say, "You!" in a tone of loathing. "I want a lawyer …" The closing door cut off any further words. Richard, raging inwardly, followed Lucile back into the main squad room.

"I'll forward it to your desk," Lucile said.

He grabbed up the phone on the first ring. "Oort!" he snapped.

"Richard." It was Pamela, and she was crying.

The shock froze him. In all the years of childhood Pamela had never cried. Not when she broke her arm when she was eleven. Not when Zorro, the family poodle, died; not when her boyfriend, the captain of the tennis team, dumped her two days before the senior prom. Never.

"It's Mama. She's dead."

His head seemed to be ringing. The words kept repeating over and over as his brain tried to process their meaning. He didn't seem to have the breath to form words.

"Did you hear me?" Pamela said, and her basic nature reasserted itself, sharpening her tone even through the tears. "Mama has died!"

I should have gone! My fault! I should have gone! They killed her and I did nothing!

"Yes ... yes." His voice was trembling. It spread to his limbs and Richard groped for the chair before his knees gave out. "How ... what ... happened?"

"She committed suicide," Pamela said, her voice thick with shame and anger. "Come home." She hung up.

That revelation briefly shook his certainty of Grenier's involvement. Slowly Richard replaced the receiver in the cradle. His mother had been fragile since Pamela's birth. Postpartum depression, the doctors had said, and recommended that the Oorts not have any more children. But they had tried again for that elusive and necessary son. The son who had let her down.

Logic whispered all the rational explanations and couldn't trump his certain knowledge. Kenntnis would never approve, but Richard felt, believed, that Grenier was behind this suicide.

Finally, the reality penetrated. His mother was dead. Hands clasped tightly between his thighs, Richard leaned forward and tried to fight back the tears. They won, but he did manage not to make a sound.

Her hands on his shoulders helping him stay upright as he learned to skate on the pond at the Vermont cabin. Curled up in his bed, chest hot and reeking with Vicks mentholated rub, the down comforter and feather pillows forming a cocoon while she read *The Wind in the Willows*. Her bell-like laughter breaking up the words as she read of Mr. Toad's delight on having seen his first motorcar. Leaning across the table in the big kitchen to hand him a beater covered with chocolate batter from his birthday cake, her gray eyes warm and sparkling. Teaching him to waltz before he became an escort at the debutante ball. Turning the pages of his sheet music as he practiced before a concert.

"Ah, itty boo, Richie's crying." And the ring of phones and smell of old, burned coffee and damp clothes and microwave popcorn was back. "What happened, Richie? Your boyfriend got AIDS? Or is it you?" The words, delivered in Snyder's nasal tones, added to the ugliness and sarcasm.

It wasn't a conscious decision. Suddenly Richard was moving, leaping up so abruptly that the chair went skittering on squealing casters across the floor. He rested one hand on his desk and vaulted across to land in front of his tormentor. Files flew off the desk like startled birds breaking from cover at his passage.

He watched his fist slicing through the air, smashing into Synder's nose. The mushy feeling followed by the crunch of cartilage giving way. The nose flattening and slipping sideways, the blood cascading hot and sticky across Richard's knuckles, staining the front of Snyder's shirt.

Snyder went down hard, landing on his butt, hands clasped across his face. Arms grabbed Richard and held him back. There was a confused babble of voices all around, but it was just sound, not words.

Then the captain was there. Richard, and half of downtown, heard his words.

"WHAT IN THE FUCK IS GOING ON?"

Richard twitched his shoulders and was released. Because of the broken nose, Synder's words were thick and phlegmy.

"I was just askin' what was wrong, and he attacked me."

While Snyder spun out his bullshit, Richard removed the pocket square from his breast pocket and wiped away the blood. He tossed it into the trash can, straightened his suit coat, and smoothed out the wrinkles on the sleeves where sweating hands had gripped him.

"Is that true?"

Richard turned to face Ortiz. "I need to take personal leave, sir. My mother has died."

All the excited chatter, query, and commentary went silent. One of the other cops muttered out of the corner of his mouth to Snyder, "Smooth, dude, very smooth."

"You hit a fellow officer. I can't just ignore that." Richard shook his head, refusing to answer. Ortiz opened his mouth, but before he could respond, rescue came from an unexpected source.

Lucile sailed across the squad room, her enormous bosom separating the gathered crowd like the prow of an icebreaker. "Captain, sir, as far as I'm concerned Rich should have hit this *pendejo* weeks ago. Snyder's been accidentally"—she made quote marks in the air.—"Spillin' coffee all over Rich's reports and then hoggin' the printer so Rich has to stay late. And sayin' things. Awful, nasty things."

Again, Ortiz started to speak, only to be struck dumb by Lucile's forefinger. It was tipped with a long, bloodred nail set with a rhinestone. She wagged it under his nose. "And you know the kinds of things. You're not on another planet when you're in that office. And if hittin' a fellow officer is against the rules, then discriminating against one ought to be, too. You're damn lucky Rich didn't bring in his delegate or file a lawsuit."

She folded her arms across her breasts and glared at Ortiz, and such was the complexity of male and female relationships in Hispanic culture that he wilted.

"You should have said something, Oort," the captain muttered. He rounded on Snyder and the clip of command was back in his voice. "Snyder, I'll see you in my office."

The tension ebbed. People returned to their desks though their heads still craned, trying to hear. Ortiz sighed and scrubbed a hand across his face. "Mom, huh?"

"Yes, sir."

"Sorry."

He wanted to scream at Ortiz that that *this wouldn't have happened if you had just let me leave!* But instead, he heard his mother's voice reminding him of the Sydney Smith quote

"Manners are like the shadows of virtues—they are the momentary display of those qualities which our fellow creatures love and respect."' The reminder had him merely murmuring, "Thank you, sir."

"Yeah, you can go. Just let us know when you'll be back. It's gonna be hell to cover for you this time of year."

"Sorry, sir," he said again.

Ortiz just waved Richard off. It was all the encouragement he needed. Richard quickly loaded up his briefcase and bolted. A few of the other detectives started to say something to him, but he froze them with a withering look.

✧ ✧ ✦

THE FIFTH SKULL was surfacing when Angela's cell phone rang. The local coroner, standing next to her, had a poleaxed expression as he stared down at a tarp covered with a jigsaw puzzle of tumbled bones. Angela had maintained a clinical aloofness, but she couldn't help wondering if serial killers were somehow linked to the Old Ones.

"Maybe that's the Fucking Big Idiots," Angela said to him. The bitter cold and dry wind hissing across the high plateau had leached all the moisture out of her skin. She felt one of the cracks on her chapped lips break open as she spoke, and tasted salt and copper as she licked away the bead of blood.

"The FBI has gotta take over. I can't handle this," the man said plaintively.

"Trust me, they'll take over," Angela said, and answered.

But it was Richard. "You don't need to go to Rhode Island." His normally lyric tenor was clipped and tight. "My mother …" There was a cough, then the voice resumed, tight with control. "My mother has died."

"Oh, God, Richard, I'm … I'm sorry."

"Yeah, me, too. I'll see you when I get back."

"I can come out as soon as—"

"*No*. Leave me alone. Please. I know it's not fair, but I'm pretty angry with *all* of you right now. Just give me some time and some space."

"I understand," she said quietly, but she was talking to a dead phone.

CHAPTER THIRTY

I T HAD BEEN a hellish trip. As he sat at O'Hare, delayed by snow and ice, Richard briefly regretted refusing Kenntnis's offer of the plane. But the Lumina corporate jet might have been grounded as well, and he would have had to accept charity from Kenntnis, whom he blamed for his mother's death.

When he wasn't blaming himself.

He finally reached TP Green Airport at 3:00 AM after catching a connecting flight at Boston's Logan Airport. Exhaustion dragged at every muscle as he shuffled down the Jetway. Behind him, the young couple who had sat in the row in front of him were still squabbling, and their tiny baby still whooped out his distress. Ahead, an elderly couple kept everyone moving at their own snail's pace. The husband, face sagging with weariness, pushed his walker like a man moving boulders. His wife, her seamed face soft with concern and love, kept touching his shoulder as if to feed him energy. Richard wondered if the young couple would last to loving old age.

My parents won't, now, he thought. *And did they ever really love each other?*

Luggage collected; he made his way out to the sidewalk in front of the airport terminal. The air was damp and carried a hint of brine from Narragansett Bay. Richard turned toward the taxi stand. It held only two cars. Behind their steering wheels the drivers dozed. A horn honked once. Richard looked back and saw a green Mercedes sedan rolling toward him. Amelia was driving, and she was alone. Relief flooded through him. He wasn't ready to face his father yet.

She pulled up to the curb, jumped out, and hugged him fiercely. He could feel her shoulders shaking. A security guard began to drift toward them. In the seemingly endless war on terrorism even family reunions had to be cut short. Amelia opened the trunk and Richard dumped in his suitcases. He noted the bag of soccer balls and the set of golf clubs. One was clearly for Paul and the other for her husband, Brent. Richard wondered if there was ever anything for Amelia.

As they drove, he studied her profile. He hadn't seen either of his sisters for two years. Amelia was the eldest. Despite being only thirty-four, her dark blonde hair had streaks of gray.

The question could be delayed no longer. "What happened?" Richard asked. "What drove her to do this?"

"I don't know." Amelia paused, shook her head sadly. "You seem to have been the only member of the family who sensed she was upset," she said. "I mean, you called me about it. But then the two of you were always close."

"Obviously not close enough." He discovered that guilt had a taste. He swallowed convulsively several times.

"You're living in New Mexico," she replied, and her tone sharpened. Richard knew it was irritation over his profession and where it had taken him.

"And Papa lived with her," Richard said, and he couldn't hide the bitterness.

"I'm not going to respond to that," Amelia said, and they didn't speak again until they had left the freeway and commercial streets had given way to residential neighborhoods.

That gave him a lot of time to reflect on his conversation with Mark Grenier in Colorado Springs a lifetime ago, the phone call after Sal Verzzi's arrival, and now this. His mother's might have been the hand that acted, but he was certain Grenier's people had been there, quietly manipulating, tormenting, goading, and encouraging.

So now he had to find them, and ... *Do what?* He couldn't prove anything. Any more than he could prove they had tried to kill him. Or killed those kids. As Kenntnis said, they never left fingerprints. Pain stabbed through the hinge of his jaw and Richard forced his tightly clenched teeth apart. Looking out the window, he drew in several long breaths to calm himself and watched the headlights illuminate their surroundings.

After New Mexico, where clean air and lack of humidity made it possible to see seventy or eighty miles, Rhode Island felt claustrophobic. Where there weren't houses, the trees pressed close to the roads. Only when they crossed over the bay heading toward Newport was there any relief from the press of humanity. No stars penetrated the smeared gray overcast. After the cumulus castles that formed over the mountains and deserts of the west, it just looked dirty.

As they approached Newport, the houses became more impressive. Small lots gave way to third- and even half-acre swathes of grass and trees. No walls disturbed the sweep of lawns between the houses. Snow lingered on the north side of bushes and walls.

But impressive is a relative term and overlooking the Rhode Island Sound were the "cottages." A coy word to describe grandiose waterfront mansions built as testaments to the power and wealth of the robber barons.

They were only a few turnings from home when Richard broke the silence. "How did she…." But he couldn't finish the sentence. Mercifully, Amelia wasn't obtuse.

"Pills washed down with cognac."

Amelia spun the wheel, taking them into a cul-de-sac. The headlights played across red brick and glittered in mullioned windows. High up under the eaves on the third floor, a round window with long pie-shaped wedges of stained glass drew his eye. The long room behind it, running the length of the house, had been his room from age five until he went away to college.

The glow from the porch light reflected off the silver bells hung on the holly wreath. They rang softly as Amelia pushed open the heavy oak door. Their footsteps were loud on the parqueted marble floor of the entryway. The air was redolent with frankincense.

Footsteps came tapping toward them, but it was the rhythm of high heels, not his father's deliberate tread. Pamela appeared in the archway. She was dressed in professional woman chic, straight skirt and long, flaring jacket in black wool, a scarf pinned to the lapel of her jacket with a pearl-and-silver pin. Her light brown hair was twisted up in a chignon. She was thirty-one and looked younger. Richard reflected that both his sisters were eighty-hour-a-week workers, but obviously a husband and child added to the toll, for Amelia looked older than her years.

His approach was wary, and Pamela bent stiffly and offered a cheek. He saluted it with a quick kiss.

"Come into the kitchen. That way we won't disturb Papa," Pamela said. "Are you hungry?"

"Not really."

"Have you eaten at all today?" Amelia asked.

"Not since breakfast."

"Then hungry or not, you need to eat something," and she made it sound like doctor's orders.

The kitchen hadn't been remodeled but left as a relic of the Edwardian era. A large brick fireplace dominated the back wall. Copper pots hung from a large wrought iron caddy. Opposite the fireplace loomed a gigantic mahogany buffet, loaded with the everyday china service and all manner of glasses. Between the two stretched a long table. Many a school project had been tackled at that table. Richard remembered making a diorama of a volcano for third grade. There had been an improbable herd of dinosaurs of all varieties grazing at the foot of that ominous peak. *Children are so willing to deal out death because they haven't experienced it,* he thought.

Someone had cooked. A turkey. It seemed a bad choice, a reminder of a now-blighted holiday. Under the warm grease smell of roasted flesh, vanilla added its richness to the air.

"Sandwich, or do you want it heated?" Pamela asked as she pulled a tray heaped with carved turkey slices out of the refrigerator.

"Sandwich."

Pamela began assembling it. "Well, she finally got the attention she craved," she said.

Richard didn't pretend not to understand. The same old game was starting with his nearest sibling.

"For God's sake, Pamela, if you can't muster up any grief, at least show a little respect!"

"I ran out of that years ago!"

They stood quivering. Amelia broke it up as she always had.

"Pamela! Stop baiting! And Richard, stop … well, just stop." Pamela hunched a shoulder and began putting away the sandwich fixings. "This isn't anyone's fault."

Yes, it is. It's mine. I knew and did nothing. But Richard didn't say it aloud because it sounded nuts and would just start another fight with Pamela.

Amelia patted him on the arm. "Here, sit down and eat."

He did, and even tried a bite, but the food seemed to enlarge as he chewed and a constriction in his throat kept him from swallowing. Finally, he choked it down, but knew he'd never manage another. Richard shredded the sandwich, hoping the destruction would hide how little he had actually eaten.

"What are the arrangements?" he asked.

"The viewing this afternoon. Service tomorrow morning with internment at noon. Naturally, we'll be home to visitors after that." The list was ticked off briskly by Pamela. "Uncle Ridley, Aunt Mary, and the kids are arriving tonight. Hollyburn's agreed to stay open a little late so Ridley can have his chance to say goodbye since the service itself will be closed casket."

Ridley was his mother's only sibling. Six years younger, Ridley Claasen had been a Wall Street banker before a car crash put him in a wheelchair. He decided that life was too short, quit his high-stress job, moved to Vermont, bought a gift shop, married an Earth mother, sired six kids, and became a general embarrassment to his family, friends, and in-laws. *Until I outdid him,* thought Richard.

"What about Brent and Paul?" Pamela asked.

"They'll be in this morning. Probably around 10:00 AM," Amelia answered.

"Tomorrow night we'll put all the kids in your old room, but you can stay there for now. We haven't got all the guest rooms ready yet," Pamela said to Richard.

"I'd ..." Richard coughed. "I'd like to see her before." The lump tightened his throat and he blinked, hoping to keep the betraying moisture at bay.

Pamela nodded. Amelia stood and picked up his plate. "Since you aren't going to eat, we should all get to bed. Grab a few hours at least."

IT WAS STRANGE to be back in his old bedroom, as strange as if adulthood had not intervened. From this side, the stained glass gathered the light from the streetlights and flung it in multicolored shards across the hardwood floor. The antique sleigh bed was covered by a handmade quilt sewn by his great-grandmother. It echoed the colored wedges formed by the window. A marble-topped antique dresser surmounted by a tall mirror, a rocking chair built by great-great-great-grandfather Nicholas Oort, and bookcases were the only other furniture.

Only a few relics of childhood remained; the model ships he'd built, and the case filled with beloved books. *The Jungle Book, The Wind in the Willows, The Chronicles of Narnia, The Lord of the Rings, Twenty Thousand Leagues Under the Sea.* Richard sank down on the floor and pulled out the Verne book. The book fell open to his favorite section, where Nemo and the Professor walked across the floor of the sea and examined the pearl in the womb of the giant oyster.

Oddly, what returned weren't memories of his mother but of his father. Robert had always been the one to read from Verne. And another memory surfaced. Being buried beneath quilts in that double bed, burning with fever while his father held him and hummed a wordless song of Robert's own creation. Those baritone notes had rumbled with comfort. Richard returned to the present and accepted emotionally what he had intellectually always known; that his music came not from Alannis, but from his father.

Why had he denied it?

Richard wasn't certain which *he* he meant. The father who rejected that side of himself or the son who couldn't accept that the father had ever possessed it?

✧   ✧   ✧

HIS SHOULDERS FELT too high, relieved of the dragging burden of the shoulder holster and gun, and it left him feeling naked. Richard looked at the shoulder rig hung on the rocking chair. The weight of the pistol pulled the rocker backward.

He couldn't wear a gun into church, to his mother's funeral. But he was carrying the sword. How was that any different?

Because it's irreplaceable and I'm afraid. They killed her.

Richard shrugged into his coat and paused before the mirror to straighten his tie. The black and dark gold paisley swirls seemed too bright against the material of his shirt. The charcoal gray suit and black shirt heightened the paleness of his skin and silver/gilt hair and turned his eyes into pale blue ice chips. He slipped on the family signet ring and his watch and squared his shoulders. It was time to face the day.

From the second floor the stairs became a great sweeping curve depositing you in the living room. His sisters had descended those stairs, long gowns trailing, white-gloved hands gripping the banister as they set out for their debutante balls. Young men with inexpertly knotted white bow ties had waited at the foot of the stairs, clasping corsages in damp hands. Richard's memories were of sliding down the banister until a broken wrist and the worst spanking of his life had made that game a lot less fun.

Three hours of sleep hadn't left him at his best. His eyelids felt coated with sand, and wisps of cloud had replaced cogent thought. It wasn't until he reached the foot of the stairs that he remembered Pamela's plans to put the kids in his old room. He went back upstairs for his piece. He would have the judge lock it in the safe. But before he faced his father with a gun in his hand, Richard decided to fortify himself with some food.

✦ ✦ ✦

"CAN HE DIE?" Rhiana asked as Kenntnis held the back door of the building open. She carried a tray stacked high with dirty dishes.

Kenntnis glanced back at the packing crate. "Yes, but not from this. This just weakens him and renders him useless to us. Fortunately, humans occasionally disgust even themselves and ratchet down the level of violence. He'll have a chance to recover then."

He took the tray from her, and they rode the elevator to the penthouse. "I admit it makes me feel more than a little vulnerable," Kenntnis said, and some of that supreme certainty that defined his personality was missing. He seemed depressed and even worried.

Rhiana followed him into the kitchen, perched on a stool at the center island, and watched as he loaded the dishes into the dishwasher. He looked up and gave her a smile. "I'm very glad you're back."

He moved to the enormous Sub-Zero refrigerator and pulled out the leftover tiramisu from last night's dinner. He indicated the dessert, then Rhiana, and lifted his brows in inquiry. She shook her head. He cut off a slab for himself.

"So did you enjoy Venice and your young man?" he asked. Rhiana flushed, angry to discover that what Madoc had told her was true. But she suppressed it, saying, "You're not mad that I lied to you?"

"You're eighteen and shacking up, and whether I like it or not I probably give off that 'daddy' vibe, so of course you lied to me even though I really don't care about your sex life." He walked over to the breakfast nook in its glass bay and sat down.

She stared at him while he ate. Cross hated her. Richard rejected her. Kenntnis used her, dared to equate himself with her father with one breath and tell her he didn't give a damn about her with another. She owed them nothing.

She considered Madoc's last words to her. *"Take a hard look at Kenntnis. Beyond the physical."* But what did that mean? Rhiana remembered another bit of advice from Madoc. *"Think of what you know of physics and combine it with your magic."*

Rhiana looked up at the lighting on its glass track curving across the ceiling. She watched the waves undulate. She blinked and the kitchen became a place of stark, angled shapes in black while the light became flashing particles that caused the room to strobe. She held out her hand palm up and felt the prickle of the light. There was an explosion of light to her left. The edges of her vision went red. Rhiana narrowed her eyes and looked to where Kenntnis sat.

Nothing human sat at the table. It wasn't like the writhing and coiling forms from the other universes. This was a whirling dervish of diamond-bright particles. They danced, while around them tendrils of light coiled up like a golden mist. It was breathtaking. Unfathomable. Beautiful.

Alien.

✧　✧　✧

UNFORTUNATELY, THE PLAN to be fortified before facing his father didn't work out. Robert wasn't in his study. He was in the kitchen, seated at the table, with the *Wall Street Journal* held up in front of him like a barricade. A cup of coffee sat near his right elbow. He wore a dark suit with a windowpane of grays and purples and dark lavender. He seemed aged far beyond his sixty-two years. Richard noticed that the judge's eyes weren't moving. The paper was just a prop.

"Good morning, sir," Richard said, and the paper crackled as the judge's hands closed convulsively on the edges.

"Good morning. Amelia tells me you arrived very late."

"Yes, sir."

Robert's eyes fell on the shoulder rig and pistol and the corners of his mouth pulled down, etching lines in his thin cheeks.

Richard hurried into speech. "We need to get this into the safe before the kids arrive."

"Yes, we do, and Brent and Paul are already here, so come along."

Robert took a sip of coffee and made a face. He crossed to the sink and poured it out.

Richard's stomach rumbled with hunger. "Just one minute, please." He opened the bread box and pulled out a slice. Saliva burst in his mouth as the rich, yeasty smell hit his nostrils.

Slathering butter on the slice, Richard devoured the bread in quick, small bites as he followed Robert across the entryway and down the hall to the study. It was a man's room. The large cherrywood desk was tucked neatly in the bay window. There were two enormously tall wingback chairs flanking a fireplace detailed in Delft blue tiles. Underfoot was a geometric oriental carpet in deep shades of red and blue. Glass-fronted bookcases were filled with hardcover books. Most of them were legal texts.

The gun was safely stowed in the floor safe under the false flagstone on the hearth.

"Do you remember the combination?" Robert asked as he spun the dial.

"Yes, sir."

"I would prefer you leave it here during the duration of your visit."

"Yes, sir. I can't imagine I'll be needing it."

"I can't imagine why you ever *wanted* it," said Robert.

It was an invitation to begin anew the endless, circular discussions that had accompanied his announcement that he'd been accepted into the police academy in Albuquerque, New Mexico.

Richard ignored the verbal gauntlet and threw out one of his own. "Sir, are you certain it was suicide?" Perhaps they had made a mistake and there would be *something* with which to attack them.

Robert jumped to his feet, whirled to face Richard. His hand rested on the mantel and the knuckles were white. "Kindly don't try to play policeman games with me, Richard. It was suicide. She left a note."

"Oh. Amelia didn't tell me that." Richard slid the stone back into place and stood.

"She didn't know about the note because I destroyed it."

"Why, sir?"

"She said things about you," Robert answered.

There was that feeling that his stomach had been replaced with a small animal consisting of only teeth and claws.

"What kind of things?"

"She offered no details but wrote that you had done things which would forever condemn you to Hell." Robert walked toward Richard. "She thought, perhaps, she could buy your soul with her life." Now only inches separated them.

Richard stared up into his father's face, suffused with blood. Robert's eyes were rimmed with red, and his expression as he looked down at his son carried anger and accusation as well as profound grief.

Not sleeplessness, tears. *He's wept for her!* The fact that Robert blamed him didn't matter. Richard knew he deserved it. What mattered was the realization—Robert *had loved her.*

Which gave him a perverse hope. *Maybe someday he'll ...*

The slamming of the front door reverberated dully down the hall. A deep baritone and a child's piping voice wove through Amelia's and Pamela's sopranos. He never finished the thought.

CHAPTER THIRTY-ONE

THE VIEWING WAS held at the Hollyburn funeral home. Robert drove Richard and Pamela over in the Land Rover while Amelia, Brent, and Paul followed in the Mercedes. Inside the Land Rover it was a silent journey.

Paul clung to Amelia's hand as they walked up to the white clapboard building. His voice tight with tension, he said, "Mama." From Amelia the little boy had learned the Oort practice (*or affectation*, Richard thought) of pronouncing the word with the French stress on the final syllable. "I'm scared." He was a sturdy youngster with chestnut brown hair and blue eyes. His features were his father's, square rather than the aquiline angles of the Oorts.

Amelia put an arm around his shoulders and pulled him close.

"Don't be. It's natural. Just a part of life. Grandmama won't be scary. She's just sleeping until the resurrection."

Brent leaned down from his six feet and muttered into Richard's ear, "I don't know why we have to put a kid through this. Christ, he's just eight."

"Because we're Oorts. Neither age nor infirmity are excuses for not doing our duty," Richard muttered back, and ahead of him he watched his father's back stiffen as he overheard them.

"Yeah, well, I'm a van Gelder and Paul's my son."

"So, take him home," Richard shot back, suddenly irritated by Brent's carping when he wasn't willing to act.

"Yeah, right," said Brent, gazing at the judge as the older man held open the front door.

The lobby swirled with color and sound. The women wore saris, the men suits, and a few of them sported turbans. The liquid sounds of some Indian language wove through the occasional sob. On the other side of the long, narrow rectangular room were five doorways. Three stood open, yawning emptily and showing only floral wallpaper and paint in soothing green and rose colors. Outside the two closed doors were discrete placards. A steady stream of mourners moved through the right-hand door. Richard walked to the left-hand door.

Amelia laid a hand on Pamela's and Robert's arms and held them back. They got it and froze. Brent took Paul over to a bench against the far wall and they sat down together.

The floral edging around the card framed her name—ALANNIS DELIA OORT. Richard drew in a long breath, laid his hand on the door handle. With an effort he pressed it down. The door opened with a soft *click,* and he entered, closing the door behind him.

Competing scents struck his nostrils. The sweetness of roses, the heavy sex scent of gardenias, the spicy tang of Easter lilies, and the delicate whisper of lily of the valley. It was either a testament to his mother's popularity or his father's clout; the room had become a garden. Wreaths curved around the coffin and there were more between the armchairs and sofa on the side wall.

The coffin rested on trestles draped with white satin. It was a heavy mahogany and brass affair. Richard walked to it and looked down on the face of his mother. She seemed tiny within the coffin's bulk.

White gold hair flowed over her shoulders. Robert had selected a smoke gray dress that would have matched her eyes. A delicate silver cross lay on her breast just above her folded hands. The gold wedding band glinted on her hand. The tiniest of smiles curved her lipsticked mouth. For an instant Richard remembered the back room of the funeral home in Denver and those rows of brilliant fluorescent colors. A shivering began deep in his belly. She would have been fifty-seven in May.

His knuckles whitened as he gripped the edge of the coffin.

"Mama, I'm sorry," he whispered.

Her skin was unexpectedly pliant, but so terribly cold beneath his fingers as he touched her cheek. Richard bent and softly kissed her brow. Eyes burning, he spun away and paced the room. *No tears. No tears.* Pulling out his handkerchief, he blew his nose. He returned to the coffin.

"I'm sorry," he said softly. "I should have come. But why didn't you call me on my cell? Why didn't you come to me with your fears? Asked me if whatever it was they told you, was true?" Richard realized his love for his mother was twined with a raging anger at her. The legacy of suicide.

Shocked by his anger, he turned it against another target. The cross. Reaching out, Richard scooped it up into his palm. The points bit into his skin as he closed his hand around it.

He spun the chain until the clasp showed and went to

unfasten it. Then he thought of his family's reaction and hesitated. He must either confess his action, which would require impossible explanations, or see Pamela and Robert accuse the staff of theft.

And Kenntnis had created a loving, merciful god. That was certainly the god his mother had revered and served with countless acts of kindness and generosity. She was one of the millions who gave strength and physical form to Cross. Richard gently laid the cross back on her bosom.

And found that his anger at the beautiful, selfish, delicate, hysterical, charming, heedless, loving person had vanished. Richard no longer prayed, but he pulled a chair over to the coffin, sat down, and talked to her. About how much he loved being a policeman. How good he was at it.

"And I learned something during the past few years. I'm not weak, and you weren't weak either. It might not have been rational, or make any logical sense, but you died trying to protect me. How many people actually have the guts to do that?"

He stood, leaned down, and kissed her one last time.

Then it was time for the public face of mourning. He opened the door, and the family took their positions. The afternoon wore on in a blur of faces, murmurs of condolence, firm handshakes, reminiscences, and a few, very few, tasteful, quiet tears. In his work Richard saw a lot of grief. Among the Hispanic families there were loud and passionate lamentations. He frankly preferred that to his own WASP culture. Violent or sudden death deserved to be railed against.

He was trapped in an exchange of platitudes with Mrs.

Van Owen. Hearing about Cindy's (they had dated his senior year) new venture in New York.

"She's not married yet, either," Mrs. Van Owen said with a suggestive little smile. "Maybe she can get up for a visit while you're still home."

A sharp and constant vibration in his inner breast pocket distracted him. Richard held up a finger to stem the flow of hopeful innuendo and hurried out into the lobby. He answered the phone.

"Okay, this is too weird," came Jennifer Salisbury's voice. "And I knew you'd want to know."

"This isn't a great time," Richard said in a low voice and looked anxiously over his shoulder toward the viewing room.

"It's about Andresson," Salisbury said.

"Okay, go ahead, but make it fast."

"I contacted the authorities in Amarillo to tell them our felony murder and assault on a police officer trumped their burglary and found out he had been released to some faith-based initiative that rehabs newly released cons and places them back in society. I pointed out that Andresson hadn't even been *tried* for the crimes in New Mexico yet."

"But they are going to pick him up, right?" Richard asked and heard his voice rising.

"No, because he's not in Texas anymore."

"He was on parole in Texas. That's a violation," Richard said.

"Yeah, and so was coming to New Mexico. The difference is he's in a church program now, and nobody wants to expend money and resources for a parole violation when the guy is, in essence, under supervision."

"What churches are associated with this initiative?" Richard asked, knowing the answer but needing the verification.

"It's funded by the Worldwide Christian Alliance, and the Amarillo authorities thought he'd gone to their compound in Virginia."

Blind rage can narrow your sight. Richard jumped when a hand fell onto his shoulder. He had neither seen nor heard Robert approaching.

"What the devil are you doing?" the judge hissed in his ear.

"Hold on," Richard said into the phone, and faced his father. "It's work. A case. I won't be long."

"No, you won't, because you are done! This is both rude and disrespectful."

"Thank you, sir, your objection is noted. Now let me do my *job*," Richard said quietly, and inwardly he was amazed at how firm and level his voice remained. Robert stared down at him, his expression both frustrated and quizzical. Then he spun on his heel and reentered the viewing room.

Richard returned to the call. "Sorry. Could you please contact Virginia and see if they can do anything?"

"Yeah, okay, this sort of gets my goat, too," said the lawyer. "Should I not call back?"

"No, call. I'll have my phone off tomorrow morning. The service …" He coughed. "The service is in the morning."

"Service?" Salisbury asked, and he realized that like all people in a tragedy he'd assumed that the entire world knew of his particular and personal pain.

"Just avoid the morning," Richard said quickly.

"I'll try to get back to you this evening," she promised.

He returned to the chapel to glares from his father and siblings and another reminiscence about his mother.

✦   ✦   ✦

THE SNOW BLEW out overnight, leaving a cold, white day. Richard had been relieved that Reverend Hoffsteader had agreed to a church service. Richard's memories of Hoffsteader's sermons were that they tended toward fire and brimstone. That he would consent to bury a suicide seemed out of character, but apparently, he bowed to the modern church's creative dodges around the suicide problem; arguing that people weren't in their right minds, or the suicide was an act in defense of another. In this case it had been true, though the reverend didn't know that.

Milling about on the sidewalk in front of the plain white clapboard church with its clear glass windows and single high steeple, Paul and his eldest Claasen cousin, Steve, kept punching each other. They looked absurd and adorable in their grown-up suits and little boy faces, even as their antics irritated the hell out of the adults. Mary, her unruly red curls inexpertly confined by a barrette, wrestled with the five younger children while the limo driver pulled Ridlley's wheelchair out of the trunk.

Inside the entryway, the women, with children in tow, headed into the church to make certain the programs were in place and the flowers arranged to their satisfaction. The men went down the hall to Hoffsteader's office. While Ridley couldn't assist in carrying the coffin, he insisted on accompanying it, in tones that indicated he expected a fight and was disappointed when he didn't get one.

The study was book-lined and terribly overheated. Hoffsteader, a pink-faced, fat man with light brown hair pulled across his bald spot, came bearing down on Richard.

"Richard." His palm was pillow soft as they shook hands. The minister's eyes raked up and down the length of Richard's body. Richard stiffened, wondering at the scrutiny, and suddenly worried that the dark purple shirt he'd selected was too colorful for good old-fashioned Protestant mourning.

"I didn't remember you were so short." That certainly seemed in character. Hoffsteader's lack of tact was well known to his parishioners. "I had thought it might be nice if you all carried the coffin on your shoulders rather than by the handles, but that's not going to work."

"No," Richard said shortly.

He had made peace with his lack of inches years ago, but he didn't particularly like having his nose rubbed in it. Two of the pallbearers, friends of his father's, were already present. The next few moments were taken up by greetings and questions.

"New Mexico, not much sailing there," from Berksen.

"How do you find police work?" from Judge Martin.

"I hear they have an opera there. Supposed to be pretty good, too," Berksen added. "Have you been?"

The questions came at Richard from all sides. He tried to answer without sounding idiotic. "No, sir. Yes, I go, and they are very good, sir. I like it very much, sir." The social platitudes felt surreal when his mother's body rested only a few hundred feet away.

"Aren't there going to be seven of you including Alannis's brother?" Richard heard Hoffsteader asking Robert.

"Oscar called early this morning. He's quite ill. I have a replacement," Robert added. "I'm certain he'll be here shortly."

The judge walked away and stood gazing out the window at the snow-covered vines snaking across a grape arbor that ran along the side of the building. It looked skeletal, the thick, gnarled vines like bony fingers clutching at the rib cage of some dead behemoth.

Hoffsteader glanced at his watch, as if death had a timetable that had to be met and beckoned them over to him with a gathering gesture of his short arms. "So, we conclude with the Lord's Prayer. When that's finished, you'll all come up and take the coffin straight down the aisle and out to the hearse."

Behind him Richard heard the door to the office open and close.

The musky, exotic scent of Kouros hit Richard's nostrils and his gut clenched in a sudden spasm of nausea even before he heard the drawling, cultured voice.

"Robert, a thousand, thousand apologies. There was an accident on I-95."

Heat raced through Richard's body, followed by a chill so deep and profound that his teeth began to chatter. His knees trembled and he seemed to have gone empty to his core. *Run, run, run!* a voice screamed in the recesses of his mind.

"Richard, dear boy."

Richard turned slowly and prepared to look into the face of his attacker, but Drew Sandringham had moved on and gathered Robert's hands in his.

"Robert, I am so very sorry. I was shocked when you called with the news, and I'm honored to serve as a pallbearer."

"Excuse me," Richard murmured and fled the office.

The bathroom was just down the hall. Richard slipped inside, locked the door, and leaned back against it. Breaths hissed between his teeth, but he still felt as if he were suffocating. Stupid, he'd been so stupid. Of course, Sandringham was going to attend the funeral. Why hadn't he foreseen that and prepared himself?

Because I didn't think he'd have the gall.

Moving to the sink, he splashed cold water over his face. It dripped off his hair where his forelock had fallen forward out of its careful part. He watched the silver drops and remembered watching the blood pattering from his badly bitten lip onto the polished inlaid wood floor of the dining room. Competing voices wove through his mind.

Pretty ... so very pretty.

... Face the monsters.

Evil and untrustworthy hands.

Shame is a powerful silencer.

He betrayed you ... His shame, not yours

... use this to hurt me?

Only if you let him.

Richard slowly raised his head and studied his features in the mirror. What looked back out of his pale blue eyes was no longer fear. It was anger.

When he reentered the office, the men had fallen back on the usual shield for grief, emotion, and discomfort. They were talking business. Money was always a good insulator.

Richard paused and forced himself to take a long, long look at Sandringham. Five years had wrought few changes. The sleek brown hair held a few more streaks of silver but the narrow face remained smooth, with only crow's feet radiating out from the tawny gold-brown eyes. Sandringham had grown an Elizabethan-style beard and mustache and it suited him. He was still a handsome man, and he knew it. He sensed the close observation and looked over at Richard. He strolled slowly over.

He gazed down. "You look well." A hand started to raise.

"Touch me and I *will kill you*," Richard said in a low, conversational tone.

Sandringham blinked, startled, and for an instant the hand hung in the air as if the older man hated to back down. But back down he did. The hand slowly lowered and brushed across the immaculately knotted Italian silk tie as if that had been his intention all along.

"So, a policeman. Quite an eccentric choice. Not what your family had hoped for you."

"Yes, I no longer have any shame," said Richard, and he laid a slight emphasis on the final word.

For an instant, Richard thought that the evening had not made the indelible impression on Drew that it had upon him, and that Sandringham wouldn't remember what he had said. Then the dark straight brows drew together, and the tawny eyes narrowed. His expression hardened.

"I'm very ... *concerned* to hear that."

"You should be." Richard said.

Sandringham stepped in even closer, crowding him, and

said softly, "Don't be fooled by the power of your little gun and shiny badge. You've got potent enemies, Richard. You want to keep me neutral."

"Thank you for the warning," Richard said.

"Just so we understand each other. I'd hate to see you hurt."

"Really? Forgive me if I find that laughable …"

Robert's voice interrupted them. "It's time," the judge said curtly.

They all filed into the church.

✧   ✧   ✧

THE HANDFUL OF half-frozen mud struck the lid of the coffin. Robert stood staring down into the grave while Richard bent and gathered up his handful. He allowed it to roll off his gloved fingers, hating the hollow, rattling sound as it struck. Amelia and Pamela added their small offerings. Ridley struggled to lean down out of his wheelchair. Richard gathered up a handful and gave it to his uncle. Ridley Ridley threw it in, and his lips moved. Richard couldn't tell what he'd said.

Their numbers were greatly reduced from the church. Brent and Mary had taken the children back to the house, and the cold and the morbidity of the cemetery had daunted most of the mourners. Only some thirty people sat on folding chairs at graveside. Hoffsteader, Bible in hand and looking like a large black buffalo in his curly wool overcoat, stood solemnly at one end of the grave. He offered the final benediction. It was finished.

Richard turned away. Ridley caught him by his sleeve. "You should sing. She loved your voice."

Richard had considered it during the long hours when he'd tried and failed to sleep. He wasn't certain his father would approve, or if grief could be controlled enough to make a sound. Finally, what the hell would he sing? The religious repertory was closed to him now. Perhaps Kenntnis was right when he said that all music was born out of human genius, and therefore good no matter what had served as the inspiration, but he couldn't say those words of false hope over his mother's grave. Richard was also afraid what it might *summon*. He would never forget that figure coming down off the cross. He looked over to Robert.

The judge didn't look at his brother-in-law or son. He continued to contemplate the grave, then suddenly he gave a sharp nod. This sign of encouragement surprised Richard. A Schubert song came to mind. Focusing, he found the opening note, drew in a long steady breath, and sang.

I think of you when the sun's shimmer
gleams from the sea;
I think of you when the moon's glimmer
is mirrored in the streams.

I see you when dust rises
on the distant road;
at dead of night, when the traveller
trembles on the narrow footbridge.

I hear you when the waves

surge with a dull roar;
often I go and listen in the quiet wood
when all is still.

I am with you; however far away you are,
you are near me!
The sun sets, soon the stars will shine on me.
O that you were here!

As the final notes echoed into silence, Richard found his father watching him. They stared at each other for a long moment, then Robert said ever so softly, "Thank you."

CHAPTER THIRTY-TWO

I T SEEMED LIKE all the people who had shunned the cemetery and even the funeral service came by the house that afternoon. The women carried covered dishes with some variety of casserole, or platters of cookies, and even whole cakes. There was so much food that they'd added two extra leaves to the dining room table to accommodate it all. Brent had made a run to the store for more paper plates and hot beverage cups.

Every room buzzed and rumbled with conversation. Overhead came the faint thunder of running feet as seven kids romped up and down the length of the attic room. The hours passed. Richard assigned himself garbage detail. He kept making sweeps through the first floor of the house gathering up dirty plates, plastic utensils, crumpled napkins, cups filled with the dregs of coffee, tea, or lemonade.

It was a slow process because he kept being drawn into conversations, sometimes about his mother but more often about New Mexico and his career choice. His first voice teacher and her partner were especially distressed that he'd abandoned music.

"Your voice just keeps getting better. What I heard today was lovely," Jeanne said as she towered over him. At five feet ten inches, a hundred and eighty pounds, and equipped with a Wagnerian soprano's bosom, she was an imposing figure.

"I wasn't going to be good enough," Richard said.

"Nonsense," said Sandra. She was an older woman, Jeanne's coach and accompanist and partner. "Tenors, like sopranos and fine wine, mature late."

"I'm really very happy with my choice," he said, sliding past them and escaping into the kitchen. His cheeks hurt from the effort of smiling and talking. Dumping the trash, he pulled out a fresh sack. Amelia turned from the stove and pushed back her hair with a forearm.

"I've boiled enough water to deliver several hundred babies," she announced.

Pamela looked up from the sink where she was washing dishes. "If I'd known this would happen, I would have hired a maid service."

"Can't we just tell them all to leave?" Richard asked plaintively.

"I thought we'd sit in the living room and *receive*," Pamela said grumpily.

The chimes from the doorbell came echoing down the hall. The siblings exchanged rueful looks.

"I'll get it," Richard said.

The woman on the front step was plump and smiling. Her belly and breasts strained against a fox-trimmed tweed coat. It had obviously been bought a lot of poundage ago. Gray curls sprang out beneath her fur hat. She held a covered Pyrex casserole pan in her gloved hands.

"You must be Richard. Your mother spoke about you *so often* and described you to a T. I would know you anywhere." She shoved the pan into his hands. "Alannis and I spent such a lot of time together after I moved here. I was afraid I couldn't make friends with her so quickly, but she made it *so* easy."

She drew out the *so*, giving it a contemptuous twist, and that's when Richard noticed that despite the pink cheeks and broad smile, the woman's eyes were cold blue and flint hard. She pushed past Richard and entered the house.

"Poor Alannis, I think she probably loved you too much," she said as she pulled off her coat and handed it to him. He juggled the pan from which rose the nauseating smell of tuna, cream of mushroom soup, and potato chips. "It wasn't hard for me to plant a few doubts, and then we'd discuss your actions over the years. Your behavior takes on a whole new light when viewed through the prism of new facts. She might have been neurotic, but she wasn't *stupid*."

It wasn't the call he had been expecting. Grenier had sent an emissary.

"Get out," Richard said through lips gone stiff with anger.

"Wouldn't dream of leaving yet. I want to offer my condolences to your *sisters,* and I understand you have a darling little *nephew*." Now an edge of fear gnawed, weakening Richard's anger. "I won't bother mentioning Robert. Alannis made it pretty clear the two of you didn't get along." She glanced back at Richard and gave him a coquettish smile, grotesque on that aging face. "And the way he controlled her life! Keeping the liquor cabinet locked, doling out a glass of wine a few times a week and refusing to allow her any sleep aids when the poor thing was so clearly suffering. I'm just glad I was able to help her find relief."

Rage exploded along every nerve ending, yanking his

muscles into a clench that set his bones to aching. Red narrowed Richard's sight, cutting off all peripheral vision, leaving only her malicious, taunting face. The coat slid out of his hand onto the marble floor. Richard spun and launched the casserole. It smashed against the paneled wall, sending gobbets of tuna and limp potato chips sliding down the wood.

"Whoops," the woman said.

Amelia and Pamela came hurrying down the hall, drawn by the explosion of breaking glass. Robert appeared in the living room archway.

The woman stepped in close and whispered in Richard's ear, "Mr. Grenier wanted me to offer you his personal condolences and remind you that you still have *so much more you could lose.* He hopes that you'll reconsider your position and give him the item."

His family reached them. "What the devil?" Robert asked.

"It must have slipped," Richard said, in a flat, emotionless voice. His sisters and father looked from the wall to Richard and the four feet that separated them.

"Mrs. Negary," said Robert, "I want to offer my apologies. It's been a long couple of days, and Richard has been under a great deal of ... stress."

Negary patted the judge on the forearm. He moved out of touching range. "I completely understand," she said. "Alannis told me a bit about the boy. How *sensitive* he is." Her tone and the mobile quirk of her eyebrows conveyed her total sympathy and complete understanding of Robert's *burden.*

Robert indicated the door to the living room. "Please, let

me get you something to drink."

Negary tucked her arm through his. "Tea would be love-ly." Pamela set her fists on her hips and glared at Richard. "What the hell is wrong with you?"

"I guess the thought of another tuna casserole just pushed me right over the edge," Richard said.

And Amelia giggled. Pamela glared at her but couldn't hold it. She began snorting with suppressed laughter. Richard forced a laugh, to share at least briefly in this moment of sibling solidarity, but the only emotion he truly felt was rage. It burned through him, but his mind was clear, diamond sharp and focused. A plan began falling into place like tumblers in a lock.

THE SAW WAS clawing through the sternum of the body on the metal autopsy table. Angela, mask, and face shield in place, stood on a riser to give her enough height to lean over the body. The wide curving light above the table threw everything into harsh relief. Damon could smell the burned yeast scent of cutting bone.

Eighties rock 'n' roll blared from the Bose player, and the bone saw howled. Damon wasn't sure if it was the saw or the very bones themselves screaming. Honestly, he felt like screaming, and he tightened his grip on the letter that had been an overnight delivery from Rhode Island. It weighed heavy in the hand, fine stationary, cream colored, swirling with watermarks. Words flowed across the page, small and precise, with that strange vertical shape of a left-handed writer.

"Angela!" There was no response. Damon snapped off the Bose and shouted, "ANGELA!"

At the same moment she whirled with an expression that was both hopeful and faux furious. When she saw it was him, she drooped in disappointment.

"Oh, it's you. What do you need?"

Wordlessly Weber offered the letter. Angela began to read. Damon didn't need to see the words to remember them. They were seared in his memory.

Dear Damon,

I know that certain revelations have caused an estrangement between us. I'm sorry for that and believe me when I say I understand and I don't blame you. But I also believe that you are a good and honorable man, which is why I'm writing to you now.

I need your help, and if any trace of affection or friendship still remains for me, I hope you will respond.

Mark Grenier is a murderer and has attempted murder time and time again. His latest victim was my mother, driven to suicide by one of his people. And I can't prove any of it. I have to bring down both him and his organization and I have to use reason's tools, not mythic weapons, to do it.

The best I have is his involvement with Andresson, removing him first from New Mexico and then from Texas. I convinced Jennifer Salisbury to have a warrant issued. A weak reed that will never survive judicial review, but it's enough to get me into his com-

pound.

By the time you read this, I will have gone to Virginia to serve the warrant and make my arrests. I'm counting on Grenier being unable to resist the chance to obtain the sword.

Everything that's been done to me and mine has been done in an effort to get me to turn over the sword. Since bribes and intimidation haven't worked, I think he'll resort to force.

Remember, Grenier has his own paladin in Andresson. They want the sword. That need will overrun any caution. So, while the other charges—aiding, abetting, and harboring a fugitive—may be bullshit, imprisoning a police offer most definitely is not.

I will try to hang on until you come … I hope you will come.

Ever your friend,
Richard

"Oh, fuck," said Angela, and shoved the letter back into Weber's hands. Tears flooded her brown eyes. "This is all *your* fault."

I know, Damon thought.

She ripped off the rubber apron, mask, and shield, throwing them to the floor. Boot heels clattered as she ran for the doors. She hit the bar with both hands, sending the door flying open.

Weber, in close pursuit, called, "Wait, we have to figure out what to do. Where are you going?"

"To Kenntnis."

"Why him?"

"He's got a plane." Angela looked back at him. "You *are* coming, aren't you?"

Weber looked down at the letter still clutched in his hand. *Yeah, I fucking am.* He set off toward his car with fast, long strides that had the diminutive coroner running to keep up.

✧   ✧   ✧

WINTER LAY LIGHTLY on the Virginia countryside. Richard, driving a rented Impala, wound his way along the curves and over the hills, following the narrow blacktop road. This was the heart of hunt country and purebred horses with high-dollar prices cropped at the still-green grass. Behind white fences, brick mansions, set well back from the road, loomed.

He had spent four days in Newport helping pack up his mother's personal effects and laying the groundwork for what he had to do. When Richard had gone to the airport that morning his father thought he was returning to New Mexico. Robert had probably learned the truth by now.

As the sun began to set, Christmas lights glowed in the trees surrounding many of the homes. No gauche Santas mounted on rooftops or wire and light deer raising and lowering their heads in robotic imitation of the grazing horses were to be seen. Money lived here, old money, and it had taste.

Seven days until Christmas and Richard's twenty-eighth birthday. The houses became fewer as he moved farther south and west.

The sun was completely gone by the time he pulled up in front of the gates. They swooped and arched before him. Pinpoint spotlights on the gatehouse gave everything a dazzling glow. Golden plaques set in the stone supports to either side read *Worldwide Christian Alliance.* The metal of the gates had been gilded with some material that made each alternating strut appear to be either gold or pearl.

"Just in case anyone misses the symbolism," Richard murmured aloud.

No, he ordered himself. *Don't be flippant. You'll blow it!*

A man dressed in a conservative suit emerged from the gatehouse. It might be civilian dress, but his muscled build and the bulge beneath his left armpit made his function quite clear—guard.

"May I help you, sir?"

"Detective Richard Oort, here to see Reverend Grenier."

"Is he expecting you?"

"Probably."

"Just one moment."

The man returned to the guard house. Through the window Richard could see him on the phone. He nodded and reached out to a control panel. The gates swung slowly open.

Don't let down your guard. There will be cameras. This is just the first hurdle.

The guard was back. "Follow this road to the fork. Go left. The house is a couple of miles farther on."

"Thank you," Richard said.

There were a number of buildings dotted along the road. Some looked like offices, others like dormitories. Judging from the enormous satellite dishes, one was a broadcasting studio. Richard reached the fork. To the right, the road ran straight up the hill and ended at an enormous white stone church. In front of it stood an even taller white stone cross.

Richard spun the wheel and sent the car up the left fork. He was driving through a mixed forest—evergreens, and deciduous trees denuded now for winter.

It seemed like a long time before Richard saw the house. It was a rustic, timbered building, but huge, two stories tall with long wings running back toward a granite cliff. Most of the windows were illuminated.

A wide circular driveway brought him to the front doors. Richard parked. As he locked the door, shielded from the house by the bulk of the car, he gave himself the final instructions.

Be angry, but a tentative anger. Unsure of what they might do next.

Be afraid.

As he climbed the stone steps, he realized the last instruction no longer required acting. He was afraid. Deathly afraid.

✧　✧　✧

THE DOORBELL PLAYED the opening chords of a hymn, so corny and so at odds with the elegant Grenier. Definitely pandering for the believing sheep, Richard thought with a curl of his lip. The heavy, carved wood doors, inset with stained glass, opened slowly. A pretty young woman in a plaid skirt and black turtleneck sweater smiled in welcome. Soft brown hair swung in a pageboy that just brushed her shoulders. She had an English complexion of cream and roses.

"May I take your coat?" she asked. Richard handed over his overcoat. Shrugged to straighten the shoulders of his suit coat and shot his cuffs. "This way." She indicated the direction with a sweep of her hand.

The public rooms contained thick white carpet, blue velvet furniture, and crystal chandeliers. The art was overly lush, overly large landscapes or religious pictures. Everything was expensive, and tacky in the extreme.

They left the main body of the house through a short hallway that ended at an ebony door. "Reverend Grenier said to send you to his private quarters. Just go through there." She indicated the door and gave him another smile. She turned and walked away.

Richard stared at the polished black wood. *Give me the strength.* Once that would have been asked of God. Now it rested only on him, his strength, his spirit, his will.

He opened the door and stepped through. Ahead, light spilled from an open doorway. A long runner, a carved Chinese rug, spread out before him. The art on the walls wasn't to Kenntnis's standards, but it was damn fine, tending toward American modern.

The open door brought him into a living room. The furniture was eighteenth century, or very fine reproductions. An enormous oriental rug in golds, blues, and creams lay on a polished slate floor. There were mirrors, but all were opaque gray like the mirrors in the South Valley trailer. It was all tasteful, elegant, and at odds with the presentation in the more public parts of the mansion.

A fireplace dominated one wall. Built of river rocks with

a granite mantelpiece, it looked large enough to roast an ox. Flames danced in the grate.

Richard heard the door close behind him and whirled. Mark Grenier stood, his hand on the doorknob, watching Richard. The minister's head was cocked to the side, a quizzical gesture. Grenier was dressed in a soft, gray cardigan sweater over a striped dress shirt in shades of green, pink, blue, purple, and yellow. Richard had a moment of both connection and dislocation. He was wearing the same shirt. Etro Milano, $$360 at Robert R. Bailey.

"You are the most unexpected young man," Grenier said. "To what do I owe the pleasure? Or have you reconsidered accepting my offer? Mrs. Negary didn't seem hopeful after your meeting."

"How could you possibly think I would work for you after what you did?" Outrage shook in his voice. Richard paused for breath and dialed it down.

"To avoid my doing it *again*," Grenier said with soft menace. "You've just had a taste of what my power can accomplish."

"Yes, well, you're not going to be able to do anything again because you're going to be in jail." His voice sounded absurdly young.

Grenier's eyebrows lifted in delighted surprise. "Oh, really?"

With his left-hand Richard removed the badge from his inside breast pocket and flipped open the leather case. With his right hand he pulled the warrant out of his coat pocket and opened it with a snap of the wrist.

"I'm here to arrest Douglas Andresson and return him to

New Mexico for trial. I'm also arresting you for aiding and abetting a felon in contravention of his parole agreement and assisting in his flight to avoid prosecution. Add to that harboring a fugitive."

For a long moment Grenier just stared at him, then he threw back his head and laughed, roaring out his amusement. When he finally stopped, Grenier mopped at his streaming eyes. "Are you completely out of your mind?"

Grenier was keeping well beyond Richard's reach, and Richard knew he was going to have to force the issue.

"I'm Mark Grenier. I pray with presidents and make and break political candidates. One heartfelt plea on my network and I can raise five million dollars in a day. An outraged commentary can bring a news anchor to their knees."

"And you bring monsters into our world," Richard said.

"They were already here. Since we developed a cerebral cortex, they've been here. A million years of human evolution and they're still here. Kenntnis hasn't defeated them yet. You can't win and I don't back losers. When the gates finally open, I won't be one of the cattle."

"No, you'll be a *sonderkommando* for the human race," Richard said. "Well, someone has to stop you." And Richard reached into the holster at the small of his back and pulled out the hilt.

Panic replaced contempt, and Grenier retreated behind the sofa, yelling, "Doug, Bruce, Willie, get in here now!"

Another door on the side of the room opened. Two big men, one black and one white, charged through, followed by Doug Andresson.

"Get that away from him!"

Richard lifted his right hand toward the hilt, but a shovel-sized hand slammed against his wrist. His fingers went numb. He dropped the hilt. The black man slapped him along the side of the head, setting his ears to ringing. Then he was firmly gripped between them.

Andresson, grinning happily, removed the pistol from Richard's shoulder holster, then gave him a rough pat down. "Like that, don't you, sweetie?" Andresson said as he clenched his fist around Richard's balls.

"Doug," Grenier snapped out. "Leave that to Bruce and Willie. Get the sword."

Andresson picked up the hilt and walked over to Grenier. He pushed it at Grenier, who recoiled. "Want to inspect it?"

"Go. Work with it."

"What do you want us to do with him, sir?" the white goon asked.

"Lock him up downstairs."

"He's a cop, sir," Willie said.

"Who is well out of his jurisdiction, and who threatened me."

The two big men hustled him toward the door. Richard, feet barely touching the floor, had a moment of panic. He quelled it and forced himself to call back over his shoulder.

"I guess this means you're resisting arrest?"

CHAPTER THIRTY-THREE

"WHO THE DEVIL are you? Why the hell are you interfering in my son's life? And what in God's name is *this*?"

The hilt landed in the center of Kenntnis's granite desk and gave its bell-like cry. Robert Oort jumped and retreated a few steps as the perfect overtones echoed and reechoed through the office, then slowly faded. Oort stared at the hilt with the air of man for whom the rules had changed, the situation had become confusing, and who resented the hell out of it.

Kenntnis also felt as if the ground had shifted when the hilt came out. He had been surprised, but unperturbed, to hear that Judge Robert Oort waited downstairs. Kenntnis assumed that Richard had tried to communicate something of his new understanding to his father, and now it was up to Kenntnis to make it explicable. The sight of the sword changed *everything*.

Resting his fists on the desk, Kenntnis levered himself to his feet and inclined his head to the judge.

"I am Kenntnis. How do you do?"

"Not well," snapped Oort.

"Neither do I ... now," Kenntnis said. He picked up the hilt. "How did you come by this?"

"My son left it for me, along with a first-class plane ticket to Albuquerque, and this … this … gibberish." Oort tossed a folded piece of paper toward Kenntnis. Kenntnis snatched it out of the air and read.

Dear Papa,

By now you've found this object and the first-class ticket on the red eye out of Logan to Albuquerque. And you've dismissed this as ravings by your son.

Don't.

This thing that I've left for you is of incalculable value. It would be impossible for me to explain its powers and purpose in a letter. Kenntnis will explain it all to you just like he did for me. Just believe me when I say it holds back the darkness, and many people's fates, not the least of them mine, hinge on its safe return to its creator. I think Kenntnis made it; at any rate he is certainly its custodian.

Thanks to Kenntnis I've realized that I'm not weak. And now I'm going to prove it to you by bringing Mama's murderers to justice. They manipulated her into suicide, trying to force me to give them this thing. Obviously, I can't have it when I confront them, so I'm depending on you to return it to its rightful owner.

I know I've been a disappointment to you. Kenntnis says it's your problem, not mine, but it still affects me and makes it hard for me to ask this favor of you now. But I must. I know your character—your honor, integrity, and sense of duty. Despite our differences, I trust you. I'm begging you, take this object to New

Mexico and return it to Kenntnis at Lumina Enterprises.

Papa, guard this thing with your life. Tell no one you have it and give it into no one's keeping except Kenntnis's. Please do this for me.

Kenntnis says I don't have to like you, much less love you. You've certainly made it hard for me to, but I've decided that I do love you, Papa. I hope someday you'll love me back.

Richard

Kenntnis looked up from the letter and met Robert Oort's furious, blue-eyed gaze. The judge made a gesture of distaste. "Richard has always had a taste for hyperbole and the overly dramatic. So did his mother." His lips twisted, a complex mix of grief and disgust.

Kenntnis dropped the letter. The paper fluttered down as broken and ephemeral as the family. "There's nothing hysterical about this. It's a masterful job of manipulation. How many times did he refer to me?" He picked up the letter and scanned it again. "Seven times. When he really didn't need to mention me by name at all. He made this about *you* and *me*. You wouldn't have come here for *him*, but you'd come here to kick my ass for interfering in his life and in what you consider your family's business." He handed the letter back to the judge.

"I think you give him too much credit," came the dismissive response.

"You really don't know this kid at all, do you?" Kenntnis

marveled, both disgusted and amazed at the man's obtuseness.

"He's my son. I think I know him better than you," Oort said.

"You'd be wrong," Kenntnis shot back. "So, let's try another question. Richard's question. Do you love him?"

Kenntnis watched the conflicting emotions play in the dark blue eyes. Kenntnis knew the type. Usually male, terrified by emotional displays because they feared the power of their own emotions. Certain if they ever expressed their feelings, they would be overpowered by them.

"I will not discuss any of this." Oort edged the words with fight. "I came here for some specific answers." The letter crumpled as his hand clenched.

"And you're going to get some, and probably not like any of them. Now, *sit down!*" Kenntnis rarely used that voice on humans anymore. It still worked.

Oort dropped into the big armchair, the same one Richard had selected all those weeks ago. The man gripped the padded leather arms and looked about as if wondering how he'd come to be there.

Kenntnis rested a hip on the edge of his desk. "Your son loves you. He won't permit a word to be said against you, even though you are clearly a son of a bitch and a self-righteous prick. He's also quite afraid of you because … Did I mention this before? You're a son of a bitch and a self-righteous prick. So, he tries desperately to win your approval, and you piss on him every time."

It was clear where Richard got his guts. Oort came out of the chair and stood quivering in front of Kenntnis.

"How dare you! I will not listen to this." He tried to move around Kenntnis toward the door.

"Oh, no, no you don't. I'm just getting started." Kenntnis grabbed Oort's arm and swung him back down into the chair. "First, you kill his musical ambitions—"

"He kept auditioning and auditioning, and never getting hired," Oort shouted. "I asked how much longer he was going to go on with this, and then he admits to me that he didn't have the talent to succeed."

"So, you demanded he quit."

"He was drifting," Oort said.

"So what? He wasn't sponging off you, was he?" Kenntnis asked.

"That's not the point. It's not what we do. We work. We're a family that serves. We gave him every opportunity, foreign travel, private schools, a fine college. He never follows through on *anything*." Oort gave Kenntnis a bitter smile. "And what does it say about Richard's character that he'd meekly quit on my say-so. You make him out to be a paragon. In fact, he's weak."

"Do you like that he's become a policeman?"

"No."

"Made that pretty clear, have you?" Oort didn't verbally reply, but the answer was in his face. "Hasn't quit yet, has he? And, by the way, he's a damn fine policeman."

"And now he's run off to God knows where in pursuit of enemies that don't exist. My wife committed suicide!" Oort choked, clenched his jaw, and looked away. "So, he'll probably lose *this* job, too."

"Ah, yes, that *other* job," Kenntnis said. "That job that

you got him. Let's talk about *that job*." Oort looked up, a sharp glance, for he'd heard the threat purring in Kenntnis's voice. Then the judge's eyes were quickly veiled by lowered lashes.

"You suspected something, didn't you?" Kenntnis said. "All this bullshit about a random mugging, but the doctors wouldn't tell you anything about his injuries because Richard wouldn't let them. Easier to blame Richard, keep thinking of him as a failure. What kept you from finding out? Fear of what you might discover? Or what that discovery might say about *your* judgment and acuity?"

Oort jerked to his feet and pushed past Kenntnis, seeking open air and relief from Kenntnis's accusatory presence. Kenntnis didn't give him any respite. He closed in once more. "Let me tell you what Richard suffered at the hands of your good *friend*."

And he did. Holding back nothing. Softening none of the ugly details while not revealing Richard's actual sexual preferences. That was not Kenntnis's to share. Oort ended up hunched over the desk, palms flat against the granite, relying on the stone to keep him upright.

"For five years, your son has carried this secret and a crushing load of guilt and shame. Never telling anyone. Until me. I held him while he cried. It should have been *you*, but he couldn't tell you. Not because he thought it would lower him in your estimation. He knows where he stands with you—the disappointment, the weakling, the failed son. He kept it from you because he didn't want to hurt you and destroy your relationship with his assailant!" Kenntnis swept up the letter, smoothed out the creases, and glanced through it again.

"You don't deserve this boy! Despite everything, he still turns to you as the person he most trusts in the world. Though you sure as hell don't deserve it. If he says he's gone to bring your wife's killers to justice—"

The office doors flew open, and Angela and Weber charged in. Kenntnis looked from the letter clutched in the policeman's hand back down to the one he held.

"Richard's gone after Grenier," Angela panted.

"We need your plane," Weber said, then hurriedly added, "Please."

"They've got the sword," Angela concluded in a tone fraught with dismay.

Kenntnis reached around Oort and held up the hilt. "No. No, they don't."

"Sword?" came faintly from the judge.

Weber raised his eyebrows and pointed at Oort.

"Richard's father," said Kenntnis shortly as he headed for the door.

"Don't we owe him an explanation?" Weber asked.

"No. He hasn't earned one yet."

"Sword?"

RICHARD WASN'T CERTAIN how long he'd been in the basement since Willie had helped himself to Richard's watch and the family signet ring. It was silly, given his overall predicament, but worry over how his father would react to that loss was his foremost thought. The ring had been given to every Oort son on his twentieth birthday since 1797. Now he had lost it.

Four concrete walls surrounded him. One was pierced with a heavy metal door. Despite his fear and tension, hunger gnawed at Richard's belly, and his tongue felt swollen from thirst.

Underfoot was more concrete, with a six-inch drain set in the middle of the floor. Overhead a high-wattage bulb burned behind a wire grate. The light reflecting off the white-gray walls made his eyes water and his head ache. There wasn't a stick of furniture or any sort of sanitary facility. Eventually he urinated down the drain.

They had taken his suit coat and emptied his pants pockets. It was cold in just his shirtsleeves, and the hard floor made his seat bones ache. Richard stood and walked in brisk circles, trying to beat back the damp chill.

He wondered how long he had been locked up. Hours certainly.

A day? He couldn't tell. And a larger problem loomed. He was a police officer being held against his will, but right now it was his word against an internationally famous evangelical minister that the imprisonment had occurred. He needed more.

A key rattled in the lock. The door opened and Bruce entered. Richard thought he came alone, but Andresson stepped out from behind Bruce's camouflaging bulk. Andresson's full under lip protruded in a childlike pout, but the eyes were mean. Richard watched the hilt flip back and forth as Andresson tossed it from hand to hand.

Andresson closed to within inches. His breath was hot, rank, and sour on Richard's face.

"How the fuck do you make it work?" He shook the hilt. "Mark and me have been tryin' and tryin', and now he's checking out some books, and maybe he's even gonna talk to the faces, but I figured, what the fuck, I got *you*."

The door stood open behind Andresson. It seemed in character to make a break for it. Richard used his shoulder to shove Andresson aside and bolted through the door. Stiff muscles seemed to crack as he barreled into a run. Glancing over, he saw the keys hanging in the lock. Stunned by their stupidity, Richard began to swing the door closed, his his other hand grabbing for the keys. Even if he succeeded in locking them in, Richard didn't figure he'd get out of the house, much less the compound.

The door shook and pushed back. Richard strained to hold it, but the combined weight of the two men on the other side overwhelmed him. Springing back, Richard went pelting for the basement stairs. The sudden release of pressure sent Bruce and Andresson plunging and staggering into the basement. The door banged against the wall.

The muscles in his thighs strained as Richard took the steps two at a time. He made it halfway up before a hand caught him by the ankle and jerked. He fell full-length on the stairs, cracking his chin, teeth snapping together on his tongue. Pain seared through his skull. Bruce twisted a hand in the collar of Richard's shirt and dragged him to his feet.

"Bring him down here!" Andresson ordered.

Choking from the pressure on his throat, Richard was half dragged, half carried back into the basement.

Bruce frog-marched Richard up to Andresson. He transferred his grip from the collar to Richard's upper arms. The confinement raised old fears. Richard felt his belly muscles quivering.

"Show me how it works," Andresson repeated.

"You were in the church," Richard said, forcing insolence.

"You had your back to me. When you came around it was there. What's the goddamn trick?" Andresson demanded.

"It's really quite simple." There was a flicker of frustration and dull anger in Andresson's black eyes, and Richard knew he had the tool to release Andresson's pent-up rage. For an instant Richard hesitated, because he was afraid, but it had to be done. He had to have proof. "Or at least it was for *me*." Richard laid a subtle emphasis on the pronoun. "But maybe I shouldn't be surprised *you* can't figure it out."

Snake quick, the sharp toe of Andresson's cowboy boot took Richard in the nuts. Pain exploded from his groin through the top of his head and a scream gurgled up, carried on a wave of rushing vomit. Richard clutched himself and curled into a fetal crouch as vomit trickled down his chin.

"Disrespect me, you little faggot. Now, you're going to tell me what I want to know. When I go up to Mr. Grenier again, I'm going to damn well know how to use this fucking thing."

"I doubt it," Richard whispered. "You're too stupid."

Andresson shoved the hilt through his belt and nodded to Bruce.

The big man jerked Richard upright and held him while Andresson laid into Richard's gut with punishing, rhythmic blows. At first Richard managed to keep his muscles taut, absorbing the punches, but pain from his abused testicles and growing terror of those clutching hands broke his concentration. His belly muscles softened, and the next punch bent him double.

As Richard folded, Andresson's knee met Richard's face in a hard upper cut, driving his lips against the edge of his teeth. The taste and smell of blood was added to the rank smell and sour taste of vomit and the sharp reek of sweat. *Just like that night ... with Drew.* Richard coughed and spat blood onto Andresson's boots.

"How does it work?" Andresson asked.

"No," Richard gasped. The fist took him in the corner of his right eye.

The beating went on. One eye was swelling shut. Blood trickled down his chin from a cut on his lip. His cheekbones hurt. Richard withdrew deep inside his mind, trying to block out the escalating pain. Tried to focus on the passing minutes. *Hang on. Hang on. Two more minutes. Five minutes. Time. I've got to buy time.*

THEY WERE GATHERED around the coffee table in the living room of the penthouse. Kenntnis swept several large art books onto the floor and set down the silver bowl. A small bit of water sloshed over onto the elaborate wood inlay. Angela instinctively wiped it up with the cuff of her jacket.

Rhiana huddled on the sofa, fingers writhing nervously through her long black hair. Cross, looking like a Peruvian mummy, just skin stretched on bone, sat in an armchair.

"Have you ever done a scrying?" Kenntnis asked the girl. Rhiana shook her head. "We take something of Richard's. We drop it into the water, you focus, and search for him."

"Based on this other letter, we know where he's gone," the judge said.

Angela studied the senior Oort from beneath her lashes. There were similarities. Richard had his father's jaw and there was the same slenderness of frame though Robert Oort was taller, perhaps five foot nine or ten. His blue eyes were unusual, with a dark halo around the iris. He had bequeathed that trait to his son. But unlike his son, Robert Oort's eyes didn't look like they ever showed much warmth or humor.

"Yes," said Kenntnis. "But there are fifteen buildings on the property. We don't want to have to search them all."

"Anybody got anything of Richard's?" Angela asked.

They all looked at each other. Weber started for the door. "I'll go over to his apartment. Get something. What kind of something you want?" he asked Kenntnis.

"Not necessary. You've got him," Cross said in a whispering croak, and pointed at Robert Oort. "Blood and bone." They all regarded the judge, whose expression went from careful control to outright confusion.

Kenntnis turned and picked up an elaborate Mogul dagger in a gold and jeweled sheath off an end table. The knife emerged with a soft shush of steel on leather. "Yes, half the DNA is probably more helpful than a psychometric object, no matter how often Richard handled it."

Angela could see the flight response struggling to overcome the judge's cool demeanor. "Are you all mad?"

Weber stepped in. "Look, Your Honor, I know it sounds

crazy, but it's all true. I've seen shit that … well … that's just unbelievable and will scare the crap right out of you. Let them try."

"And if nothing happens?" Oort asked.

"Then your old lady was fucking somebody else when she got knocked up," said Cross. He pointed at Rhiana. "She's good. If Richard's your kid, she'll find him."

"Or we're all insane and you can have us arrested or committed, your choice," Kenntnis said.

Oort considered for a moment then walked up to the table and held out his hand for the knife. Kenntnis gave a little half bow and handed over the dagger. Oort gripped the jeweled handle, and flexed his left hand several times, preparing himself to cut.

Angela took the knife away from him. "Look, I'm trained to cut flesh with sharp objects. Why don't you let me?"

Oort looked down at her. "You're a scientist, a physician. Do you believe any of this?"

"All of it," Angela said. They looked at each other for a long time; then Oort gave a sharp nod and held his hand over the silver bowl.

Angela tested the edge on her thumb. It was razor sharp. She weighed the balance of the blade and cut quickly, parting the skin. Drops of blood struck the water, and swirled away in slow eddies, deep red in the center fading to rose at the edges.

"That's probably enough," Cross croaked.

"Get me some bandages and antiseptic," Angela ordered.

"There's a first aid kit in the cabinet in the front bathroom," Kenntnis said to Weber. The cop went.

"Got a penny?" Cross asked Rhiana. She nodded.

Weber returned with a first aid kit. Angela went to work bandaging the judge's hand. Rhiana chanted quietly. The penny flared. The judge jumped.

"Now what?" Rhiana asked, looking from Cross to Kenntnis.

"Since you've never done this before, I'd put it in the water," Cross whispered. "Give yourself all the help you can."

Rhiana dropped in the penny. It spun beneath the water, creating a whirlpool effect. The bloodstained water glowed.

"Now find him," Cross ordered.

Rhiana, her face tight with concentration, held the edges of the bowl between her hands and bent over the water.

Angela gave the bandage a final pat, and edged closer to the table, craning to see. She felt Richard's father standing stiffly behind her, his sharp, nervous breaths ruffling her hair.

The water swirled wildly, then froze. Richard hung limply in the grip of a big man. A smaller man was delivering a brutal beating. Blood ran from a cut over Richard's eye, his nose, his lips. Both eyes were blackened.

"Oh, God, Richard," the judge said.

"Pull back," Cross instructed Rhiana. "Show us the fucking building." The water swirled and stilled again, showing a large stone and timber building.

"Cocky, cocky," murmured Kenntnis. "That's the main house. Okay, let's go."

Kenntnis began issuing orders. "Weber, contact local law enforcement and try to get a warrant and backup. Given Grenier's standing in the community it won't be easy but try. Angela," he turned to her. "Judging from the scrying,

Richard's going to be in bad shape. You need to get him on his feet … fast. Have something special, and I don't care if it's legal, in your black bag."

"Okay, then I'm going to have to meet you at the airport."

"Do I want to know what you're getting?" Weber asked.

"No."

Angela turned away to grab her purse and found herself looking at Rhiana as the girl fished the penny out of the bloody water. Rhiana brought the penny up to her lips. There was a spark, and the fire jumped from the penny and vanished between her lips. Angela was dimly aware of Kenntnis telling Cross that as soon as they found Richard, Cross should get the sword into his hands, but it didn't really register because she was watching Rhiana lick the blood delicately off her fingers. It was disturbing, but before she could say anything or even ponder the significance, an altercation had begun.

Angela heard Cross say in a loud, rude, and aggrieved voice, "Excuse me!" When she looked over Oort senior and the homeless god each had a hand on the hilt.

"My son left this in *my* keeping." There was a tug of war, then Kenntnis with one of his sly smiles nodded to Cross who, grumbling, released the hilt.

"Excuse me," said Rhiana and there was a catch in her voice. "I need a minute." She ran out of the room.

"I believe you said you have a plane?" the judge said. Angela, Weber, Kenntnis and Cross exchanged glances.

"Quick learner," grunted the homeless god.

CHAPTER THIRTY-FOUR

"*W*HAT THE HELL *are you doing!*" It was Grenier, roaring out his fury. He seized Andresson by the hair and yanked him away from Richard. Bruce released Richard like he was toxic. It didn't even hurt to hit the floor. It was just a relief to lie there.

"I didn't want a mark on him. We were the injured party here, and now you've gone and done this!" Grenier pulled the handkerchief out of his breast pocket and fastidiously wiped his fingers and hand.

Richard realized he was wiping away the grease from Andresson's unwashed hair. He also realized that Grenier was no longer wearing the twin to Richard's now blood-stained shirt. A day had passed, and that gave him hope.

Andresson climbed to his feet, glaring hatred at Grenier. The older man gave him a look of disdain. Which Richard thought took some real guts, because Andresson frankly scared the crap out of him.

"Well, it's too late now," Grenier said. He walked over to Richard, and bending down, began to blot the blood flowing from Richard's nose. Richard felt his nose shift in a way it wasn't supposed to. He whimpered. "Richard, dear boy, please tell Doug how to use the sword."

"No," Richard said thickly.

The butterfly knife came out and opened with a rattle. Andresson lunged toward Richard's eyes. "Tell me or I'll fucking blind you."

Richard cried out, shrinking back. He threw his hands up in front of his face. The point of the knife slashed across his palms. Grenier clotheslined Andresson and thrust him back. Andresson swung hard at Grenier and popped him on the temple. Grenier couldn't seem to credit that *he* had been hit. But Richard had seen the behavior often enough. Violent criminals didn't have an edit button. Andresson wanted to hurt Richard. Grenier had gotten in his way. Andresson had struck out without thought of the consequences. But Bruce knew who paid his salary. He kicked the knife out of the young man's hand and gathered Andresson into a bear hug.

Grenier's eyes flicked between Richard and Andresson. Richard found himself thinking about the Italian shirt again, and suddenly Richard knew what he was seeing. Even bloodied and bruised, Richard was of Grenier's class. Andresson was a tool forced upon Grenier because of an accident of genetics.

"Do you really want to give him the sword?" Richard whispered. "He'll have the power to destroy you."

"What choice do I have?" Grenier said in an equally low tone. "You persist in playing the hero."

"Maybe you just haven't offered me the right incentive," Richard said. It was hard to look coy with his eyes swelling shut, but he tried.

"Bring Detective Oort upstairs," Grenier said to Bruce. The big man released Andresson, grabbed Richard under the arms and hauled him to his feet.

"Hey! What the fuck is this shit?" Andresson began.

Grenier walked over until he and Andresson were nose to nose.

"Douglas, you are on thin ice right now. You are proving to be a disappointment to me, so I suggest you *stop* disappointing me, and try not to annoy me further."

"Fuck you!" And Andresson flung himself away up the stairs.

"You want me to get him, boss?" Bruce asked.

"He won't go far. Tell Willie to bring him and the hilt to my office. Or just the hilt if Doug isn't inclined to join us."

✦　✦　✦

Cross, Rhiana, Angela, Robert Oort and Kenntnis waited on the tarmac beside the Gulfstream GV. Kenntnis cocked an eyebrow at the sight of the large duffel Weber carried as he joined them.

"Guns and body armor," Damon grunted.

"I suppose I should be grateful that private air travel is exempt from security inspections," the judge muttered.

"All right, this is us going now," Cross said and started to climb the stairs into the plane.

The others followed. Kenntnis remained on the tarmac. Rhiana looked back. Her expression was troubled. "You're not coming with us?"

"No. Cross will help you."

"Look at him! He's barely functioning. He could shatter at any moment. I need someone to help me, advise me. I need *you*."

Kenntnis looked up at Cross, who stood in the door of the plane. The homeless god shrugged. "Do as you please, but I told you I got a bad feeling if you come along."

Rhiana gave Kenntnis a tremulous smile. "I didn't think you could be spooked by 'I've got a bad feeling about this.'"

Kenntnis swallowed his doubts and joined them on the plane.

✧　　✧　　✧

THE PRETTY, PERKY assistant provided an ice pack, aspirin, and a glass of cognac. She seemed unfazed by Richard's condition. They sat in Grenier's study, an elegant room filled with glass-fronted bookcases, a Queen Anne desk, and a number of opaque mirrors. A Perisan rug filled with flowers and twining vines was underfoot. Grenier sat behind the desk, a copy of the presidential Resolute Desk, his hands folded serenely on the blotter. To either side of the desk, floor-to-ceiling windows looked out on a grove of pines. A wind had risen and sang with a bass groan in the branches, shaking loose the thin layer of snow that had fallen. Judging by the light and the position of the sun, it was midmorning. Richard realized he had been imprisoned for two nights and a day. His thoughts went to the miles separating New Mexico and Virginia, and where along that route his friends might be. Assuming anyone was coming, of course.

The cognac stung the cuts in and on his mouth, but Richard forced himself to keep taking small sips. He needed the stimulant.

"So, what is it you want?" Grenier asked.

"I know you've been making inquiries about me," Richard said.

"Please don't state the obvious," Grenier drawled. "You don't have a lot of leeway here."

"Well, I'm assuming you found Drew."

Grenier maintained the bored tone, but Richard saw the subtle tightening of his shoulders. "Yes."

"And he's talked to you?" Richard asked.

"Yes. Your behavior at the funeral got him quite worried. He thought you were going to break your silence. Our offer to prevent that was all the incentive he needed."

"Well, that's what I want. I want to hurt Drew. I want him to go to jail. I want to wreck him financially." Richard shrugged. "If you can make and break presidents, Drew should be easy."

"Simple vengeance? And here I thought you were a little hero," Grenier said.

"Sorry to disappoint," Richard said.

Grenier keyed the intercom on his desk. "Ellie, has Willie found Doug? I want him now."

Richard held up a finger. "No, you start the ball rolling first."

"You make a lot of demands."

Richard forced a smile. He wasn't sure if it came out as cocky or just a grimace. "I'm worth it."

Grenier left the desk. "And by the way. Willie is going to be holding a gun to your head, literally, when you do draw the sword. You will not threaten me. Understood?"

"Understood."

The door opened and Andresson walked in. *No, correct*

that, thought Richard, *he's swaggering. That can't be good.* Willie, his brow creased with concern, walked behind him. He was carrying a piece of newspaper. On it were small pieces of gray Lucite.

There was a sudden tightness beneath Richard's breastbone. "Mr. Grenier, Doug was out at the wood pile using the ax on that … hilt … thing. I'm sorry, sir, I hope this isn't a problem." He laid the paper gingerly on the desk in front of Grenier.

Grenier stared at the shards as if he'd just heard the stock market had dropped to zero.

Andresson strolled up to the desk, perched on the edge and began cleaning under his nails with the sterling silver letter opener. "Just doing a little *experimentation*, Mark," Andresson said with a grin. "Is it supposed to … uh … fall apart like that?" Andresson gave a braying laugh. "He played you, dude, and you never even *saw* it."

Grenier's hands shot out and gathered the fragments to him.

When he finally looked up his expression was so cold and so hateful that Richard began to tremble.

"Let me kill him," Andresson said eagerly.

Sadness and regret closed on the back of Richard's throat. He hadn't thought he would die. He had really thought they would reach him in time.

"No," said Grenier.

"But he played you. He's gotta have the cops coming."

Nauseating colors began to roil and twist through one of the mirrors. There were the outlines of something that might have been a face, and that strange guttural language that

Richard had first heard out of Rhiana echoed from the mirror. Grenier listened intently then nodded. The colors vanished.

Grenier turned back to Andresson. "His associates are coming, but they'll never be able to get help. He's a rogue cop out of his jurisdiction, they have no proof, and I'm Mark Grenier."

"And we want these people here why?" Andresson asked. Richard shared the psychopath's confusion.

"For reasons you don't need to know about. But in the meantime, we may as well convince Richard to tell us where he left the *actual* sword. It will be useful even after—" Grenier broke off as if suddenly aware he was saying too much. "Where is the sword, Richard?" Richard carefully set aside the ice pack, took one final sip of cognac, and remained silent. "Well, all right. Actually, I'd just as soon hurt you," Grenier said cheerfully.

Richard briefly wondered if he could take what was coming. *But I manipulated Andresson into beating me, and I endured that.* And he remembered what he'd said at his mother's casket. *I'm not weak.* It sure as hell hadn't been meant for her. He had been the only person in that room who could listen and hear. Richard took a deep breath and met Grenier's eyes. He'd hold on.

✧ ✧ ✧

WEBER WORKED THE phones from the moment they reached cruising altitude and got nowhere. No local Virginia cop was going to roll into the Worldwide Christian Alliance on the say-so of an Albuquerque cop. Now, if he could get them any *evidence* that a police officer had been kidnapped that would definitely change the equation, but of course he mustn't harass Reverend Grenier while *obtaining* that evidence. After his last useless call, he pocketed his phone and addressed the group.

"I won't kid you, this ain't good. If we were rolling up with a line of cop cars there's less chance of Richard getting killed." He pushed aside the sick feeling just saying the words had elicited. "Flunkies tend to give up when they see cops, and not want to face a capital murder charge, especially not of a police officer."

"What about the FBI?" Kenntnis said. He turned to Richard's old man. In Weber's estimation Judge Oort had all the warmth of a glacier on a granite cliff. "You're a federal judge."

"What's the allegation?" Oort asked. "I *think* my son's being held prisoner by one of the country's foremost evangelists?"

"Maybe your wife," Weber began. "We could do a little hand waving about finding new evidence that the suicide wasn't—"

"What about nuclear terrorism," Rhiana said quietly. Everyone looked at the girl. Weber felt like the plane had just dropped ten thousand feet.

"Why am I just hearing about nukes?" he asked plaintively.

Rhiana ignored him and focused on the judge. "I'm a physics student. I was building a nuclear bomb for them."

"You would testify to this?" the judge asked.

"Yes."

"They'll take you into custody," Oort warned.

"And they'll have to come to Grenier's compound to do that, won't they?" Weber said. He shot an approving grin at Rhiana. The momentary flicker of pleasure and hope didn't do much to loosen the knot of tension in his gut.

"But will they come?" Kenntnis asked. "The current administration has close ties to Grenier."

"And after 9/11 and the rise of domestic terrorism and white supremacy the FBI's motto is CYA," Oort replied. "An abject apology for inconveniencing Mr. Grenier is preferable to congressional hearings over the failure to prevent a nuclear attack. Oh, I expect they will come."

Since they were only moments away from landing, that call had to wait. As soon as they were wheels down at the private airport in Virginia, Judge Oort turned on his cell phone. It started ringing immediately. He answered as they hustled across the tarmac toward a waiting helicopter and a large Land Rover.

"Hello …? Pamela, I can't talk right now. I have to make a call—" Weber could faintly hear a woman's voice. She sounded stressed, panicked, and pissed, but Damon couldn't distinguish any of the words.

Oort stopped walking, and as he watched, the blood flowed out of his face. "No, I can't say when I'll be back. You handle things." He listened and two dull pink spots blossomed high on his cheeks. "What I'm doing right now is pretty damn important!" He snapped his phone shut and turned to face them. "That was my daughter, Pamela. My house in Newport has been burgled and set on fire." He slowly took the hilt out of his overcoat pocket and gazed down at it thoughtfully.

"Looks like those nuclear terrorists heard you were after them," Weber said. Oort met the cop's gaze and nodded. He opened his phone and called the FBI.

✦   ✦   ✦

Weber was a rapidly dwindling figure standing next to the big Land Rover. Angela, peering down through the side door of the helicopter, thought he gave them a salute before climbing into the car.

Even with the headphones, the chatter of the blades was a bone-shaking presence.

"Poor guy," Cross said. "Maybe one of us should have gone with him."

"The FBI was not going to allow any of us to enter the compound with them. They *will* take Weber," Kenntnis replied over the comm.

"And treat him like shit," Angela added.

"Boss," said the pilot, "the FAA is grounding air traffic around our destination."

"Damn, I thought we'd timed this better," Kenntnis grumbled. "So, fly *real* low," he told the pilot.

The man's thumb shot up. "They'll think we're a car."

Angela could see the pilot's teeth, white and straight as he grinned beneath his helmet. She hated him for his cheerfulness. She hated helicopters. She hated Richard for taking this insane risk. She hated Grenier for making it necessary for Richard to take this insane risk.

She touched the rough material and ceramic inserts in her vest, and then the barrel of the shotgun nestled beside her seat; party favors from Weber's Duffel-Bag-O'Mayhem.

They swooped down the road. The bare branches of the trees trembled under the assault from the rotors, and a few withered but stubborn leaves that still clung to them were whirled away in tatters. The few cars they encountered swerved in dismay at the sight of a large helicopter skimming just above their roofs.

Oort senior had been totally silent, but he stirred, leaned into Angela, and indicated for her to lift her earphones. She did. He yelled into her ear. "Who is he? How can he arrange all this?"

"Money," said Cross in a perfectly normal tone of voice that somehow carried over the noise of the motor and blades. Oort's eyes widened. "It's the ultimate magic power."

"Boss," came the pilot's voice. "We've got an FBI helicopter closing fast. If I leave the road, I can take us over that ridge and straight down into the compound."

"Do it."

"You're going to have to get me out of the hoosegow later," the pilot warned.

"I'll handle it," Kenntnis said.

Angela forced herself to keep her eyes open, but she was sure the skids scrapped the rough granite outcropping as they roared over the top of the bluff. Suddenly another helicopter drew up next to them. The armored, helmeted and heavily armed figure in the doorway of the chopper made hand signals. The bottom fell out of Angela's stomach as their pilot took them straight down the cliff. Below her spread a beautiful snow-covered valley dotted with blue-green evergreens, bare-branched oaks, and chestnut trees. Their pursuer overshot them. Their helicopter buzzed the peaked roof of a three-story house.

✧ ✧ ✧

There was the sharp, stinging scent of an ammonia ampule being broken beneath his nose. "Richard." The voice was soft and reasonable.

Richard jerked back to awareness. The room spun around him, and slowly things came back into focus. He was still tied in a chair. His ankles lashed to the legs; arms wrenched behind the back. His wrists were swollen and blood slick from his maddened attempts to break free. It hadn't taken long for his confinement phobia to kick in. His trousers were unzipped, and his genitals pulled free of his jockey shorts. His balls ached and burned. He bit back a whimper.

Grenier stood over him. "We searched your father's house. The sword isn't there." He picked up the ends of the frayed electrical wire and brushed them against each other. Electricity arced. Richard's back arched in anticipation.

"My people were very unhappy. I'm afraid they burned the house down. It's unfortunate about your father. Now, where is the—"

A pulsating roar shook the house. Followed closely by another. *Helicopters,* Richard realized. *I did it. I hung on.*

Grenier dropped the wire, walked to the study window, and looked out. "Ah, they're here." He suddenly frowned.

"Why are there two—"

Willie entered the office. "Boss, the front gate called. The FBI is here."

"This wasn't part of the plan," Grenier said, his frown deepening. "Stay here with him. We still don't have the sword, so I'd like to keep him alive, but if it looks like they're about to rescue him—kill him." Willie pulled out his .45. Grenier shook his head. "That's not going to work much longer. Cut his throat."

Grenier left. Willie holstered the pistol and pulled a heavy hunting knife out of its sheath. He didn't look happy.

✧ ✧ ✧

THE ENGINE STUTTERED, and the pilot fought the stick as they slalomed between a couple of tall pines kicking up snow. It dropped into a clearing and landed hard.

"Go! Go! Go!" the pilot yelled, and Angela figured he was mentally back in Afghanistan.

Kenntnis slid the door open, and they all piled out. Angela managed to grab her medical bag then remembered the shotgun. She turned back, but the judge had already grabbed it. The look on his face was grim as he pumped a shell into the chamber. Behind her she heard the helicopter engine die with a whine.

Their improbable Scooby gang scurried in five different directions like quail exploding from a covey, heading into the cover of the trees. The judge stuck close to her, but she soon lost sight of Rhiana, Cross and Kenntnis.

"Great, leave the two ordinary humans on their own," she

panted, as they paused under the low sweeping branches of an evergreen. They stood on a deep carpet of richly scented needles free of any snow.

Oort carefully parted the branches and looked. "The house is only a few hundred feet to our left."

"Let's go." She glanced back at him and couldn't help adding, "Think you'll still be a judge after today?" To her surprise a small smile played across the thin mouth.

They ran for the house.

✧ ✧ ✧

"CROSS AND I will scout," Rhiana said. "You wait here. That way if Cross's … feeling is right you'll be safe." She pulled out her cell phone. "I'll call you when we're sure it's okay."

Kenntnis hesitated and glanced over at Cross. The three of them were pressed against a thick hedge. "I'd rather stay with you," Kenntnis said.

That show of insecurity, almost fear, shook Rhiana's resolve. But if she didn't go through with it no one would ever believe that she *could* have done it. She wouldn't be the one they had worked so long to create. She fanned the embers of anger and resentment as she said, "We need to know the extent of the magical incursion. Only Cross and I can do that, and if we run into something we don't want to be trying to protect you too."

"Who made you queen? You're not in charge here," Cross snapped. The embers became flames. She gave the homeless god a thin smile. "Well, you're pretty useless right now, but maybe you can help me a little."

Kenntnis nodded. "She's right. We need to know how far Grenier has gone. If they managed to open a gate."

"What about Richard?" Cross asked.

"He's got his father," Kenntnis said.

Rhiana nodded and ignited a penny. It led the way. She didn't look back at Kenntnis.

✧ ✧ ✧

WILLIE HADN'T STEPPED close enough to use the knife, and that gave Richard a small flicker of hope. Also, Willie seemed to be smarter and less vicious than Bruce. Richard's throat was so raw from screaming that he wasn't certain he could make a sound. He tried; a squeak emerged. He tried again, harder, for the sound had brought the Willie out of his thoughtful funk.

"Please, it's just … worse … for … you … if you … kill … me." The words were a thread of sound.

Somewhere down the hallway they heard the thunderous roar of a shotgun discharging. Willie's head snapped up. Willie adjusted his grip on the knife hilt and sprang toward Richard.

The door to the study flew open. Richard couldn't turn to look. There was the sound of a pump working, a steel clash that said death was coming.

The chair was solid wood, heavy. With his last strength Richard threw himself hard left. The chair listed, teetered, and went over with a crash. Willie's slash cut the air where his throat had been. At the same time the shotgun bellowed. The exertion had Richard's vision narrowing to a dark tunnel. His last sight was of the front of Willie's chest, exploding into hamburger as the shotgun pellets ripped into him, and his last thought was *guess there isn't enough magic around to fuck up the guns... yet.*

CHAPTER THIRTY-FIVE

Rhiana ran through the thin blanket of snow toward the cliff face. The penny danced in the air in front of them.

"What the fuck is it sensing?" Cross panted behind her.

"I don't know. I guess we'll we'll find out when we get there. It's powerful, whatever it is." She darted through a modified shoji gate into a small dell shielded on one side by a spur of gray granite.

"Yeah, no shit. I feel like I'm swimming there's so much magic."

Wind chimes hung from the thin birches around the perimeter. Even though there was no breeze, a dissonant overtone hung like a sigh in the cold air.

It was a sculpture garden of glass. Green, gray, red, purple, black, pebbled, swirled, and clear monoliths, some with straight angles but more often twisted lines, stood in the dell. In front of some the snow had melted away, revealing matted brown grass, and in front of one a char of ash.

"What the fuck is this?"

Rhiana stopped, turned slowly, and stared at him. Cross looked down to where the snow was melting from beneath her feet.

"Oh, fuck."

Rhiana smiled, enjoying his fear. Payback time had finally come. She spread her arms wide. Cross's splinters, his deadly brethren, flowed out of the sculptures and through her body. She became the lens, focusing them into a single ribbon of power. The bands of pulsing color enveloped Cross and forced themselves between his lips. The human form bloated and swelled. The belly burst through the dirty jeans and flannel shirt. Soon it no longer resembled a human, just a mass of viscous colors, twining and coiling.

Cross's wailing fear and rage as his essence was diluted flowed hot into her. As their minds touched, Cross read the full magnitude of what they planned, and fear became despair, unleashing a jolt of power so great that it knocked Rhiana to the ground. The fractals blew apart and vanished. Cross was gone.

A shadow bubbled out of a purple-colored monolith. It resolved into Madoc.

"That was impressive," he said, and held out a hand to help her to her feet.

"Thank you."

"All set?" he asked.

"Kenntnis isn't carrying the sword."

He seemed disappointed but not surprised. "You rarely achieve perfection. I do have one tiny question about another deviation from perfection. Why is the FBI at the gate?"

"It made everyone more comfortable. And more deaths mean more power." But Rhiana couldn't meet his eyes.

"Yes, but the components for the bomb are here," Madoc said.

Rhiana covered her mouth with a hand. "Oh, God, I'm

sorry, I didn't think … I thought it was just a ruse."

"It was … partially. But we had intended to have you detonate it. You know enough now that you wouldn't have been hurt, and we could have ushered in the Armageddon that the humans are so eager to enjoy."

"Isn't that going to happen anyway?" Rhiana asked.

"Yes, but a nuclear bomb exploding in the United States would have started the wars much more quickly. Ah, well, I'm certain the monkeys will find ample reasons to kill each other." Madoc caressed her cheek and twined his hands in her hair, shaking her head from side to side. "So, you want your little human alive. That's all right. You shall have him if that's really what you want." He dropped a kiss onto her forehead and laughed. "You can have anything you want if you pull this off."

✦　✦　✦

HANDS WERE ON his face. Richard remembered them being larger the last time they'd cupped his cheeks. He opened his eyes and looked up into his father's face.

"Papa," he whispered, and his voice broke. "You … came … I … tried not to tell … hoped … knew … maybe … you would come … hurt so bad … they burned … the house … I lost my ring … I'm sorry, I'm sorry, so sorry." The words ran together. A cry for forgiveness, a litany of guilt.

"Shhh. Quiet. Angela, help me. These cords are embedded in his skin. I'll watch the door."

Richard tried to process the sight of his father, in a tailored suit, holding a shotgun leveled and at the ready. Then

Angela was there.

Kneeling next to Richard, she opened her bag and pulled out a scalpel. Her hands were cool on his abraded skin. He gazed unbelieving at her gamine face. She cut the cords, but relief soon gave way to new agony as blood flowed back into Richard's hands and feet.

They pulled him to his feet. Richard fumbled at his crotch, trying to tuck himself away. Angela took command, and soon had him zipped. They got him over to a couch and laid him down. Angela ordered the judge to shatter one of the darkened mirrors, but he knelt next to his son, gently chafing his hands.

"You're going to be all right. The FBI is coming," his father said.

"The sword. Do you have it?"

"Yes."

The judge pulled it out, and Richard clutched it to his chest with one hand with one hand while with the other he gripped his father's shoulder.

Angela grabbed up the shotgun, and a moment later Richard heard the sound of smashing glass. She returned carrying a large piece of one of the darkened mirrors. Opening her case, she took out a square of aluminum foil and a Dairy Queen straw. The foil peeled back to reveal a small folded white paper. Richard and Robert watched, bemused, as she poured out two neat lines of cocaine onto the glass.

She positioned the straw. "Snort," she ordered.

"Are you crazy?" the judge said.

"I'm a cop," Richard said at the same time.

"Analgesic, and upper. He needs both real bad right now."

"His mother," the judge began, and laid a hand on hers.

She pushed it away. "Look, if he becomes an addict, I'll pay for the Betty Ford Clinic myself, okay? But he won't." She smiled warmly at him. "He's not the type."

But I am, Richard thought, remembering, or rather *not* remembering, a lot of nights. A new consideration entered the calculation. Grenier was still free and powerful. Richard snorted.

A tingling jolt seemed to go straight up into his brain. The sore tissues of his nose went numb. A few seconds later there was a bitter aftertaste on the back of his tongue, but Richard didn't mind. He felt *great.*

Angela held up the glass. "Lick off the last of it. It'll help your mouth." He obeyed and the same numbness pervaded the cut tissues of his mouth and tongue.

Richard found himself on his feet. "Yeah. Okay. This is *good.*"

✧   ✧   ✧

"KENNTNIS, COME QUICKLY." Rhiana's voice crackled on a rapidly decaying cell connection. "We've found ... thing, but we don't under ... d ... it."

"Where are you?"

"At ... base ... cliff. We need—*It's trying to get Cross!*" The phone went dead.

Kenntnis considered retreat, but Cross was irreplaceable. There was no option. He went.

✧   ✧   ✧

RICHARD, ANGELA, AND Robert reacted to the faint, distant crack, and chatter of gunfire.

"The cavalry," Robert said.

Richard couldn't help it; he glanced over at Angela. She understood the unspoken question. "With Weber leading the charge," she said, and grinned.

He came back. He doesn't hate me.

They listened to the tempo of gunfire. "And meeting some opposition from the sound of it," the judge said, frowning. "Idiots. Who resists the FBI?"

"Desperate or really confident people. Either way, we should get the hell out of here," Angela said.

"You go ahead," Richard said. "I need to find Grenier and use the sword on him." Angela put her hands on her hips and glared at him. Richard became aware of the gunfire beginning to stutter into silence. He knew what that portended. "It's going to be a lot harder later," Richard warned.

Seeing the sense in what he had said, Angela nodded and turned to gather up her medical bag. Richard saw her eyes widen in horror.

"*Richard!*" She grabbed him and spun him around.

Now he could see what had so frightened her. Grenier stood in the door of the study. A fountain of light cascaded off the folded reading glasses that he held in his right hand.

The light splashed across Angela's booted feet. The intricate leaves and vines on the thick oriental carpet writhed and shot up out of the nap, twisting themselves around her body.

Robert cried out in shock and alarm as the vines wrapped

tightly around Angela's neck, forced themselves up her nose and down her throat. Guttural noises erupted from Angela. If she hadn't moved him, it would have been Richard choking instead.

The entire rug was seething now. The judge, with admirable presence of mind, jumped up onto the desk, but it was only a momentary respite. The vines pursued.

The vines thrust into every orifice of Willie's body and seemed to find nourishment in the dead flesh. They grew even more quickly there.

Richard leaped away from Angela's clawing hands. Her eyes showed mute desperation. He nearly fell as the vines tangled around his feet.

Richard drew the sword. The overtones climbed beyond human hearing, then began again with a bass groan and a rapidly ascending scale. He swept the star-swirling blade across the vines at his feet. They screamed and liquefied into a foul-smelling black ooze.

Angela lay on the heaving, writhing rug. Her body was almost invisible beneath the leaves and vines.

"All of you die!" Richard yelled as he thrust the point of the sword deep into the rug where the spell had first landed. They did.

He heard his father's careful, precise voice, now carrying an uncontrollable quaver. "… Hallowed be thy Name. Thy Kingdom come—"

"Shut up, sir! Don't call them. There are openings everywhere." Richard thrust the sword at one of the opaque mirrors.

Richard turned, and he and Grenier measured each other

across half a room and an intellectual divide a universe wide.

"There's so much magic flowing we could drown in it," Grenier said. "And I can throw spells until whatever you took wears off. And, of course, you have to protect *them*." He jerked his head toward Angela, lying still on the rug, and Robert perched on the desk. "That's the problem with being a hero."

Robert glanced over toward the abandoned shotgun. Grenier caught the look. "I expect it's been rendered inert, but just in case...." And fire arced from the glasses, striking the metal, and the barrel melted. Grenier laughed and advanced a few steps into the study. They circled each other warily.

"Papa, take Angela. Leave by the window," Richard ordered.

Fire flared in the lenses of the glasses. The windows vanished as the walls grew closed, obliterating doorway and windows. The stench from the dead vines made Richard's gut heave. Grenier flexed his free hand, grinning wildly.

It's like he's drunk, Richard thought. *What is going on? It's supposed to take enormous power to do this much magic, and he's unfazed.*

But there was no more time to ponder the problem. The lenses of the glasses were pulsing with changing colors. Richard decided to try to parry the attack rather than attacking whatever outcome the spell produced. He dropped his weight, knees bent, balance evenly divided between his feet. He had fenced epee in college. The sword was more like a rapier and heavier. Richard hoped the high from the cocaine would last long enough.

Grenier's hand shot out, releasing a spell. Richard lunged and parried high left. The fire vanished into the blade, but it didn't blow back onto Grenier the way it had with Delay in the church, perhaps because this was no young apprentice but a master of sorcery, or perhaps because there was so much magic present, as Grenier had said.

Richard rushed Grenier, a swift advance ending in a long, deep, groin-pulling lunge. Grenier grabbed a book off a small table and slapped the point of the sword aside. Richard pushed back onto his back leg. Grenier threw the book into his face. Richard knocked it aside with his right hand. Fire flew. Toward the judge this time. Richard parried.

Richard weighed the options. An all-out attack on Grenier, and hope he could neutralize him before the sorcerer landed a spell on Angela or his father? Or fight defensively, and try to protect them?

Richard tried to reach a wall to neutralize the magic that closed the cage. If the judge and Angela were free, Richard could concentrate on Grenier. The minister sensed his intent, and pushed hard, keeping Richard from ever reaching the blank walls.

They circled each other, exchanging feints, waiting for the other to attack. The attacks came in a flurry of fire and night. Golden light arced and soared across the room and was eaten by the darkness of the sword. Once Richard missed, and the spell reached the glass-fronted bookcases. Glass wasps swarmed out with an eerie chiming buzz and headed for his father. Running full-out, Richard managed to bring the sword through them in an overhand cut. He couldn't control his momentum and slammed into the desk.

Robert grabbed Richard's shoulders, helped steady him, and got him turned around. His father's lips were against his ear.

"Try to maneuver him over here," the judge whispered.

Richard gave an almost imperceptible nod and, bouncing lightly on the balls of his feet, advanced on Grenier.

✧   ✧   ✧

Kenntnis entered the dell. The chimes stirred and echoed in one perfect chord, but his effect ended with the bells. The glass sculptures were stained red in the light of the setting sun. In the distance he could hear the real-world sounds of a very real firefight going on by the gate. Kenntnis realized he didn't recognize any of the artists in the garden, and a cold hollow formed at his core.

Rhiana stood on a small knoll in the center of the sculpture garden. Pennies spun at her feet, creating the illusion she stood in the midst of a fire. Her right hand was outstretched. Balanced on her palm was a tiny speck of darkness.

Kenntnis recognized the creature who sat on one of the smaller sculptures, watching.

Oh, Richard, now would be a good time for you to arrive "in the nick of time."

Rhiana flung the darkness into the air, crying out the spell. Kenntnis felt a cold more profound than any he'd experienced in the vast emptiness between the galaxies. He sensed the bosonic atoms falling into the lowest possible quantum state. It was a stunning blending of physics and magic, and he was powerless, trapped between the two forces. The matter that shaped his human body blasted into pieces. Icy claws settled into him, holding him like a butterfly on a pin. The spinning darkness released by Rhiana fell over his glittering form and swept him up in the whirlwind. Time slowed. The world became a smear and a blur as human time raced forward … and … he … froze …

✧　✧　✧

PARTS OF RICHARD'S beaten body were starting to make their presence known. Richard could feel sweat stinging in the cuts on his face and mouth. His abused testicles hated it every time he lunged, and his quads popped each time he pushed back out of the lunge. His breath was loud in his own ears.

Suddenly, Grenier's reading glasses began to blaze constantly. It distracted even their owner. Grenier stared down at them.

"She did it," Grenier said in a fierce whisper.

That can't be good, Richard thought, and he realized the sound of gunfire was gone. *And that's really not good.* He forced himself to focus and used Grenier's momentary inattention to rush the older man.

Richard came in slightly to the left. It forced Grenier to half-turn and step closer to the fallen chair, the desk, and Willie's body.

The swirl of stars around the sword broadened and widened until Richard was looking through a hazy shield of stars at his foe. Out of the corner of his eye, Richard saw his father move. Hunching, Robert circled around the end of the desk. He reached down and came up holding the electrical cord.

Richard flung himself forward in a wild attack to keep Grenier focusing on him. Robert rushed forward and wrapped the cord around Grenier's neck. The man screamed, his free hand clawing at his throat.

Richard spun on his back foot and brought the edge of the blade across Grenier's exposed right wrist. The hand holding the glasses dropped onto the sticky floor. The glasses went dark. Blood fountained from the severed stump. Grenier fell onto the floor and went into a violent seizure.

"Get a tourniquet on him," Richard ordered.

"Let him bleed. Demon," spat the judge.

"No. I want him alive, in jail, and robbed of his power."

Robert's normal icy control reasserted itself. He nodded, pulled off his necktie, put a knee in Grenier's chest to control him, and tied off the gushing arm.

Richard touched the wall. The windows returned.

He broke out several mullions with the hilt of the sword and briefly breathed in the cold, pine-scented air, then he whirled, ran to Angela, and gathered her into his arms.

"Oh, Angie, sweetie." He felt beneath her jaw for a pulse. "Be all right. Be all right." He found it, but it was faint and jumping.

Robert was pacing nervously. He skirted Willie's half-decayed corpse, perforated with holes so both bone and viscera showed. Richard wondered how he would explain that to the feds. His father bent down briefly, then went to the window to watch for the FBI.

The high from the cocaine was starting to wear off. Richard tried to marshal his whirling thoughts. "Papa, can you take—"

The sound of pounding feet coming down the hall had him tense until he saw Weber come panting through the door followed by four FBI agents in tactical gear.

"Jesus Christ, Rhode Island. You are the biggest ass—"

"Damon, we need a medic and quick. It's Angela. And Grenier could use help, too."

"What did you do to him?" Richard nodded toward the severed hand. "Shit." Weber ran a hand through his hair and turned to the agents. "So, I don't suppose you fellas could—"

"All that broken glass must have caught him just right," said one of the helmeted men.

Richard interrupted the posturing. "*Please*, this lady needs medical attention."

"Fucking cars all died," said another agent. "But we'll get her out of here." The man swept Angela into his arms. Another agent heaved Grenier over his shoulder in a fireman's carry.

A hand was suddenly in front of Richard's face. "Come on Rhode Island, let's get the fuck out of here," Weber said gently. Richard gripped Weber's hand tightly and was hauled to his feet. "You did good," Weber said softly against his ear.

Richard's throat tightened. All he could manage was a nod. His father's voice broke through his chaotic thoughts.

"Richard, I think you better come look at this, and tell me what it means."

✧   ✧   ✧

WHAT ROBERT HAD seen through the window were bands of light thrusting into the sky off to their left along the cliff face.

Where the light touched the rock, it looked plastic, and it seemed to be breathing.

Richard carried the drawn sword. Despite all of his objections and remonstrations, his father was at his side. Weber had wanted to come, but Richard had begged him to stay with Angela. At least that way he would know that two of the people most dear to him were safe.

He felt Robert's hand on his shoulder. "It's yes," his father said suddenly.

Richard shook himself out of his haze. "What?"

"The answer to your question. It's yes."

Richard nodded, swallowed hard. Ahead of them was a crooked shoji gate. For some reason it felt disturbing.

"Let's not walk under that," Richard said.

He and Robert left the gravel path and walked in the snow. They passed close to a tree on whose bare branches hung a number of steel, glass, and ceramic wind chimes. They had all been fused into undifferentiated lumps.

Glass sculptures glowed dark orange, red, purple, sick green and threw their light into the night sky. The temperature was dropping, frosting the top of the snow with ice crystals that crunched beneath the soles of their shoes. There was a strange metallic smell in the air.

In the midst of the colored glass forms, a clear glass piece wove a serpentine shape across the snow. It was reminiscent of the sand eddies left in ancient sea beds by long dry waves. It stood about six feet tall and ten feet long.

At the heart of the clear glass there was a core of spinning darkness. Orbiting the darkness was a glitter of silver bright lights dancing through a swirling golden mist. It looked like someone had trapped a dust devil comprised of diamonds and gold dust. Tendrils of light were being dragged into the darkness.

Richard walked around the clear glass piece and retreated with a yelp of pain. He had never felt such profound cold. He looked down at the patch of frostbite across the back of his hand.

Next, he approached the pulsing cliff. *Picture it closed.* But it was an enormous rip in reality, much larger than anything he'd faced before. He struggled, but the tear continued to solidify, the opening widening. Pillars began to form on the sides, and there was the suggestion of an arch in the rough stone of the cliff face. From behind him his father gripped his upper arms and pulled him away. Richard retreated, exhausted.

"It's too big. It's a gate. I'm not sure how—"

"You can't close it. Not with Kenntnis gone."

Richard whirled to find Rhiana regarding him from in front of a dark purple sculpture. She was dressed in a form-hugging dress that seemed constructed of snowflakes and spiderwebs. Diamond pins glittered in her long hair, which floated up behind her and coiled around her arms and neck in defiance of the slight breeze.

"Rhiana, what have you done?" Richard breathed, struggling for calm.

"I chose."

Richard held out a hand toward Rhiana. "And I chose you. Cross wanted to destroy you. I told Kenntnis I would *never* allow that."

"So, choose me now. I'll protect you." She held out her

hand to him.

A black-and-purple shadow boiled out of the monolith. Robert gasped and his grip on Richard's shoulders tightened. The colors transformed into a sharp-faced man. He came up behind Rhiana, laid a hand possessively on her shoulder, and smiled at Richard, an expression both triumphant and mocking.

"You're human, Rhiana, at least partly. Don't do this," Richard pleaded.

She laid her hand over the man's. "And this part is better. I finally *belong* someplace."

"You belong to both. Why reject us?"

"Because they appreciate me. I've done something none of them could ever do. I blended magic and physics. You just wanted to use me, use my power to ultimately destroy my power. Why would I do that?"

"Because they're—"

"Evil?" Rhiana scoffed. "People throw that word around too easily. And besides, we don't see it that way. Everyone's a hero in their own little personal drama. Don't be a dead hero, Richard. Come with me. I'll protect you," she repeated. Richard shook his head. "You can't stand against us, not with Kenntnis trapped. He's ours. Your world is ours." She gestured at the clear glass sculpture.

Richard stared in shock at the gold and diamond swirl in the glass. Tried to square that with the huge man who had dominated his life for the past months. He crept toward the glass but had to retreat from the unrelenting cold. Nothing human could survive it.

"You can't get close enough to use the sword. Absolute

zero gives you slow glass. Slow glass traps light. That's all Kenntnis is… was," Rhiana said.

"Hush!" the man said. "You give them too much." Power flowed out of his hand and into Rhiana's shoulder. They began to dissolve into pulsing colors, black and purple, and vanished back through the purple glass sculpture.

"Richard!"

It was Weber, followed by two of the agents from earlier. They were all running through the shoji gate.

"Damon, *don't*," Richard yelled.

Weber and the African American agent made it through safely, but something black and glistening, as if it had been dipped in oil, came undulating out of the crosspiece of the gate and seized the other agent.

He was pulled, kicking, and screaming, into the air. Weber and the other FBI agent whirled. The captured agent's screams echoed around the dell. Richard charged and barreled between Weber and the African-American agent, knocking them off balance. He was beneath the shoji gate. There didn't seem to be enough air, and what was there was tainted with a harsh, metallic smell that was almost a taste. Richard knew he stood between worlds, and he had very little time. Swinging the sword up, he managed to touch the Old One. A keening, howling wail began. The agent fell heavily to the ground.

Weber and the other other agent rushed in and dragged the man away.

Richard drew the sword across the uprights of the gate. *Picture it closed.* This time it worked, because it was a tear, not like the structure that was being constructed on the far side of the dell. The shoji gate collapsed in a jumble of splintered wood. Richard retreated, the point of the sword flicking from side to side. It was less a conscious thought than a sense that he had to weave a net of protection around the humans.

The agent was administering CPR to his fallen comrade. While he compressed the chest he kept yelling, "What the *fuck* is going on? What the *fuck* was that? What the *fuck*?"

Weber grabbed Richard's shoulder. All around them the glass sculptures were coiling with light. The enormous gate in the cliff was almost complete.

"Can you stop this?" Weber demanded.

"No," Richard admitted.

"Then we've got to get out of here."

Richard pointed at the clear glass form. "That's Kenntnis. If we leave him…" He shrugged helplessly. "I don't know how we ever get back."

"We worry about that later. Because if we don't get out of here right the fuck *now,* we're not going to get to worry about much of anything ever again. Let's *go!*"

His father grabbed Richard by the shoulders and gave him a shake. "He's right."

Richard looked around and realized that the five human men were in a circle of sanity. Beneath their feet was scuffed and dirt-stained snow and winter grass. Just beyond them was madness. Colors whirled and coiled. Viscous shadows crawled across undulating ground.

"Carry him," Richard ordered and pointed at the fallen agent. "Stay together."

Step by step they retreated from the dell. Fortunately, the

madness didn't follow. Beyond the ruins of the shoji gate the world was once again the world, familiar and safe.

But for how long? Richard wondered.

CHAPTER THIRTY-SIX

RICHARD GAVE THE nurses at the station a nervous wave as he walked past. The small package of Oreos weighed like a guilty conscience in his coat pocket. He had promised Angela cookies. He figured she deserved them after having her stomach pumped. He carried a carton of milk openly. He didn't think they would object to that.

The nurses gave him smiles that were almost grimaces. Angela was making herself nicely hated by the medical and nursing staff of Walter Reed. That meant she was probably ready to be discharged, and everyone, friends, and staff alike, were fervently hoping that would occur today.

To his relief, Richard avoided a stay in the hospital. They had set and packed his broken nose, clipped shut the cut over his right eye, bandaged his wrists and ankles, and given him a salve for his burns.

Then he belonged to the FBI. Fortunately, the three of them, Richard, Weber, and the judge, had had time to rehearse their stories before the interrogations began.

They had questioned him for ten hours the first day, seven on the second, and another eight on the third day. Richard had stuck to his story—he had come to Virginia to arrest Doug Andresson. No, he didn't know why his father had said there was a nuclear bomb on the premises. Maybe the judge had just said that to get help in rescuing his son. No, Richard didn't know what had happened to the girl who said she'd been recruited to build the bomb. No, he didn't know why Reverend Grenier had imprisoned and tortured him.

Fortunately, Richard had sheathed the sword before the authorities found them. The FBI was baffled by the twisting hilt, but it never occurred to them that it was a weapon. When asked about it, Richard had said it was an early Christmas present from his father. Just an objet d' art.

What saved them from closer scrutiny was Robert's status as a Federal Court judge, and the fact that Richard and Weber were cops. Though local police were often viewed as lowly scum by the federal agents, they were still law enforcement officers. Weber had gone in with the strike team, and it was pretty damn clear that Richard had been a victim, and the judge had called in a few political favors from the Rhode Island senators.

Richard also suspected that the authorities were far more concerned with the dimensional gateway that had appeared in rural Virginia, though they never brought it up to him. They had been well away from the garden before the rest of the FBI strike team found them. Richard thought the agent would have told them of his presence in the sculpture garden. Apparently, he hadn't.

Richard made the turn toward Angela's room. A big man was waiting for him, leaning against a wall. Richard recognized the African American agent from the dell. The man stepped out and blocked Richard's way.

"Agent."

"Bob Franklin," he said, and held out his hand.

Richard shook it cautiously, then asked, "I thought we were done with the questioning?"

"I'm not here … officially," Franklin said. His expression was blank, his dark brown eyes giving away nothing.

"Then maybe you would be willing to answer a few of *my* questions?" Richard suggested.

"No, but I will give you a heads-up."

"About what?" Richard asked.

"Why don't we go in here?" The agent gestured at the empty visitor's room.

The man shut the door. "So, Reverend Grenier says that you broke into his compound and attacked him. That you cut off his hand with a sword. Of course, nobody can find a sword." The agent stared down at Richard.

"But, of course, you know differently," Richard said softly.

"Yeah, I do, but I haven't said anything."

"I had been wondering why you hadn't."

"Because I saw the monsters in that garden, but my superiors won't let me talk about that, not to anyone. And my partner, Syd, is catatonic in the psych ward, and since I can't tell the docs what he saw, about that … thing that grabbed him, they can't do shit for him."

"What do you want from me?" Richard asked.

"You seemed to understand what was going on there. I thought maybe you might be able to help," Franklin said.

Richard started to shake his head, then an almost forgotten conversation came back. *When it's drawn it makes people sane.* Richard heard Kenntnis's rumbling bass and was suddenly aware of the hilt resting in its holster at the small of his back. He also faced once more the grief and fear that accompanied the loss of his mentor.

"No promises," Richard said. "But I might be able to help. Can you get us in to see him?"

"Watch me." And the agent grinned like a happy wolf, his teeth white in his dark face.

Syd Marten sat in a chair in his small room. His chest rose and fell beneath the thin hospital gown. The sour smell of unwashed human hung in the tiny room. His brown, gray-tipped hair hung in lank strands across his forehead. Occasionally his eyes blinked. Nothing else marked him as alive and human.

"His daughter, Samantha, is frantic. She's in the Bureau, too," Franklin said as they looked down at the man.

Richard's eyes scanned the walls and ceiling. "No cameras," he said.

"No."

"Shield me in case someone looks through the window." Richard indicated the small glass pane in the door. Franklin placed his bulk between Richard and the door.

Richard drew the sword. Marten's head slowly turned toward the source of the sound.

"Jesus," Franklin breathed.

Richard gently touched the agent on the shoulder with the flat of the sword as if he were knighting him. Marten cried out in pain and shuddered. His eyes closed. When he opened them, an intelligent presence had returned.

"Make them go away," he whispered through dry, chapped lips.

Richard rested his hand briefly on the man's shoulder. "I'll try."

"Syd," Franklin said, and pushing past Richard, he gripped his partner's hand.

Sheathing the sword, Richard returned it to its holster and stepped back. After a moment Franklin looked back at him.

"Those questions you had … What do you want to know?"

✧　✧　✧

"… THEY'VE THROWN a cordon of National Guard around the garden, but they keep retreating a few feet each day. If they don't, the soldiers start hallucinating. That's how Franklin put it. They'll suddenly shoot each other or themselves or walk off the cliff because they think they can fly, become catatonic. This is wrapped in so much secrecy that Franklin thinks he'd be sent to Gitmo if they ever found out he told me," Richard concluded.

He was sitting cross-legged on the foot of Angela's bed. Cookie crumbs were scattered across the sheet. Angela had a milk mustache, and with her tumbled curls looked like a wicked urchin. Bouquets of roses lined the window ledge. Since Richard had been locked up with the FBI and hadn't been able to visit before now, he'd arranged to have bouquets delivered every day.

His father stood near the door and occasionally peeked out into the hall. Weber sprawled in an armchair.

"And what do we think this means?" the judge asked,

coming over to the bed to look down at his son.

"I think it has to do with Kenntnis. Rhiana bound Prometheus. Who knows what the effect will be?"

"What about Cross?" Angela asked. "He might be able to explain it to us." Her voice was hoarse and husky from a throat abused by the attacking vines and the stomach pump.

"I think we have to presume he's gone," Richard said. "There hasn't been any sign of him, and I have to believe he'd contact us."

"So, what happens to us?" Weber asked. "Last thing I heard from my interviewers was 'Don't leave the area.' Are we stuck here forever, or are we on our way to being 'detainees'?"

"Franklin says we've been cleared," Richard answered. "Because the lie you told them actually turned out to be true. They found components for a nuclear bomb in one of the buildings."

Weber shook his head. "Those dumb bastards."

"No," the judge corrected. "Overconfident and supremely arrogant."

"Whatever the motivation, it still comes out as dumb, *que, no*?" Angela added.

Robert Oort nodded. "Point."

"And falling under the 'my, isn't this ironic' category, there's the little matter of a piece of paper with traces of cocaine on it found in Grenier's office." Richard chuckled. "Franklin said he couldn't tell which one bothered his superiors more, the bomb, the dope, or the monsters."

Weber gave one of his sharp, single cracks of laughter. Angela started to laugh, then abruptly stopped.

"Oh, shit, my fingerprints are all over that paper."

The judge swept the crumbs off the top sheet and into the palm of his hand. "I don't think you have to worry about a drug charge. I expect we're all going to become very big, very public heroes, very soon."

Weber and Angela stared at the older man, who stood serenely brushing the crumbs into the trash can. Their faces were a study in confusion. Richard suspected his expression mirrored theirs.

"I beg your pardon, sir?"

"Consider," said Robert in his best "from the bench" tone. "The government has evidence of a plot to construct an atomic bomb. They also have a hole in reality, disgorging demons—"

"Monsters," Richard corrected.

"Whatever, it doesn't matter what you call them. This area of chaos is expanding every day and driving soldiers mad. Which do you think is going to be more terrifying to the American people? The press knows something occurred at the WWCA compound. The authorities must give them *something*."

Richard whistled. "And a nuclear bomb is a hell of a smoke screen for the real threat."

"Watch your language," his father said automatically.

"So, Grenier is screwed, blued, and tattooed," Weber said.

"No, Grenier will undoubtably make bail. He has cash, connections, and clout. Whether he stays around for a trial is … questionable. There are countries with no extradition treaties. If he should come to trial, he'll blame it all on out-of-control underlings, and quite possibly escape with only a slap on the wrist," Robert said.

"Bummer," Weber said.

"I know we ought to stay close, and try to free Kenntnis," Angela said. "But …" She shivered. Richard took hold of her foot beneath the covers and gave it a comforting squeeze. "I want to get as far away from that place as possible."

"Maybe I ought to go to the authorities. Tell them what I know. Offer to help," Richard mused.

"Not a bad idea," Weber said, and Angela nodded.

Resistance came from an unexpected source. "No," said the judge. "I think you need to be free to respond to what, I think, is going to be a constantly changing and probably ever more dangerous situation. The government will lock you up tight, send that weapon off to the DOD to be researched, and in general fiddle while the world goes to Hell."

"Watch your language," Richard said, and gave his father a quick smile.

"I use the word in the literal, not the profane sense," Robert shot back, and the creases at the side of his mouth deepened briefly.

"Okay, but where's our headquarters while we try to save the world?" Weber asked.

Richard's mind suddenly filled with the scent of piñon fires and the chest-aching bite of clean winter air, vistas of blue-gray mountains against turquoise skies.

"New Mexico," he said.

"Why?" his father asked.

"Kenntnis was there. Of all the places in the world he could have lived, he chose New Mexico. There must have been reasons."

"It is a place where science and magic rub close," Angela mused. "On the one hand you've got Los Alamos and the Bell Lab at Kirtland Air Force Base, and White Sands missile range and space port, and the Santa Fe Institute, and on the other you've got sacred tortillas and kachinas, and crystal healers, and skin walkers, Tarot readers, people who will balance your aura, and past life gurus, and mediums—"

"Whoa, whoa, whoa, I'm starting to feel totally outnumbered," Weber groaned.

"And the Lumina," Richard said softly. "Don't forget us."

✦   ✦   ✦

ORTIZ STARED, AMAZED, at Richard standing in the doorway of his office. "Oort, my God, we've been hearing about what happened, but what are you doing back here? I thought you'd stay out east with your family through Christmas," Ortiz said.

"No, sir. By the way, I don't mind working tomorrow. If you can use the help."

"Can I ever. Nobody wants to work Christmas Day." Ortiz stood and held out his hand. "Welcome back. Glad to have you."

They shook. "Thank you, sir."

Richard went into the bullpen. Snyder was staring in amazement at Weber, who was unpacking a box and arranging mementos and personal items on his desk. Snyder's head snapped around when he heard Richard's footfalls.

"You're back," Snyder said, and it wasn't clear which of the two men he was addressing.

Both Weber and Richard looked at him and said together, "Yes."

Richard sat down on the edge of Synder's desk. "And Dale," Richard said, leaning in. "I'm here to stay."

Snyder met Richard's cool, level gaze and dropped his eyes down to the report he held. "Yeah, well, welcome back," he concluded weakly.

The few other detectives present had been watching with the interest a wolf pack shows in a clash for leadership. Now they came over and offered hellos, expressed curiosity and congratulations about the events in Virginia, and offered best wishes for the season.

A few hours later Richard's phone rang. The man on the other end of the line was a lawyer. After Richard hung up, he called his father.

✧　✧　✧

GEORGE GOLD WAS a short, round man with a heavy mane of dark hair that brushed the top of his collar. Judging by the creases in his fat cheeks and the crew's feet surrounding his brown eyes, he was a man who smiled a lot. He wasn't smiling now.

They were in Kenntnis's office. The wide expanse of the granite desk held legal documents and stacks of balance sheets and account books. Richard stood staring almost blindly around the room while the judge perused the documents.

"Mr. Kenntnis had a system whereby he would contact us every twenty-four hours. If that contact ever failed to occur, certain events followed. That contact ended five days ago. We had a little trouble contacting you initially, Detective, and I didn't want to draw the attention of the press. At any rate, I apologize for the delay," Gold said. Richard waved off the apology. "You understand that according to Mr. Kenntnis's instructions, control of Lumina Enterprises, all assets and operations, has been granted to you under a Durable Power of Attorney until such time as Mr. Kenntnis should return or be declared legally dead at which point the company becomes yours."

Richard scrubbed his hands across his face, and winced when he inadvertently touched his nose. Panic fluttered in his belly, and he couldn't seem to get control of his whirling thoughts. The only coherent thing he knew was, *I can't do this!*

"It's all in order," the judge said, looking up from the paper he was reading.

Gold pulled out an engraved card case, fished out a card, and offered it to Richard. It read, *George S. Gold, Chief Counsel, Lumina Enterprises.* "If you need anything, don't hesitate to call, and I'm certain the other officers will be in touch with you shortly." The heavy door closed behind the lawyer.

Robert began examining the balance sheets. Richard trailed his hands along the edge of the desk, moved to the chair, sat down.

The judge looked up at him over the top of his reading glasses.

"This company appears to be worth more than Microsoft."

"Oh, God." Richard dropped his face into his hands. "I can't even manage to balance my checkbook. Will you help me?" He looked up at his father and felt ice forming in his belly at his presumption. He quickly backpedaled. "Sorry, sir, you have your own work, I can't expect—"

"Richard." He jumped at the peremptory tone in his father's voice. "I intend to resign from the bench. After what I've seen and experienced, hearing legal cases doesn't seem very relevant right now. As Detective Weber said, we have a world to save." The judge paused and busied himself with tapping straight the pages of the balance sheet he'd been reading. "And I have children and a grandson to protect. So, yes, I will help you. Here is my first piece of advice—get a new desk. You look all of twelve behind that monolith." There was again that deepening of the creases in his father's cheeks.

Richard smiled wanly back. He looked down at the swirling colors of the granite, the flecks of mica, and remembered the glittering lights in Kenntnis's dark eyes.

The pressure from his father's hand on his shoulder made him look up. "I don't know why I waited, but now seems the right time." Robert reached into his pocket. When he opened his fingers the gold signet ring glinted on his palm.

"The family ring!" Richard reached out for it, then pulled his hand back. "Where did you … How did you …"

"Apparently those demon weeds only had a taste for flesh and fabric. It was on the floor next to the body." Robert took

Richard's hand in his and slipped the ring onto his finger.

✧ ✧ ✧

THEY WERE ALL staying at Angela's condo. It made sense. Richard had a one-bedroom apartment, and her townhouse had three bedrooms. Richard knew he had the right to the penthouse at Lumina headquarters, but he couldn't bring himself to make the move. Not yet. It felt too much like trespassing.

The only light came from the flames of the candles. The votives sat in small triangular glass holders in gemlike colors. Flames licked across the wood in the kiva fireplace. The room was redolent with the scent of posole, piñon, and the anise in the *biscochitos*. The judge had made great-great-grandfather Oort's homemade eggnog. It was a big hit with Angela and Damon. Richard contented himself with a glass of milk.

Outside, the cul-de-sac was dark except for the flicker of candles in the *farolitos*. The next-door neighbors had bowed to community pressure and removed the electric luminarias. Someone had even managed to get the city to turn off the streetlights for this one night.

The little sacks glowed with a golden light, but it was diffuse, softened by the snow that had begun falling. A thin layer already covered the sidewalks and yards. The *farolitos* wouldn't last much longer.

It was just the four of them. Angela had managed to join her family just before sunset at the cemetery, but she still wasn't fully recovered from the events at Grenier's compound, so she begged off joining them at the family home and, instead, returned to her townhouse and what remained of the Lumina.

When it came to the Oort family, Amelia had refused to disrupt her family on such short notice and on the eve of Christmas. She seemed piqued that the judge had chosen New Mexico over Boston. Pamela had also refused, but surprised Richard by saying she would come west for New Year's. The prospect left him with more than a few misgivings.

And miraculously Weber was there.

The cop shook back his cuff and looked at his watch. "Shit, it's 1:00 AM. Merry fucking Christmas everybody."

"Happy birthday," the judge said to Richard.

"No shit?" Weber said.

"Yes, I'm afraid so," Richard responded.

Weber pushed up out of the armchair. "I'd better head home. I've got to stop by Carol's for a little while tomorrow," he said, he said, referring to his wife.

"So, things are looking up for the two of you?" Richard asked, and vowed to be pleased with the answer, whatever it might be.

"Nah. I just became momentarily more attractive because I've been interviewed on the *Today* show. The divorce is still happening."

"Don't tear yourself down," said Angela. She was laying on the couch, her feet tucked under a knitted comforter.

There was a soft knock on the front door. They all froze, then exchanged glances.

"You expecting anybody?" Weber asked.

Angela shook her head. "Certainly not at this hour."

She disentangled her feet from the comforter. It slid off the sofa with a whisper. Richard helped her up.

Weber unclipped his holster and drew his gun. Richard pulled the hilt of the sword free. He kept his hand in position to draw it as they moved cautiously to the door.

"Who is it?" Angela called.

"It's me," came a familiar, aggrieved voice. "Somebody threw away my damn box."

But Richard had been fooled before. He looked to his father.

Robert took Angela by the arms and pulled her back into the living room. Richard drew the sword. The chords echoed in the barrel vault. He He nodded to Damon. Weber yanked open the door. But it was Cross. Their Cross, and he looked better than he had in weeks.

"Hey," he said. "Thanks for putting a light in the window." He jerked a thumb back over his shoulder, indicating the *farolitos*. "So, to speak."

"Get in here!" Richard ordered as he grabbed the homeless god's hand and yanked him into the hallway.

"So, what happened after I got splintered?" the Old One asked, and while they told him, he ate his way through three bowls of *posole*, five butter-drenched tortillas, six tamales, a dozen cookies, and four cups of eggnog.

He sat on the banco near the kiva fireplace, leaned back against warm plaster, and gave a huge belch. Angela picked up the tray.

"Fortified enough to answer a few questions?" Richard asked.

"Shoot."

"What happens with Kenntnis captured?" Richard continued.

"I'm not exactly sure. He's reason and order incarnate. It's why he couldn't use the sword. He made it. It's a part of him, but too much order is just as bad as too much chaos."

"So, the sword is weakened?" Richard asked.

"Maybe, maybe not. We'll have to see."

"It's one thing to close a tear," Richard said. "Those gates are pretty damn terrifying."

"And there's more than one," Cross said. "Got a big one breaking through in Jerusalem, another in India, and I didn't look any further. I wanted to get back to you."

"So, what happens to our world? To reality as we know it?" the judge asked.

Cross shrugged. "I'm not sure. I guess we all find out together." His lips parted, showing teeth in a humorless grin. "Won't *that* be exciting?"

"Kenntnis told me at our first meeting that the Lumina's weapons are science, technology, and rational thought. The Old Ones can't change scientific principles, and technology exists, but they can affect our reality where magic is in play," Richard said.

"So, the world goes nuts?" Weber asked.

"In places, and it does seem to affect people inside those areas," Richard answered.

"Which would fit with what the FBI agent told you about the soldiers," his father said.

"I still can't believe Rhiana betrayed us," Angela said sadly.

Richard closed his eyes briefly, remembering all the times he'd mishandled the girl. "It's my fault."

Cross made a rude noise. "Yeah, I figured we'd get around to you feeling guilty about *something* sooner or later. Kenntnis said you have a bad habit of trying to take responsibility for every fucking bad thing that happens. Get over yourself. And, hey, of course she went with her monster daddy; I mean, ichor is thicker than water, amirite?" Angela threw a *biscochito* at him. It bounced off the Old One's nose and fell onto his chest, leaving a trail of sugar crystals. He snatched it up and ate it in a single bite.

Cross's mien became serious, and he pinned Richard with a look. "So, what are your orders, *jefe*?"

Richard gulped. "I sort of hoped that *you'd* tell *me*."

"*You're* the head of the Lumina."

They were all looking at him … *to him*. Cross, the vessel holding the faith, hope, and charity of millions of believers. Angela, scared but determined, believing in him totally, accepting him. Weber, solid, and ready to march if he had a direction. Friendship restored. *And I mustn't hope for more,* Richard reminded himself. His father, steel incarnate with a cold, analytical mind, ready to advise him.

And support me.

And Richard realized he didn't have to do this alone. He drew in a long, steadying breath. "Rhiana said she bound Kenntnis with magic but holds him with physics using something called 'slow glass.' So, we find some physicists."

"We got 'em. Lumina has a big lab up in Rochester," Cross said.

"Okay. Good. So, if reason is under threat, then I'll need

all of my advisors thinking clearly and protected from any magical attack. Damon, you asked me weeks ago to use the sword on you. Well, it's time."

"For me, too?" Cross said hopefully.

"Be quiet. Sit down," Richard ordered. The homeless god sat.

"Okay, let's do it," Weber said.

He drew the sword. The tonal echoes seemed to shake the walls.

Weber stood up as Richard approached. Richard looked up at the taller man, started to raise the sword. "You want me to kneel, Short Stuff?" Weber asked, his tone whimsical. "Or you wanna just whack me on the leg?" Richard glared at him in mock outrage, and Weber reached out and ruffled his hair.

"Hey," said Cross, waving his hands excitedly in the air. "You want to do this up right?"

Richard was grateful for the distraction, it helped cover the blush he felt rising into his cheeks.

"It hasn't been done this way in a long, long time, but this might be a good time to revive it."

"What?" Robert asked.

"Where do you think that whole knighting ritual came from?" Cross asked. "Of course, it's gotten garbled over the years, and there's been a lot of religious shit thrown in to undercut its power, but it worked *good*. None of my kind ever infiltrated the Lumina because you had to get touched with the sword, which kills us, and it strips the magic right the hell out of a human candidate. Win/win, right?"

"So, what do we have to do?" Angela asked, clearly intrigued by the prospect.

"Say the oath. Let him touch you with the blade."

"And what is the oath?" the judge asked, his tone cautious.

Cross closed his eyes as if summoning some distant memory, and recited:

"Here I do affirm my desire to serve the light. To seek knowledge and understanding in all my endeavors. To defend the world and all mankind. To close gates and open minds. To teach what I know and learn what I can. To be true to reason and truth in each area of my life. This do I swear upon my life and my honor."

One by one they came to him. Richard hated to hurt them, and it was evident the touch of the sword was painful. He, who possessed no magic, wondered what they felt. Was it like losing dreams, or waking to cold reality without any softening and comforting veils? As expected, Angela was the person least affected. His father had the strongest reaction, which Richard initially found surprising, but considering his father's strong religious beliefs he probably shouldn't have.

Weber eventually left for his apartment. Robert, most affected by the sword, went upstairs to bed. Cross went outside to keep watch. Angela started to carry the dishes into the kitchen, but Richard took them from her and sent her upstairs to sleep as well. After loading the dishwasher, he sat staring into the dying embers of the fire, looking forward and trying to plan, looking back, and remembering. He wasn't certain when he fell asleep.

He woke at first light. The townhouse was silent. He checked on Angela and his father. Both sleeping peacefully. He cleaned up in the downstairs bathroom. Though rumpled, his suit still looked better than anything he'd ever seen his fellow officer's wear. It would do for what, he hoped, would be a dull shift.

He stepped outside, the snow squeaking beneath his shoes, breath forming a white cloud in front of his lips. The storm had blown out overnight. Under the rising sun the snow glittered as if it had been frosted with diamonds. The Sandias, their blue-gray splendor iced with snow, bridged Heaven and Earth, seeming to touch the turquoise-blue sky.

Richard went to work.

Ready to hold back the monsters.

If You Liked ...

If you liked *Lucifer's War* you might also enjoy:
Morningstar's Heir
One Fatal Tree
To Reign in Heaven

About the Author

Melinda M. Snodgrass studied opera at the Conservatory of Vienna, graduated Magna cum Laude from U.N.M. with a degree in history, and went on to Law School. After 3 years as a lawyer she realized she hated lawyers and turned to writing.

In 1988 she accepted a job on Star Trek: The Next Generation and began her Hollywood career where she has worked on staff on numerous shows and has written television pilots and feature films. She currently has two television series in active development.

In the prose world she writes for and co-edits the shared world anthology series Wild Cards with George R. R. Martin.

In addition, she writes her own novels. She is working on a fourth novel in the Carolingian series and a fourth novel for her White Fang Law series.

For fun she rides her dressage horse, plays video games and spends a lot of time in the gym. (Or she did before there was a pandemic).

Book Club Questions

1. Now that you've finished do you think this book is a fantasy novel or a science fiction novel?

2. Does the juxtaposition of present-day setting, police work and the supernatural make for an interesting opening for a story?

3. Would you rather have magical powers or do you agree they would be dangerous?

4. Did the information that Richard could walk in darkness work as foreshadowing for what Richard will discover about himself?

5. Did the idea that magic warps Euclidian reality raise interesting questions about the idea there are multiverses and how gravity, time, the strong and weak forces behave in those other universes?

6. Did the use of Cross for a character's name spark questions about who and what he might be?

7. Did you look up Kenntnis' name before Richard realized what it meant?

8. Lucifer's War explores questions about allowing mankind to eat from the fruit of the tree of knowledge. Is knowledge and free will important for humanity?

9. Was Richard right to protect Rhiana or should she have been neutralized?

10. Family dynamics are an important part of the theme of Lucifer's War. What other novels delve into issues of family?

11. Is Kenntnis a hypocrite because he uses magic to fight and defeat magic?

12. Why do you think Damon asks for a transfer when he learns Richard is queer?

13. Did the author do a good job acknowledging the abuses in law enforcement while still honoring good cops who try to serve with integrity?

14. Why do you think Grenier chose to use psychological pressure on Richard rather than just killing him to take the sword?

15. Can parental expectations be a form of child abuse?

16. You have Richard's father and Rhiana's father, are they two sides of the same coin?

17. Did the juxtaposition of New Mexico as the place where the atomic bomb was developed and also a place where mysticism runs deep make you want to know more about the state?

18. Who was more at fault Richard for not being honest with Angela, or Angela for pushing for a sexual encounter?

19. Was there a better way for Richard to have handled Rhiana's crush?

20. Did you think Richard had taken the sword to Grenier? Do you think he had a good plan for how to arrange to be rescued?

21. Rhiana is torn between two worlds. How do these stresses manifest in the real world?

22. Do you think Richard's rapprochement with his father will last as the series continues?

OTHER TITLES BY MELINDA M. SNODGRASS

Circuit series:
Circuit
Circuit Breaker
Final Circuit
Queen's Gambit Declined

The Edge series:
The Edge of Reason
The Edge of Ruin
The Edge of Dawn

The Imperials Saga:
The High Ground
In Evil Times
The Hidden World
The Currency of War
The Thucydides Trap

White Fang Law:
This Case is Gonna Kill Me, Book 1
Box Office Poison, Book 2
Publish and Perish, Book 3

www.ingramcontent.com/pod-product-compliance
Lightning Source LLC
Chambersburg PA
CBHW061103310726
48974CB00002B/371